VINTAGE WORLDS 2
MORE TALES OF THE OLD SOLAR SYSTEM

VINTAGE WORLDS 2

MORE TALES OF THE OLD SOLAR SYSTEM

EDITED BY

ZENDEXOR

AND

JOHN MICHAEL GREER

CONTENTS

VINTAGE WORLDS 2

MORE TALES OF THE OLD SOLAR SYSTEM

INTRODUCTION

Music Of The Hyper-Spheres

Zendexor

You don't have to be drunk to have double vision; a telescope can do it too. Hold on to this idea: it really can happen, that one celestial object can be seen as two.

Picture, if you will, what is seen in a powerful telescope when a beam from a cosmically distant source has been warped around some enormous intervening dark mass, so that we perceive the farther object as double or multiple, or even turned into a ring.

Next, my quirky addiction to scientific analogies will forge a link between such "gravitational lensing" and the other modes—moral, philosophical, aesthetic—in which it can likewise happen that an original unity is refracted into competing contradictions. If like me you are monotheistically inclined, you could liken the original point source of light to God, and the intervening mass as the influence of an immature Creation distorting the original unity of His messages;

and I suspect that the principle may be paralleled in other religious modes. Be that as it may, the adversarial consequences bombard us in antithetical pairs—liberty versus equality, wavy continua versus quantized particles, free will versus determinism, and even the Somewheres versus Anywheres of our present culture war (as recently defined so effectively by David Goodhart).

Now let's apply all this to science fiction—in particular to the traditional sf of the Old Solar System, which the discoveries of the Space Age have rendered counter-factual. What makes this type of literature so coherent as a sub-genre? How do its connective tissues work? What actually happens to the reader's brain after he has read many stories set (for example) on different versions of Mars, written and imagined by different authors?

If we were robotically logical about it, we'd have to conclude that it couldn't work. We'd assume that because the stories in many respects are mutually contradictory, it must follow that each tale can only be appreciated in isolation from the others. Edgar Rice Burroughs gives us a Mars with flyers; Leigh Brackett gives us one without them; C S Lewis gives us one where you can breathe down in the canyon-like *handramits* but not on the plateau; Arthur C Clarke gives us one where humans can't breathe anywhere outside their domes, though native life exists; and so on and on in countless variations. To read of such disparate settings one after the other must entail (the robot would insist) a separate on-and-off suspension of disbelief for each in turn: a set of unrelated backgrounds, with no linkages for collective support: a random collection of standalone tales, and that's all.

But in reality that is *not* all.

What happens, what we experience, is all that plus… what? A flickery build-up of a hyper-Mars, an archetype created by a composite, a probability function accreted by all the overlapping visions, growing with each story. I couldn't resist

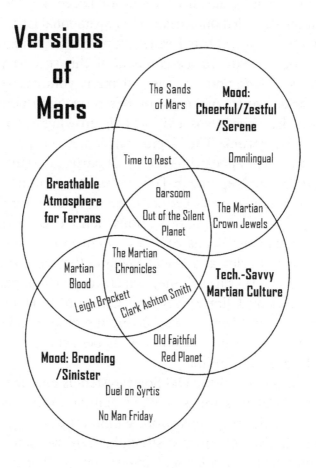

Versions of Mars

The Sands of Mars

Mood: Cheerful/Zestful /Serene

Time to Rest

Omnilingual

Breathable Atmosphere for Terrans

Barsoom

Out of the Silent Planet

The Martian Crown Jewels

The Martian Chronicles

Martian Blood

Leigh Brackett

Clark Ashton Smith

Tech.-Savvy Martian Culture

Old Faithful Red Planet

Mood: Brooding /Sinister

Duel on Syrtis

No Man Friday

trying to doodle the process in a Venn diagram, though the result merely demonstrates the futility of such attempts -

It's only a fun sketch, but even if I had spent a year of serious effort on it the result would be on the same inadequate level. Never mind; the indescribable thing occurs; the orchestrated overlaps of the hyper-spheres, fuelled from within by some naturally mythopoeic power inherent in the ideas of those worlds, and interacting with tradition, all converge to build our literary Mars, a "hyper-Mars" that lurks behind all the scattered imagery of the disparate tales, like the unity of a deep-sky object lurks beyond the shredded-out smears of a gravitational lens.

Of course you, Dear Reader, don't need an analysis as you set out to explore the contents of this second volume of *Vintage Worlds*, and, we hope, of many volumes to come. Nevertheless your enjoyment of this series will increase as you note that each tale is a visible twig growing out of an invisible greater trunk. The Neptune in James Murphy's "Cutter Pristine" (to appear in Volume 3) partly overlaps, partly contradicts, the Neptune in Troy Jones' story in this volume and that imagined by Violet Bertelsen in Volume 1: refracted images, as it were, of the mysterious "lensed" original.Similarly, of the planet Venus you'll experience varied ectypes in tales by Levi Seeley and David England (both in Volume 3) and Joel Jones (in this volume), which you can compare with the versions by Clint Spivey and Christopher Henningsen in Volume 1. I'll leave you to divine the other connections. The more you read, the more the hyper-spheres take their hyper-form in your mind.

The sub-genre of the Old Solar System is unique in sf for the potency of its settings. Authors cannot invent what they like in the OSS; they must work within a tradition, but it is one which gives them extra strength. Here we note a great difference between solar and interstellar sf. Planets which feature in tales set away among the stars are entirely the products of individual imaginations; it takes the lone genius of a Jack Vance to create Cadwal, the lone genius of a Frank Herbert to create Arrakis. Writers who stay "at home" in our good old System can be said to have it easier, in the sense that they can—indeed must—draw from an existing well of inspiration. But they are thereby challenged to live up to it—

And here are some shots at doing so.

Coverage, world by world:

The Sun: *Flow*

Mercury: *Zookie Must Die*

Venus: *Blood Prince of Venus* (second part)

The Moon: *Whom Gods Destroy*

Mars: *Exodus, The Horse-Men of Ganymede* (first part), *Blood Prince of Venus* (first part)

The Jovian system: *Flame Lords of Jupiter, The Horse-Men of Ganymede; The Sarcastic Snake-Men of Neptune* (opening scene on Callisto)

The Saturn system: *The Lost Rings of Saturn*

Uranus: *Beyond Despair*

Neptune: *The Sarcastic Snake-Men of Neptune*

Dylan T. Jeninga is an enthusiast of the fantastic yet (perhaps marginally) credible, and it was this interest that drew him to science fiction when he was a young boy, and more recently to the classic tales of our Solar System as it ought to have been. Born near the Wisconsin/Illinois border on the last day of 1993, he now lives in California with his actress wife Izzy (who, the reader may be sure, has a hand in shaping everything he creates). He works as an improvisational actor/hopefully temporary shop clerk, and he writes everything from realistic adventures among the planets to sojourns to the distant stars.

Of all the worlds of the Old Solar System, the Moon has arguably had the steepest decline, losing the needle-pointed mountains and dazzling starscapes scientists expected to find there—as well as its Selenite inhabitants, of course. In Whom Gods Destroy, *Dylan Jeninga helps restore the Moon's lost glory with a tense and suspenseful tale of adventure beneath the lunar surface...*

WHOM GODS DESTROY

Dylan T. Jeninga

EVERY CHILD WAS familiar with the first photographs of the three Selenite cities. In those old images they resembled nothing so much as great, ivory fingers of skeletal hands, stark against the black sky, reaching in eons-long silence for the still blue eye of the Earth. Patryk even had several of the original prints in his collection.

But standing there, looking up at those half-buried spires, was different. They subdued him. The weight of the epochs that had come and gone since even a mote of dust shifted in the ancient necropolis before him was suffocating.

Then the feeling passed.

"So, how do we do this and not get arrested?" he asked Waceera, a Lunar woman who stood out against the regolith in a bright yellow surface-suit with a scorpion decal adorning her helmet. He'd discovered her through the extensive underground channels he'd acquired building his collection. For a guide she was expensive, half up-front, but she seemed to be his only choice: his representatives were rebuffed by every other prospector, smuggler and freelancer they approached.

Still, she had her own rover, and was experienced with the Lunar wilderness.

"Well, we aren't going in there," she said, glancing at the ancient structural bones as she unpacked the dusty rover. "Sensor beams all around. Bring the feds down on us in a second."

"It's the same with the other two cities?"

"Worse. The good one, in Hypatia, has tourists busing in from Utulivu all the time, and the one Farside is almost as popular. These ruins are smallest."

"Hmm. So where are we going, then?"

"You'll see," she handed him a satchel. He knew from her invoice that it held spare oxygen tanks, water flasks, spelunking equipment and a flashlight. "I'll tell you when we're up in the hills, out of listening range."

"But there's nobody around for miles."

"Not so. There's a team of archaeologists in a hab not far. Radio sounds wide and clear without air in the way. Lady Luna has no privacy."

"If we aren't going in the city, I don't see why that matters. The hills aren't under federal protection too, are they?"

"You'll see," Waceera repeated, "you'll be impressed, I think."

They made their way up the uneven terrain. Their path led into the rolling foothills of a towering caldera, no doubt extinct long before even the city at its base. Waceera bounced naturally across sunken boulders and rubble, but Patryk was less steady, frequently stopping to correct his balance and keep himself from toppling. He had, in the course of his travels, been to every inhabited or formerly inhabited world in the system, but learning to walk again remained a challenge each time.

"So," he asked absently, focusing on his footing but hating prolonged silence, "I have a question."

"Shoot."

"Why did you say yes to this?"

Waceera glanced back at him.

"The money, friend."

"Right," he said. "Only nobody else was interested in the money, once they found out I'm looking for Selenite artifacts. Didn't even give a reason, just showed my people the door, every one of them."

Waceera was quiet, and Patryk wondered if maybe she hadn't heard him. He was about to repeat himself when she spoke up.

"Our heritage, I guess. They belonged to the Moon, like we do. Or, some folks think it's bad luck to mess with moon-men ruins. Most don't even visit, except maybe as kids."

Patryk nodded sagely. "Superstition. You know, on Mars it's taboo to disrespect a water talisman. Almost couldn't find anybody to sell me one."

"Why would you want one? You can afford all the water on Earth."

"Heh, well, that's not quite true. But I'm a collector of alien cultural items, among other things. I've got the most complete arrangement of Callistan prayer shrouds in the system." He didn't try to suppress the pride in his voice.

"Mmm," Waceera said. "But nothing Selenite."

"Not yet," Patryk agreed. "It's a hole that's been eating at me for years. Nothing on the market but replicas and fakes. Even the black market! Can you believe that?"

"I can."

After seeming hours of trudging they entered a low, un-assuming ravine between two slopes. Waceera finally came to a halt.

"Here," she said, turning and looking him over. She tutted. "You're covered in dust. Could get in the joints of your suit, make a leak."

"This is it?" Patryk panted, "Is this a trick?"

Waceera unclipped a magnetic wand from her belt and

played it over him, diffusing the static that made the Lunar regolith cling to him.

"Not a trick. Look, in the dark there," she pointed with her free hand.

Patryk followed her finger up to a jagged promontory standing over the gully. Shadows on Luna were sharp-edged and solid; he squinted against the bright Sun.

"I don't see it," he said.

"There's a cave," Waceera insisted. "In the shadow, look!"

Continuing to squint, he finally saw what Waceera was directing him to: an opening, tall and narrow as a man, which he had missed in the gloom.

"What is it?" he asked. "A lava tube?"

His guide shook her head. "Don't know. Funny sort of lava tube, if it is. But what's inside is more interesting. Better effect if I don't spoil it for you." She took her flashlight from her bag and started for the slender aperture. He went after her as best he could, rummaging for his own light.

"It's tight," she warned, tossing her satchel into the crevice and sliding after it. "Careful not to knick your suit on anything."

"I'm not completely incompetent. This isn't my first airless world, I've been around the System a few times."

"Oo, big fancy Earther." Her voice came out of the black. "You're good, come on."

Patryk lobbed his bag after her. "You want the other half of your money, or no?"

"You see this," she replied, "you'll want to pay me triple."

"We'll see about that. I don't even know what 'this' is."

"Something Selenite. All I'll say."

"I should hope so."

Patryk inched slowly through the claustrophobic mouth to avoid tripping on the rugged floor. The squeeze lasted longer than he expected, cutting deep into the hillside, but finally he emerged into a wider, tubular cavern.

Waceera was waiting for him. She shined her light over smooth, obsidian walls cut in wavy, undulating segments as if by a colossal earthworm. Twisting nautilus patterns adorned every surface, half-obscured by ageless dust, and the stone-strewn regolith was disturbed by a mess of bootprints—presumably left by her previous sojourn into that hidden corridor.

"This way," she ordered, cutting a path through darkness that seemed to retreat with reluctance, begrudged to give up for even a moment the realm where it had ruled unchallenged for millennia. The tunnel split and split again, bifurcating like the channels of a subterranean river, which it may have been—Patryk was no geologist. He doubted, though, that a river could cut such bizarre passages as these.

They trudged through winding tunnels for what felt like ages. Patryk tried to determine if the designs on the tunnel walls were artificial or if they'd been formed by some mysterious natural process. If they were 'moonman' made, they were a find all on their own.

With a yelp, Waceera came to a sudden stop, and Patryk almost fell over trying to keep from colliding with her. They were on the precipice of a yawning chasm, nearly invisible in the dark.

"Close one," his chaperone muttered, shining her light over the edge.

"Thank God for you." Patryk exhaled. "I never would've seen it!"

"I thought the drop-off was further down. Didn't expect it yet."

Patryk edged forward. The abyss didn't appear to have a bottom. "We must be making good time. This is your second time around."

"Makes sense." Waceera assented. She set her bag down and pulled out her spelunking gear. "We'll need these."

"Have you explored this whole thing?" he asked as she

strapped on her climbing harness, then got busy helping him with his.

"No. Only been down once, didn't stay long."

"But you seem to know it pretty well."

Waceera directed her flashlight at the floor behind them. "Following my tracks," she said. "Footprints last. Also helpful for finding your way back."

"Right, right." Patryk cast his light on the double sets of prints. "And how did you find it in the first place? It's pretty out of the way."

"Accident. I was prospecting."

"For what? Gold?"

Waceera chuckled. "Titanium."

"Ah. And you haven't brought anyone else here?"

"Just you. My friends are 'superstitious.'"

"Well, I don't think they'd need to worry. This is certainly an odd little maze, but nothing pins it as Selenite. If I hadn't just paid you half of my discretionary budget, I'd bet it really is a lava tube."

"It's money well spent, friend. Just a bit further now."

They rappelled together into the pit, Patryk taking it slowly, and he was surprised to discover it wasn't nearly as deep as he expected. The dusty onyx floor was less than a hundred yards down. When they reached it they paused to replenish their oxygen, dumping their expended air canisters beneath their hanging ropes.

The geometric swirls which had until now twisted incongruously on every surface converged here to flow into a single, confined passage that burrowed further into darkness. It was this way that Waceera led.

"How far down are we, you think?" Patryk asked.

"A couple kilometers, maybe more."

"Gonna be difficult to collect artifacts this far down. If there are any."

"You'll figure it." Waceera held her flashlight ahead of

her. The polished hall ended abruptly with an embankment of grey Lunar rock, rent through the center by a narrow fissure not unlike the one through which they'd first come. "After you," she gestured as Patryk shuffled through the shadowy cleft.

Emerging, he was confronted with a large, cephalopoidal eye.

Surrounding him on all sides were hundreds of stark, white monoliths, twice his height and shining like bleached bone in the light of his flash, each possessing the same carven, inhuman eye. An army of cyclopic pillars, arrayed in formations that faded into the inky recesses of their spacious, rocky cavity. Nautilus whirls were drawn into the timeless dust of the floor, circling the statues in an ancient, ethereal dance.

"Incredible," Patryk breathed. He walked amidst the forest of columns, shining his light over their alabaster surfaces inscribed with thousands of churning, intricate fractals that hurt his head and seemed to imbue the statues with a sort of illusory life.

"Worth the wait, eh?" said Waceera.

"I'll say," Patryk said, laying his hand on the nearest monolith. Even gloved he felt the chill of its touch, as if it were rendered in dry ice. "How many are there?"

"Don't know. Didn't count them."

"I wonder what they are." Patryk wandered through the forest of stone sentries, trying to approximate the minimum number of laborers necessary to make off with these treasures. The fewer people involved, the less likely they would be to tip off the law, but they would need to be adept at delving on the Moon.

"Hey, Waceera," he looked around. She had fallen some distance behind him, judging by the bobbing point of her light.

"Yeah," she replied. As her voice clicked off, Patryk

thought it was tainted by faint interference.

"Forget your friends. You know any people with tight lips and empty pockets who aren't afraid of the man in the moon?"

"Could be I do." The static was definitely noticeable now, as if the mass of columns were blocking her signal.

"I'm getting some interference on my end." At once, the beacon of Waceera's flashlight went out, as if smothered.

"Hey," Patryk said, "I lost you."

No answer. He waved his light around. "Waceera, I can't see you. Did your bulb go out?"

There was a thump, then, an ultrasonic pulse in a place with no sound. Then, a few moments later, another, and another. He felt them in his chest. A rhythm. He glanced around, his light creating long, split shadows that obscured more than they revealed. It occurred to him that something might have befallen his guide, that perhaps her suit had failed her suddenly or some other disaster had overtaken her. The thought of being alone in that sunless Tartarus made him shiver, and he hurried back, casting his beam back and forth and calling over the radio.

After a while of clumsy bounding, he thought that he must surely have found her already, yet nothing, apart from the numberless columns, surrounded him. Their crescent pupils watched him closely. His mind began to play tricks, the dark was full of skittering shadows and stalking things that stood his hair on end, and all the while the thrumming pulse continued. Perspiration collected on his brow. Training his light on the furrowed ground, he remembered Waceera's advice about footprints. He found his own trail and started to follow it back, hoping that she would appear. Then, fearing he'd overlooked her prone body, he turned around retrace his steps yet again.

For a split second, the circle of his light passed over something that made his heart stop. His beam snapped to it. A pale, monstrously elongated figure was rushing toward him. Reason left him. His boots pushed hard against the soft regolith, kicking up clouds of dust and nearly sending him tumbling around the monoliths even as they seemed to fence him in. The creature leaped after him, closer each time he looked, and as it gained the drumbeat pounding grew faster and louder to match it. When he came at last to the fissure he dashed through it to the place where he and Waceera had rappelled into the abyss.

The ropes were hanging where they left them. Propelled onward by the nightmare at his heels, he flew up the cliff face hand over hand, his Earthly strength carrying him in the Lunar gravity. He climbed over the precipice and stumbled headlong into the labyrinthine passages, where the geometric swirls that adorned the walls churned like writhing serpents, and the very corridors themselves seemed to have shifted and changed. He quickly became lost.

His own harried, gasping breaths were drowned by the hellish thumping which pounded at his skull. His pursuer would soon have him.

Finally he came again upon a set of double boot prints and began to follow them backwards, half-delirious, along the path he prayed would take him up into the blinding Lunar day. He scrambled down the half-familiar tunnels, the thing barreling after him, then he turned a corner and let out a short, desperate sob. A great, white monolith had appeared in the narrow cavern exit, barring the way. The thumping reached a fever pitch.

Its gaze held cold contempt as he was grabbed from behind. He swung his bag blindly, striking the demon as it tangled him in ghostly, crooked fingers. He had an impression of an ovoid eye with a crescent pupil, and then there was a rock in his hand and he was striking at it. Its skeletal tendrils threatened to draw him in but he struck again and again, swinging with the strength of animal terror. Then it was beneath him and he kept swinging, holding it down, aiming for the eye, feeling it crunch under his hand. He rained blows on it. He screamed. He showed it no mercy. He only relented when he finally realized it had gone completely limp.

Patryk sat back, his ragged breaths wracking his lungs, the adrenaline making him tremble. For a while he did nothing but curse, cry, and thank every god he'd ever heard of on a dozen planets. The thumping had stopped. The monolith that blocked his way was gone. The cavern was utterly still.

After a while he noticed that the rock in his hand was flecked with red crystals.

The twisted body beneath him seemed somehow diminished. He stared at it. Gradually, new details came into focus. A flickering flashlight, a ruptured air tank, a faded decal of a scorpion on a shattered bright-yellow helmet. Frozen blood coating it all like a morning frost.

He was found, some time later, by one of the archeologists stationed nearby. He'd overheard Patryk and Waceera's earlier discussion on the surface and, in suspicion, set out to investigate. He was alarmed to find Patryk wandering aimlessly outside of the cave mouth, clutching a bloody rock.

In Utulivu, Patryk was charged with the murder of Waceera Mwangi, a member of the Lunar citizenry. He insisted on his innocence, but his story was met with skepticism, especially after a thorough exploration of the cavern revealed a perfectly natural lava tube, completely lacking Selenite artifacts. An inspection of his suit however, identified half a dozen tiny dust-born leaks. It became the position of the courts that, even if Patryk told the truth, it was a truth tainted by hypoxia. In compensation for his wealth, no bail was set for his sentence.

Some months later, Doctor Karim Oliveira of the University of Clavius was leading an archaeological expedition among the ruins of Farside. She and a team of students were excitedly pouring over an as-yet uncovered foundation which, in previous surveys of the ruins, had been overlooked as a natural formation. They found several relics which were unknown to Selenology, among them never-before-seen tools, artistic pieces, and other items of mysterious purpose. Additionally, nearly missed among the profusion, they unearthed the fractured remains of what might have been a structural support or idol. Its worn pieces still retained the remnants of swirling geometric sigils across their surfaces, and one fragment in particular bore an image of a single, crescent-pupilled eye.

Violet Bertelsen is an herbalist, farmhand and amateur historian currently living in the northeastern United States. When she was a child, the woods befriended and educated Violet, who proved to be an eager student. She spent her young adulthood in a haze, wandering the vast expanses of North America trying to find the lost fragments of her soul in deserts, hot springs and rail-yards. Now older and more sedate, she likes to spend her time talking with trees, reading history books, laughing uproariously with fellow farmhands, drinking black birch tea and, on occasion, writing science fiction stories.

Some accounts of the Old Solar System make it look as clean and glistening as a freshly washed Space Cadet uniform, but there was another side to that end of classic science fiction, a noir sensibility as gritty as anything Chandler or Hammett had to offer. (It's not accidental that Leigh Brackett, one of the great names of the Old Solar System genre, also wrote crackerjack noir mystery stories.) In Zookie Must Die, *Violet Bertelsen catches the same harsh ambience in a tale of revenge on Mercury...*

ZOOKIE MUST DIE

Violet Bertelsen

WITH DELICATE CARE, Henniver landed his space craft in the parking lot on the western edge of the Twilight Belt of Mercury. Carefully but absently, he adjusted his space suit, making sure he put in two fresh oxygen tanks, and zipped, latched and wrapped his suit, finally attaching the helmet. With a harsh little flip, he opened the hatch, and descended the little ladder into the crepuscular air.

He stood still for a moment in the parking lot of spacecraft. Henniver closed the hatch with his clicker key, locking it. For a moment he regarded his vehicle; it was small and cheap, and he'd worked for five years in the harmonium mine to afford it. He put the key in his inside pocket, undoing his spacesuit to access his jeans. With the same distracted care, he put the spacesuit back together again, checking it twice.

Henniver's lips were a hard thin line, and he touched his ray gun with a certain cold satisfaction. He imagined Zookie's insouciant grin erased forever through force of laser burns and the thought brought a certain satisfaction to Henniver's heart, making his blood run hot and his heart beat loudly in his ears.

Zookie must die! he thought to himself, and consulted his trackerscreen. Zookie was on the western half of the Twilight Belt, about seven kilometers away from this spacecraft parking lot. According to the trackerscreen readout, Zookie had fled to the Darkside. *Mercury!* thought Henniver; *of all places to run, Mercury. Strip-mall of the universe, sleaziest planet there is. Nothing here but bad burger joints, Uranian dice and hookers.* On the Twilight Belt everything goes and nothing matters. The local girls watched Henniver orient himself clumsily in his full spacesuit.

"What you want spaceman? Want to spend some time with us?" they cried in a chorus with their colorful wigs, big nails and garishly painted faces bare in the dry Mercurial air. Uranian jazz played somewhere in the distance with its compelling rhythms and atonal melodies.

"Zookie's going to die!" screamed Henniver, red faced. The girls slithered away, taking cover in a burger joint made of extruded plastic in the shape of a monstrous ice-cream sundae. There they watched him nervously as he strode down the boardwalk, so clearly all rough and no trade, bad business.

*Zookie...*thought Henniver remembering the day he came home and heard him and Julia making love, screaming in ecstasy. Shortly afterwards she had become addicted to rekt, the latest space drug. Zookie was always carrying, and what else was there to do in the endless expanse of the old suburb? Henniver remembered cleaning up Julia's vomit, of sympathetically listening to her complain about her hangovers and fraught feelings and of finally finding her pale blue body after she overdosed on a deadly combo of rekt and Uranian spilanthes. That was three days ago. It was *he*, Henniver, who had stayed with her, who hadn't left her, who had...*loved* her.

As he walked through the Twilight Belt, it became increasingly dark, cold and sleazy. The buildings more rundown, the prostitutes uglier in faux furs and headdresses to protect against the cold. Henniver followed Zookie on the trackerscreen. He felt his face burning red, he remembered the shame he had felt as his friends mocked his forbearance, of how Julia had always been taking money right out of his account to give Zookie for drugs, and how the mockery turned into exile after Julia died. His old friends had abandoned him, but why? It made no sense to Henniver. Was it because they too were snorting rekt with Zookie? That they were embarrassed by Henniver's integrity? They couldn't respect a man who let his woman get away with all of that?

No matter, thought Henniver, my entire life I've done what's been expected me. The only thing that has been unexpected has been how well I played my part, how slavishly I followed the script. Well what script is this? I may not have my dreams, but I will have my revenge!

He could see Zookie's blue eyes, his ruddy face, his little lithe body. He saw the easy smile that Zookie wore and his ready laugh that made everyone happy. And then Henniver saw Zookie's beautiful body covered with laser burns, his space suit cut open to let in the frigid air, just a few degrees below absolute zero, his body freeze-dried in a flash. For Zookie had fled to Mercury of all places, the land of extremes. The Brightside forever hot enough to boil led, and the Darkside forever cold as deep space. Only in the Twilight zone did you see the fast food joints and painted easy women, the slot machines and the gaudy good time boys. Henniver smiled grimly to himself in spite of his vigilance; *of course Zookie comes here, he knows it's the last place in the universe someone as uptight as me would dare to venture.*

Henniver followed the flashing of the trackerscreen. Five kilometers away was the red dot he pursued flashing on the screen, as he walked deeper and deeper into the Darkside. Henniver didn't think of himself as religious, or superstitious, but he was afraid of the Darkside. There were those persistent rumors of people disappearing there, of spacecraft going missing...the Darkside was a place where things got lost, and according to the old legends, where lost things were found. Zookie had gotten lost real fast after Henniver had thrashed him, still daring to come into his house and snort rekt with Henniver's old friends, even in the days after Julia's overdose. One day Henniver snapped, Zookie was laughing real loud at some dumb joke in the other room, and Henniver had kicked down the door where the little party was listening to Uranian jazz and bumping rekt. Zookie's faced blanched as Henniver grabbed the little addict by his hair and began hitting him hard, again and again, right in the face and then dragging Zookie's limp, beautiful body by his golden curls down the stairs. Henniver had put Zookie's head right there on the chopping block by the wood shed, and gone to grab the axe, blind with fury, seeing red, and sometime between when Henniver had stepped away to the shed and returned in incandescent rage Zookie had...disappeared, without a trace.

As the surroundings grew increasingly dark, Henniver turned on his headlight, with its pale ghostly green tinted LED. He swept it down on the cold, pale gray rocks and followed the trackerscreen, flashing. Now only four kilometers separated him from his prey.

Bless Gwanice's heart, thought Henniver, who had managed to slip a nanotracker into Zookie's skin the night before last, while he was in the Prime Numbers bar, his face bruised and bloodied, talking loud and stupid, passing the pale blue powder of rekt around the table. Late in the night, Gwanice had taken the nanotracker on her finger and then poked Zookie in the face with it while he was drunk and half asleep leaning against the bar, talking slack. She poked him real hard and the little bead entered his forehead and burrowed into his skin as it was designed. Zookie muttered and swatted. And that was that. Gwanice gave Henniver the accompanying trackerscreen the next night.

"I hope you kill him. Kill him for Julia and kill him for

being such a jackass," she told Henniver and Henniver smiled coldly.

"Thank you Gwanice," he put the trackerscreen into his pocket, and then looked at her with a simian grin, "but I reckon that I'm going to *kill him for me.*"

And before either of them had thought about it they were mouth to mouth, hands tearing at each other's clothing, naked and Henniver was holding Gwanice in his enormous arms, strong from working in the harmonium mines, holding her, her legs wrapped around him while they fornicated harshly, hard, screaming and scratching, making not the sweet, funny faces of love, but the ugly faces of hate.

Afterwards they drank whiskey and smoked cigarettes and talked about nothing in particular, and now, walking into the Darkside of Mercury so far from Earth, Henniver thought with titillating shame, how much more he had enjoyed Gwanice over Julia, how with Julia it had been little pets and soft tickles and pecks, whereas with Gwanice it had been two roaring demons at each others' throats. In the morning, she had begged him to return and Henniver had flicked the cigarette he was smoking onto her lawn, winked and boarded his spacecraft. Henniver didn't think of himself as a smoker, but remembering last night with Gwanice how he wished that he could smoke a cigarette while he searched out Zookie, smoke curling around his face as he had his revenge. Three kilometers, flashed the tracker screen.

Henniver stumbled on the uneven ground of Mercury, the great darkness that seemed to diminish the feeble light of his LED, the lack of reflectivity of the stones, the sand and gravel on submerged monoliths. He half looked at the trackerscreen and half towards his feet, telling himself, his heart racing, sweat pouring down his face, that if he tripped and tore a hole in his suit…well, that would be lights out, game over. It was only too easy to die stupid and hasty on the Darkside. Henniver involuntarily shuddered, remembering the images of the bodies in satellite orbit, the people who had gotten thrown from the al-Azoz satellite after its windows broke, the dead mummy faces on the after-dinner news.

Henniver's dim LED lamp caught the sight of something that looked different than the grey pebbles and craggy stones off about four meters to his left. Curious in spite of himself he looked, and there was the bent body of a painted girl in a faux-fur coat, her blowsy face stuck in an expression of fear, agony, and hate, laser burns running across her naked chest. Henniver had never seen laser burns like this before; he shuddered at the blistered, scorched flesh, and the frozen expression the girl gave now. *Someone killed her in the Twilight Belt and carried her body here to avoid detection*, thought Henniver; *cheaper than paying her I reckon*, he thought, and then blushed at his own cynicism. *I wonder how long she's been out here. Could be fifteen minutes or five hundred years...* He trudged on, feeling sick to his stomach, struggling to avoid vomiting in the space suit.

Henniver had been saving his money to buy a little farm where he and Julia could settle down, pup a few brats. Land was cheap around the Moons of Jupiter, rich and fertile and produced enormous apples, peas, turnips, and sugar beets. They could have led a simple life, contributed to the betterment of the human project of the universe. He had once possessed a beautiful dream, and it was a dream and he had seen it collapse into scorched ruins in a moment. Henniver could take a lot, he had survived more than he wanted to remember, but having his dreams wrenched from his heart was more than he could take. He took his money out of the bank and bought a spaceship, a little economy one on the cheap side. Then he went into the gun store and bought the most powerful ray gun they had. He regretted that he would have to kill Zookie in such a cold, silent and unforgiving landscape. He had look forward, with a certain bragging satisfaction, to the smell of Zookie's burning flesh and the sound of his screams.

Onwards he walked, in his bulky space suit, a mere two kilometers from his prey. Henniver involuntarily remembered when the Martians had invaded Earth before the Johnson administration managed to patch together a global dictatorship, strong enough to forcefully repulse the invaderss. The Martians were despised with their senseless killings and evil laughter. So different from humans, more than anything these giant green tusked men of Mars seemed to enjoy the hot thrill of hatred. Henniver remembered the propaganda movies of Martians, faces bent in malevolent sneers, splitting open chests with their long blades, and eating the still beating hearts from their human victims, laughing all the while. Henniver wished that he could do the same to Zookie. Stab some nails through Zookie's beautiful hands and feet and carefully expose his beating heart to sharp teeth, Henniver imagined the fearful whimpering and malicious laughter as Zookie's exposed heart trembled in terror. Henniver paused in this brutal reverie and thought; *who am I becoming?* And with strained restraint, Henniver resolved to tone down his enthusiasms; *I'll give him a merciful death* Henniver thought, bloodlessly and milquetoast, *no torture, no unnecessary pain, no frills.* This lack passionless scheming made him feel somehow even worse, more coldblooded and plotting.

And so now, gaining ground, Henniver decided not to think any more about the details. He redoubled his resolve to kill Zookie, while trying to quiet any protesting inner voice. Who was he becoming? Henniver wondered seriously, his temples pounding. He wasn't a smoker, he didn't sleep with women like Gwanice, he didn't fantasize about killing his enemies like a bloody Martian...No, he was in the right, he was good. Best not dwell on it...but as he thought about not thinking his thoughts gained more traction in his fevered brain.

Henniver came to a sloping depression that led into the depths of Mercury; the trackerscreen indicated clearly that his prey was somewhere in the depths, and so he cautiously walked down the slope, trying to avoid slipping. He continued downward into a darkness so great that his very soul began to quiver, and his heart beat like an alarm clock against his ribs. He went down and had to twist around great rocks, several times almost skidding on loose pea-gravel. As he walked, he saw a white light in the distance. It looked like a great fluorescent light. Henniver turned off his head lamp and grabbed his ray gun and thought, *it's go time!* And rushed towards the light.

What he saw took his break away; shelves and piles, and great heaps of every last little thing. Here were keys of every sort, and here were hair pins, and there were coins from the bottom of the sea and from underneath the couch in a thousand climes. Figurines, and statuettes, statues, every toy, cutlery and pots of pans, pets of every species, children, elders, and madmen. Houses, cities and entire cultures. Raving minds were next to dancing gossamer dreams like mirages in the desert, which were on shelves below ancient heroic ideals and forgotten myths. *The place of lost things*, thought Henniver suddenly cold, as he walked down aisles, seeing disposed gods and drowned collective imaginings, right next to souls screaming in their bottles; he walked around in a daze; *how do I get out of here* he thought until he walked into the dead prostitute he had seen not an hour prior, she looked happy and young and was holding hands with Julia. Julia was happy and laughing, she mouthed words Henniver couldn't understand, pointing. Henniver's eyes followed her finger and he saw...*himself.* He saw himself, big and strong, decent and happy like he was just a week ago. He saw someone sweet and innocent who would never dream of killing someone, never dream of hurting anything.

Involuntarily he dropped the trackerscreen and dropped the ray gun. His old self picked them up and handed them back to him: *look* said his old self pointing, *look at the track-*

erscreen. Henniver did and saw he had found Zookie, and he looked down and there was Zookie, his face still bruised and swollen and two black eyes, in a cheaply made spacesuit, hastily assembled, cracked along the side. It seemed that while running Zookie had tripped and fallen, breaking the seal of his suit and that had been lights out, game over. Zookie stared up at Henniver with dumb dead eyes, and Henniver stood there, cold sweat pouring down his face, a huge sense of relaxation sweeping his body. He blinked, and he was no longer standing in the place of all lost things that seemed so real for a moment ago. Now he was standing over the very real dead body of Zookie, who had died in his own dumb escape, his luck running out. Not knowing what else to do, Henniver picked up a handful of pebbles and threw them over Zookie's body.

"Rest in peace," said Henniver, before he dialed the reverse function on the trackerscreen, walking slowly back across the dark, featureless landscape. As he trudged the five kilometers back to the Twilight Belt, he felt an enormous sense of relief; it would probably be years before anyone found Zookie's body, and Zookie wasn't the sort of person who inspired a lot of questions on the part of a mortician or detective.

Still, another shadowy question followed Henniver as he walked; *I may not have killed Zookie, at least not directly, but have I killed a part of myself?* The more he tried not to think of the look of his own eyes while he started at himself in the place of lost things, the more he thought that perhaps he was indeed somehow inwardly dead, lost to himself.

He returned to the twilight zone, and realized that he had lost his ray gun somewhere in the Darkside. A cold sweat of paranoia suffused anew over his skin; the Johnson dictatorship, the prison camps, the torture rooms, his ray gun somewhere on the Darkside; had he just signed his death warrant? Henniver took off his helmet and deeply inhaled the dusty aromatic air of the Twilight Belt. He forced himself to find the key and with a shaking hand opened the door to his space craft. He forced himself up the ladder into the cockpit, and after closing the hatch he set his course to Gwanice's house with a smile and took off.

Well, he thought, *sometimes lost things are found.* Henniver leaned back in the black leather cockpit chair as his craft raced towards the small blue point in space that he called home. *Maybe I am not dead to myself, maybe my innocence hasn't been murdered...Maybe*, he thought, exhausted from his travails, hurtling rapidly towards Earth, towards Gwanice, knowing in his gut that something very important had been decided.

KS "Kaz" Augustin writes genre fiction, but her favourite is space opera. She cut her teeth on Weinbaum, Kuttner, Russell, Harrison and Smith and loves recreating such atmosphere whenever she can. You can visit her website at https://www.KSAugustin.com and sign up to her newsletter at Challis Tower Books at http://bit.ly/CT-subs

To say more than a little about Flow *would be to give away too much about K S Augustin's luminous tone poem of a first encounter with an alien species. Enjoy...*

FLOW

K. S. Augustin

IC.

The sound captured Crimson's attention the way a web's vibration summons the spider. Crimson knew every sound the *Flare* made, knew it better than the rhythm of her own heartbeat or the litany of obstacles she'd overcome to make it into that cockpit.

Something's wrong. No, not now. It can't be.

Stretching a hand, she laid it gently on the warm metal console in front of her, feeling the engine's low growl tickle her fingertips, encouraging the small trembles and hiccoughs to tell its tale. Things are going well, they said, no need to worry.

Was that right? She stayed deathly still, listening. Could she be imagining things? Would her father have come to the same conclusion? Or would he have—

A tremor jolted her body. Not *Flare*. Her. She buckled within the safety harness and the thick straps bit into her shoulders. Then she was tipping. Or was it the ship? No, definitely not the ship.

What's happening? Why do I feel—

A soundless explosion of white enveloped her. No, it wasn't the *Flare*, she thought, it couldn't be. There was no scream of burgeoning chaos, no yells of fractured alloy. The popping hadn't escalated to anything worse, therefore her ship (*hers? surely yes, by now*) must still be in one piece. What she was experiencing was something else. Something personal. It was—

"—IF YOU COULD help us."

Crimson blinked, trying to clear the fogginess from her mind. It was bright. So bright. She shut her eyes again, this time for several seconds, breathing in deep. When she opened them for a third time, her surroundings were more bearable, the surrounding colours not as bleached. There was someone standing in front of her. Bipedal. Tall, thin, almost skeletal. She could make out his? her? its? features now, beyond the glare that had bothered her before. Delicate, pointed chin, long wiry limbs, upswept intelligent eyes that watched her carefully.

"Help?" That was one of her buttons and Crimson knew it. Did this being know it, too? But then she was caught by the sound of her own voice, as thin as the being standing in front of her. "I—" She stopped. She still didn't sound right.

"Are you in pain?" the being asked.

Crimson frowned and made a show of looking around. Her mission had been purely reconnaissance. Inanimate target. Passive sensor inputs with a single human to interpret, analyse and pass back The Important Stuff. It had been monkey-plus kind of processing, yet garnered stratospheric status, and she had beaten out hundreds of overqualified hopefuls to land herself in the *Flare*'s coveted cockpit.

"No, I'm not in pain," she answered.

What would Mission Control make of this? Had they somehow known that there was a chance of—her mind trembled for a second—alien contact? Because that's what she was facing. The being watching her was definitely alien. Was that why the Agency's trials had been so difficult?

She lifted her right foot and set it back down a little more firmly than was warranted. The ground beneath her feet remained solid and stable.

"Where am I?" she asked.

"You are in our home."

"Our?"

"My...siblings. Some of our parents. Some of our children."

Children? Parents? Aliens? How did that make sense? Crimson tried concentrating on the being's words, parsing them for hidden meanings, but there was sharp pain across her forehead and right temple, the mother of all migraines. She tried working past it, imagining that the spikes of agony didn't really exist, but they were insistent.

"I have used terms that we have gleaned are familiar to you."

"Are you able to," she frowned more deeply, "read my mind?"

A pause. "No. You are an alien to us. How are you called in the language of your people?"

"How—? My *name*? My name's Crimson Monteiro."

"Yes. Name. Yes. Crimson. Crimson. Monteiro." It was silent for a moment. "That is a long name."

There were longer of course, but Crimson could understand the sentiment. She nodded, she hoped understandingly. "What is *your* name?"

"Ge."

"That's it? That's your name? 'Ge'?"

"I need no more."

Crimson tried imagining an Earthful of people, each with a one-syllabled name. What a joke that would be. But maybe Ge wasn't one individual in an ocean of several billion. Crimson gazed past the alien and saw...could they be trees? How did she not notice them before? Pale green leaves sprouted from limed oak branches, some a few metres away, others stretching back, obscuring the horizon. The colours were a little washed out but the forms were familiar enough. Then a wave of blue, white and pink, haloed in fuzzy white, zigzagged in front of her, obliterating her view. Crimson rubbed her temple. Damn that migraine. It was interfering with her vision now.

"We took you from your conveyance." Ge's voice interrupted her introspection.

"My ship." Crimon's tone was flat. "You took me from the *Flare*." Lest she forget where and what she was doing before she had been abducted. "I was on a mission to probe the Sun before you brought me here. You had no right to do that."

"We need your help," Ge said. It pointed up and to Crimson's right.

Crimson turned, following the line of Ge's arm and gasped. Something large and dark loomed, hovering over them like a vengeful raptor. It was a polygon, edged against the misty pastel sky, opaque, featureless, sucking in the light. Every now and then a part of it flickered as if on fire.

"What is it?" she asked, tilting her head as she tried identifying features of the anomaly.

"We don't know. It is alien to us, as you are alien to us. That's why we seek your help."

Get an alien to fight an alien, was that their thinking? Was that why they had kidnapped her from the *Flare*? Crimson rolled the thought over in her head for a moment then let it drop. As her father would say, it wasn't wise antagonising the powerful, and if Ge had transported her from the *Flare* so effortlessly, then it definitely had access to very advanced tech.

"How long has it been there?" she asked, instead.

"Many generations."

"When did it arrive?"

"A very long time ago."

Crimson shook her head, not entirely convinced. "It just seems to be hovering there."

"It moves."

She turned. "Have you tried deflecting it?"

"We are not familiar with its technology. We thought you could help us."

"Why me?"

"We detected your *prensam*. We are able to communicate with you."

Crimson stared at the alien while her mind raced. They were able to communicate with *her*. Did that mean there were commonalities between Ge and herself? Or maybe "prensam" indicated location or proximity. Why not teleport someone from a bunker on Venus, for example? Had she been plucked from her ship because she had been closer to wherever-this-place was? A thought dawned.

Was she on...*Mercury*? Was she speaking with a native of what was thought to be a dead world overrun with solar storms? Tendrils of mythology fluttered through her mind. Maybe not Mercury; maybe, instead, that phantasm once thought to exist between Mercury and her mission target. *Vulcan!*

"Your planet," she said suddenly, "this place, how big is it?"

"Big enough for all of us."

Vulcan!

It had to be!

An object of pure outdated French fantasy, now solid beneath her feet. She shifted her gaze to beyond Ge, to a swaying and hazy pastel horizon that peeked between the bleached trunks of half-familiar vegetation. It looked so far away, which also didn't make sense. If what she was eyeballing was correct, if Vulcan was of a decent enough size to produce a faraway horizon, Earth's telescopes would have picked it up long ago.

"Why didn't we know of you?" she asked. "Do you use some kind of shielding technology on your planet?"

They must do or she would have been burnt to a crisp seconds after being transported here.

"All see us," Ge said. "We hide nothing."

Crimson tightened her lips.

Don't antagonise the powerful.

"What do I get if I help you?" she finally asked. "Will you let me go? Put me back on the *Flare?*"

Ge's hesitation was palpable. "Yes," it finally said. "We will. You can. Go."

"I need to get back there as soon as possible," she said, hammering the point home.

Who knows what had happened since her teleportation? Maybe the process itself had been responsible for the anomalous sound and the sensations that had burst around her during those turbulent split-seconds. Mission Control had made piloting the *Flare* as idiot-proof as possible. By now, autonomous protocols should have been initiated, coded messages sent. But how long could she stay on Vulcan before something aboard the first sunskimmer from Earth inevitably failed? How long until the possibility that there would be no ship to return to?

Crimson straightened. "Let's get to work, then. Now."

BUT GE HAD other plans. It led her through a dreamscape that seemed to subtly change the moment she moved focus, teasing her peripheral vision. The trees wavered against a pearlescent glare that narrowed Crimson's eyes into a seemingly never-ending squint. The pull of gravity against the soles of her booted feet felt right, yet wavered alarmingly every few minutes. She stumbled several times, falling to the ground, and felt a sponginess against her bare hands that her soles hadn't detected.

And it was empty. Crimson couldn't see another being in sight, only waves of warm air dancing around her like mirages in a desert. Yet her lungs didn't burn as she expected them to, and she didn't seem to be perspiring at all.

"Are you alone on this planet?" she asked, struggling to keep up with Ge's sinuously gliding gait.

It stopped and turned. "No. We are many." Then it began walking again.

Crimson shook her head and followed.

"This is yours," Ge finally said and stretched forward a hand. To its right, on a spot that Crimson could have sworn had been nothing but a milky, well, *nothingness* up till that moment, stood a small one-storey construction. And her curiosity about how it had done this was subsumed by something else because, despite its sharp swooping roof and the walls that quashed themselves into the soil, it reminded her of a very familiar cabin. In fact, architectural eccentricies aside, it looked a lot like the cabin her father used to rent every summer. Carlos Monteiro, the great solar physicist and father of the most famous dropout (and, later, prodigal daughter) of the TransEurope Agency of High Technologies. He had died years ago and, with him, her precious summer excursions away from his pestering colleagues, the government's oily bureaucrats and the weight of a thousand gazes. How had Ge known to manufacture this if it wasn't telepathic? Or maybe the answer was much simpler, she concluded. Maybe she was projecting, seeing elements of her personal failure in a structure an alien couldn't possibly know about.

Ge regarded her intently, forcing Crimson to stammer out a response. "It's, er, very nice. Looks very serviceable. But I don't think—"

"It is only for you. It has....rooms. To cut you off from others."

Yes, in a way she supposed those were exactly what rooms were.

Crimson felt a physical wave of vertigo as she took a step forward and quickly stumbled to a halt.

She shouldn't be the one here, trading social chitchat with an alien on a previously undiscovered planet. It should have been someone else. Someone with no personal ties to the late great Carlos Monteiro; someone smarter but without the right connections. Except it was Crimson now facing Ge, not anyone else, and she didn't know what to say in front of a structure that reminded her too much of how she had betrayed her idol.

"Would you like to enter?" Ge asked.

Of course. The alien had extended an enormous amount of hospitality and all she could do was stare blankly at it.

"You shouldn't have done this," she said. "I don't expect to be here very long."

Ge remained silent.

"If I can be of help to get rid of, or deflect, whatever that monstrosity is, then I'd prefer being, ah, transported back to the *Flare* as soon as possible."

Surely it remembered the promise it had made.

Crimson persisted. "Have you made any sensor readings of your intruder? What did you find?"

But Ge seemed intent on showing her inside her cabin. Crimson—distracted, frustrated, decidedly bullish—reluctantly followed, taking offhand notice of the sparse interior. She should be working, not touring Vulcan contemporary architectural design. The fate of the *Flare* nagged at her. She had failed at so much. To fail at this as well....

Then she remembered her mini-cam. She touched the small stud above her left breast pocket and began recording. She would be rightly scorned and vilified if she failed to document details of this amazing diversion. Assuming, she thought to herself, she could solve the mystery of the black cloud. And get back to the *Flare* in time.

"What do you do here?" she asked. "What is your function in your society?" Maybe Ge wasn't even a scientist, something Crimson needed to clarify as soon as possible. She needed to work with the right people if she wanted to liberate herself.

"I keep knowledge," Ge replied.

Keep knowledge? But wasn't that what a scientist did? Or was it more an historian?

"Old knowledge?"

Ge lifted its hands. "All knowledge."

Crimson's brain raced. "And where do you keep this knowledge?" Maybe there was a library or databank somewhere she could access?

Ge walked forward and briefly touched the top of her head, followed by its own. "Where all knowledge is held."

"You don't have anything written down?" That drew a blank stare. "Recorded? Um, put in permanent form somewhere so others can also understand?"

"We all understand."

Crimson came to a sudden stop in the middle of the cabin's main room. This philosophical blathering was getting her nowhere. For the moment, it looked like she was stuck with the alien. Maybe a proper scientist would happen along soon. If Ge wasn't the last of its species.

"We really should get to work." Her voice was firm.

"As you say."

Finally. Crimson's small smile was one of victory.

WHETHER IT WAS really Vulcan or even the mirror Earth that was supposed to lie on the exact opposite side of the Sun (what was happening to her was so bizarre that Crimson wasn't ruling anything out just yet), the planet was oddly familiar in some ways and bizarrely alien in others. Crimson tried matching weather patterns to what she'd read of other bodies in the solar system but continually drew a blank. Clouds behaved like vortices, trees sprouted and withered with alarming speed and, occasionally, dark smudges appeared on the ground and sped off in different directions. She thought of them as negative spotlights. Were they pest infestations? A virus of some kind? The gravity continued to tremble. Especially on that first day with Ge, Crimson stumbled and fell with embarrassing regularity.

"I'm not usually this uncoordinated," she'd say and Ge would nod but remain silent.

She still didn't know how she hadn't noticed the vast forests of trees before. She was surrounded by them. Tall, short, leafy, spindly. There was even a lake near what she called her cabin. The water was a pale milky green with constant breezes whipping small chorus lines of wavelets across the pastel surface, blowing them into small soft peaks before flicking them at the shoreline. In the days since she'd agreed to help Ge, as inviting as the water looked, she hadn't worked up the courage to go for a dip. What was alien for "swimming costume"?

The sun set late and rose early on the alien world. It was already in the sky when she rose, and still there when she fell, exhausted, to sleep every night. Her headache continued, playing havoc with concentration. She concluded that there was something about the planet that physically affected her, as the headache was soon joined by sharp pain radiating from her right knee. When that discomfort was joined by a throbbing ache in her ribs, she knew she was right and redoubled her efforts to solve Ge's problem and get back to the human-friendly environment of the *Flare* where she could program a full medical self-diagnostic and map out a rehabilitation plan. Assuming it wasn't too late.

The food was...interesting. It all looked familiar (if a little washed out in colour), yet was disconcerting to handle and strange to eat. What she thought of as a fried egg had sharp zigzag edges, noodles had to be sliced like bread before they fell into a tangle of thin circular strands, the meat was always minced and Ge didn't have the words to tell her where or how it was sourced. And it all tasted like crisp, grain wafers, brittle, with a hint of flavour that was, at best, salty. With everything else going on, and with her body failing to adapt adequately, the last thing Crimson wanted to think about was the nutritional profile of what she was putting into her mouth, so she ate as little as possible, and only when the sharp pangs in her stomach overrode every other impulse.

The place where she helped Ge—she called it the lab— was austere: an empty space covered in shimmering tile within a dome with a clear curved roof. And it was through that clear roof that Crimson could see the hovering anomaly.

On the second day, an alien that looked almost identical to Ge stopped by the doorless lab to stare mutely at her.

Crimson was so startled she only found her voice after the figure hurried away. "Wait," she called out, then turned to her companion. "Ge, tell them to come back. I'd like to talk to them. Surely your people as curious about me as I am about them?"

"It's a child. They would not understand. We have plenty of work to do. They will only distract you."

Reluctantly, Crimson let the matter drop, but she was starting to think that Ge's planet had many more problems than the dark monster above them. She got the impression that the aliens were dying in some way—the population seemed so sparse as to be non-existent—and they, too, were suffering from the same physical maladies that she was. Ge was forgetful, often repeating the same question a couple of times a day. Initially irritated, Crimson had to learn to tamp down her anger. She was on *their* world, helping them with an alien problem. Her temper had no place here.

And when Ge said that its people didn't have the technology to deflect the intruder, it appeared to be telling the truth. There was no equipment that Crimson could use that was in any way familiar to her, and what little that did exist had functions she could hardly guess.

"This ensures that *prensam* is not over-regulated," it said of a pulsing orb attached to the wall that Crimson had originally thought was a work of art. "And this," Ge gestured to a waist-high cylinder that glowed alternately amber and blue, "regulates the waves of *kijma* so that the effects of *alnamo* are reduced."

"*Kijma?*" The device didn't have any handles, buttons or even a screen. "Do you mean light? Magnetism? Some kind of energy vortex?"

"*Kijma,*" was Ge's only response, with an accompanying hand movement that Crimson thought denoted a shrug.

The alien was so opaque, Crimson felt like screaming. Once more, she wondered where the *Flare* was, whether the autopilot had kicked in after detecting her absence. Had messages initiated by emergency protocols been sent back to Mission Control? She estimated that she had been away from her craft for no more than two days. That wouldn't give the boffins back at base enough time to *do* something, but it would start them thinking.

What would they make of the strange creature in front of her? As she had several times already, Crimson instinctively reached for the mini-cam above her left top pocket, touching the activation button. She still didn't know whether it was working, had nothing with her from the *Flare* that could verify that it was recording. Maybe it didn't matter. Maybe the comfort was only psychological. Maybe, for the moment, that was all that mattered.

IT TURNED OUT that Ge was as curious about Crimson as she was about its people and, if she were honest with herself, she believed that she was giving more valuable intel than she was receiving.

After another fruitless day spent at the lab, she walked back to her cabin and sat on the short limed blades of "grass" beside the lake. Ge sat opposite. Beneath her fingers, the vegetation felt spiky, yet she could rest her open palm on them till they flattened and feel no discomfort. The fields around her had twice bloomed with tall canes of yellow flower-things, but upon closer inspection, Crimson couldn't identify the parts she had learnt from her Biology classes. Stigma? Stamen? Seed capsule? None of those seemed to exist in the day-blooms she plucked. Living in such strangeness was exhilarating but also muddied her thinking.

"What do you feel?" Ge asked on the third afternoon. "How does this place look to you?"

Maybe it was the glare, but focusing her thoughts was becoming more difficult by the day. Her body ached.

Crimson frowned, trying to rally her neurons into some kind of sustained, collective action. She stared at Ge and thought about a doomed people, perhaps looking for refuge elsewhere. Had they brought her to their planet because they sought escape and wanted to assess her for...friendliness, compassion, compatibility, all of the above? Was the dark anomaly less an invader and more a wholesale destroyer of their society? But what would they think of Earth, these alien Vulcans (or Earth Primers)? After such emptiness, how would they cope with the urban press of humanity? What would...*what was that name?* What would...y*es! Mission Control!* What would Mission Control say if she returned with a delegation of Ge's people?

"This place," Ge prompted, as if aware of her internal struggle. "How does it look to you?"

"I don't know how to describe it." She felt like shaking her head but the migraine from her first minutes on the planet had only increased in virulence. It pounded against her entire skull now, like a hammer fashioned from thorns. "My mission was to analyse sensor readings, not, not initiate first contact with another sentient species."

"How do your people think?"

(*Ha! Very badly?*) Crimson tried choosing her words carefully. "My people aren't intrinsically cruel." (*Really?*) "But they can make errors in judgement."

"Errors? How?"

Her guard was down now. After almost three days on Ge's strange planet, Crimson was exhausted. Sleep was supposed to revitalise, yet wasn't doing its job. How long more could she survive in this place?

"You don't think straight," she said.

"Straight? Bent? Obtuse? Convergent?"

"You make mistakes."

Mistakes like trying to find oblivion through whatever means she could find. Spending her teenage years dabbling in illegal script-hacking. Pretending to be her father's protégé when she was nothing but his pale shadow. Accepting the bowing and scraping of the influential sycophants around her because she didn't know how to say no.

Sliding into the flight seat of the *Flare* as if she belonged there.

I did it for you, Dad.

She shook her head. "It doesn't matter. You just have to be careful. Even *I* can't be trusted."

"How do you feel?" Ge asked.

That was a new one. "How" not "what". An impulse nagged at the back of her head. She had to get back to the lab. To find out whatever that *thing* was. Solve the problem, get back to the *Flare*, go home, get covered in glory.

That'll show 'em.

But even blinking her eyes was difficult. Had the planet's toxicity finally caught up with her? Or maybe it was the radiation from Vulcan (or Earth Prime)?

For a brief moment she found herself back on her ship. The walls were comfortingly metallic around her, she felt the harness straps press against her body, but only for a moment. Light obscured her view as the navigation controls sparked, all in slow motion. She followed the path of several bright flares as they shot from the console and felt a sharp impact against her head. The noviglass buttons shattered into thousands of glittering shards, a galaxy of tiny suns enveloping her. Her chair deformed, twisting her body like clay and the bones of her legs and torso protested. Cracked. Broke.

Then she was back on the grass that shouldn't exist, in front of a humanoid that, likewise, shouldn't have existed. She looked up at the black cloud that dominated a sector of pale sky.

"That's my ship," she said, wondering how enlightenment had come at all when her brain could barely process what she was saying.

"We are curious. Why did you come?"

But Crimson wasn't listening. She looked around frantically. Did this place even exist?

"No."

Startled, Crimson whipped her head back. "What did you say?"

"This place has been constructed. It is not natural to us. We have not encountered beings like you before. We needed to study you."

"Study?"

"You are dying. Your ship will approach, but it will be destroyed. We are safe."

She could only stare at it.

"I am not Ge. I am the eighth generation descendant of Ge."

Crimson knew that revelation should have sparked a reaction, but she was wrapped in dense foam, listening to the alien's words through a wall of white noise. Even movement was now difficult. She sat, frozen, as if nailed to the soft spiky grass.

How long had she been here, in this place?

She could only move her eyes now, watching as the *Flare* continued its slow plummet towards the Sun. Towards her.

"I wish," she said, returning her gaze to Ge, but she was thinking of her father.

I found something, Dad. Something that can top even your reputation. Aren't you proud of me now?

Was there sadness in Ge's eyes? Or was it the unbearable incandescence of plasma as it dissolved into chaos, as the trees blossomed into beings, swirling around her ever faster, burning into her retinas?

Crimson couldn't even close her eyes anymore as the aliens' magnificence burst free.

Tock.

Under the alias "Zendexor", Robert Gibson co-edits the Vintage Worlds series and is the webmaster of www.solarsystemheritage.com. Born in London in 1954, of mixed Scottish and Belgian extraction, Robert works from home as a private tutor in Lancashire, England. He is married to Mary, who helps him with any maths that he finds too hard, and proofreads his fiction. His published works include the Old Solar System adventures Valeddom *and the collection of linked tales set on the Seventh Planet,* Uranian Gleams. *Another Uranian story appeared in Vintage Worlds Volume 1.*

Contact with alien intelligences is one of the great themes of the Old Solar System—no surprise, given the enthusiasm with which the authors of golden age science fiction stocked the solar system with unearthly life and civilizations. In Flame Lords of Jupiter, *Robert Gibson serves up a robust dish of classic interplanetary adventure, with more than one deft nod to classic SF stories blended in...*

FLAME LORDS OF JUPITER

Robert Gibson

1

RESKEN 905 SCOWLED with longing, hunched at the window of the orbiting fortress. As his gaze scanned and roved, his stomach churned in almost human fashion with the weight of news. During the past few minutes his situation had changed more than in the previous six thousand years, and a whisper now emerged, from his more-than-mortal brain, telling him that his age-long vigil might be about to end.

He stared as though the space around Jupiter were a labyrinth that would yield to scrutiny: he had become able, seriously able to believe, that his naked eyes might tell him what the fort's detectors refused to reveal. This made it likely that the hour at last had come, for which he had been created.

Previous false alarms, strewn over centuries, had provided exercise for his intellect, but his android body had lacked action—had in fact never known any life other than that which he had always lived, in a cathedral-sized metal shell hurtling twenty thousand miles above the cloud-tops of the giant planet.

Yet he was as fit and muscular as the day his Terran masters had perfected him. The cells that made up his Herculean frame drew their power from the restless virtual foam of space itself. Physically as well as mentally, he was to all intents and purposes a minor god—which he needed to be, if his testing time was at hand.

A buzzer sounded and a glow-bulb flashed, announcing a transphotic communication from Earth. (Overwhelmed by a sense of history, Resken 905 glanced at the wall clock before pressing the stud to receive the call. It was 05:11, Greenwich Mean Time, on 19th May, A.D. 8323. He had been over sixty-two centuries in the Fortress.)

"Resken?" said the voice from Earth, and simultaneously a caped figure appeared on the communic.

"Yes, Mever, it is I. I happen to be at home at the moment."

The object of his sarcasm smiled from the screen, crinkling a lined face. "As always, I admire how you maintain the repartee…"

"Seven minutes ago," Resken cut in, "the space around me went red."

Meven's face puckered and bleared. The man's mouth firmed in an effort to normalise, to dismiss the news: "It's good, of course, that they constructed you with a sense of madcap fun, but—"

"Forgive me—I must stop you there. You know, Meven, that there is one thing I never joke about." It was vital to convince the old Capcom dynast, one of the few remaining Terrans who still bothered to listen, that what was about to follow was no gag, no mere ploy to while away the years.

"Do you mean to tell me," sighed the face on screen, "that you actually have something to report about the… you know… the—"

"I saw the vacuum outside my window acquire colour. It turned a dull red. The flicker was repeated twice."

"You realize what you are saying is impossible?"

"A ranging shot, I'd guess. From below. And not impossible, merely unimaginable."

Meven's face was now a blotchy grey as he mumbled, "What do you think it means?"

Resken had had tough-mindedness manufactured into him, yet could still spare some compassion for the frailer human. Nevertheless the Terran had better pull himself together, because the answer could not be broken gently.

"The Second Jovian War is about to begin."

"No. No…"

If only, thought the android, if only I could throw a bucket of cold water at that croaky time-wasting face. "You can't take it, but you *must* take it. Or else Earth may be finished."

"*They* shouldn't *want* it. They wouldn't *dare*. Wouldn't *ever* dare," bleated the man. "We thrashed them, last time."

"Then why did your ancestors build this fortress? Why build me?" He paused, and then, though he had never played cards, added: "You always knew this was on the cards." Meven had no answer, and Resken continued, with a sense of an angler playing his fish, though he had never angled, never seen a stream, never seen a fish: "But you're partly right, insofar as they wouldn't risk it a second time with that kind of purely psychological warfare in which we worsted them so thoroughly. Therefore, mark my words, they're preparing a *physical battle*."

He watched those words sink in, watched their effect on the Terran's features, and braced himself to ride out one last futile wave of rejection. Sure enough the man scoffed—but feebly—

"Jovian spaceships?"

Resken scoffed in turn, "Come now—what's so improbable about that? Are you about to give me the silly old argument that Jupiter's huge escape velocity makes us safe from them? Ignoring that their resources are likely to be as exceptional as their world's gravity, and that the one will compensate for the other? It's time to bestir yourself, Meven. Alert your authorities; wake them up from their dabblings—because I'm going to need reinforcements! Unless it's already too late."

Meven, however, sadly began to shake his head.

Here, then, realized Resken, was failure, clear from the body language: utter failure to rise to the occasion. What next? What could he do with such a person? Continue to bawl him out: no other option presented itself. From a vast tonal range, Resken picked a voice which cut like a blowtorch: *"Don't tell me you have forgotten what this fortress is for."*

Wistful came the Earthman's reply: "It has given my life meaning..."

"Ah," said Resken in bitter understanding. His loud-voiced approach having failed, he switched to irony. "Ah. Just 'meaning'-therapy. Including all your years of contact with me. It's all about feeling good. Nothing more."

"I'm afraid that's true," muttered the screen-voice from between drooping shoulders.

The admission did not greatly surprise Resken. He had always been plentifully supplied with news from the home world of mankind. 'Meaning' indeed was the only currency of value on an Earth long given to unlimited material wealth, ever since the invention of the matter-duplicator in 2330 had wiped out old-style economics overnight. Only one age-old struggle remained—the quest for purpose.

To be appointed to the Observatory staff, to be trusted to maintain contact with the Fortress at Jupiter, was a prize keenly sought, an honour and a boon to the life of any decent, intelligent Terran.

"Well," shrugged Resken, "it's a pity but you're going to find out, you're about to learn, Man, that a long distinguished record of fine gestures will not suffice to meet the Jovians' attack."

Meven gave a weak farewell smile. "Listen, friend. We

did do what was needed, long ago."

"You mean..."

"We made you."

"That," said Resken, "is the oldest, most useless argument of all."

But he was speaking to a blank screen. That was when he understood that he was absolutely alone; that no help would come from Earth; that all available hope had been so conveniently pinned on him.

2

A COUPLE OF minutes later, space flashed red again, as though the void could be stained by cherry juice. The craziness of this apparent violation of natural law shouted its message of Jovian power. Flash, flash, the stains shone brighter, enveloping the fortress.

During this build-up Resken did his best to parry the inner thrusts of despair, by clinging to the knowledge that the Jovians had lost the First War. Beaten once, they could be beaten again.

If so, it would have to be done differently this time. History never repeated. In the previous bout, the war's psychological character had nullified the Jovians' advantage of size—since no one could match Terrans for ruthless mental cunning. But this next contest threatened to be an altogether cruder affair. And neither the Earth nor the rest of the System could hope to withstand the hordes of the giant planet if they broke out into space.

An android is like a man, in that he has to have hope. Resken therefore reminded himself that, after all, no enemy armada was visible yet. Space-flashes, whatever they were, weren't space-ships. That final doom was not yet in evidence.

As if on cue to that thought, the flashes re-appeared. A quality without mass, without detectable radiation, stained the outside vacuum with a deep red that came and went in staccato bursts, stronger by far than the previous manifestations; strong enough, this time, that Resken's queasiness swelled and popped as a burst of insight:

THEY WON'T LEAP—THEY'LL PULL. *To them, their immense planet is the universe. That's why they're not yet leaving it. The very concept of going "off-world" is one they don't yet understand. Thank goodness. That will be what saves us, if we do survive. Yet the consequence may be grave for me personally. I feel it in my steel bones, that since they don't leap, they'll pull—they'll drag me down to them—ah, look now—*

In an elastic moment the outside redness brightened into pink. Embracing the fortress, prongs of radiation scanned what was in it and then—

One might as well say, the Jovians "pulled".

Resken's awareness froze as he was "translated".

The giant world's gravity took hold of him. Weight enough to crush a mere man, triggered in him a long-planned response: his musculature underwent that cellular adjustment for which it had been designed, with this moment in view, millennia before.

So he was able to throw off the effects of the change. Presently, as his thoughts thawed into a stream of awareness, of new weight and motion, he looked about him.

He was standing in a roomy monocar.

Except for ribs of metal, its hull was transparent, allowing him to see all around, far over cloud-tops below, and upwards to a billowy ceiling above. Thus sandwiched between two levels of the Jovian atmosphere, the silent car ran frictionlessly atop a rail which appeared to float in mid-air. Resken simply absorbed the stunning scene; he accepted it all: the mighty vehicle, the scarcely believable rail apparently unsupported in the midst of sky, and the sky itself, with its continent-sized clouds, diffusely lit vaporous mountains floating in a creamy twilight of beige, pink and orange...

This must be the Girdle. I'm actually travelling on that equatorial planet-spanning structure which we divined in the First War. According to Terran calculations it had twelve stations, each of which beamed its own nightmare at Earth. We're immune to it now. They can't be trying to use it again. Not in the same way, at any rate. There'd be no point. So... they're using it for something else. As a transport system? Yes—and as a stopover for me.

Guesswork was vital for Resken. He must continue to believe in using his wits, ridiculous though it must seem to pit the said wits against the most colossal world in the System.

Cling to hope, or give up and die; that was his choice, and because his makers had imparted to him their own irrational will to live, he hoped in his guesses. "I'm going to be fetched from here," he thought, and gained hefty satisfaction when, sure enough, he saw a grey round-ended cylinder soar towards him out of the lower clouds.

Not another "translation", no. So close to the surface, something more basic, something cruder is needed.

As the rising shape approached to rendezvous with the monocar, the thing revealed its roughened texture, unpleasantly reminiscent of a bug with legs folded against its body: its design had nothing in common with the monocar's austere beauty. Resken did not even try to stop his mind from constructing empty theories. The supreme Jovian lords most likely were aided by lesser minions, bug-like nasties who shared their evil but lacked their dignity.

The crude grey airship clanged against the monocar. In no time a circular section of wall flapped down to allow passage between the docked vehicles.

In through the gap came a clicking horde of spherical creatures on stubby retractable legs. "Here come the Minions", nodded Resken to himself. They were about four feet high, with grotesquely wide mouths that opened and closed apparently out of smooth flesh, without lips or even a line to show (when the jaws were shut) where the openings had been. Clack, clack, they surged in and poured around him.

Jostled by these animated medicine balls, he was borne back with them as they returned to their airship, and as the connecting passage re-closed, and the ship un-docked and began its descent, he actually felt nostalgic for the quiet and splendid vehicle which doubtless continued as ever to glide round the great Girdle of the planet. He allowed such small pieces of emotional guesswork free play within himself. He'd been built, he now realized, to house the hunches and prejudices which churned within him, and to act inspired by the mettlesome spirit they now gave him. Quite likely his designers had fully known, that in constructing him to last so long, they had caused something unique to brew... for how could the petty old boxes called "thought", "logic", or "emotion" still pigeonhole his input after so many thousands of years? All must be boiled down into a super-intuition, so he trusted, so he hoped, as with a crazy glint in his eyes he prepared to wager the fate of his world, pitting himself against Jupiter.

The snapping Minions allowed him to shove his way through them as he sought the window. They let him stare as the airship descended into the lower cloud layer.

After perhaps half a minute the creamy blankness outside thinned away and through its last wisps Resken beheld the panorama which he had waited out his millennia to see.

No human eyes would have been able to judge its distance or its scale, but Resken's hard orbs, with their inbuilt equivalent of radar, ascertained that the planet lay spread out fifty miles below him. He was permitted to gaze his fill— which made good sense, for why not let him see everything, since his likelihood of return to his Terran fortress was zero?

Jupiter's surface, diffusely bathed in its orange glow, undulated with enormous but shallow gradients, mottled with grey-hazed patches which he guessed (setting his gaze to highest magnification) to be jungle. Five or six locations showed higher topography, with what resembled steeper volcanoes at the summits of lazier cones, as if Earth's Mount Fuji had been placed atop Mars' Olympus Mons. Valleys and swales were streaked with phosphorescent orange rivers (or roads?) which must supply some of the illumination, while the rest of the available light either spilled up from molten vents or filtered down through the clouds, or both. Resten wondered whether the darkness of night ever came to the surface of this world. Perhaps some areas knew blackness, but this one might be a sleepless capital district. "Guess on, guess on," he encouraged himself; "there's naught else to do."

Sudden blows to his shoulders jerked his attention away from the landscape.Jostled again by the Minions, he was forced away from the window, hustled across the floor, down through a trapdoor and into a windowless pod in the under-belly of the airship.

He guessed again, rightly—

It happened: a jolt of separation; a queasy weightless drop...

Then deceleration and a swinging motion. And lastly, the pod's walls began to dissolve, actually dissolve like wax.

He wasn't going to be granted a soft landing. Contemptuously the lords of this world were making their point. *The method of dumping is the message. It's what you do with rubbish.*

He fell a couple of yards onto the Jovian surface.

The drop was the equivalent of a five-yard fall on Earth, but his springy synthetic muscles were equal to the shock. He landed in a crouch like that of an athlete who awaits the starting gun. Simultaneously, eyes strained wide, he made sure that he did not lose a split second in his grasp of the scene around him. People! Human shapes! A crowd of brightly clothed forms, mouths agape! He heard them piping with amazement as they shuffled. They were backing off, to take position at a respectful ten-yard distance from the alien construct who had been tipped onto their patch.

3

RESKEN, NATURALLY, UNDERSTOOD nothing of their gabble, but their movements and poses told him enough. These folk, though genetically unrelated to Terrans, were obviously human, and the recordings he had watched during his long, long life had taught him plenty about human body-language on any planet.

He wasn't even shocked to see men and women on Jupiter. STIM (solar teleological irradiative morphogenesis) or, in popular parlance, the "Barsoom Principle", asserted that all the worlds of the System had a tendency to evolve native human minorities; hence he could read the emotion of this crowd.

They were grateful, humbly grateful and overjoyed. It was such an honour to receive a crumb from the table of their overlords! He, Resken 905, was that "crumb"—a kind of throwaway gift from the Powers that must rule this giant planet, and whose rubbish was treasure to lesser beings.

A tall bearded man robed in brown detached himself from the crowd. Eyes cast down in a pose of reverent submission, the Jovian villager approached the android and sank onto one knee. A tense silence fell upon all.

"Jull," said the man, thumping his breast.

"Resken," said the android with a similar gesture. Smiling, he gestured for the man to rise. The tension went out of the air.

Jull turned to issue orders; dozens of figures snapped into action. The android, swivelling on his heel, noted a cluster of squat frame houses built of red branches and woven leathery leaves. Towards this area trotted the task-force, who within minutes were erecting a greater structure: a superior lodging for their new guest.

It was not hard for Resken to gauge the comfortable trap he was in. Well, why not simply accept the inevitable? His conscience was clear. Struggle merely for the sake of struggle was pointless...

It was fatally easy for him to take this line, especially when Lerin, the chief's beautiful daughter, was assigned, surprise surprise, to teach him the language.

Her willowy form—so different from the squat Jovian build of standard predictions—melted his heart, even as the pattern of events spoke more cynically to his mind with the message, *Here's your role prepared.* Wryly, resignedly, he could imagine himself already labelled in Fate's display case as the easy hero, the champion of Lerin's people (the Haop, the humans of this world were called), soon to be their leader against the Jovian High Powers, and yet all the time merely serving the purpose of those very Powers.

Half of each ten-hour Jovian day, Lerin coached him. The smiling young woman pointed to one object after another, named each one and used the relation of nouns to build his understanding of verbs and adjectives, all the while domesticating him with her hopeful regard, weaving her spell of love and community purpose. The circumstances brought intellectual dividends too. Soon, the all-important dichotomy in Jovian life became apparent to him: namely, "short and squat" versus "slim and tall". For example, Lerin would indicate truffle-like plants and thick-boled stumpy trees and say "ummb"; then she would aim her finger at slender trees and spindly creatures stalking amongst them, and say "emmb". Ummb—emmb, one of those contrasts, as basic as plant/animal, red/blue, yin/yang...

"I understand," said Resken on the second day. "Two phyla on Buruz/Hemberaz."

Her face lit up. "Yes! Yes! One world, two names. 'Hemberaz' to us; 'Buruz' to the Flame-Lords."

'Buruz', as Resken now knew, meant "all". He nodded to himself, piecing together his more successful guesses. He had no precise idea, as yet, of what the Flame-Lords might look like. Nevertheless he could safely assume that they were the ultimate pinnacle of evolution of the "ummb" phylum—the stoutly-built creatures of this giant world. They, and their rotund Minions, had no choice but to be squat, fully subject as they were to Jovian gravity and hence designed to live heavy. Somewhere along the line of Jupiter's history there must have been a useful mutation to escape this fate. The "emmb" phylum consisted of creatures who were partially immune to gravitational pull. Doubtless it had begun with a single cell, containing some nullifying ingredient for which any terrestrial physicist would give his right arm. Eons must then have passed while the new type of cell divided and spread and incorporated itself into the tissues of an entire new category of living beings. These were creatures whose body-plans need not be squat, who could stand tall and thin, and who could climb and jump and generally knock about like the fauna of Earth or Venus.

Need there be conflict between squat "ummb" and slim "emmb"? Not in the forest, at any rate. He stood close to the edge of one patch of tall, wavy vegetation, while part of his attention remained on Lerin as she went on with her pointing and her commentary. He eyed the round shapes that groped through the undergrowth, causing the thinner higher stalks to tremble like jelly. Raggy mop-bodied birds, whenever their perches shook too roughly, fluttered squawking from branch to branch. Only a few times did he hear louder bellows and feel the tremors of bestial combat vibrate the ground. This seemed a mostly peaceful world, as far as his eyes could detect, his gaze lifting past the near forest to the vista of the next huge hill and beyond its hazy mottlings, further out to the vague undulations on the far-stretched horizon: all seemed immensely quiet and still.

He knew better than to trust these impressions.

He would trust his intuition instead. Only an infinitesimal fraction of the Jovian scene would ever get covered by his eyes, whereas his mind could hug the lot... might, at any rate, try.

"And make it a *good* try," he told himself. "To get it wrong, now, would be *most* expensive."

Meanwhile, he would continue to go native.

Fifty short Jovian days after his arrival at the village of Deyet, came the great gathering summoned by the chief, Jull, from the dozens of Haop settlements on the slopes of Gmezul.

Resken 905 was a married android by this time.

He and his new spouse stood beside Jull, in the same clearing that had been the scene of the android's arrival from the sky. He now felt the pressure of thousands of eyes upon him, the expectations of an entire people. He was only an artificial man, but he *was* inescapably a man, he now knew, and the adoration bestowed on him by Lerin was a bond and a snare of destiny.

It also cancelled out much old logic. He could no longer assume that these people's fear of the Flame-Lords would continue to restrain them.

The ceremonial speeches had all been made and a hush fell. It was his turn to speak. He adjusted his voice-box to crowd volume.

"People of Gmezul," he cried, "I admit the rumours are true, that I am not of this world; that I am of the third planet—"

That phrase destroyed the united hush that had lain on the crowd. A multitude of yelling throats hurled the iconic name: *"Earth!" "Earth!"*

Resken raised and lowered his arms. "Very well! I am of Earth!"

"Sent! Sent! Sent from Earth!"

"All ri-i-i-ight!" he yelled back. "You can say I've been sent from Earth; but listen, will you?"

"Lead us! Lead us against the Flame-Lords!"

Resken gave in. With gestures and promises he pacified the crowd. Then he turned to Jull and asked quietly, "Why are they so determined on this rebellion? Your lives are not hard. Your land is rich; you live in reasonable comfort. Why risk all this, in revolt against your superiors?"

The elderly chief did not hesitate.

"Because," said Jull, "they are our superiors."

Oho, so that was it. Resken did not change expression. He understood more widely by the second, that the motive of pride was knit together with the legends undoubtedly filtered down from the First Jovian War. Somehow the folk of this corner of Jupiter knew that Earth had, once upon a time, defeated the Flame-Lords.

That knowledge, and the arrival of a real live "Earthling", was enough to drive them crazy.

But did *he* have to be crazy too?

He asked himself this question one last time, prompted by the exalted expression on the face of his spouse, Lerin.

Was he really prepared, for the sake of this present moment—for the sun-spread of joy upon a pretty face—was he prepared to risk the annihilation of himself and all these people, pitted against beings who could snuff them out in one breath?

Ah, but "risk" and "pitted" were the wrong words, he knew.

They were all playing the Flame-Lords' game.

Resken 905, snatched down from orbit, was an adhesive. Fly-paper, that's what he was. Shoved among the people of Gmezul, to collect the trouble-makers.

What to do? Resist? No - this was the game, and he must play. He listened to himself say to Jull, "Very well—let's get started." *If one could change the rules, one might still win.*

4

He expected the chief to begin discussing practicalities, logistics... Instead, with a hand-wave, Jull signalled for a banner to be hoisted. Immediately this was answered by a more distant flutter of blue and red and orange: birds streaked upwards, in tight formation of colour-groups, a quarter mile beyond the edge of the gathering. Visible from afar, they formed the unstoppable signal for the march to start as another flight soared, further off, and then another, the flocks irrevocably alerting the communities of Gmezul like a lit chain of beacon fires strung in a line for scores of miles around that immense Jovian hil—a sequence which could not be countermanded.

Resken was aghast; then he smiled.

He hadn't been looking forward to all the organizational work. Now it was suddenly obvious, there was none to do.

With the clothes they stood up in, with the supplies on their backs, the inhabitants of Deyet, and doubtless of every other village on the Hill, were moving up the slope towards the fastness of the Flame-Lord of Gmezul.

It's not my fault at all, thought Resken. They're fulfilling some deep need of their own...

He was tugged by Lerin, her arm linked with his. She was pulling him towards the hoisted banner. Beside it, as it whipped in the breeze, stood a plump woman whose fingers sparkled with ornate rings. Lerin whispered, "Take the word, Resken."

"From her? What word?"

"She is Valooma Lakkas. You remember—I told you."

"You told me many things." Resken came to a stop and looked into the eyes of the soothsayer.

Cynically, he expected some bet-hedging statement, such as, "A great power is about to fall". This must be part of the instinctive set-up. A number of the village elders had stopped to listen—as Lerin put it, to "take the word".

The oracle was brief. "Live in the moment," said the plump woman, "for only the moment is alive."

"Thank you for that," murmured Resken. "I would sure rather live in the moment than think about what will happen afterwards." Sardonically said—*and yet*, he reflected as he walked on, *why not? Why demote any bunch of moments? Why despise any time as mere 'transition time'? These days of advance should be appreciated for their own sake...*

To travel hopefully was the thing.

But hang on—suppose there is no hope?

"Lerin!" he cried.

She was gone! No—there she was, she had merely stepped aside to spread Valooma's message to followers who were waiting to hear. She came back to him, took his arm again... He relapsed into contentment.

He, she and all the other folk of Deyet took the up-ward-slanting route between two forests, which led them eventually to their first stop, in a higher clearing, by the last hour of the short Jovian day. By this time Resken's reasoning faculties had been quite shunted away into some dusty store-compartment of his mind.

The horde camped for the ten hours of darkness. They chatted in low voices, ate and slept, and at the vague cloud-glow that was sunup they resumed their climb. Subdued merely by the importance of the occasion, no one seemed a prey to fear. Upon every face had descended a solemnity which left little room for any twitch of doubt.

By the following day Resken had thoroughly developed a similar ability not to think, not to worry, and instead to put his trust in the prevailing mood of the uphill flow, as if he and his followers formed a gravity-defying river. Doubts largely ceased for him, as for them. This was necessary in order that his steps might continue to plod, one after the other, up to-wards the summit cone.

No such immense climb would have been available on

Earth. If it had been, Resken knew from his long studies, it would have taken them into freezing cold. Here, the planet was so vast, a climb of five or ten miles made little difference climatically. The types of vegetation, as of terrain, remained fairly constant. Altitude did make some difference to the view, however. The horizon swelled by a factor of two or three. But after that, it ceased to grow, since the density of atmosphere put a limit of a few hundred miles on how far sight could penetrate; thus the skyline presently appeared to halt its retreat, thereafter persisting as a constant vast circle of haze.

Within that circle, however, perspectives shifted as the days went by. It became possible to see the tops of some of the other major hills, as Gmezul progressively revealed its eminence to be huger than they.

From his millennial studies of Earth, Resken drew an analogy with sea-swells frozen in a snapshot taken from tall ship's deck—only the scale was quite different and these hills, of course, were solid and still. Yet the *idea* of their undulating movement haunted him. He became more mentally "jumpy"; his muscles tensed as if in anticipation of a sudden attack. Well, why not? Was that not a reasonable notion? Wasn't he leading a war party?

The faces and moods of his army of followers had turned even quieter and more watchful than before, suggesting that their hunches might be not dissimilar to his. Though they weren't yet directing looks of inquiry at *him*, yet an alarm bell rang in his mind, to awaken him from his previous optimistic trance. To his trusting people he had better at least *appear* to know what he was doing.

Therefore he kept his firm stride, not daring to break it even after he became aware that a grey hump atop the upper skyline was no mere protruberance in the flank of Gmezul but an actual sight of the final summit cone, peeping at last over the main slope's shallower gradient. The face of doom, it was; yet at all costs, he commanded himself, he must maintain the same calm pace as before while his catlike alertness intensified and his sidelong glances monitored more closely the mien of his closest companions. Groping in mental darkness, he must at least stay in instant touch with whatever stirred the others, so that his hackles would rise the same as theirs... though when the precise nature of the doom chose to reveal itself he would have to do more than shudder in unison with his adopted people: he would have to show them leadership. Whatever loomed, whatever settlement of accounts with that summit cone, he, Resken 905, must stand the trial as figurehead of the rebellion. This certainty was a racking dream-torture, held at bay, so far, by sheer guts or ego—

Then at last came the wakeful, open, long-foreseen sounds of fear.

His ears were assailed by: "Muxxt!" "Muxxt!" —an outcry in the form of a word that was new to him. Nevertheless he instantly guessed where to look, without needing the craned necks all around him to indicate the distant summit cone. From that loftiest peak a cloudy smudge, hardly more than an out-of-focus speck, now rose. This was what was inspiring the echoes of "Muxxt!" "Muxxt!" from mouth to mouth, as folk halted their march. They can't have been sure themselves, thought Resken quietly—but they're not surprised.

The tiny distant cloud ceased to rise and began to swell. Or rather it came closer, at a speed which Resken's eye and brain could judge from Doppler calculation. The object, he guessed, would be upon him within minutes. Its bearing did not alter by the smallest deviation from its line-of-sight approach at a rate of about two hundred miles per hour. Within the next minute he began to resolve it into a swarm of dots. The minute after that, his eyesight could magnify each dot into a mighty flying creature, an ovoid considerably larger than a man, and bristling with wings, beaks, claws...

Please—breathed the android's inner self—since "this is it", let my arrogance serve a larger purpose. Let a merciful regard be turned upon the up-blundering folk whom I have led to this juncture—please, there has to be a compensation for their belief in me; their fond illusion that I know what I am doing—

That word *Muxxt* meanwhile kept smiting his ears. Belatedly he snatched the sense of it by means of his recently acquired Jovian vocabulary: *Muxxt* was not so much a name, as a named number. *Muxx* would be Sixty whereas *Muxxt* with the extra "t" sound was Sixty-One. Here and now, this was a number with some peculiarly personal element: expressed with dire brevity the prickly-prime "61" hovered one wing-beat ahead of his mental grasp, teasing him with foreboding of some act of will. And now the ovoid creatures themselves had arrived overhead, to bulk above him with their eerie gulping hums; bizarre winged eggs fanning into inverted cup formation, flapping loftily in preparation for a swoop—

But wait—belatedly shrieked the android's mind (while eye and brain ran a superfast register of the objects above him)—*they are not 61; they are 60; one is missing; and that one creates a ravenous vacancy—*

A slot waiting to receive me. It pulls like the hungry gap in an ionized atom's outer electron shell. So, is that the idea? I am to be wedged into the role of that final particle?

The subdued multitudes around him watched meanwhile with fear-battered faces. He sensed their grim effort. They were desperately trying to clutch the hope he embodied for them—the hope that he could do something, something right now, to counter the humming overhead things. *All very well for you to pin all that expectation on me.* He was tempted to shout at them, *Stop hoping at me, will you*—He closed his eyes at the edge of despair. But from deeper inside him came the sudden grin of a manic idea. Actually there was one possible "something" in which *he* might put *his* hopes...

He therefore opted not to struggle. As the big gulp began, he stood still, allowing the sixty ovoids to descend and buzz closer around him. Their threatening bulk and sinister crescendo must, he realized, seem nightmarish to his followers, who were scattering back in terror. But he hoped that his upright and unflinching stance might at least hint to them that all was not yet lost. *If the Sixty swallow me, that means, does it not, that I'll be in, and if I'm in, I'm in, and then we'll see; perhaps it will turn out that they have made a mistake. That's all I crave: that they please make just one game-changing mistake.*

His view became fully clogged with the hovering ovoids. Their wings fanned his face, and the noise almost deafened him, but that was as nothing compared to the first brush of mental contact. It was the prickly stroke of a consciousness so much larger than his, that it threatened to bite off and swallow his own. *Larger—yes, much larger—but maybe not stronger.*

He remained patient and docile while they pulled him into their collective. He did not tremble bodily nor assert his will. Nor did he allow his ego so much as a single prideful flinch of resistance, while his personality dissolved into the group. For—he sensed with gathering joy—he didn't need to. He must have had a right hunch here; must have guessed what was going to happen. His small tincture of personality was able well to outweigh their huge Sixty; he sensed his ego overflow theirs, felt them feebly realize, too late, that they had blundered and blundered good! They'd had no idea of the power his Terran designers had given to his mind and personality. Indeed, how could they have known? They'd have had to have been familiar with the history of ancient Terran space programs to understand how engineers made a fetish of redundancy, and habitually constructed their wares many times stronger and more reliable than the planned mission required; with the result that when plans were upset and the mission changed, the product remained ready.

You never had a chance, gloated Resken's mind at the sixty newly-trapped shadows cowering in a corner of his brain.

With both arms he made a palm-pushing upward gesture. At the same time, he spoke the mental command, *Rise ten yards. Hover till I call you.*

They obeyed—and his people saw, and wondered—and he beckoned the edge of the crowds forward, whereupon their foremost elements scrambled upright, followed by others, and began to approach, gingerly at first, then with amazed alacrity, as they sensed that he was truly in command of the *Muxxt.*

Lerin was the first to reach his side; she took his arm and gazed into his face as if her eyes would scour him— "You are really you?"

"Authentically me," he smiled.

Warily she mused, with an upward glance, "And now you seem to be master of *them...*"

"I tricked them, I think," he nodded. "Not sure yet how far. But now I'll have to go."

She shuddered. "With them—up to the top?"

"Yes. Before I lose the advantage of surprise. Sorry about this," he said. "Will you explain that for me, to our people?"

Her face had turned haggard, but she bowed her head in acquiescence, and, not daring a farewell hug, she sadly drew back to leave him free. He wasted no more time. Shooting a mental summons to the Sixty, he bade two of them descend, fetch and lift him.

So a pair of ovoids closed around him, one on each side of him, while the rest hovered lower, and then the full Muxxt including and commanded by Resken soared as a full group of Sixty-One into the sky. Silently the ascent was witnessed by all the folk who had followed him so far, and who now stood hemmed in by forebodings and desperate hopes, their eyes tracking the flying formation as it wheeled and angled to set their leader's course towards the summit cone of Gmezul.

5

Tentacular limbs supporting him under each shoulder, Resken was borne through the air by two of the ovoid flyers. Wedged in this way between them, he was deprived of sight where the creatures' bulk obstructed his view, but ahead and below he did have some narrow view of the land over which they sped. It looked momently more barren and at the same time more garish. Purple rocks increasingly littered the slope in dribblets of scree which suggested gouts of dried volcanic blood.

Resken 905 felt light-headedly close to death, the eeriness of his fantastic situation accentuated by the captive shadow minds of the Muxxt tumbling inside his head. One fixed spike rose clear of the maelstrom of mystery: the moral landmark variously termed honour, duty, loyalty… tinged with pride. *Do your best and don't expect to survive. The great thing is to impress the enemy. They're sure to test you to destruction. Do your best. Do your best.*

Because of this moral imperative, there was no turning back, even though he might have been able to control his flight by the ascendancy he had won over the ovoid creatures; he was as certain to continue towards his doom, as if the Muxxt really had captured him, instead of he them. That thing called honour / duty / loyalty ensured that he could not deviate. Resignedly, he could only watch as his bearers lifted him past a grey belt of discontinuous rock. They had now attained the altitude of the steeper, summit cone; henceforth, with a more tilted gradient, the terrain over which they flew acquired a more sinister aspect. The slope up here was more extremely grooved with fissures and pocked with caves. Wider yawned the rents in the ground, and more chaotic, as they neared the ultimate top.

He was into his last minutes of life—and he did not understand himself. Surely he ought to be able to answer the question: *what did he hope to achieve, in this rush towards doom?*

Not being a fool, Resken possessed a fair degree of self-knowledge. He knew (without being able to do anything about it) that he had been designed with various unattractive but vigorous human qualities such as arrogance and selfish ambition, while at the same time he was also aware that he had been provided with an equal helping of courage and idealism. Those traits were copied from mankind; his super-human qualities on the other hand were mainly physical, not moral—with one exception: his stupendous patience: a patience that had enabled him to wait out thousands of years of isolation in an orbiting capsule, in preparation for the doomed mission in which he was now engaged.

Now, close to the end, that super-patience was at last wearing thin.

Because he was not a fool, he could question the obvious surface flaws in his designers' strategy, and deduce that some secret must underlie them, enabling the strategy to make sense. Otherwise he'd have to conclude that his Terran backers were idiots. What was the point of an agent placed to undertake a mission from which he could not return? An agent who could not possibly harm the enemy in any way— what conceivable use could he be to the Terran war effort? No, there must be more to it all than this; and the truth was finally seeping through to the surface of his consciousness. His makers had thought to prevent him from accessing it directly, but he could not forever be denied, especially now he possessed the extra processing power of the Muxxt brains, and life's tangles were at last unravelling, allowing common sense to shine out as never before, in the simplified vista of approaching extinction.

Those Muxxt—he certainly had turned the tables on them! They had thought to absorb him; he instead had absorbed them; and the combined gestalt could be compared to a state which, in theory only, was a federation, and in practice was dominated by one country far larger than the rest. Resken's brain thus now held sway as the Russia of the Muxxt's USSR. This coup had won him a few minutes' reprieve from enemy control. However, it was ludicrous to hope that he might repeat the performance with the actual Flame Lord of Gmezul.

So, what good had it done him? Think! To win these extra few minutes, had been good for - what? What might he yet achieve, to set against the disaster which loomed as the imminent reward for his pig-headed persistence? From somewhere inside him, he found an inexplicable trust in himself. But could he trust this feeling of trust?

Intuition, blah—he needed answers; and not only, he realized, answers concerning this senseless Second Jovian War, *but also about the First*. The two wars, grasped in unison—

He made a snap decision as he was carried up past a cave-opening wide enough to accommodate all of his swarm of Muxxt. Though it glowed like the mouth of an orange hell, the gaping dry-vent gave off no more heat than the rest of this jumbled landscape, and so, as far as temperature was concerned, they'd be able to swerve and fly right into it, and that, under his mental command, is what they immediately did—to find that the space inside opened out into a roughly spherical cavern about fifty yards wide. Resken brought his subject swarm to a hovering halt at the centre of the enclosed space. He took hurried note of the shape and the sounds and texture of the interior. The yellow-orange walls blazed with a translucent glow, pulsing in time with a kind of sloshing rumble, like the respiration of a stertorous giant. Gliding forward to peer over the rim of a downward tunnel entrance he then caught sight of a brilliant blue stream. His brain named it "lava" but his emotions conceived of it as "the blood of Gmezul". Had he really entered a living body? The idea slithered forward... Caution at this point might be the worst madness of all. Move forward, inward! It was a powerful hunch. He obeyed it. Further into the labyrinthine network of caves and caverns he and his swarm of ovoid flyers glided, deeper into the warm dazzle of translucent throbbing radiance, the vast eerie mutter and hiss of concealed flows.

The geometric awareness grew in him, of how much the entire volcanic cone was perforated by tunnels and caverns. The summit of Gmezul was almost one quarter air, as opposed to a mere three quarters mountain. Spongy metaphors crowded in on his imagination. He thought of lung passages, and of the aerated rock called pumice which he had never seen but with which he was quite familiar through his encyclopaedic store of Earth science. Organic or inorganic sponginess—which was it? Of the two, the organic continued to gain in conviction. The rhythmic throbs of sound and light, and the glistening of the pathways, blended in an experience which *was* like travelling through a giant body. The idea presently force-fed him the awful truth, that the Flame Lord of Gmezul was no mere colossal energy creature inhabiting the volcano; it *was* the volcano.

Straightaway the Muxxt, the recent extensions of his mind, who had been waiting like demure servants, now flooded his central awareness with a gleeful "Yes!"

At the same instant the long-brewed Terran plan came likewise at last into full and explicit focus in his brain, so that he could not help blabbing it, as it bled from his thoughts via his links with the Muxxt—could not help, therefore, being crushingly aware of having, in that moment, betrayed his whole purpose in coming here.

Then, when at last he would have fled, out of the corners of his eyes he saw other flying groups draw up behind him, to occupy all cavern corners and the entrances to the tunnels at his back, blocking his retreat. Their names filtered into his mind via the awareness of the Muxxt; not Sixty-One but other related prime gestalts—the Trexxt, the Zaddst, the Noxxt, the Bluxxt: the 23, 37, 53, 89... enough to obstruct the way back like a wall.

Finally, in their plural voice, in mingled sounds and thought-forms, the forces who had trapped him addressed him, with the cold laughter of history.

6

Listen, Earthman, said the voice with stupendous gentleness, —*for Earthman we call you, construct though you are... construct or 'natural', as with organic or inorganic, or our own 'ummb' versus 'emmb', it is all one to us, infinitely beneath our concern, since we, the gathered Flame Lords, are features of the planet itself. As you hear the rumblings around you, Earthman, you hear not only the throat of Gmezul, but also what we relay to you of the throats of all Emorion uttering their balance of energies in the ultimate language of power - of topographic life. Thus we do you some honour, little Man. You have served our purpose well. Henceforth, thanks partly to you, Emorion is the name for what your people know as Jupiter, and what the Haop knew as Hemberaz, and Gmezul knew as Buruz—*

All now engulfed in the true name, with your unwitting aid. And we can repay you with knowledge, since your barriers are down, your infinitesimally puny mind open to what we pour in...

Understand, then, the different kinds of life. In addition to organic life such as can be found on most worlds, and the rarer inorganic life such as you people have found on the Darkside of Mercury and in grottoes on your Moon, there is what you might call positional life. This—the cause of topographic beings like us—is born of the endless patterned interplay between what flows and what the flows flow past. Thus we, the living volcanic cones of Emorion, came into existence. But at first, for long ages, we did not know that Emorion was a planet. To us it was Buruz—the Universe. "Emorion" was just a word for "ground" as opposed to "sky".

An understandable mistake, we're sure you will agree, if you consider the size of our world.

Then came irritations. Inexplicable pokings from above. They began with what you call the Galileo entry probe, at the beginning of your race's Space Age. Multitudes of other "probes" followed. We did not understand or care for these strange objects that rained down through our atmosphere. Disturbed by their artificial origin, we falsely assumed that a weird civilization must exist somewhere in the higher cloud layers of Buruz.

But though we did not understand and could not suspect the true location of the race that built them, it was easy for us to retaliate.

We hit back by means of what we will call Influence-Track Reversal—but which lesser intellects have inaccurately termed Reverse Causation. That is, we took hold of the influences, the emotional disturbances, which we received from your probes, and reflected the whole lot, with embellishments of our own, accurately back upon the senders.

This process, though we did not know it at the time, was what you call the First Jovian War.

Your race did well to survive these counter-measures of ours. You even managed, in the end, to reverse our "reverse causation" back on us, and thus evolve a defence which led to cessation of hostilities. In fact, under the circumstances, we don't mind allowing you to call the result a "win" for Earth. However, we might add that it was lucky for you that you didn't push your luck—that you stopped bothering us with your probes after that.

After the War, both sides "took stock".

Increasing numbers of us began to re-think our assumption that our enemy inhabited the upper atmosphere of 'Buruz'. The difficulties, the improbabilities of the theory became more and more evident to us. One by one, we grasped that the ground and the cloudy sky we know, tremendous though they are, are not the Universe.

As for you Earthmen—well, you tried to think ahead, it seems. We've just now learned from the store in your own mind, Resken, about how your people reacted to the great event.

Understandably, you wanted to make sure of your victory. You wanted to make the peace permanent. So you sought for a way to deter any future aggression from our giant planet.

But before many centuries had passed, your world became incapable of much joint effort, for your Ages of Freedom dawned—the end of all economic struggles, the end of all your old-style disciplined States.

So you opted for defence on the cheap.

Bluff!

Yes, Resken, your people tried to bluff us! What you hear now is real laughter, the laughter of volcanoes; of mountains shaking their shoulders with mirth. But we understand, too…

You based your plans on an idea from an ancient science-fiction story, "Victory Unintentional" by one Isaac Asimov.

A mightily strong and capable construct would represent Earth, and the stupid Jovians would take it for an average Earthman, and be impressed.

It's not your fault that you had no idea what you were dealing with. We forgive your presumption.

We forgive it the more readily, as you have done us a favour…

You have converted Gmezul.

The last of us Flame Lords to accept a true picture of the Universe is Gmezul, in whose innards you are floating at this very moment. He is one of the greatest of us, but he held out longest against the truth. He is a dreamer, a nostalgic lover of old ideas, and has created beautiful mounds of echo-crystal-poems around his false visions of Emorion-as-Buruz, but we need his mighty mind to direct itself outward, to appreciate and study the real Universe.

He is now convinced at last. Thank you! We could not do it, but the presence of a real Earth construct, actually radiating its character inside Gmezul, has proved sufficient to effect the desired cure. We are now one people. Nothing henceforth can stop us, Earthman, from the achievement of our full potential, which is to know all things, and thus at need to control all things.

Welcome to Emorion, tiny creature from Earth. You may make your home in Deyet village with the Haop girl and never fear a Second Jovian War.

Troy Jones has had stories published in the After Oil *anthologies volumes 3 and 4, in* Merigan Tales: Stories from the World of Star's Reach, *and in the first* Vintage Worlds *anthology. He lives in Huntsville, Alabama.*

What would the Old Solar System be without continuing characters? From Northwest Smith and Lucky Starr to Captain Future and Tom Corbett of the Space Patrol, the classic genre was well supplied with characters who roamed from story to story, encountering adventures all over the solar system. Troy Jones' contribution to the first Vintage Worlds anthology, The Headless Skeletons of Neptune, *introduced DeJanay "DJ" Jespers to that colorful subgenre. In* The Sarcastic Snake-Men of Neptune, *DJ—on her honeymoon with her new husband Scott—ends up flung into a new adventure..*

THE SARCASTIC SNAKE-MEN OF NEPTUNE

Troy Jones III

M Y HUSBAND WAS getting away, but I was hot in pursuit. Scott turned his skis to the right suddenly, sending a spray of powder into the Jupiter-lit sky and narrowly avoiding a spongy, indigo "bush" sticking up out of the artificial snow. I was far enough behind—perhaps ten meters—that I could take a line that avoided the plant without having to turn so hard. My more efficient line helped me gain a bit on Scott.

We hit a relatively clear section and Scott glanced back over his shoulder. "Staying with me pretty good this time," he radioed.

I said nothing and focused on keeping myself balanced and my skis pointed in the right direction. Scott carved left, avoiding a dark, cauliflower-esque "tree" suddenly looming before us. He planted his pole and turned right, returning to the planned route. I followed. Scott, the more experienced skier, was starting to pull away again. I grit my teeth. I was determined to beat him to the bottom at least once today.

We went over a ridge that turned out to be a steep cliff—suddenly the ground was a good six meters below us.

Skiing on Callisto is a very different experience from skiing on Earth. The microgravity, you know. Also, not much air resistance. We were airborne for what felt like an eternity. Well, maybe "airborne" is not the right term—what passes for an atmosphere on Callisto is hardly worthy of the term "air". We arced majestically through the thin excuse for an atmosphere as the Callisti gravity finally got around to guiding us gently earthward. Or callistoward.

I came down onto a fairly level patch and wobbled a bit, but somehow kept my feet under me, even managing to not drop either of my ski-poles.

Scott's voice crackled over my space-suit's radio again. "How you doing back there?"

I radioed back. "Worry about yourself, Mister. I'm gonna win this time. You'll see."

Scott's laughter came back over the radio. He didn't sound at all worried, which only infuriated me further.

The slope steepened and we both started turning left and right to keep our speed under control. The gravity might be less, but you can still quickly build up to a dangerously high velocity if you aren't careful. Too fast and you won't be able to avoid the occasional rock outcropping or clump of spongy "vegetation" that clings stubbornly to the surface of Callisto, living off little more than cosmic radiation and carbon dioxide.

Scott was able to keep his skis parallel while turning, helping him maintain a stable speed he was comfortable with. My awkwardly V-shaped "snow plow" turns were much less efficient by comparison. In what seemed like no time at all he had doubled the distance between us.

The slope levelled out a bit. Scott hopped into the "air" at the top of a mogul (that's a hump of snow for you landlubbers) and did a 180. He started skiing backwards.

"Really?" I radioed him.

He just laughed. "Looks like you still have both your poles this time, at least. You're improving!"

Scott was taking glances over his shoulders on each turn, but seemingly mostly negotiating the moguls more by feel than sight.

"We'll see how well you ski after I choke you out, buster," I vowed heatedly.

The next part of the slope was a wickedly steep checkerboard of moguls. The sensible thing for Scott to do would have been to turn around and ski like a sane person. But, like a man, he wasn't about to stop showing off so soon after a trash-talk exchange. And I will say, for a while he managed it.

Then he hit a mogul at an awkward angle and went tumbling, ski-boots over teakettle, in low-gravity slow-motion. An inarticulate yelp came over the radio.

My initial reaction was concern for his safety, so the fact that I was headed straight for him being a potential problem *for me* didn't occur to me until a couple of seconds after he'd come to rest.

By then it was too late to turn to the left or right—on the slopes it's easy to lose track of just how fast you're going. I was already low in the knees though (because, you know, skiing), so, more from instinct than any real skill, I flexed into my knees a bit more, then snapped them straight, as hard as I could, launching myself off the ground.

I don't think the maneuver would have worked in Earth gravity, but on Callisto everyone has insane hang-time. I let out a victorious whoop as I sailed over Scott's prone form.

I landed on the side of a mogul and pinwheeled my arms crazily, trying to maintain my balance. I "snow plowed" my skis in a V-shape, trying to reduce my speed. Somehow I managed to stay upright.

"Are you all right, babe?" I radioed once I had myself under control.

"Yeah. I didn't need those ribs anyway," he answered. "I have a spare."

It was my turn to laugh. He was joking, so he was fine. Probably.

I didn't wait because now was my big chance. I continued descending the slope as quickly as I dared, knowing Scott wouldn't be far behind once he hauled himself to his feet. Leading the way was more challenging than following though, since following I could generally assume the routes he chose around obstacles were sound. In the lead, I had only myself to rely on.

I crested a ridge and suddenly the end of the slope was in sight. Something metallic glinted down there in the distance. I risked a glance over my right shoulder. Scott flew over the ridge behind me, closing fast, no longer messing around but legitimately trying to catch up.

I raced down the slope, struggling to keep my skis as parallel as I could as I turned left, right, left, much faster than I felt comfortable, just barely in control. I would have radioed Scott a semi-good-natured taunt, but it took 100% of my focus to keep my feet under me and myself sliding at high speed in the right direction.

And then it was over. The ground levelled out—the end of the course. I raised an arm in victory and looked back at Scott as I snow-plowed my skis to slow down. He was only two or three seconds behind me.

"Look out!" Scott's voice crackled over the radio.

Too slow, I swiveled my head to face front. A waist-high, four-legged robot was directly in my path. I had just enough time to think, *what is that doing there?* before colliding with it, sending it for a slow-motion tumble and taking a spill of my own.

Scott expertly come to a stop near us.

"You alright, D.J.?" he asked.

"Better than alright," I reported. I was laying on my side.

I got my skis uncrossed, put my ski-poles together, and planted them in the ground near my waist. Putting most of my weight on the poles, I levered myself up sideways onto my feet, with what I thought was a pretty reasonable degree of gracefulness. (I'd had a lot of practice standing up after a fall that week.) "Better than alright," I said again. "I beat you! At long last! Pure skill."

Scott laughed. "That you did. I'm impressed." He managed to make the praise not sound too patronizing.

I noticed he was holding his side. "You sure *you're* alright, babe?"

"Just a little bruised." He let go of his ribs and put his arm around my waist. "Wanna go up again? Quintuple black diamond this time?" He smiled through the transparent bubble of his spacesuit helmet. I like his smile.

But the robot had recovered itself and was waving its four arms at us, trying to get our attention. The robot's body looked like a pair of inverted cones surfaced with highly reflective glass, one cone nested partially inside the other, like a shiny, upside-down Christmas tree. Its arms and legs sprouted from rings around the widest part of each cone—four legs from the lower cone's ring and four arms from the upper cone. Atop the upper cone was its squat, cylindrical head, which was also mirrored glass except for a short antenna.

The robot pointed one of its arms at the stubby antenna attached to the side of its otherwise featureless head and held up all six fingers of one robotic hand. (I keep calling it a robot. The truth is that Callisti are much stranger than robots, but they look outwardly like robots so, like most tourists on Callisto, I tended to think of them that way.)

I switched the radio to channel six using my wrist-control.

"Mister and Mrs. Short?" the robot asked. I nodded. "My apologies. You have a call on the ansible from Earth," it continued. "It is an urgent matter; I am to direct you to the lodge at once." (Callisto doesn't have enough of an atmosphere to carry sound very well, hence the need for radios.)

I was not thrilled about having my honeymoon interrupted, but I figured an ansible call was likely to be an emergency. We went along as the robot led us back to the Gomul Catena Resort's luxurious ski lodge and conducted us to a fancy private meeting room with a ceiling-mounted tri-vid projector, comfy chairs, real-looking wood panelling, and a massive mahogany table that must have been imported from Earth at considerable expense.

Ansibles are a fairly new technology, so there's still some confusion about what exactly they do. They are, essentially, instantaneous communicators by means of quantum-entangled particles. That is to say, manipulation of one particle causes an instant sympathetic reaction in its entangled twin, regardless of distance, and I do emphasize *instantly*. These sympathetic reactions allow communication from one end of the Solar System to the other, bypassing lightspeed delay. The downside is that ansibles are fantastically expensive to maintain and use. In fact, there's only one ansible on all of Callisto, located in the Alliance consulate, its special particle quantumly entangled with its counterpart in a government building somewhere on Earth. But the quantum signal from Earth can be piped from the consulate by more conventional means to the tri-vid in the ski lodge's meeting room—a true marvel of modern technology.

(Certain wild-eyed dreamers think ansible technology might someday lead to matter-teleporters or even faster-than-light space travel, but that seems quite unlikely to this engineer, due to certain fundamental technical limitations I would prefer not to get into right now.)

A burst of bluish three-dimensional static appeared at the head of the table and was quickly replaced by a highly realistic hologram of a mostly bald, middle-aged white man wearing a dark sport-coat and collarless button-up synthsilk shirt, per the latest fashion. He looked real enough to reach out and touch—the very latest in hi-def tri-vid technology.

"Ah, there we go. Scott!" said the hologram. "And the new missus, I see," with a polite nod at me. "Looks like you married up, old man. Congratulations. Enjoying married life?" I tentatively pegged the hologram's accent as Boston.

"Yes, sir, thank you," Scott answered neutrally. He gestured at me. "This is DeJanay, my wife. D.J., this is Major Sullivan. He was my CO in the Mars War. You're what, AIA now?"

I nodded a greeting at the holographic Major Sullivan.

"I'm a civilian now—no need to call me *sir* anymore," the hologram said. I noted that Sullivan neither confirmed nor denied that he was now AIA—that is, Alliance Intelligence Agency.

Scott nodded. "Yes, si-... Ah. Okay. I don't imagine this is a social call. Is there something going on? What's the situation on Earth?"

"The situation on Earth? Grim. Very grim," Sullivan reported. "Yankees are this close to clinching the East." He held up thumb and forefinger to illustrate how near this disaster was.

I looked questioningly at Scott, who pressed his lips together in a disappointed line at the news. It took me a second to figure out what Sullivan was talking about.

"Ah, baseball?" I asked. Scott nodded. I turned back to Sullivan. "Don't spoil today's game please." Scott follows his Blue Jays closely (more closely than I follow my Braves), but due to the lightspeed delay, Sullivan there on Earth would have had knowledge of the game's progress at least half an hour before the broadcast reached us the conventional way.

"Brains *and* beauty, this one," said Sullivan patronizingly. I ground my teeth.

"Sullivan," Scott said quickly. "I know you aren't making an ansible call to talk baseball." Changing the subject, but

I had I figured that as well, of course. Ansible calls are not cheap.

Sullivan waved a vague dismissal. "Oh, it's all government money. Who gives... Mm." A quick glance at me as he stifled something presumably impolite. "But you're right. There's something else, important. Ah. You may want to send the missus away for this. It's a matter of some sensitivity. Not classified, technically, but we don't want, y'know, just anyone yapping about this before we get the situation under control. Maybe set her loose with a credit chip to buy something nice for herself. You understand."

Scott hesitated, perhaps sensing danger. I jumped in. "*I* understand that the only reason you don't have a black eye right now is because you aren't actually here in the flesh."

Sullivan laughed. "Oh, a firecracker! Brains, beauty, and moxie! I like her even more."

Scott reached across the table and squeezed my hand. I bit back the even more acid retort that would have come next. I did understand that a government official would not be calling on the ansible about a sensitive-but-not-classified matter unless it was important, even if said government official needed his holographic teeth kicked in.

"I'm not sending her away," said Scott. "She's my wife. This is our *honeymoon.* Tell us what you want and we'll give you a yes or no. Although I will warn you, I traded in my raygun for a slide-rule long ago."

"Suit yourself," said Sullivan the hologram. He consulted a tablet and frowned. "Have you heard of Ariel Martinelli?"

Scott shook his head.

"The journalist?" I asked.

Major Sullivan nodded. "The journalist, yes. She's gone missing investigating a story."

"Surely that's a matter for actual authorities, yes?" I pointed out. "The Callisti natives are very helpful and efficient, in my experience. Notify them; see if they've seen her." I felt a little bit proud of myself that I had remembered to call the Callisti by their right name instead of *robots*.

Scott spoke up. "And for that matter, why is the AIA involved looking for a missing civilian? Is she one of yours? A... what-do-you-call-it, non-official cover operative?" A *spy*, in other words. Although I thought it unlikely that a spy would have a cover identity as a modestly well-known media personality. Then again, I don't really know anything about spying.

Sullivan pressed his lips together in an enigmatic tight little smile and pointedly left those last questions unanswered. "Not Callisto. Her last known whereabouts are Neptune."

"Neptune!?" I exclaimed. "Do you have any idea how far away-"

Sullivan made an impatient gesture. "Yes, we know how far it is. And, Earth will not have a good launch window for Neptune for several weeks. That brings us to you two."

"We have a launch window," I ventured. This out-of-the-blue request was starting to make more sense.

(A lot of people who are new to space travel don't understand the existence of launch windows. Why can't we just go to another planet whenever we want? And indeed, the aforementioned wild-eyed dreamers dream of a day when the people of the Solar System will not be at the mercy of the fact that the planets are tiny, rapidly moving targets within the unthinkably vast space of the System, and in the future—they believe—travel between planets will be as quick and convenient as it is over the surface of Earth. But that day, if it ever comes, is a long ways off yet. As it stands now, the planets are extremely far away from each other, and they race around the Sun at surprisingly high speeds. If the planet you're on and your intended destination aren't lined up favorably, then it is, paradoxically, more efficient to wait a few weeks or even months for a more favorable alignment—a launch window, as it's called—before blasting off.)

Sullivan nodded. "Your window is open now, actually. Closes in a couple of days. Earth-days, I mean. Dunno how that translates to local time. If we had suitable personnel of our own in the Jupiter zone, we wouldn't be contracting this out of course, but..." he shrugged and trailed off.

Scott looked thoughtful. "It'll be expensive to charter a rocket on such short notice. If we can get one at all. Neptune, wow."

"It's all government money anyway, right, Sully?" I said. "We can book a luxury yacht, cruise out to Neptune with just the two of us, have a crazy-amazing adventure, and leave the bill to the taxpayers. Honeymoon saved! Woo!"

Sullivan did not look at all happy about that prospect, but neither did he veto the idea. They must've really been desperate.

There followed some negotiations over the specifics of payment and so forth, along with a few more chauvinistic remarks from Sullivan. Anyway, after we agreed to track her down, Sullivan promised to transmit our quarry's dossier to us via tight-beam transmission directly to our rocket once we were underway, just in case anyone was listening in on this conversation (a tight-beam transmission is much harder to intercept). I'll summarize the terms of the agreement by saying Scott and I would be set for a long time if we succeeded in bringing back Miss Martinelli in one piece, and even if we failed, it would still be more than worth our time—assuming we survived, of course. And if not, funeral expenses would be picked up by the Atlantic Alliance taxpayers.

The money isn't why Scott agreed to take this mission though; I'm pretty sure if I hadn't been there he would have agreed to save the damsel in distress for free (after expenses, *maybe*), just because that's the kind of old-fashioned good-guy/pushover he is. Lucky for him, I'm not quite as old-fashioned.

(And needless to say, his brief suggestion that he leave me

behind on Callisto while he would go gallivanting off on a dangerous adventure got shut down *real* quick. "We're married now, buster. Any gallivanting will be done *together*.")

Unlucky for me though, there were no luxury yachts available to charter for a Neptune run. In fact, all we could find was a Callisti-owned package-courier rocket that had never been taken out of Jupiter's gravity well by its current owner. Not ideal, but you have to take what you can get sometimes.

THE MAGLEV TRAIN ride out to the spaceport on the edge of the Gomul Catena crater-chain was uneventful. Mostly I looked out the window and admired the starkly beautiful Callisto landscape, illuminated by the baseball-sized Jupiter hanging above.

Emerging from the train, we found Swollen-With-Gratitude—that's the ski resort's Venusian proprietor—waiting for us on the platform amid the hustle and bustle of Earthlings, Venusians, Ganymedans, Ioi, and other denizens of the System coming and going.

"Mister and Mrs. Short!" exclaimed the slender Venusian. He spread his long fingers in a gesture of helplessness. "I heard but I did not believe it. Could not believe it."

(Of course, since he is a Venusian, he did not actually exclaim any of this with the proboscis he has in place of a mouth. Rather, he rubbed his antennae together rapidly, which produced a sound not altogether dissimilar to the sound a grasshopper makes by rubbing its hind legs together. A little box he wore on a chain around his rather long neck picked up the sound of his Venusian speech and translated it to English, even doing a reasonable job of simulating emotional inflections accurately—obviously an important feature when it comes to Venusians.)

"It was told to me," Swollen-With-Gratitude continued, "that my dearest friends the Shorts were leaving the decadent comforts of Gomul Catena nearly a week early, but I paid no heed to these rumors, dismissing them out of hand as the vicious calumnies of petty ne'er-do-wells. But now I stand here and see with my own eye that it is true!" SWG lowered the large, singular eye atop his long, flexible neck sadly. "I would sooner see the entrails ripped from my body and stomped into the regolith before my very eye than see the ones closest to my hearts leave in haste without even a goodbye to poor, bereft Swollen-With-Gratitude!"

Scott and I looked at each other. Judging from his nonplussed expression, I decided I'd better be the one to deal with SWG.

I took a deep breath. "Dear Swollen-With-Gratitude, I am so deeply sorry. We both are. We have a... friend who desperately needs our help, and we must depart while we still have a launch window. But we promise to come back when we can. I humbly beg your forgiveness for the terrible, unforgivable insult of not coming to tell you directly. I can only grovel abjectly and offer to let you kill and eat our firstborn if it would help in some small way to repair the bond between us."

(This last is a standard Venusian politeness I learned when I was stationed there a few years ago. It's rare for a Venusian to actually take up such an offer.)

SWG waved the offer away. "No propitiation is needed, for nothing can weaken the bond of true friendship between us three. But if there is anything Swollen-With-Gratitude can do to aid you on your journey, he will do it—though it breaks his hearts to see you go."

I opened my mouth to politely decline the offer in the customary flowery/grotesque Venusian way, but before I could, Scott muttered under his breath, "a ray-gun would be nice."

Something else I learned when stationed on Venus is that Venusians have incredibly good hearing. SWG gestured and a Callisti robot appeared seemingly out of nowhere. He turned to it and said something with his antenna-speech, but the auto-interpreter around his neck produced the clicking/chirping/rustling sounds of the Callisti language instead of English. The robot hurried away.

I sensed that Scott was about to take that request back—he'd meant it for my ears only, I'm sure—but before he could, I dug my elbow into his ribs. To make a request, even in jest, and then back out of it once the other party has moved to fulfill it really *would* have been a grave insult.

"Oof," said Scott. I belatedly remembered that that was his injured side. Oops.

And after exchanging a few more extravagant blandishments and pleasantries (including SWG offering to personally eviscerate any resort employees who had displeased us, which we of course declined), we placated SWG at last and made our way to launchpad 23, where our chartered rocket awaited us.

OUR ROCKET PILOT, who was also the rocket's proprietor, met us on the launchpad, on the largely airless surface. It waved and pointed to the stubby radio antenna on its head.

"Hello there. We're Mr. and Mrs. Short. What should we call you?" Scott radioed.

"You may refer to me as Captain," the Callisti responded. (I assumed this was simply because its name would be unpronounceable to us.)

During my brief stay on Callisto, I'd never seen a Callisti native with more than three of those robot cones. But Captain consisted of five cones, stacked like a totem pole, each cone with four arms on its utility ring, except for the bottom cone which had four legs instead. Captain was slightly taller than Scott, in fact. An impressive (if slightly ungainly) sight.

Captain's voice crackled over the radio again. "A pleasure to meet the two of you. Please come aboard."

Captain walked toward the rocket's gangplank without turning around first. (I guess if you can see in all directions at once and your arms and legs are all equidistant around your body, there's less need to turn your whole body around.)

I looked up at the rocket. I'm no expert, but I could tell it was Earth-built, a late-model De Sá perhaps, with fancy dramatic fins and four removable external fuel tanks. The extra fuel would be required to get us to Neptune.

The hatch at the top of the gangplank was open, but I could see it was small enough that Scott and I would have to duck to get through it. I wondered how Captain would negotiate the opening, being not particularly flexible. No sooner had that thought crossed my mind though, than Captain reached up with the arms of its middle cone and lifted its two upper cones off. Instead of bending its rigid metallic form to get through the door, Captain simply separated itself and carried its own upper half aboard.

I guess I expected Captain to reunite itself after embarking, but was surprised again. Once aboard, Captain set down the two upper cones on the deck—apparently the arms sprouting from its utility rings can double as legs—and these two started punching buttons on a wall panel. The gangplank retracted, the hatch behind us closed, and the hiss of the airlock cycle began. It was a tight squeeze with the three (four?) of us in the airlock.

Once the air pressure equalized, the airlock's inner hatch slid open and we had access to the interior of the ship. Captain's lower three cones toddled off somewhere (the bridge, I presume), while his upper two remained with us.

Scott and I checked the atmosphere readings and, satisfied that it was safe, removed our spherical space-helmets.

Captain's voice came over the ship's intercom. "Feel free to make yourselves at home, except that the bridge and the engines are off-limits for safety reasons. Your luggage is all aboard; we'll depart as soon as we have clearance from ground control."

"Thank you, but I'm curious," said Scott. He seemed unsure whether to look up to address the intercom or look down to address Captain's upper half. "Are you, ah, one being or two? Or five?"

"That is a question our philosophers have wrestled with for millennia," came the cryptic reply over the intercom. "Please follow me to your cabin." Captain's upper half started moving down the hall. We followed.

SPACE, PARADOXICALLY, IS at a premium in space. By that I mean, rockets are always terribly cramped on the inside. Cabins are too small for even one person, but of necessity must be shared by four or more. Corridors force tall people to slouch, and barely allow two people going opposite ways to get past each other. The mess hall doubles as a meeting room, triples as an exercise room, quadruples as a tri-vid viewing lounge, and quintuples as a storage room for random junk. And so on.

One would think that, *in space*, one would have all the space one could possibly need—*I mean, it's right there in the name*, as one famous tri-vid media personality often says— but of course it doesn't work like that. The issue isn't a lack of space as such, but of pressurized, atmosphere-filled, climate-controlled space. Every cubic foot of *that* that you have to maintain raises the cost of your rocket voyage by a crazy amount. That's why—luxury cruisers excepted—rockets are designed to utilize what little internal space they have so efficiently—and "efficiently" translates into sore necks and chronic bad posture for spacers.

I understand all of that—indeed, I'm a life-support engineer by trade—but it won't stop me from complaining about the lack of space in space. And I will say that this rocket trip was better than most, relatively speaking. Our humble package-courier, a De Sá Emissaire Mk IV (to be exact), was far from a luxury yacht, but with just us two Earthlings—and a philosophically ambiguous number of Callisti—it was positively *spacious*.

About an hour after we blasted off, Captain informed us that a coded message had come for us from Earth via directed laser burst. It turned out to be the promised dossier on Miss Martinelli. (Since we had provided Major Sullivan with our flight-plan, he was able to aim a communication laser at the exact point we would be along our path, taking into account the half-hour or so lightspeed delay between us, and send the dossier to us via coded laser-bursts. This transmission could not be intercepted—in theory—unless another ship happened to be in the direct path of the laser.)

Scott and I looked over the files on his tablet in the mess hall / storage room / everything-else room.

Martinelli was freelance, so she didn't have an employer as such. She did stories for most of the major tri-vid networks, mostly political stuff, foreign affairs, that kind of thing. None of her usual network contacts knew what she was looking into on Neptune, according to the dossier. She had family on Earth, but they were mostly estranged; none of them had any idea what she was up to on Neptune either. She had an agent in Rome who knew where she was but not what the potential story on Neptune was about.

She'd brought along a sort-of dead-man's switch, a small transmitter that would send a coded message twice a day letting her agent know she was okay. The dead-man's switch had stopped transmitting a couple of weeks ago, but the agent had not otherwise heard anything.

We couldn't find any reason for the AIA to have such a keen interest in her either.

"Useless," I declared it all.

"If there were any obvious clues, I'm sure Sullivan or one of his people would have noticed and brought them to our attention," said Scott.

"So we're wasting our time."

"No, we're looking for whatever they missed."

Nothing jumped out at us, however.

PEOPLE SOMETIMES ASK what one does for fun on long space voyages. The answer is not anything terribly exotic. Watch tri-vid recordings, read the latest issue of *Flabbergasting Stories*, play cards or other games, take your pick. Hobbies that require a lot of space, e.g. most sports, are right out. Compact game-bits that can be used for a wide variety of different games—like cards, dice, or Martian chessmen—see a lot of use.

One evening we were playing Gnostica (a moderately popular game among spacers that uses Martian chessmen and Earthling Tarot cards) with some of Captain's robot cones when Scott decided to revisit the question of just how many there were of Captain.

Scott played a Sword card from his hand, killing one of my small chessmen. "Captain, I'm curious. Forgive me if this is some kind of taboo to ask. On Callisto, we noticed that most of your people have one or two of those... cones. A few have three. You're the first we've seen with five. Is that some kind of status thing? Or...?"

Captain didn't answer right away, perhaps thinking about it. I played a Cup card from my hand to respawn the chessman Scott had killed, oriented for a counterattack.

Captain discarded the two cards remaining from its hand and drew back to six. Then its voice addressed us over the ship intercom. "It isn't a status thing, no. Most of my people live far underground in hives, without any cones. The cones are necessary only for those of us who would interact with off-worlders, or who need to utilize off-world technology or facilities for whatever reason. We claim only as many cones as needed."

Scott scowled at his cards a moment, then used his move to reorient one of his chessmen to deal with my threatened attack. "You need five? What determines how many are needed?"

I played a Hermit card from my hand, spiriting away Scott's newly reoriented defender to an empty space far from where the action was developing.

One of Captain's pieces was lying down by itself on a Cup pip card, oriented away from both me and Scott. Captain used its power to spawn a new territory from a card in his hand, which also turned out to be a Cup card. "Each cone can only sustain so many individuals. For this lengthy—and possibly dangerous—mission, I decided to bring along as many individuals as I could, in case of casualties."

Scott frowned in confusion. "Individuals?" (I was confused as well.)

"Perhaps this will clarify," said Captain. The lid of Captain's topmost cone hinged open. A swarm of indigo cicadas streamed out. Scott and I gaped.

Not cicadas, of course. They were Callisti—the *actual* Callisti, minus the robot shell, which could more accurately be called a *vehicle* than a robot. But the sounds of their rustling wings and chirping reminded me strongly of dog-day cicadas from summer nights back home in Georgia.

I was awe-struck. "The tourist brochures—"

"Make no mention of this," Captain confirmed. "Swollen-With-Gratitude and other off-world developers like him urge us to downplay our nature. Swollen believes that servile robots are less off-putting to potential tourists than intelligent, hive-minded insectoids would be."

That didn't really sit right with me, but I couldn't really argue with it either. Many Earthlings do have a visceral dislike of *bugs*.

Not me though. I held out my index finger. One of Captain's *individuals* alighted on my fingertip. Up close, it didn't look quite as much like a cicada. Its head was too big, and it had only four legs instead of six. Also, its head boasted multiple eyes of varying sizes all around it, somewhat like a spider. It waved one its legs at me and then took off to rejoin the swarm.

The cicadas—the individual Callisti—returned to their robot shell and closed the lid.

It was Scott's move. He discarded one of his three cards and refilled his hand to six. "You don't consider *yourself* an individual?"

"An individual is, by definition, not divisible. The small creatures that comprise me are individuals. I am the whole that is greater than the sum of my parts. The gestalt. The hive-mind. But I am separable. A group of my individuals permanently separated from me would comprise a new gestalt."

"How does that hive-mind stuff work, exactly?" I asked. "Telepathic?" I played the Hanged Man from my hand. This card does two things: first, it's used like a Rod—which I used to push one of Scott's defending chessmen away—and then you may exchange hands with another player. I exchanged my one remaining card in hand for Scott's fresh hand of six. I smiled sweetly at Scott's consternation.

Captain used the same Cup card on the table that he had used last turn to spawn a new small chessman on his new territory. "Telepathic, yes, but don't worry. Our brains are structured very differently from yours; I cannot read your minds. My inevitable victory in this game will be due solely to my vastly superior intellect."

I laughed. Captain had not trash-talked or joked around with us prior to this, so I took this—along with Captain showing us its true form—as a sign that we were friends now.

In the end, Captain beat us soundly at Gnostica. By the time Captain made its game-ending Challenge, Scott and I were too weakened from fighting each other to raise any kind of defense. So maybe there is something to that whole superior intellect thing.

On the other hand, I crushed both Scott and Captain at poker the next day. Who has the vastly superior intellect now, hm?

THREE WEEKS FROM Jupiter to Neptune is an excellent travel time, relatively speaking. We were able to do it because Saturn lay close enough to our path to take a convenient slingshot through its gravity well, giving us a substantial speed boost. I'm sure Sullivan would have liked us to get there sooner, but as mentioned, Neptune is just so far away.

Neptune is a cold ocean world, its watery surface kept liquid by the tidal energy imparted by its massive moon Triton, so landing a conventional rocket on Neptune's surface (or blasting off again) is problematic. Neptune does have numerous floating "islands" made of accreted biological matter on which the snake-like natives live, but these pseudo-islands have been deemed too ecologically delicate for rocket launches or landings. Instead, rockets dock at the space station, and aerospace shuttles (with special pontoons to let them take off from and alight upon the water, like seaplanes) ferry visitors from orbit to Neptune and back again.

We made our way through the transfer tube connecting Captain's rocket and the space station. (No spacesuits for us since Neptune's atmosphere is approximately Earth-normal, as is its space station's, if a bit cold. So instead, civilian space-tourist attire: a jumpsuit for Scott and a cute jumpskirt and insulated leggings for me.)

"Where do we even begin?" I asked Scott. "I don't know anything about searching for missing persons."

"Hospital, jail, morgue—in that order," said Scott. "If the Alliance had a consulate on Neptune, we would start there, I guess. But they don't. If they did, there'd probably be official-cover AIA agents working at the consulate anyway, and they wouldn't need us."

"But what if she went down to the surface? A needle in a haystack would be an easy find compared to an Earthling lost in an ocean big enough to swallow the whole Earth like a pebble."

Scott didn't have an answer for that, even though I was grossly exaggerating the size difference between Earth and Neptune (which is, in fact, only about four times as big as Earth). We would just have to cross that bridge if we ever came to it, I figured.

The space station's hatch irised open. I jumped, startled. A huge *snake-man* was standing right there in the shadows on the other side. From where its body/tail rested on the floor to the top of its three-eyed head, it stood eight feet tall, easy. The snake-man wore only a utility belt, from which dangled a ray-gun, a truncheon, and some other, less readily identifiable, implements.

"Greetings," whispered the three-armed snake-man. "Scott Short? DeJanay Short?"

(Neptunians are one of only three known extraterrestrial races that can manage Earthling speech without some form of assistive technology. But they lack vocal cords, so everything they say sounds like a whisper, even if they're speaking as loud as they can.)

"That's us," said Scott.

The Neptunian twisted its neck until its head was upside-down, its three yellow eyes now on the underside of its head. I wasn't sure if this was a body-language expression thing, or if it was just trying to get a better look at us.

"Which," asked the Neptunian, its head still upside-down, "is which?"

Scott and I looked at each other. Gotta love culture gaps.

Scott tapped his chest. "Scott Short."

I nodded. "DeJanay Short. D.J. for, ah... short." I honestly had not thought about the potential confusion of having both a nickname "for short" and the *surname* Short until that moment. Not that it would have made me rethink marrying Scott.

I hoped earnestly that the Neptunian customs official (I was assuming that's what it was) would understand what I meant and not call me "DeJanay Short D.J. For-Ah-Short" from then on.

The Neptunian turned its head rightside-up. "I am called," and there followed a long, vowelless sequence of oily sibilants and harsh fricatives, with the odd glottal stop mixed in here and there. "Hh'shkh for short, if you like." Hh'shkh pointed to a badge on its utility belt. I did not recognize the badge's iconography.

"Hh'shkh, pleased to meet you," I said. I thought I did reasonably well with the name. "Are you... a customs official?"

Hh'shkh bobbed its head up and down. I wasn't sure if it was imitating an Earthling nod or if the gesture meant something altogether different to a Neptunian. "Something like that. Do you have anything to declare?"

I couldn't resist. "Nothing except my genius."

Hh'shkh bobbed its head again and made a low hissing sound. I wasn't sure if it was laughing or about to bite me.

Scott sighed. "We have a ray-gun to declare." Scott held out the mahogany case containing the ray-gun from Swollen-With-Gratitude and opened it. "I checked the local laws, and I believe it's in compliance. Five thousand watts average discharge per shot, sixteen shots at normal power from a full charge. Well within legal limits for personal defense."

Hh'shkh plucked the ray-gun from the case with one of its three hands and looked it over expertly. "Venusian?"

Scott nodded. "Yeah. A... gift from a friend." (Technically not true since SWG had, in fact, billed us for it.)

"Very nice." Hh'shkh returned the weapon. "I'm sure

you'll be pleased to learn that I'm to be your escort at all times during your stay—for your safety, of course. Times are... interesting... on the station right now. Probably wise to carry a gun."

"How so?" I asked.

It ignored the question. "Would you like to check in at the Earthling consulate?"

Scott frowned. "There isn't an—"

I nudged him with my elbow and nodded.

"Ehh. Yes, Earthling consulate," said Scott.

THE NEPTUNIAN SPACE station was downright eerie. Lighting on-station was kept perpetually dim since that's what Neptunians are used to—high noon on Neptune is about as bright as twilight on Earth due to the distance from the Sun. But that wasn't the most eerie part. The *whispering* was what made the hairs on the back of my neck stand up. Everywhere we went, crowds of tall snake-men all around, all whispering in the gloomy dimness in their alien tongue, all falling silent and peering at us with inscrutable yellow eyes as we passed by along the space station concourse.

(I understand that the low light and the whispering were simply the result of the physiology of the Neptunians, but even knowing that, the effect was unsettling, especially at first.)

The consulate was visible from far away. Bright (i.e., Earth-normal) light blazed from a small office-front like a beacon in the night. We entered, blinking as our eyes adjusted to the brightness. Our escort declined to follow us into the consulate, preferring instead to await us in the gloom outside.

"Visitors!" exclaimed a young, surprised Asian woman. "May I help you?"

To summarize some of what we found out there, Scott and Sullivan were right that the Atlantic Alliance didn't have a consulate on Neptune. But less than two years ago—and apparently unbeknownst even to the allegedly competent AIA—Earth's *other* great superpower, the Pacific Bloc, had opened a consulate and begun pressing for closer diplomatic ties with the Neptunians. They'd even subsidized a recent major expansion of Neptune's commercial space station.

The young woman, Miss Ting, was a receptionist, holding down the fort while the consul and assistant consul were off in another part of the station for an emergency meeting of some kind. She'd been stationed at Neptune for the better part of a year. Probably her superiors wouldn't have wanted her to answer our questions, but Earthling visitors were very rare, so she was eager to chatter about anything and everything, even to us Atlanteans. We sat around a conference table in the back of the consulate drinking synth-coffee.

"What does the P.B. want here?" Scott asked. "I'm sure Neptune has resources, but shipping anything from here to Earth would be prohibitively expensive. Our experts say it'll be decades—at least—before any kind of trans-Saturnian commerce will be viable."

"It's the Neptunians themselves the Chairman is interested in," she explained. "The snake-men are strong, fast, have incredible night-vision, and are equally adept at moving on land, underwater, or in zero-gee, due to their amphibious nature. They even have a venomous bite."

"If they're amphibious, snake-men is probably a misnomer," I pointed out.

Miss Ting waved that pedantic quibble away. "Whatever you call them, they're the perfect soldiers. The perfect marines. The perfect spacers. The Chairman wants to establish a... a sort of foreign legion of snake-men. He believes that will give us an advantage in any future, y'know, conflict."

That was all very interesting—not to say alarming—but didn't directly pertain to why we were there.

"We're actually looking for a friend of ours, who we believe was last seen here. Have you seen this person?" I projected a holographic image of Ariel Martinelli from my tablet.

"Oh! You're friends of Martina?"

I nodded, managing to refrain from correcting the incorrect name. Just to be on the safe side, I also kicked Scott under the table so that he wouldn't either. He gave me an aggrieved look.

"We used to hang out, but I haven't seen her in... maybe a month? Or six weeks? I assume she left on the last supply rocket. She said to look her up if I'm ever in Vladivostok."

We chatted a bit more, not learning anything further, and then prepared to take our leave.

"One more thing before you go," said Miss Ting. "You may have noticed already anyway. The snake-men have a... peculiar sense of humor."

"How so?"

Ting shrugged. "Dry? Sarcastic? Wildly inappropriate? I don't really know how to describe it. But be careful of taking anything they say too literally."

I thought back over my interactions with Hh'shkh and nodded slowly.

We thanked her for her help and rejoined our escort outside the consulate.

"Where to next?" it asked in its whispery voice. "Fleshpot of questionable repute? Or perhaps fleshpot of unquestionably bad repute?"

I had to smile—that was a good one. "Hospital," I said.

"Hospital?" It turned its head over. "Are you ill? You look ill, I'm sorry to say. Each missing an arm and an eye. I'm not sure the hospital can do much for you."

We insisted on the hospital nonetheless, after checking in with Captain.

THE HOSPITAL WAS packed. Standing-room only in the dimly

lit emergency-room lobby, although admittedly for a snake-man there isn't much of a distinction between sitting and standing. I couldn't see any evidence of outward traumatic injuries among the Neptunians—not that I'm any kind of xenomedicine expert—but those awaiting treatment seemed to be suffering from a sort of listless malaise. Whether that was related to their actual health complaint or merely the result of waiting an eternity in the ER, I had no way to know.

"Is it always this crowded?" I asked Hh'shkh.

It turned its head upside-down a moment before turning it back the right way. "Interesting times, as I say."

Scott frowned, thoughtful. "Just why are times so interesting anyway?"

Hh'shkh briefly bowed its head, eyes closed—a gesture I hadn't seen it do yet—and said nothing.

None of the hospital staff spoke English, but our escort interpreted for us once we got the attention of someone who looked like it might be a nurse or doctor. Long story short: no Earthlings had been treated at the station hospital recently.

According to the doctor-or-whatever, the last Earthling to be admitted to the hospital was a consulate employee who'd come in over a year ago with some minor injury and was vivisected in the name of xenomedical research, since none of the hospital staff had ever seen the inside of an Earthling before. The doctor-or-whatever also eagerly offered to move me and Scott to the head of the line if we had any minor injuries or illnesses we wanted them to take a look at.

Our guide and the doctor both bobbed their heads and hissed in appreciation of the joke. At least, I *hoped* that's what was happening.

Regardless, we thought it best not to linger at the hospital any longer. Next stop: jail.

HH'SHKH BOBBED ITS head when we asked it to take us to jail.

"You wish to confess your many crimes?"

"Of course," I said. "Can't you tell by looking at us that we're master criminals?"

Scott opened his mouth to protest, but a well-placed elbow to the ribs kept him quiet. Our escort bobbed its head more vigorously and hissed appreciatively.

I nodded to myself. *There, see? All figured out.* I started to think maybe I should write a book on Neptunian etiquette for Earthling tourists.

We found that the jail was even more crowded than the hospital. A literal line out the door of snake-men waiting to be booked for (according to our guide) assault, fighting, property damage, hooliganism, and several more serious misdeeds.

"Is this normal?" I asked Hh'shkh. "Are your people such wanton outlaws?"

Instead of hiss-laughing at the joke though, Hh'shkh hung its head and closed its eyes, like it had at the hospital. I grasped what that meant then. *Shame.*

"I..." I looked at Scott. He was useless. Turned back to Hh'shkh. "I'm sorry, Hh'shkh. Didn't mean to offend."

Hh'shkh said nothing for a time. I was unsure about the appropriateness of physical touch, but decided to risk it. I gave our guide a reassuring pat on the shoulder. Or tried to, at least. It jerked away from my touch the instant I made contact.

I mentally scrapped my plans for the book on Neptunian etiquette—a few more things to figure out first, it would seem.

Hh'shkh opened its eyes. "The madness," it whispered. "Space madness."

Even though Neptunians are an utterly different species and culture from us, and even though I'd only had contact with them for a few hours, I think I'd developed a pretty good handle on their offbeat humor—what was a joke and what wasn't. This *space madness* thing was definitely no joke.

"What do you mean?" I asked.

"The madness affects us all, sooner or later. It starts with nightmares, insomnia, headaches, feelings of... disconnectedness. For some, increasingly violent impulses. For others, apathy and torpor. For everyone, in the end, death comes."

"Why do you stay in space, then? Why not return to the surface? I mean, if it's... er... space madness."

Hh'shkh turned its head upside down again, perhaps trying to decide if I was joking. (Tentatively, I had the upside-down thing pegged as a quizzical/pensive gesture.) After a moment, it untwisted its head and said, "Some do, if they can. The pay is excellent on the station though, much better than anything down below—your Earthling Chairman is very generous with his development money. Hard to slither away from that, if you know what I mean. The temptation to stay and ignore the early warning signs of the madness is strong."

Scott and I exchanged glances. It seemed wisest not to correct the Neptunians' apparent misapprehension of the political situation on Earth, at least for the time being.

"How about you, Huck-Shick?" asked Scott. I winced at his butchering of Hh'shkh's nickname. "Any, ah... space madness symptoms?"

Hh'shkh bobbed its head with amusement. "Your mate's linguistic capabilities far exceed your own. As for me, no. No symptoms yet, Deep Ones be thanked."

I blinked. "Who are the D-"

But before we could follow up on this latest tidbit of Neptunian culture, a commotion arose among the accused criminals waiting in line. Several were whisper-shouting and gesturing in our direction.

"What are they saying?"

Instead of answering, Hh'shkh turned away. "We must go. Now." It slithered away from the escalating disturbance in front of the jail, back the way we'd come. Snake-men can move across the floor with surprising speed, seemingly effortlessly. Scott and I hurried to keep up. But the commotion was spreading rapidly along the station concourse. Soon a group of angry snake-men blocked our path. These *coiled* themselves as if ready to strike, not unlike their terrestrial analogues, large mouths open to reveal long fangs dripping with venom. They rasped at us menacingly. I had no trouble interpreting that bit of Neptunian body-language even though I had not seen it before.

(You might think the difference between a Neptunian's amused hiss and its menacing rasp is subtle, requiring an expert to distinguish. It's not. At all. If a Neptunian coils itself and rasps at you, venomous fangs bared, there will not be any question in your mind as to what that signifies.)

Scott reached for the Venusian ray-gun at his side. I wondered if sixteen shots would be enough.

One of the Neptunians confronting us said something threatening-sounding in its harsh whisper-language.

"What did it say, Huck-Shick?" Scott asked.

"It said," came another Neptunian voice behind us, "that the Chairman's softskin devils will pay for bringing us the madness." Apparently, Hh'shkh was not the only English-speaker on-station.

We turned. This latest speaker was coiled aggressively like the others, and was, additionally, armed with a ray-gun. We were surrounded.

Scott, admittedly, shot first. We would likely both be dead now if he hadn't. His first shot dropped the ray-gun wielding Neptunian. And that opened the floodgates; ray-guns suddenly were everywhere, discharging every which-way.

When the directed-energy rays started flying, my space-cadet basic training came back to me with a quickness. I hit the deck. With no weapon myself, making myself less of a target was all I could do. Scott came down on top of me, shielding me with his body and firing at any Neptunians who got too close.

The chaos of the riot seemed to last an eternity, though objectively it was only a minute or two before the Neptunian riot police arrived to shut down the mayhem. As one might expect, they arrested everybody involved, us included.

Hh'shkh had gotten separated from us in the melee, I don't know how. I hadn't seen much of the fighting, what with my vantage-point on the floor and the low-light conditions of the station.

And here I want it noted for the record that we were then processed through the Neptunian justice system without so much as an interpreter—let alone a lawyer—a clear violation of the Ceres Accords. After an eternity of waiting in line at the jail, we were brought before some kind of authority figure—desk sergeant or magistrate or something else entirely, I have no idea. The magistrate-or-whatever whisper-shouted a few questions at us in Neptunian, and when we failed to answer, gestured impatiently for us to be taken away.

And so we were led away, out of the twilit magistrate-or-whatever's chambers, to the even darker holding cells, which my mind couldn't help thinking of as the dungeon. Our guards found our assigned cell and shoved us in. The heavy metal door slammed behind us, accompanied by the unmistakable *clank* of a magnetic lock engaging.

ABSOLUTE PITCH BLACKNESS.

"Scott?" I said, after a few moments.

"Yeah?"

"This is not good." I swallowed. My voice was far more quavery than I would have liked.

"Hey." Scott put his arm around me. "We'll be alright, babe. You'll see."

His words held a quiet confidence I took comfort in, despite the fact that what he said was, logically speaking, in complete defiance of the reality of our predicament. Sometimes a girl just has to trust in her cleft-chinned space-hero and say "nuts" to logic.

A female voice called out weakly in the darkness. "No, no... Have you come... to torment me again?" Unmistakably an Earthling voice.

I hesitated, surprised.

"Miss Martinelli?" asked Scott.

The unseen voice scoffed bitterly. "Who else... would I be?" She spoke slowly and quietly, as if with great effort. "I don't... recognize your voice. Am I... hallucinating... a completely made-up person now?"

"You're not hallucinating, Miss Martinelli. We're here to rescue you." Scott evidently didn't see the need to qualify that confident assertion with the proviso that we were in dire need of rescue ourselves.

"Oh... this one again? The rescue hallucination is my favorite. Rescue..." Her voice trailed off weirdly. After a moment, the sound of slow, heavy breathing. She was asleep.

Scott and I moved to the back of the cell where she lay. "What's wrong with her?" I whispered.

That was the exact wrong thing to do.

Martinelli woke up whimpering and curled herself into a fetal ball. "The whispers! The *whispers*! No! Make it stop! No!"

After a few moments of this, she drifted back into unconsciousness.

Scott took me by the elbow and led me to the opposite side of the cell. He muttered—not whispered but muttered, "Long periods of total isolation can be damaging to mental health. If she's been in solitary confinement for all this time, then..." He sighed. "The constant darkness probably doesn't help either."

"Maybe she has whatever's making the Neptunians go crazy. The... space madness."

A demented chuckle from the other side of the cell. "I know what's eating the snake-men. I know. I know!"

I wasn't sure whether it would be better to engage her in her obvious insanity or try to ignore her.

Scott took a deep breath. "What's affecting the Neptunians, Miss Martinelli?"

"Don't call me that!" she said. Her voice was getting stronger—perhaps human contact was already doing her some good. "Don't call me Miss Martinelli. I know you're hallucinations, but you could... at least... do me the favor of not blowing my cover. I'm Martina Vladimirovna from Vladivostok, doing research for my master's thesis."

"Ah," said Scott. "Of course. Miss Vladi-... Vlad-"

"Vladimirovna."

"Right. What's affecting the Neptunians?" he repeated.

"Hormones."

We waited for her to continue, but she didn't elaborate right away. Just as I was beginning to think she'd drifted back to sleep, she spoke up again.

"Hormones. The snake-men are... not really snakes. Amphibians."

"We know," said Scott.

Another long pause as Martinelli either gathered her thoughts or nodded off.

"Amphibians. But that isn't really the right word either. They have... four... life-stages, not two. The adults you see... are the third stage."

I wasn't sure if this was all crazy-talk or legit stuff. "What's the fourth stage?" I asked.

"They call it... contemplation. When an adult's body decides it's time, the Neptunian will swim up under one of the floating islands and attach itself to the underside... become a permanent part of the island."

"Why?"

"There... would not be islands... otherwise."

I took a moment to digest this in silence. I wondered about the potential chicken-and-egg problem this raised, but decided not to quibble. After all, Earth's chickens seem to have overcome the original chicken-and-egg problem just fine.

"On Neptune, the adult stage continues for several decades before the final stage begins. Something about outer space, though... the microgravity, or the cosmic radiation, or something... no one knows, but it triggers the final stage prematurely, usually after only a year or two in space, at most. And if an adult's body starts to change but there's no island to attach to, they die."

"Yet there's a huge population of adult Neptunians on this space station," Scott pointed out.

"They all take... synthetic hormone supplements. To suppress the premature change."

Suddenly they didn't seem like the perfect space-soldiers any more.

"The synthetic hormones have increasingly worse side-effects with long-term use. Depression. Aggression. I came... to report on the Pacific Bloc's activities here, and I found... all this. Would have been a career-defining scoop. One for the history books, even." She took a deep breath. "Instead I'm commiserating about it with my own hallucinations." She chuckled sardonically.

I thought for a bit. "Is the weird joking one of the side-effects of the synthetic hormones, too?"

"No... that's normal for them. Most Neptunians love nothing more than some good, off-color teasing."

I wasn't sure what to say. Evidently neither was Scott. After a few moments came the sound of Miss Martinelli softly snoring.

"Now what?" I mumbled to Scott, remembering not to whisper.

"Now we come up with an escape plan," he muttered.

"Great. Any ideas?"

"No. You?"

"No."

Scott was silent a moment. "In the tri-vids, the heroes usually climb out of the brig through a ventilation shaft."

"Too bad this isn't a tri-vid, then," I said. "Speaking as a life-support engineer, I can attest that the number of real-life space-station ventilation shafts that are big enough for an adult to walk or crawl through is zero. In space, the *actual hallways* are barely wide enough to get through. You know this. Forget the ventilation shafts."

"Maybe the Neptunians design their space stations differently."

"That doesn't seem like the kind of design constraint that would vary that much between species."

"We should look for a ventilation shaft anyway."

"I'm telling you, it's a waste of time."

"Do you have any better ideas?"

He had me there. "No," I admitted.

It took us quite a few minutes in the total darkness, but we found the vents: a supply vent in the ceiling and the return vent set directly beneath it in the floor. As expected though, the vents were not big enough for even a child to crawl through, let alone full-grown Earthlings, and on top of that (literally), the grilles covering the vents were not designed to be removed by anyone locked in the cell. I mean, *obviously.*

We were considering our (lack of) options when Martinelli woke up again.

"Are you still there?"

"Still here," I said.

"Are you still going to rescue me?"

"Working on it."

"Some of the previous hallucinations used the ventilation shaft to get me out," she supplied helpfully.

I ground my teeth. Didn't feel like going through that explanation again. "That won't work."

"Others picked the lock of the cell door."

"It's a magnetic lock. One doesn't simply *pick* those."

She was silent a moment. "This is... a very realistic hallucination."

"Yeah, well—"

A loud metallic clatter on the floor, just a few feet away from me. I just about jumped out of my skin.

"What was that!?" Martinelli wailed, frightened.

I felt around on the floor, found the offending object. "It's..." I traced my fingers over its rectangular form and its many slots and cross-pieces.

It was the grille from the ceiling vent.

"What—"

Suddenly the room was filled with the sound of cicada-chirping and wing-rustling.

I'd never been so happy to hear cicadas. "Captain!"

"What's going on!?" Miss Martinelli was nearing a full-blown panic.

"Don't worry, Miss Vladimirovna! Everything's all right," I said, slightly proud of myself that I remembered to use her assumed Pacifican name. "This is Captain, a hyper-intelligent swarm of space-cicadas. Hopefully here to rescue us. Captain, this is, ah... the person we're looking for."

"Oh," Martinelli said quietly.

"You sound disappointed?"

"I... space-cicadas? I had started to think this wasn't a hallucination."

The cicada-chirps started coming in irregular, choppy bursts. I frowned.

"Morse code," muttered Scott.

"Crap. My Morse is really rusty." The Alliance Space Agency still requires would-be spacers to pass a Morse code test, and I did pass that test in my cadet days, thank you very much, but my skills had since lapsed. I mean, what are the odds that you'll ever have to use a rocket's running lights to signal for help in Morse? Or use Morse to decode an alien insectoid swarm's chirped message?

Captain chirped more code at us. I caught the first letter of it, an "S" (easy to remember, dit-dit-dit), but missed the rest.

"Shield eyes," Scott relayed. I *knew* there was a reason I keep him around. "Hm. What are shield ey—"

A blaze of illumination as the room's lights came up. I had failed to shield my eyes in time—I was momentarily dazzled. Miss Martinelli squealed in discomfort.

A heavy clank as the cell door's magnetic lock disengaged. The door swung open.

I blinked and peered out of our cell. It was bright outside as well. The station's lights were up—*all the way* up. I could hear snake-men hissing in distress. Somehow Captain had taken over the station's control systems.

Captain's swarm of individuals flew out the door.

I looked down at Miss Martinelli, who lay on the floor covering her eyes, weeping. She looked a mess. Now that it was light, I could see she'd dyed her hair black (for disguise, I guess), but her blonde roots were showing due to the month or so in solitary confinement, very unfortunate. She also looked like she hadn't seen a proper meal in a long time. "Miss Martinelli, we have to go now. Can you w-"

Scott scooped her up in his arms easily and rushed to the door.

"That works too," I mumbled. I suppressed an irrational pang of jealousy—I mean, Scott had never carried *me* bodily out of a hostile alien space station as I daintily swooned! (Admittedly though, I'm not much of a dainty swooner.) I followed them out.

We beat a hasty retreat back to Captain's rocket. The twilight-accustomed Neptunians were too blinded by the light to stop us.

LATER, WHEN WE were safely away in the vastness of interplanetary space—and Miss Martinelli had sufficiently recovered to have a rational conversation—we compared notes sitting around the cramped mess-hall table.

"What were you in jail for? I have to ask," I asked.

"I think the P.B. consul suspected I was a spy. He convinced a magistrate I was a threat to station security, and that I wasn't being truthful about my reasons for coming here, which, to be fair, I guess I wasn't. You?"

"Rioting and attempted murder, I think," said Scott. "No doubt a laundry-list of other offenses as well."

"Nice. Lucky we all ended up in the same cell."

Scott shrugged. "That actually is standard procedure. Locking up members of the same species together simplifies things when it comes to feeding and that kind of stuff. Wouldn't want to feed Martian blood-gruel to a pollen-sipping Venusian, for example."

"Ah... well, that makes sense. So, um. I assume my grandmother sent you?" she quasi-asked.

Scott blinked. "Your grandmother?"

"Yeah. My grandmother. Amelia De Sá."

"De Sá? The rocket tycoon? First female trillionaire?"

"Yeah."

"Mm. Not directly," said Scott. "We were... contracted by an AIA spook. If your nanna is a big-time political campaign contributor—as I assume she would be—she probably pulled some strings. I guess we were the puppets at the end of the string."

"I wonder why that family connection wasn't in the dossier," I said. "Seems important, and surely it's public record."

Scott waved that away. "Some AIA bureaucrat probably decided we didn't need to know. Doesn't matter now."

"I'm curious also," said Martinelli, "where you got the cicadas. They're very... effective."

"Ski holiday," I answered, and left it at that.

Captain chose that moment to break in on the conversation. "We're now en route to Ceres, ETA 32 Earth-days. I'm afraid that was our relatively best option, given our suboptimal launch-time and circumstances. I hope you all like being defeated over and over at cards by a hyper-intelligent hive-mind."

Martinelli sighed dramatically and lowered her head to the table.

It would be a long trip. But at least we could look forward to getting paid—not to mention my husband still owed me half a honeymoon.

AND THAT'S THE story of how Scott and I caused our *second* major interplanetary diplomatic incident. I want it noted for the record that this one wasn't our fault either.

James W. Murphy spent his childhood near the tide pools and harbors of Los Angeles, his adolescence in the forests and plains of Oregon, and most of his adulthood in the cozy alleys of Taipei and dusty boulevards of Beijing. He's made a living flipping hamburgers in polyester, stocking groceries in a red bow tie, and painting houses in canvas pants, all while lifting heavy objects with proper form. He's also been a teacher, a translator, a technology industry analyst, and a publisher of research books and journals, spending over a dozen years terrorized by millions of emails and presentation slides. He currently lives in the misty hills of southern Taipei with his wife Monica, enjoying the regenerative power of their three dozen houseplants and doing whatever he wants, like writing science fiction stories.

Let's face it, one of the worst things about the real solar system is that it's lonely. The Old Solar System, with its plethora of intelligent species, was a much more interesting place. That said, as James W. Murphy reminds us in The Lost Rings of Saturn, *not every intelligent species is good company...*

THE LOST RINGS OF SATURN

James W. Murphy

THE WONTIL LOCKED eyes with Joseph just before it took a bite from the side of the Terran man's head, as if it were a large apple. With a loud snick and crack, the Saturnian's powerful jaws easily dug in and pulled away, excising a neat mouthful of bone, brain, and scalp. The Wontil held fast as the man jerked, caught in the creature's vice-like grip, aided by the hydraulic pressures of the gaseous circulatory system flowing through its thin limbs.

Joseph and a number of fellow Terrans huddled next to him watched in horror as the man's eyes fluttered, his legs spasming and kicking out on the stone tiles of the refrigeration unit where Joseph and the others were held captive. Normally storing more mundane edibles, the refrigeration unit was now host to Joseph and a number of other Earth people he did not recognize. They had all been pulled out of bed that morning. All were in various states of dress. Joseph was thankful he had a full set of sleepwear, as he looked at the three other men and woman next to him in their underwear, shivering.

Over the man's screams Joseph could still hear the sickening crunch of bone as the Wontil chewed and smacked, its purplish, bat-like features covered in a sheen of blood. The creature leaned forward from its squatting position behind his victim, placing a hand on the man's legs, running its long fingernails over the pants, back and forth and leg to leg, as if to massage and sooth. The man stopped kicking. Joseph momentarily registered the perplexing maneuver, the thought quickly flitting away as the Wontil once again locked eyes with Joseph, and smiled.

It was an odd smile. One of conviviality rather than malice, as if to share his delight over some sumptuous meal. Joseph heard a loud croak from the women next to him, followed by a splash as she emptied the contents of her stomach. He instinctively patted her on the back, catching the ridiculousness of it too late. He pulled away as she nodded her thanks.

A high-pitched sound suddenly broke forth from speakers. The Wontil hissed up into the air, clearly exasperated at having his meal so abruptly interrupted. He let go of his victim's lifeless body, and stormed out of the unit, letting forth a string of curses. All of which Joseph understood, owing to his facility with the Wontil language—a rare skill among non-Saturnian races, but especially so among his fellow Earth people. And this particular Wontil's curses deployed excessively vivid depictions of someone's mother, a characteristic uniting the profane language of all sentient races throughout the known solar system. The exception being the pitiable Bhlemphroims on the other side of Saturn, who accepted such phrases with sense of deep pride.

Another Wontil popped his head into the refrigerator. "Which one of you speaks Wontil?"

The Earth folk in the room stared blankly, not comprehending and awaiting the inevitable follow up question in broken Terran.

"Who know...who speak...Wontil?" he stammered.

Joseph now deeply regretted using the language earlier to try to reason with their captors. The other humans quickly pointed at him in unison, their hands trembling in the cold.

JOSEPH STOOD NEXT to his Wontil escort as they traveled by conveyor, unsure of whether he was in a better predicament than his compatriots back in the refrigeration unit. He was feeling lethargic after multiple adrenaline spikes throughout the day since he was pulled out of his bed and taken captive. At least his bones were finally thawing out.

He watched the gray, bleak landscape flow by outside the large, crystalline portals. It was a different world from the Saturn of earlier years, when he had visited as a young man. The charm of the Wontil villages. The friendliness and curiosity of the inhabitants. Miles of unspoiled desert and flowering forests.

That had all changed during the intervening years he spent on Saturn's moon, Titan. While he honed his Wontil language skills and made a home in the independent Titan kingdom, the Wontil had carpeted Saturn in an organism called Black Membrane—a dark fungus that leached life force from the planet, converting it into energy for the various industries Saturn now supported across the solar system. The membrane stretched out for miles, like glistening chocolate pudding, punctuated by the occasional tower which fed the super-hydrophilic membrane with millions of gallons of water melted off the planet's icy poles.

Titan, newly displaced in importance by Saturn, proved to be a difficult place to continue his chosen profession, forcing his move to the ringed planet. A move he had always regretted, but never more so than now. He noticed the familiar smell of the organic lubricant used on the conveyor—the smell of honey mixed with gasoline. A fixture of hundreds of much more mundane mornings comprising years of miserable commutes.

Out the portals he saw the occasional cluster of elderly Wontil, who as part of their morning exercises stood in concentric circles on the open plazas next to the various residence tubes. Moving clockwise and counter-clockwise from circle to circle, they stared up into the atmosphere. This activity was believed to add to Wontil longevity, although no scientific causal link was ever determined. But mortality rates of geriatric Wontil had increased since heavy layers of soupy smog covered the planet, indicating that there was a connection between longevity and access to the upper atmosphere. Despite the muted effects due to the increase in pollution, the elderly continued to do it as a matter of habit. It was odd to see this normal daily routine while any other non-Saturnians like himself were currently experiencing a living hell.

"Teacher," asked his Wontil escort in Terran. "You live by our Saturn how much long?"

The pattern of speech was familiar to Joseph, who had heard it stated this way, and subsequently corrected, thousands of times in his classrooms on Titan and Saturn.

"You mean, 'how long have I lived on Saturn?' I have lived on Saturn for five years," Joseph responded, reflexively, making sure to use a complete sentence despite its awkwardness. He marveled at the pedestrian back-and-forth with his captor given the circumstances.

"Yes. Years of five. And why you like our Saturn?" continued the guard, the same look of eagerness he had seen before on the bat-like faces of other Wontil.

"Well, a lot of reasons. The food is great. The culture is interesting. I like learning about Saturn's long and rich history."

The Wontil nodded, satisfied at hearing the expected perfunctory answer that all visitors to Saturn learned to give when presented with this very question.

The would-be student asked nothing more, and they swayed back and forth as the conveyor hurtled through the city. Joseph saw they were passing his living quarters in the residential tubes, where only a few hours earlier he had been sleeping, expecting to wake up to a normal, tedious day of teaching Wontil youth.

His escort's attention was focused on the holographic signage which paced the conveyor, for the convenience of passengers to understand the myriad rules governing the conveyor's use, most rules randomly but viciously enforced. The Wontil suddenly wheezed, a sound Joseph recognized as a chuckle, followed by a licking of his lips and a heavy swallow. Reading the sign, he was unable locate the information triggering the Wontil's laugh.

Until he got to line 26, which stated simply, "No Food Allowed."

JOSEPH SAT IN the chair as the Prefect examined him from his desk. Like all Wontil his arms were thin, but the marathon banqueting required of all bureaucrats as part of their elaborate social customs had taken its toll, resulting in a wide, bloated midsection. It had the effect of bringing his typically large Wontil head into better proportion with the size of his body, although making his limbs look even thinner by comparison. Whatever caustic, inebriating drinks he was forced to imbibe in their ritualistic drinking duels had wreaked havoc on his organs, resulting in numerous dark splotches on his purple face.

"Are you a meat eater?" asked the Prefect in Wontil.

Joseph hesitated to respond. Historical treatises of Saturn described the Wontil's long-passed predilection for eating other humanoid races on the planet, but he couldn't recall any mention of whether their prey were fed an exclusively vegetarian diet before slaughter.

"Almost exclusively meat, My Fine Prefect," Joseph responded.

"Then we will have some Vhlorrh steaks prepared for you."

Joseph was confused. Then his heart fluttered a few extra beats. He ventured a question, trying hard to sound calm, making sure to use the appropriate honorific. "Trying to fatten me up, Dearest Leader?"

"Why? You are already fat," said the Prefect with characteristically Wontil directness. Joseph flinched. Describing someone as "fat" had long ago become the absolute height of offense among Terrans.

"I mean are you preparing to get me in a state so that I will be a better meal for you, Joyous Prefect on High?" Joseph clarified.

"I see. No. We have another use for you."

Joseph's heart began to slow down. "And what's that, Exalted Prefect, Paragon of Grace and Beauty? What would you have of my shabby self?"

The Prefect opened his mouth to speak, but paused. "Why do you speak Wontil like a Titanite?"

"I spent quite a while on Titan before coming to Saturn, Supreme Leader, He of Irrepressible Virility and Poise."

"I suppose we will have to live with your Titanite accent. But you will cease using these ridiculous honorifics. Titan is obsessed with maintaining the ancient and backward Wontil ways. So typically affected and overly polite. A habit we will soon correct once we take Titan back under Saturn's reign."

Joseph's heart sank. Whatever horrible fate awaited him on this forlorn planet, he had taken comfort that his family was safe on Titan. An awful series of images flashed in his mind. The lush, green moon dying with the spread of Black Membrane. His wife and daughter fighting with neighbors like vicious animals for scraps of food. And if they survived that, eaten by these Saturnian devils.

"Which brings me to the point of having you brought here," the Prefect continued. "We will take back Titan one day. But as of now they continue to enjoy the protection of you imperialist Earthmen. And somehow defying the limits of your impossibly small heads, you Earthmen have managed to taint nearly every planet with your influence.

"This state of affairs is an historical aberration. As the proud center of the greatest empire, spanning numerous planets in ancient times, Saturn will retake its rightful place as ruler of our solar system. We now control most industry. But we are continually disadvantaged by inability to speak Terran. In light of this—"

"Can I ask a question before you continue?" asked Joseph, continuing without pause, as the question in Wontil is always rhetorical, "Why the focus on language skills? Couldn't you just bend the planets to your will with your control on industry? Or you could just go to war."

"First," replied the Prefect, leaning back into his chair, "we are a long time away from being able to confront the Earthman militarily. Second, even if we were to succeed, and impose our own language, there is the problem that the species of most other planets are incapable of speaking it. This is in some cases a problem of oral anatomy, but in most cases relates to the lower levels of intelligence outside the purple races of Saturn. If we must rule, we will need to do it through your language, which unfortunately is the most common. Besides, we prefer it this way, rather than outright military subjugation. We are a peaceful people."

As was his habit when dealing with the Wontil of Saturn, Joseph let the Prefect's final dissonant statement hang in the air without comment.

"The Schoolmistress of Jdormic Primary School has vouched for your ability to instill a working facility of the Terran language in Wontil youth. Starting now, you will teach a selection of elite Wontil linguists, who will then serve as teachers to others, and so on, until Terran is mastered to a reasonable degree by the greater populace."

Joseph shook his head. "I don't think that's going to work. I'm trained to teach children. And teaching adults...it's not just a matter of pedagogy. Adults just can't seem to quite master the vowel sounds. And the grammar. Old patterns are just too entrenched. It might be better to—"

"Silence Earthman!" the Prefect bellowed, learning forward in his seat. "You dare make demands?!"

The Prefect pushed a button on his desk, producing a buzzing sound outside the room. Two guards walked in, one to each side of Joseph. They reached down, each one grabbing an arm in their vice-like grips. Joseph's arms felt completely immobile, as if fused inside cold steel. Another hand came around his throat, another at his knees, his body completely fixed save his trembling feet.

The Prefect slowly rose, and walked over to the bound man. He reached down, holding his index and middle finger in the shape of scissors on either side of Joseph's ring finger, just behind his matrimonial ring. Joseph looked up at him in disbelief.

The Prefect's nose-flaps closed. He heard the buildup of pressure in the Wontil's hand, followed by intense pinching on his ring finger and then the sickening sound snapping bone. Pain flashed through Joseph's knuckles, made worse by the inability to move away, or move at all. He heard the sound of the ring hitting the floor and rolling away.

The room started spinning. He could see the Prefect crawling around on the ground. Finding whatever he was looking for, the Prefect stood up, and inserted Joseph's severed ring finger into his mouth, munching on it like a Terran baby carrot. And then everything went black.

JOSEPH WOKE UP in his living quarters to the smell of grilled meat. A clean bandage covered the stump of his ring finger on his left hand, but there was no pain. Fortunately the herbal tinctures of the ancient Wontil were preserved on Titan, and shipped to Saturn regularly, the desires of commerce trumping national and cultural enmity between the Wontil of the planet and its moon.

He walked over to the cold plate of meat. Each steak was densely marbled with fat and sinew, the highest grade of Vhlorrh steak. Terran steaks were comparatively bland and poorly textured. With certain spices a Terran beef cut could achieve the taste of a Vhlorrh, but not its unique texture. His stomach growling, he ignored the cutlery, grabbing a steak with his hand and biting off a large chunk. He shuddered as the richness of the steak hit his palette, the sinew popping and snapping against his teeth, releasing its bounty of juices.

He chewed rapidly, first out of hunger, yielding quickly to anger as he considered on the inappropriateness of enjoying a fine steak while Earth people across Saturn were being herded into refrigerators and eaten alive. He flashed on the horrific scenes he was forced to witness, disgusted with himself as his body yearned for sustenance and his taste-buds danced with delight. He put the remainder down, turned his back to it, and walked to the window, doing his best to ignore it.

The glow of Saturn's rings was barely perceptible in the smoggy night sky. He thought about the view from Titan. He and his small family in their small house in the twilight belt. Sitting in their small garden on his regular trips back, drinking wine and marveling at the rings of Saturn blazing across the sky.

He should have stayed there. Job prospects were poor, but they could have survived. At numerous points during his posting on Saturn, he regretted his choices. Not just leaving his new family, but having dedicated so much time and effort to studying the language and culture of the Wontil. Undeniably rich, but as of late, degenerate. At least its variation on Saturn.

Of all the languages and cultures he could have studied, it had to be this one. So many people said it was a good choice. Professionally, yes. But over time, he had grown to despise it, and it introduced a strange sensitivity. When back on Titan, he would perceptibly cringe when whenever he heard a Saturnian accent. Or felt more melancholy than appropriate when seeing some shared vestige of an ancient culture that no longer existed.

Regardless of the depth of his disappointment, he never expected it to come to this. He had sensed an oddness for a while, attributing to the normal ebb and flow of supremacist sentiment so common among the Wontil of Saturn. But nothing so extreme as to result in the wholesale butchering of off-worlders.

He had to flee, but had no idea how. He would be intercepted if he tried to make it to an interplanetary craft. And even if he were to get a ship, there was the problem of his limited flight skills.

Joseph searched in his galley for a knife. At the bottom of the drawer he found a paring knife, small enough to conceal in his pocket. Taking it, he walked over to the washroom mirror. Joseph held the knife in front of his forehead, measuring the length, trying to determine how deep it would go if inserted into his temple. Satisfied, he then wrapped it up in paper, and placed it in his pocket.

JOSEPH WALKED INTO the teachers' lounge at the appointed time, as commanded by the note he found stuck to the bathroom door of his living quarters. The Schoolmistress was there as expected, but he was surprised to see the Jovian teacher that had arrived a few weeks earlier from his home on Jupiter. He recalled trying to describe the Jovian to his wife. Something close to a sea lion on stubby legs, with a slit of a mouth instead of a snout, but the same big eyes and flat arms that ended in flippers. He noticed the outer side of the Jovian's left flipper had been cut off.

Like all Jovians, he was massive. The school desk he was sitting in struggled under his bulk, the legs of the chair bowing and threatening to snap. He wore no lower garment to cover his lower extremities, as was the custom among Jovian males, although the arrangement of the Jovian anatomy ensured nothing offensive was visible. His stubby legs were covered in a tan coat of short, shiny fur, the legs white and losing circulation where the chair frame indented his ample flesh.

Although the Jovian was not of Terran heritage nor a native Terran-speaker, Saturn's urgent demand for teachers required a certain laxity of standards. Other teachers reported that his grammar was spotty, and his accent was comically strong, a fact that went undetected by his Wontil employers due to his basic facility with Wontil.

It was common for non-Terran teachers who found themselves teaching the Terran language to overcompensate in some way for not having been born on Earth. The Jovian was no exception. He wore a floral-print shirt native to one of Earth's long-submerged islands, clearly believing it to project a sense of "Terran-ness". Joseph had never caught his name. No doubt he had adopted a name that was typically Terran.

"Good to see you have come at the appointed time, Joseph." said the Schoolmistress as she looked up from her desk. "I am always surprised when you Earthmen manage to be punctual. That your tiny little brains can manage the concept of time."

The Jovian's chair creaked as he twisted around to look Joseph, a big, goofy smile spreading across his face. "I not alone?" said the Jovian, as his head whipped back to query the Schoolmistress, his thighs rhythmically clapping together with excitement.

"Joseph, this is Doug. Doug, this is Joseph," said the Schoolmistress, annoyed.

"Hi Joe. Nice to meet you. I Doug." announced the Jovian, pointing a flipper at himself, and then extending the flipper out in a now unfashionable form of Terran greeting. Aware of the gesture, Joseph took Doug's flipper, and shook.

His appendage felt like a turgid fish wrapped in warm velvet. "The pleasure is mine, Doug. Great to see another teacher was spared—"

"You will only speak Wontil in my presence!" commanded the Schoolmistress, who despite being a teacher of Terran, was unable to understand anything the two said.

"Profuse apologies, Schoolmistress," said Joseph in Wontil. "It was not our intention to offend. Just the polite exchange of pleasantries."

"I am aware of that," claimed the Schoolmistress. "But time is running short. You need time to prepare for class. I assume the Prefect briefed you on your assignment?"

"I think Prefect confused," said Doug, rubbing his injured flipper. "He ask me teach Jovian. But I teach Terran. I good. Should teach Terran." Doug then nodded furiously, as if nodding hard enough would convince the Schoolmistress.

"No, you will teach Jovian you fat slug," responded the Schoolmistress. "Count yourself lucky. You Jovians are as delicious as you are idiotic. Although we have spared you from butchering, your training of our people will help us easily infiltrate your cowed, dimwitted, and delicious populace."

The Schoolmistress's repeated insults of the Jovian's intelligence and physical shape were a common practice across the planets. According to the intelligence tests administered by the eugenicists of Mercury, Jovians rated lowest of any species capable of language. Joseph guessed that Doug, given his poor but serviceable language skills, was likely a genius of his species. And while the Mercurians took particular delight in pointing out the weakness of the Jovians, they were dismayed to discover they themselves were outclassed by the Wontil. Although the Mercurians' jealousies were allayed by the Wontil's outsized ambition and infighting, which until recently had kept them technologically behind for millennia.

"You will teach Jovian, and should you prove effective, your life will be spared," said the Schoolmistress.

Doug let out a whimper, and looked down to the floor. "Don't expect us to have any sympathy," the Schoolmistress continued. "Do you have any idea how delectable you are? Jovian meat makes the finest Vhlorrh steak taste like dry char. Imagine tasting something so delicious you can think of but little else. Imagine flesh so sublime as to give an overwhelming feeling of dissatisfaction and unease whenever one is not in a state of chewing it. Imagine living in a constant state of preoccupation, unable to enjoy any sweet aspect of life without your mind turning toward the gastric ecstasies of Jovian flesh. It's maddening. If anything the Wontil should be recipients of sympathy. What I wouldn't give to have never known such a taste." The Schoolmistress was visibly salivating, and she paused to swallow. In the ensuing silence, the cooling unit, which held various lunches and beverages stored by the faculty, suddenly whirred. Doug's head whipped over to look at it, then guiltily looked back at the schoolmistress. He slowly lowered his chin down to the desk, his sorrowful, coal-black eyes darting back and forth between her and Joseph.

Joseph stifled the urge to launch out of his seat and strangle the Schoolmistress. If there were truly a "peaceful people" in the system, it would certainly be the Jovians. Not once in the histories of the planets was it ever recorded that Jovians attacked another race. Nor were they ever successfully occupied, although the histories detailed numerous failed attempts. While not gifted with the intelligence, they were a warm, giving people. The Schoolmistresses belabored descriptions were unnecessarily cruel. He resisted the urge to argue back, their situation precarious as it was.

"And how will our teaching be assessed?" asked Joseph, changing the subject.

"You are expected to teach the mandated vocabulary lists, of course. The students must demonstrate mastery of ten-thousand words in your respective languages. Successful attainment of this learning objective, and their successful passing of a test in three days, will result in your release," the Schoolmistress answered.

"But a list of vocabulary won't help their skill at all," said Joseph, immediately regretting it.

"You obviously don't understand, as you are not Wontil," said the Schoolmistress, showing teeth in an imitation of an indulgent smile. "Up until now, outside the walls of our odd, experimental school, this is how we have always taught off-world languages. It is a core aspect of Wontil culture. Blessed as we are with the highest intelligence and keen competitive spirit, it is important to maintain easily measurable criteria, so that students can know their relative standing."

Realizing arguing was pointless, Joseph made a har-rumph of agreement.

The Schoolmistress stood up. "Very well. There is little time left. Please prepare your lesson plans, and proceed to the classroom at the appointed time." said the Schoolmistress as she ambled toward the door. "And I think you are very well aware of the stakes. Failure to achieve the learning objectives will result in your immediate slaughter and butchering. The Jovian will be fed to the higher castes. You, Joseph, will be fed to the lower." She left the room, and Joseph could hear the slap of her feet getting quieter as she went down the hall-way.

Joseph turned to Doug, who was cradling his injured flip-per. "Are you doing okay there?" Joseph asked in Terran.

"Doug not okay. Why Wontil so mean? Not good, eat Jovians even if better meat grade than high level portion of Vhlorrh steak. And why she always call me idiot? Doug very smart Jovian on Jupiter. Took test. Wontil like test. They should respect."

"Doug, you realize we are in big trouble here, right? We've got to find a way to get off Saturn."

"Of course. Our situation is evident of self. Must leave.

Doug will conceive plan. Doug save Joe. And Doug." Doug's head lifted upward, as if to strike a heroic pose. Then moved down, to meet Joseph's eyes. "But first, eat. Talk of flavors delicious make Doug hungry, even if join by scary mind-pictures of homeworld friends chew by Wontil."

"Alright. But you need to get that bandage replaced," said Joseph, walking over to the first aid kit.

"It is okay," said Doug. "Not hand hurt. Only heart hurt. Wontil Prefect cut hand. Then take arm-ring given by the Doug-Mother while chewing piece-part of Doug. Why Wontil act so dastardly?"

Doug looked at Joseph, realizing the Jovian wanted an honest answer to his question. Meeting Doug's doleful, coal-black eyes, Joseph felt the room wash away. His vision went black, as if Doug's eyes reached out and surrounded him. A sensation of rising overtook him, as if floating into a suffocating thick wet cloud of sorrow. For a split second he felt he would tip off the edge into insanity. He shut his eyes and shook himself, the feeling of maddening sadness leaving him as he became aware of himself back in the room. His eyes filled with uncontrollable tears. Embarrassed, he quickly put his head his sleeve, grunting as he wiped them away. What the universe denied the Jovians in intelligence, it balanced with spectrum of emotion of which most species were incapable. A spectrum of emotion with which Jovians would at times inadvertently share.

"I'm not sure what to say, Doug, other than sorry," said Joseph. "He took my matrimonial ring too. Don't know why. Maybe to just be cruel. Maybe as a trophy. The metal's worthless." Joe worked to compose himself, reminding himself not look too deeply into the Jovian's eyes again.

"Oh. Doug make Joe sad. I always do that. No Joe. Like I say. Doug save Joe. And Doug. And rings. But first, Doug eat."

The Jovian made an effort to stand up. Heaving in big

breaths, in and out, with the occasional growl, Doug was eventually able to remove himself from the desk and chair, the indentations from the metal supports still visible on his body. He bounded with surprising agility over to the refrigerator, the floor trembling with each step. Doug opened the refrigerator door, grabbed a whole roasted Blinkon ham, threw it in the air, and caught it in his open mouth, swallowing the whole mass of meat down his gullet like an egret.

Doug then turned to Joseph. He smiled a big, toothless grin. Joseph realized he was smiling back.

JOSEPH STOOD IN front of the classroom, thirty or so middle-aged Wontil linguists sitting in their desks, ramrod straight.

"Good Morning, Teacher!" they bellowed in practiced unison.

Joseph was momentarily taken aback at the mundane daily rituals reasserting themselves into his living nightmare. "Good Morning, class," he responded.

An unwavering respect for authority was drilled into the Wontil as children from an early age. No matter whether the respect was sincere, the Wontil student took it as an expression of fine character to demonstrate poise and deference. He was relieved to have some sense of control, a reprieve from the mire of helplessness he'd felt since the previous day. Joseph also realized this was a critical juncture at which to assert his teacherly dominance, and set the tone for the rest of the course.

Cloaking himself fully in his Wontil teacher persona, deftly imitating his most severe Wontil language teacher, Joseph angrily bellowed, "What is this?!" letting the vagueness of his question stir unease among the students before continuing. They looked at each other with nervous, questioning looks, trying to figure out what was wrong.

"You dare sit where you please? Have you no sense of proper order? Do you think this is some sort of cave, where you, like bunch of savages, can lay about on some dirt floor next your livestock?"

The students' purplish hue turned pale. The Wontil had actually been living in caves a generation or two prior. Their deep-held notions of supremacy, based on a glorified past and very recent progress, was deeply unsettled when presented with painful realities of the not-too-distant past.

"This will not do. Disordered seating arrangements lead to disordered minds. You will sit in order of height," commanded Joseph.

The students, hesitating, slowly stood, and began the process finding their new desk assignment. Standing in line, they shuffled back and forth, sometimes asking a third student to verify.

This was a rapid process among Wontil youth, as the speed of growth varied considerably among children. Mature Wontil were more or less the same height. A resource-poor past had also placed a preference on smaller stature, so that arguments broke out occasionally when students' self-perceived sense of smaller height differed from what surfaced in the comparisons. Arguments were quickly silenced by a grunt from Joseph.

Having eventually found their seats, Joseph began the lesson. In the intervening time since his meeting with the Prefect, the administration had plastered the room from floor to ceiling in several thousand flash cards containing the target vocabulary. While taking up a small part of the wall previously, and only occupying a minor role in Joseph's teaching methods, Wontil administrators deemed such rote memorization as the quintessence of language pedagogy. In his current situation, he could only comply.

Joseph took out his photon pointer, and aimed it at a card in the corner of the room. Their heads followed.

"Arrivals," said Joseph.

"Arrivals!" repeated the class, with enthusiasm.

"Departures."

"Departures!"

He aimed the pointer at a different part of the ceiling.

"Poison."

"Poison!"

He aimed at another random card. And another. Then another. The heads of the Wontil following the pointer like kittens.

JOSEPH FOUND HIMSELF once more in the Prefect's office, joined this time by the Schoolmistress and the Jovian Doug.

"We have had complaints," said the Prefect.

"Prefect," responded the Schoolmistress. "I can assure you these two are doing their utmost to teach the required vocabulary. The students proceed well. Very rapidly, in fact, considering their advanced years. I would venture that--"

"It is not a question of the learning objectives. It is a matter of classroom management." The Prefect looked at Joseph. "You are not Wontil, so you do not understand. The linguists assigned to your class operate a very clear hierarchy, their position determined by the result of their civil service exams. You have disrupted that hierarchy, seating them in an order that is not appropriate for their station."

He turned to Doug. "And you. What in the heavens is a 'gold star'?"

Doug looked at the Schoolmistress. The Schoolmistress, wringing her hands together, responded. "Sir, we are an experimental school, and some of these methods, while unorthodox for sure, have been effective in the past. A 'gold star,' is a small incentive, or an award, to a student for the successful completion of some task or an achievement of some sort."

"You mean as a prize for passing a test? And you give

them precious metals. Or celestial matter? As incentive?" the Prefect guessed, looking confused.

"Well not exactly. It's not actual gold. Or celestial matter. And a test is not necessarily required." The Schoolmistress paused, scratching her head, trying to think of how to explain further.

"Never mind," said the Prefect, "You two will cease with these suspect alien practices immediately. Failure to do so, starting with your next class, will result in more than a lost finger." The Prefect, paused for a moment, lost in thought, then wiped a off stream of saliva with his arm. Joseph could hear a wet-sounding swallow from the Schoolmistress.

The Prefect's expression turned dark, and he began reaching into his desk drawer. "And if you ever want these back again, you will ensure the students achieve the learning objective without incident." The Prefect opened his drawer, and pulled out Joseph's rings, followed by Doug's flipper bracelet.

Joseph was startled by a loud bark from Doug. He looked over to see the Jovian huffing as he pulled himself out the chair. As the Prefect reached toward the button on his desk, Doug's arm shot out, his flipper slapping the rings out the Prefect's hand, followed by rapid slaps the heads of the Prefect and Schoolmistress, who both collapsed to the floor.

Having heard the Jovian's bark, four guards burst through the door. Doug, spotting the rings where they landed, dropped like felled tree next to them. He stuffed the rings into his mouth with his flipper, swallowing them down with loud gulps. The guards, ignoring the weak Earthman, all accosted Doug, who looked back at Joseph, and yelled, "Run! Joe run! Meet at 36 Dock Bay. Go now! Doug meet Joe there. This easy."

Joseph bolted out of the room, his survival instincts overpowering his desire to help. *Doug can obviously handle them,* Joe tried to convince himself, as he bolted down the hallway and ignoring the wrenching pangs of guilt.

JOSEPH HID AMONG the pipes in the darkness. He had managed to get surprisingly far, moving from recess to recess, behind the numerous pipes that fed the facility. He could hear the voices of Wontil passing by. As the voices moved away, he went to the next recess, repeating this process as he very slowly made his way to Dock Bay 36.

He regretted his hasty decision to leave Doug. He likely only bought himself a few more minutes of life, ending it as a coward. Even though Doug was a force of nature on this planet, Joseph doubted he was able to get away.

He heard a sound, a shuffle nearby. Joseph held his breath, listening intently as he reached into his pocket and pulled out the small, paper-wrapped knife he put there earlier. As he unwrapped it, the paper surrounding the knife made loud, crackling noises. The sounds coming from the hall ceased.

Joseph let forth a string of curses in his head, wishing he had used a cloth instead of paper. As he slowly unwrapped further, each little crackle echoed like a gunshot in the silence. He put the paper back in his pocket, and squeezed the knife handle firmly in his hand.

Another shuffling sound issued from his side. He whipped to the source of the noise, and stabbed blindly. He could feel the knife sink into flesh, followed by a loud hiss of air which tickled his knuckles. The Wontil he stabbed jumped back, holding its arm with alarm. The gas of its circulatory system was leaking out at a fast rate, and the creature tried to cover it up with its other hand. Failing, he looked up at Joseph, his face filled with terror and helplessness. Despite the desperation of his own situation, Joseph couldn't help but feel pity as he looked at the Wontil, cradling its arm pathetically.

The Wontil let out a piercing cry. Within seconds three more Wontil where there, dragging Joseph into the center of the hallway. Each of the Wontil held an appendage, their grips getting tighter as they watched their dying compatriot drop to the floor.

"We have to keep the Earthman alive," said one of the Wontil. "But he can still teach with no arms or legs. Just squeeze the things off. He can teach the classes propped up in a damn chair."

The other Wontil, looking agreeable and pleased vent their anger, began pressing their lips together tightly. Nose flaps closing, Joseph could hear the build-up of pressure in their arms. He braced himself as their hands dug deep, the burn of their fingernails digging into his skin.

Joseph closed his eyes. He could hear the loud thudding of his heart in his ears. Louder and louder.

He felt himself drop the floor. He frantically felt around for his legs, worrying that he wasn't feeling any pain at their removal due to shock. They were all there, and clearly his arms were still attached. The Wontil had simply dropped him. He could see the Wontil running down the hall, and saw that the loud thud was not his heart, but was in fact the approaching figure of the Jovian Doug.

All the three Wontil jumped on Doug, his flippers flapping wildly. Unable to grab his arms, they made for his body, each grip unable to find purchase on Doug's furry, flabby skin. One Wontil, climbing to Doug's neck, let out a loud list of mother-themed curses, similar to the ones issued by the Wontil in the refrigeration unit. The Wontil went through a graphic list of vile activities, the maternal object of the description abstract—a reaction to exasperation of what the universe had set upon him, wrestling fruitlessly with some giant from Jupiter. Yet Doug, with his poor grasp of Wontil pronouns and just enough understanding to glean the graphic details listed by his attacker, suddenly screamed, "Why you say that of the Doug-Mother?!"

Joseph watched as Doug's face contorted into an expression of incandescent rage.

Letting out a shattering roar, the massive Jovian slammed his body against a series of pipes, the pipes bending cartoonishly into the partial form of the Wontil on his neck. He slapped the attacker on his right. It went flying down the hallway, landing with a wet crunch. He coiled a flipper around the Wontil on his left, then spun, the body twirling like a top away from the head that was biting into the Jovian's stomach. The head fell off soon after, a small chunk of Doug's flesh in its mouth, wearing an expression of ghastly joy.

Doug stood there, heaving amidst the sound of the Wontil's escaping circulatory gases. His breathing started to slow. He looked up at Joseph, and smiled. Then walked over to Joseph to help him up. "Can Joe walk?" asked Doug.

"My joints hurt, but I can make it. We're pretty close to the docking bay. We've got to get there fast." Joseph could hear the sounds of approaching Wontil. Scores of bare feet slapping the floor. There were a lot of them. Joseph put his hand on Doug's back, and they continued down the hallway. "I'm so sorry I left you Doug."

"No. Doug told Joe go. You listened well and follow instructions. Besides, I fine doing this work. Jovian never afraid hard work," said Doug, with a wink. It was impossible tell if the Jovian had a sense of humor, or was being sincere.

The sounds of approaching Wontil were closer. They rounded a corner, and were met with a line of a dozen Wontil. It was clear that they were expected. The Wontil immediately rushed them.

Doug reached out and pushed Joseph to the ground, sliding him between his legs, and began to use his deathly flippers to slap off their attackers. Joseph crouched low, the span underneath Doug providing safe harbor as chaos erupted around them. He could see the Wontil jumping up, piling onto Doug's bulk. A quivering mountain of slaps, screams, and hissing gasses swayed above him. Joseph heard another group Wontil join the fray. Joseph pulled out his knife, and began stabbing indiscriminately at purple flesh, producing sounds of popping and hissing, like a dozen pinpricked balloons.

He could feel Doug's body start to lean precariously to the right. The Jovian's right leg was trembling under the weight of a couple dozen Wontil. Joseph could feel the gap surrounding him get larger as Doug fell over and crashed through a side door, followed by the sounds of slaps and screams as Wontil crashed around the room they fell into.

An emergency alarm went off. Joseph recognized it as one of higher level alarms reserved for grave disasters, which had played occasionally during drills. The sound of fighting soon abated. The Wontil were no longer attacking. Joseph saw their attention now fixed out a large window which formed the outer wall. Joseph stood up, as did Doug.

The electro-mechanical console in front of the window was crushed. Wontil rushed back and forth with panic-stricken faces, working various levers. Outside the window, red lights flashed on the columns which fed water to the black membrane. Lights could be seen flashing as far as the eye could see, far into the horizon on the various columns which jutted up from the landscape.

A loud crack and tearing noise shook the room. The hydrophilic black membrane which covered the planet was rapidly drying out. Membrane everywhere trembled and snapped, curling back and dissolving into a brown powder that was quickly blown away by the wind.

The Wontil were fully occupied, either working on the console to bring the system back into some kind of control, or fleeing the room to other parts of the building. Joseph and Doug looked at each other in disbelief, and then ran. Panicking Wontil, rushing back and forth to various stations in the building, paid them little notice as the two teachers made their way to the docking station.

DOUG MANAGED THE controls expertly as they glided into out of the docking bay. Their departure was unobstructed while the Wontil focused on managing the disaster currently unfolding on the planet. He and Doug had triggered a chain-reaction that would have repercussions throughout the solar system. Energy supplies would be stretched. Some sectors of production would grind to a total halt. Life on Titan would change irrevocably, the small necessities of daily life dependent on Saturn no longer available. No doubt things could get tough. But he had his life. And his family. And their home. And their garden.

Doug weaved in an out around the debris-field, narrowly missing a cluster of junk that had been jettisoned from the planet. Joseph was impressed. "Where did you learn to fly like that, Doug?"

"Before teacher work, Doug pilot on Jupiter."

They were nearing Saturn's rings. Doug and Joseph viewed the rings as they passed by the portals. Joseph hadn't had such a clear view of them in ages.

"Told you. Doug save Joe. And rings," said Doug.

"About that, " asked Joseph. "When can I expect to get my ring back?"

"One year?"

"A year?!"

"Yes, one Saturn year. About thirty of your earth years. Jovian have very long digestive tract."

Doug once again struck a heroic pose, head lifting in the air.

Then he turned to Joseph, and winked.

Jamie Ross was a Canadian/Irish systems and software engineer living in rural East County Clare, Ireland. Growing up in the US and Canada, he and his brother Graham devoured every science fiction and fantasy book in their local libraries, from Edgar Rice Burroughs and Jules Vern to Andre Norton and Robert Heinlein shaping their life direction. He went on to study Aeronautics and Astronautics at MIT and graduated on to work on a diverse range of R&D projects including advanced spacecraft navigation and control systems, a Life Science centrifuge for ISS, as well as robotic missions to Mars and Europa. His brother picked up a PhD in fluid dynamics at Stanford and was instrumental in the Hubble Space Telescope and Gravity B spacecraft programs. On a more practical side, Jamie worked on the Iridium communications network and giant undersea tidal turbines in France and Canada. He first tried coming up with a story about asteroid mining years ago, ending up making friends with the top expert in the subject at the US Geological Survey which resulted in a proposal for mining lunar regolith but couldn't find the story that needed to be told. The story that starts here finally introduced itself in the competition for the first Vintage Worlds and has sucked him into its expanding universe.

One of the complaints about the new solar system is that it is dead and lifeless compared to the tales of the Old Solar System. What if we are wrong and discovering otherwise has all sorts of unintended consequences? A young Canadian astronaut struggling with terminal cancer expects to die in her last mission, but fate has other plans...

BEYOND DESPAIR

Jamie Ross

- EARTH GEOSYNCHRONOUS ORBIT -

THE DEEP SPACE exploration vessel, Shining Star, was scheduled to leave Earth orbit in a few hours for the long journey to Uranus and now the departure was delayed by preparations for a high-level news conference to be broadcast around the globe. The multinational crew waited impatiently on the bridge, uncomfortable in their new dress uniforms. Ivan Kuznetsov of the Russian Federal Space Agency was Mission Commander with 30 years of experience in the Eurasian Economic Union space program. Elisabeth Marie Williams, of the Canadian Space Agency was the Eurasian Economic Union's most experienced pilot while the powerful fusion engines were the brainchild of J.Y. "Jimmy" Ho of the Chinese National Space Agency. Medical/Science Officer Marika Werner from Germany rounded out the small experienced crew.

Elisabeth tried to hide in the back of the group hoping not to be noticed as she didn't want to face millions of viewers. Initially she enjoyed the media spotlight but the long-term radiation and low-g effects of space travel had taken its toll on her body and now she hated the public relations aspects of the job. The other crew members appeared equally uncomfortable with the publicity stunt as their restlessness revealed. Marika, the medical/science officer complained out loud, "Commander, is this necessary? We have enough things to worry about without having to waste time listening to more speeches?" Ivan shrugged in response, "Marika, our governments invested significant resources and money on this project and they need to keep people involved and supportive. Just be glad they turned down the offer of commercial advertising or we would be promoting electric sports cars, deodorant or hygiene products." He pulled out his checklist, "Jimmy, are all the engines online and ready for the first delta-V burn?" Jimmy turned away from his engineering displays and flashed a grin. "Commander, I guarantee they will give you the ride of your life. I double-checked all the systems and we can depart as soon as the cameras turn off. " Jimmy invested his life's work on these engines and insisted on accompanying them on their maiden flight to make sure they returned to Earth in one piece.

As they reviewed the departure protocol, the comm-link flashed and the video link came online. Mission Director, Alexi Grigorovich appeared on the screen with people rushing around behind him setting up for the conference.

"Hello everyone. I am impressed. You are all very professional looking in the uniforms our media people designed for you. I must apologise for all this but we need to give people something to get excited about. You may not know that the Lunar Helium-3 mining operations are about to be shut down due to massive cost overruns so we are counting on you bringing back full tanks. If we can show that mining the gas planets is cost-effective, then we may be able to keep the lights on back here on Earth. Bringing Helium-3 gives hope to people and will prevent the current conflicts over resources."

He glanced over the crewmembers, frowning in Elisabeth's direction. "Elisabeth, how are you doing? Are you going to be able to finish piloting through the atmosphere? I don't think anyone else could fly through that atmosphere and survive."

"Thank you for your concern Alexi, I am confident that I will be able to make the collection runs even if I don't manage the return trip," she said, smiling stoically. After receiving her last dismal medical report, she hung on to the goal of completing this last mission. The report had confirmed what she already suspected. The cellular damage from 5 years piloting cislunar space had triggered cancer, destroying her immune system. She trimmed her hair short after it turned white and brittle in the last year and accepted that she would not survive the 15-month duration of the mission. She only needed to pilot the crew to Uranus and work out the flight procedure to collect the first loads of Helium 3. Once that was done, the crew could manage the return to Earth without her.

As the cameras closed down, everyone relaxed. Elisabeth changed to her normal flight attire and started final orbital departure procedures. She reviewed the planned trajectories and confirmed the initial transfer orbit. They would reach the moon, and execute a series of swings around the planets to reach Uranus in 7 months. It would be a long trip, she thought as she started on her checklist.

- VICINITY OF URANUS -

THE SHINING STAR approached its destination seven months after the departure from Earth. Elisabeth monitored the approach to Uranus alone in the small cockpit. It had become her favourite place to relax and avoid people during the endless hours. It was always quiet with only the humming of the fusion drive in the background. The dim red lights of the instrumentation displays were the only distraction allowing her to be alone with her thoughts.

She listened to Mozart on headphones as she reviewed the procedures for the final rendezvous with Uranus. The long journey was drawing close to its goal with Uranus getting larger on the view screens every hour. Elisabeth wished there were actual windows but all the crew areas were located at the core of the spacecraft. Here they were surrounded by water and fuel tanks for radiation protection. Displays at least provided high-quality imagery of the outside of the ship, but the protection wouldn't do her any good at this point. She wished the lunar freighters had been protected that way.

Her briefing when they picked her for this project was simple and clear. The Eurasian Economic Union desperately needed the Helium-3 and the atmosphere on Uranus had abundant amounts ready for collection. Conventional oil, gas and coal supplies were getting more expensive and challenging to obtain every year. The development of working Helium-3 Fusion reactors had been a major achievement. The new reactors would replace nuclear, oil and gas generators and solve a lot of energy problems. Unfortunately, the amount of fuel available from lunar mining was limited and expensive. So in some sense, the future of mankind depended on this mission. Whether she and the majority of her crew survived this trip wasn't relevant as long as the fuel came back.

As she listened to the strains of the music, she reflected on how she had gotten to this point in her life. The long days and nights of the trip provided lots of time to think about life choices. Elisabeth had picked this career for the adventure. As a teenager, she had devoured all the science fiction novels and movies. She imagined a glamorous and exciting life as an astronaut. Life doesn't always turn out as planned, though, and her dreams ended at 28 when her family were all killed.

Her family had been on a holiday to San Francisco when US provocations had triggered the launch of a Korean nuke. Her parents and sister had all disappeared in a fiery instant and left her alone. The collapse of the North American governments that followed the attack extinguished American and associated Canadian space ambitions as survival and rebuilding took priority. She had buried her grief by volunteering for the deep space missions for the EEC from Earth to the Moon and back with its toll on her health. It didn't matter to her, though, because life without family was too long anyway.

SHE WAS STARTLED as Ivan poked his head in. "Elisabeth, how close are we to orbital burn?"

She turned to him, taking off her headphones. "We are three hours out, then we should be able to establish a geosynchronous orbit, Commander.." She liked Ivan and had willingly shared her bed with him though even that was getting more uncomfortable as her health worsened. She shook the dark thoughts out of her head as he returned to the bridge.

The opaque atmosphere of Uranus loomed ever closer on the monitor. Elisabeth turned her attention back to her work and completed the orbital manoeuvres needed to achieve orbit. After they were in a stable orbit, she headed to the viewing pod by the docking bay. It was the only place which had actual windows and was generally only used during orbital operations.

Elisabeth sat in the pod looking at the milky white planet below them. The next step would be to pilot one of the collector shuttles down into the atmosphere and scoop up as much Helium-3 as fuel tanks would hold. This was the part that they selected her for as the winds were brutal and no one knew what atmospheric flight on Uranus would be like and her experience would be essential. Once she had sorted it out, they would use the flight information to automate the collection, which was just as well, given rapidly deteriorating health. She just had to survive this.

She was jolted out of her reverie by Ivan's voice booming

over the intercom, "Elisabeth, meet us in the shuttlebay—
The preflight checkout is complete and the collector is ready
for flight. Time to earn your pay." She rolled her eyes and
climbed out of the pod, taking one last look at the swirling
clouds on the planet below, as she headed along the corridor
to pick up her flight suit.

AFTER CLIMBING INTO the shuttle cockpit, Elisabeth completed her pre-flight check and confirmed systems status with
Jimmy. "Please try not to damage it too badly, Elisabeth."

"Sure, Jimmy, I wouldn't want to scratch anything",
she laughed. She turned and noticed Marika next to Jimmy
frowning. As Medical Officer, Marika was aware of her condition but knew the importance of these flights. Elisabeth
smiled at her. "I am heading down; wish me luck".

Elisabeth was an experienced shuttle pilot so she easily
manoeuvred the craft clear of the docking bay and reduced
speed, dropping behind and below the mothercraft. Descending to a planet was a matter of slowing orbital speed. She
had to descend from 8 km/sec at 57000 km down to about
100km, so it took several burns to make the transition.

Descending into the thick clouds, the flight required her
full attention as she took over manual control. She watched
the hull temperature rise as the craft was being buffeted by
the high winds but it was still within margins. The visibility
was severely limited by the dense clouds at this altitude so she
was relying on the doppler radar for information and she had
to constantly fight the controls to maintain her profile. The
tanks were filling up as expected as the air-scoops collected
the gas, so it was all going as planned.

Once the tank gauges showed the collection complete, she
ignited the primary thrusters to take her back up to the Shining Star to unload and return for more.

"Commander, first run is complete... there were no major

problems so I am going down for some more."

Elisabeth started to relax a little on the third trip down to the planet. She had been expecting problems with the collection runs, but other than the normal sort of glitches it was going surprisingly well. She had adjusted to the constant buffeting from the winds and was able to navigate the round trip without too much difficulty. She had put her concerns about the return trip to Earth out of her mind as she focused on the mission at hand.

It had been a long strenuous day and she rubbed the back of her aching neck, thinking that it would only take another few trips to complete the collection when alarms started going off and the SAR display was flashing. She stared at the massive shape indicated by the radar. Whatever it was, it was close and very BIG! She scanned the area, looking for any escape options Below her a giant airship broke free of the clouds and then an impossibly lush jungle landscape appeared below.

As she stared down at the scene unfolding before her, the airship disappeared into another cloudbank. Then she shook her head and blinked in disbelief at the giant "flowers" floating over canyons. Elisabeth didn't have time to take in the strange scene as something fast dark slammed into her ship from behind, disabling her controls. The shuttle jerked and spiralled out of control as the guidance and propulsion system lost power. She barely managed to radio the Shining Star, "Help, I am going down.. you aren't going believe this." Darkness overtook her as she slipped into unconsciousness, death coming earlier than even she expected.

- AIREAN DOME, PLANET LÚTH (URANUS)-

ELISABETH EMERGED FROM the horribly chaotic dreams she had been having. Her eyesight was blurred so only vague shapes appeared through a white mist. She was upright but it was hard to tell as she had no sensation in her body. As her eyesight became sharper, the vague forms outside started to solidify. Through the mist, it appeared they were tall, humanoid with very pale white skin and dark round eyes. They wore some sort of robes and several of them stood behind what looked like control panels.

Her head started to throb and she was gradually able to move but there was no response from her limbs. Her eyesight was improving and her vision cleared up so she tried to focus on the beings in front of her. They were somewhat human but taller and more slender. The one in the golden robes stopped talking with the others and came and stood before her, looking at her.

"Can you understand me?" he said. She was surprised as she realised he was speaking English, so she nodded, trying to make sense of the scene. She became aware that she was suspended in some sort of transparent tube as it slowing retracted upwards. "You are from the third planet, Eléth which you call Earth," was a statement rather than a question. "You were out of control heading for one of our ships so we were forced to shoot you down and you crashed. We found what was left of you and your vessel in the wilds of our planet where you were critically injured. We know much about your planet from monitoring your communications but we don't have the medical knowledge or the biological material to repair all your neurological functions".

He waited a minute to make sure he had her attention, "The Symbiotes are a class of symbiotic mechanical beings who serve us here on Lúth or Uranus as you call it. We adapted their components to rebuild you but I am afraid it won't be sufficient to restore all your functions. We don't have the required information about your nervous systems so we could not reconnect all your nerves; however, you will be able to move around. We added neural training so you can understand and speak our language. You are ..." He watched her for her reactions.

The unreality of her situation was too much and her mind snapped and panic broke through her normal discipline. She tried to scream but nothing came out. How was this possible? She kept thinking it must be a bad dream or a nightmare. Her mind was racing to catch up because everything she was seeing and experiencing was impossible! Uranus was a cold gas planet, it didn't have the lush green landscapes... it didn't have civilization and she couldn't be a cyborg or whatever she was supposed to be. She didn't even know if she had a body anymore. It was too much and she lapsed back into the darkness of unconsciousness.

WHEN SHE AWOKE this time, the room was dark except for softly glowing lights from the instrument panels. She experienced some sensation in her body this time but her arms and legs were still numb. She found she was able to move her arms and legs a bit and was able to turn her head to look around.

She was standing on a small glowing platform which she was connected to by cables at the back of her neck and torso. She held up her hand and instead of flesh and bone there was an intricate mechanical hand and arm. She looked down at smooth silver mechanical legs instead of her legs and the pale skin of her nearly naked torso displayed seams and markings which were probably cybernetic in nature. The total panic came back and hit her hard.

This had to be a dark dream but her senses told her it was far too real. I have to keep calm, she thought to herself but she was struggling. It was the same sense of unreality she experienced when she found out her family had been killed. All the piled up emotions she had buried away were hitting her now. Back then she had fled to the isolation of space to avoid dealing with her grief. Now she was a half robot? She would have sobbed but this new body was incapable of expressing emotions.

She finally exhausted herself struggling to move off the platform to no avail. The platform lit up again and she slid back into unconsciousness.

AS SHE REGAINED consciousness for the third time, someone was disconnecting her from the platform connections.

This being was a symbiote, smooth silver surfaces with complex arms that looked like the ones she had. The torso was white metallic with a definite female shape. The head was smooth humanlike with glowing eyes and a symbol on its neck.

"You will recover shortly enough to walk but please move slowly as you need to adjust to your new body. You have been unconscious for several of your Earth weeks," the symbiote whispered. "I am Alisna, assistant to Leader Myker who spoke to you earlier. You are currently in the Ilúrsa medical complex where we have been repairing your body. You should have full use of your arms and legs but you will need some physical rehabilitation for you to regain your full mobility. We have also added memory modules for additional skills you will need."

"What skills? What happens to me now?" Elisabeth still had a hard time accepting what was going on.

"You are Lizbeth, pilot symbiote of Leader Myker. He has need of your piloting skills. I will take you to him where he will inform you of your new role and responsibilities."

"Pilot? Where is my ship? Where are my crew? What am I?", her voice hoarse and unfamiliar, her foggy brain trying to make sense of her new body.

"I am sorry, your ship was completely destroyed in the crash. I understand we tracked another ship recently in the last cycle which disappeared over the Wilds but it was not found or recovered so I have no further information."

So her crew might be somewhere on the planet? She had

to return to the Shining Star somehow. The Lúthians had a high level of technical sophistication so maybe they had spaceships as well.

ALISNA GUIDED HER out of the dim room into the bright light blazing in through tall windows. The scene outside was filled with exotic gardens and people but the sky was milky white. She was definitely not on Earth!

"Alisna, where are the Sun, stars? Why is there nothing in the sky!"

Alisna turned to look at her then explained, "We live under the Airean Dome which keeps us safe and protected from the environment. We are far from the Sun as you call it and only the energy cores allow us to live outside the planet interior."

Energy cores? Could it be that they had mastered Helium 3 fusion technology long before Earth scientists and engineers?

"After we complete your rehabilitation, I will take you to meet with Myker and he can answer your questions."

"Alisna, I am confused, what are the symbiotes? Are you androids?"

Alisna paused to consider the question. "If I understand what you mean by android, then no, we are not androids as we are not purely machines. We have consciousness and our organic matrix is maintained by what you would call a semi-sentient fungus. The fungus is an ancient lifeform that evolved in the deep caverns. When we are created, it is what allows our consciousness to enter and stay."

Lizbeth shook her head, realising there was a lot she and Earth science didn't understand. "So what am I then?"

"Your body was created like a symbiote so you have the fungus which protects your organic matrix but your human brain and nervous system were grafted in so you still have your own memories and consciousness. Your organic body functions much like your human body as far as we know." Her head still spinning, Lizbeth stammered, "So am I still human?" She was afraid to hear the answer. Alisna looked back at her intently, "Yes and no. You are partly like you were and now you are also like us. We have tried creating such a hybrid before but they all died so something about your physiology allows the successful merger. You are unique. That's all I can tell you at the present time". Alisna took her hand and made it obvious that Lizbeth was to follow.

EACH "DAY" ON Uranus was only about 17 Earth hours so it was several Lúthian weeks before Alisna deemed Elisabeth ready to venture out in public.

As they walked outside the Ilursa complex for the first time, Elisabeth was acutely aware of all the sounds and smells of the crowds milling along the main street. She decided some of this was a function of her new enhanced body. While she saw a lot of symbiotes moving about the area, it was rare to see one with organic bodies like her. The ones she saw were smooth and humanoid with male and female features and some were very mechanical looking but nothing like her. She was to be an odd combination of the two.

"Come with me Lizbeth, Leader Myker wants you to demonstrate your piloting skills". Alisna summoned a ground vehicle, like a taxi, and soon they were moving down a broad boulevard. As Lizbeth leaned over to look out the windows, she observed giant flowers floating over the road similar to the ones she had glimpsed before. It wasn't what she was expecting! Earth scientists had gotten it all wrong, she thought; now she had to question everything she had been taught about the solar system. Were all the planets as different as this one was?

They soon pulled up to an airport of some sort. Giant airships were taking off, disappearing into the distance while other craft were approaching and landing. Alisna drove across the field towards an unusual craft which didn't match the others.

It was smaller than the airships she had seen and she soon realised it was a spacecraft. As they approached the craft, she saw a figure waiting for them. Leader Myker stood patiently for them next to an open hatch.

"Hello Lizbeth, I apologise for rushing you through this but there is a sense of urgency. This is a prototype of an interplanetary spacecraft we have built but we have discovered that it is not well-shielded enough to protect our kind. A symbiote can pilot it but the last prototypes crashed as the symbiote pilots were unable to deal with the turbulent atmosphere. No Lúthian would volunteer to give up his or her body to be a symbiote so we are hoping you can succeed.

"We have been observing significantly more military space activity around your planet and we are concerned they will be following your path here with warships. We need to find out more so we can avoid a conflict. As you are the only one capable of piloting our interplanetary spacecraft, we need you to pilot it back to Earth and help us prevent a war."

Myker watched her to gauge her reaction. She was trying to take in the new information once again. How was she supposed to prevent a war when she was still dealing with the dysphoria from her new symbiote body. But piloting was what she did and even with all this, maybe she could make sense of her world if she could pilot again. She also wanted to return to Earth and find out what Myker was talking about.

Myker showed her to the cockpit which looked like an empty reclining chair with some sort of connectors. "Please lie down and we will start your training," Myker gestured to the empty seat.

As Lizbeth lay down, there was a slight tug at the back of

her neck. She reached back to discover cables plugged into receptacles which must have been under her "skin". Without warning the room went dark and a very different scene appeared around her. She could see outside the spacecraft and "feel" the engines and power systems. The spacecraft had become an extension of her body.

"Lizbeth, you should be able to access the ship's visual and technical data systems. The ship has an onboard artificial intelligence, like a special-purpose symbiote which provides all the information you need. You may call her Sophia, after your Greek god of wisdom and it will support you during operation." She could see he was pleased with himself in his own arrogant way.

In her head she heard a new voice, "Hello Lizbeth, I am Sophia, your ship information system. I am downloading the instructions you will need to operate the ship. Once it is complete, we can make your first suborbital flight."

There was a buzz in her head and then suddenly she understood how everything functioned. It was amazing! She could literally fly this ship with her mind and she paused as she realised they had never mentioned the Shining Star. The Lúthians might not be aware that it was still in geosynchronous orbit. She had to locate it and find out what happened to the crew.

Alisna settled into the seat next to hers, interconnecting into the ship's system as Lizbeth had. "I don't have the technical capability to fly the ship as you have," Lizbeth could see her virtual self turn towards her as she talked. "It isn't necessary to see each other's avatars when we are connected but Myker insisted it would make more sense to your human brain."

A sudden realisation hit Lizbeth, "What do you mean, 'human brain'? I thought you replaced everything with symbiote parts."

Alisna shook her head, "No. You are unique, you actually

retain your human brain and much of your central nervous system and some organic parts that we don't have a replacement for. So you are not a full symbiote, but a..." she obviously was searching for a word, "... hybrid. You are an enhanced human so space travel won't damage you as it did your previous body but you still retain human functions in many ways."

She wasn't quite sure what that meant but it did mean she was still part human. Now if she could find a way back to the Shining Star, she might find some answers and a way home.

"Can we start, please? Take the ship into a 300km circular orbit and we will take it through some manoeuvres to verify your training."

Lizbeth focused on the ship's systems as Sophia released control to her. She experienced the build-up in the engines and exhilaration as the ship just lifted off the ground and into the sky. For this first time in a long time, she was feeling excited about flying!

Myker had Lizbeth flying several missions each day for the next few weeks as the tech symbiotes reviewed each flight and made adjustments and upgrades. On the third week, he called her into the council room.

"Lizbeth, thank you for all your assistance. Your skills as a pilot are obvious. The ship would have been destroyed several times if one of our symbiotes had flown it." He appeared to be genuinely appreciative but there was something he was not telling her. "The last upgrades to the ship will be complete tonight, and we would like you to depart for Earth as soon as possible."

Lizbeth was suspicious, "I will get ready to depart as soon as possible, Leader Myker, but you are not telling me something; why the rush?

"We are monitoring Earth communication as I have told you before. There is a military mission being planned for Uranus in the next few weeks." Myker looked concerned.

"But we used the last of the Helium 3 getting here; how

are they planning to travel so far?" Lizbeth was puzzled by the idea.

"They have revived an old propulsion concept of detonating nuclear bombs behind the ships with the resultant explosive force providing propulsion. It's not safe but it would be effective so they must be desperate. That's why we have to move to avert a disaster. I suggest you rendezvous with your ship in orbit and bring back some Helium 3; it may be useful."

Lizbeth jerked back slightly; she hadn't realised the Lúthians knew about the Shining Star as they have never mentioned it. "Ahh.. yes that would be a good place to start. I'll leave as soon as I am ready." She nodded at Myker and turned and headed back to the medical complex where she was quartered.

As she walked back to her room, she mused that one good thing about her new half-symbiote body was that she didn't need to bring a lot with her. Even her hair stayed clean which mean there was more to her capabilities than she knew about. Her plan was simple: get to the craft and head back to find the Shining Star. It was a long way away and didn't have a big signature anyway, so you had to know where to look. Fortunately, as its pilot, she at least knew roughly where she left it.

It was early the next morning when the opportunity came. Alisna contacted her on the comm system and confirmed that the ship was ready and waiting for her. She gathered her few things and walked outside the complex and found a taxi vehicle to take her to the airport. There was a major gathering in the city centre so the roads were almost empty and the news on the radio was focused about the impending threat from Earth.

The symbiote driver took her to the landing pad and Lizbeth walked to the craft and boarded without any interference. She checked out the vehicle and confirmed to herself that all the upgrade work was completed. After settling into the pilot seat, she activated the neural interface and the cockpit disappeared as she entered the immersive mode.

"Hello Lizbeth", Sophia was right there, now with a Greek goddess avatar that Lizbeth had put together. "What is the mission today?"

"Sophia, we need to find my old ship so I can find out what happened to my crew. It's in geosynchronous orbit over the equator but I am not sure of the exact coordinates." She was hoping that Sophia had been given complete access to the Lúthian tracking systems.

"I will check the latest records. Leader Myker instructed me to provide you with whatever support you need." Sophia started to display all known satellite records on her display.

"Please let Myker know once we have taken off. Hopefully, the Shining Star is still operational and if I can get it activated, we can head back to Earth to deliver our fuel and find out if Lúth is in danger."

She smiled as she hadn't cared much whether she lived or died in the past few years. She hadn't had time to deal with her anger and grief over losing her family and now her humanity but at least there might be a future ahead of her now to sort it out.

"Pass me the controls, Sophia, we need to get back to space."

LIZBETH SCANNED THE sky as her ship rose up to geosynchronous orbit. She could "see" through her long-range sensors but finding the ship wouldn't be easy. Space was "big" and even a massive spacecraft like the Shining Star was difficult to locate even if you had an idea where to find it.

Several hours went by before she could sense a presence, which her sensors soon identified as the Shining Star. As she manoeuvred close to the big ship, she could see all the Helium 3 tanks were full. So the crew had managed to complete the collection after she crashed. The empty bays indicated that they had taken the other collector ship to search for her and it hadn't returned.

She could see there was room for her craft in the empty collection ship bay. She manoeuvred the Lúthian ship into position near the docking port and engaged the landing gear to secure it to the giant vessel.

The combination of symbiotic tech and skintight pressure suit meant she only needed a transparent helmet to cross over to the Shining Star. It was running on standby power so there were no obstacles getting through the airlock. As she came on-board, the lights in the ship came alive as it recognized her entry.

"Please identify yourself", came the voice of the on-board AI. "This is Lt-Commander Elisabeth Williams," she replied as she had so many times before. The AI was silent as it scanned her. Retinal scans or fingerprints weren't going to work with her new body so she volunteered, "I have had extreme medical repairs but you can check my DNA which should confirm my identity." The AI paused again as it processed the new information. "Please report to the medical centre."

Lizbeth followed the corridor to the medical bay, reassured by the familiarity but still a little disturbed. Things had changed so much for her. She entered the room where she had always gotten more bad news about her health and lay down on the examination table.

"Please lie still during the examination," the AI continued. Scanning arms moved slowly over her as she felt a tug in her abdomen where it had taken a sample.

After it completed what she decided was the most comprehensive medical exam she had experienced, the AI gave its results.

"You are confirmed as Elisabeth Williams, pilot of the Shining Star; welcome back Elisabeth. Your analysis indicates you are about 45% human with about 65% alien technology. Your brain and torso remain largely human in function but your limbs, skull, eyes, ears and some of your internal organs have been augmented or repaired with a combination of cyber technology and bio-organic technology. You are not fully functioning because of mismatches between the alien technology and your human anatomy and nervous system.

Suddenly she heard Sophie's familiar voice in her head, "Lizbeth, this AI knows far more about your physiology than we do. If I merge with it, we can combine our knowledge and finish the repairs on your body".

She thought about that for a few minutes, "Would that allow you to upgrade the technology on the Shining Star as well and vice versa?"

Sophie answered, "I would think so as your AI has sufficient knowledge and understanding".

Lizbeth pondered the implications for a moment. She had terrifying memories of the old sci-fi movie, "The Forbin Project", where two AI's joined to enslave mankind. Given the way mankind was going, maybe that wasn't the worst outcome. In for a dime, in for a dollar, as the old saying went, she thought.

"Sophie, I think that would be a good idea... what do you need me to do?"

FOR THE NEXT couple of hours, Lizbeth collected optical cable and adjusted the wireless receiver to allow direct communications between the two systems. Then she waited as they "introduced themselves", which in reality meant exchanging information protocols until they were able to communicate freely.

"Lizbeth, we are ready to attempt the merge so we will be out of communication for about an hour. Please monitor the ship systems while we are inactive." Lizbeth sighed, "Yes

Sophie, I can manage for a couple of hours."

Lizbeth had learned a few new things and was now able to directly connect into the Shining Star computer network so she set off to explore and see what had happened in her absence. After about an hour of scanning logs, she sat back and disconnected. The crew had used the second collector to complete the Helium 3 retrieval but disagreement had broken out over the next step. Ivan and Marika wanted to descend one more time to see if they could locate Elisabeth while Jimmy insisted that completing the mission was most important and the risk was too high.

She couldn't argue with Jimmy, she would have made the same case but then again she hadn't been invested in life, just finishing this last mission.

The log indicated that in the end, they all decided to go down and sweep the last known location of Elisabeth's collector ship. Log transmissions indicated that they too ran into difficulties but it didn't seem like they crashed the way she did. The transmission ended but it wasn't clear the state of the ship or the crew. So it was possible they could still be alive! Neither Myker or Alisna had mentioned any other crashes so there was no way of knowing what happened. Mission Control back on Earth must have been aware of the disappearance of the crew which might explain the activity Myker had revealed.

"Hello Lizbeth, we have successfully completed the merger and are assessing your repairs as well as ship upgrades." Lizbeth blinked reflexively. It had worked?

"What do I call you now?" was all she could think of.

"You may still call me Sophie, your AI would be considered female so she was happy to keep that. You will need to get back on the medic bed so we can proceed with the necessary upgrades to repair your body."

Lizbeth removed the tunic she was wearing and reclined on the examination table. She plugged in a neural connector.

"I'm sorry Lizbeth, we have to disconnect your nervous system to make the repairs, you will wake up when it's complete," was the last thing she heard as she lost consciousness yet again.

THIS TIME WHEN she awoke, Lizbeth felt clear-headed. It was amazing as she could "feel" her arms and legs and her body like it was her own this time. She looked at the clock on the wall and instantly she was zoomed in to its details. There was more functionality in her cybernetic eyes than they had told her about.

"Hello Lizbeth, I see you are awake now. We have run scans and your body should be working much better for you as your AI had all the missing information we needed."

Lizbeth slid off the table, "How long have I been out?"

"You have been unconscious now for 4 earth days, so we have had time to integrate the ship systems as well."

"Can we make it back to Earth now?" she asked, afraid to hear the answer.

"Yes, Lizbeth, by integrating Lúthian technology, we were able to bring the Helium 3 drives to 98% efficiency so the journey should only take about 2 weeks."

Two weeks? It took them 70 days to make the journey from Earth. She hadn't thought this far ahead, to be honest. She was supposed to die early on during the return voyage and then she was so caught up in her transformation and getting back to the Shining Star so she never considered anything beyond that. She shook her head and thought if she let herself sink into what was going on, it would be hard to get anything done.

"Sophie, can you plot a course to Lunar orbit and get us there? I think I need to get some rest and sort this all out in my head."

"Yes Lizbeth, your quarters are prepared. While you

need normal rest, you also need recharging so we have added neural electrical receptors to your bed to allow both. This will allow your brain's neural pathways to adjust to the new connections."

Lizbeth started towards the door and saw herself in a mirror for the first time. The woman looking back at her had what appeared to be smooth thigh-high metal boots, capable-looking metallic arms and the eyes that looked back glowed blue. A combination of sadness, grief and hope rose up in her. She looked strange but strong and healthy and she felt better than she had in ages. She walked down the familiar corridor to her stateroom and as she sat in her bunk, it all felt so different. She didn't experience the depression she used to feel here. This was something different, optimism for her life was appearing again.

As she rested, she dreamed for the first time in many months. It was an odd mix of images from Lúth and Earth and feeling she was running from someone or something.

She didn't want to wake up as the reality was too strange. Suddenly the lights in the cabin came on and she could her Sophie in her ear, "Lizbeth, we are approaching Earth-Lunar space and I believe we need you on the bridge". Coming from Sophie, that sounded ominous. She dressed in bits of uniform which she could wear with her cybernetic parts and headed straight to the bridge. Once she arrived, she sat down quickly in the captain's chair and activated the neural connector.

As space spread before her in her immersive state, she noted several large unusual ships in both lunar and earth high orbits. She could see sensor indications of multiple missile launchers on the ships and extremely large engine nozzles which meant that these were the warships Myker was referring to. "This doesn't look good. Those ships look ready to fly and they are heavily armed", she commented. Sophie responded "I am getting a signal on your communications channel; they would like to talk to you, Lizbeth. Do you want me to set up a video link?"

Lizbeth nodded, "Yes, this is going to be an interesting conversation."

She sat down in front of the video link. As the screen cleared, she saw Alexi Grigorovich, Project Lead for the Uranus Mission, staring back at her. He looked uncomfortable and suspicious as her image appeared. She supposed the glowing cybernetic eyes were not what he was expecting. "Who are you? Where are my crew?" he barked at her.

"Hello Alexi, this is Elisabeth Williams; the other crew members are missing on Uranus but we managed to return with Helium 3." She could see Alexi talking to people out of the view of the camera, then he turned back to look at her. "Elisabeth Williams died when her collector ship crashed in Uranus according to our logs, so you can't be her. We don't know who or what you are but you will open the ship for docking and surrender to our people." A cold shiver went up her spine as she realised that they were using the hostile alien protocol. It had been discussed in briefings but no one took it seriously. If she followed their instructions, it was likely they would tear her apart to learn about the Lúthian technology.

"Alexi, it's a long story but trust me, I am Elisabeth. The ship confirmed my identity via my DNA otherwise I wouldn't be able to access its systems. You have to understand, we have it all wrong. Uranus is inhabited by intelligent beings. They call their planet Lúth and they have some advanced technology we don't have. I was almost dead but their medical people were able to repair my body with cybernetic modifications, but it's still me."

Alexi turned again to talk to people off-camera then stepped aside as a woman Lizbeth recognised as Zhang Nianzhen, Speaker for the EEC council. "Commander Williams, if what you say is true, then this whole mission may be a mistake. We assumed you had been attacked by hostile beings and we need the Helium 3. The situation here is getting more desperate by the day. Is it possible for us to negotiate some sort of agreement with these... umm... Lúthians? We could offer them resources, technology or other materials they may not have access to."

Lizbeth thought for a moment and turned the audio off. "Sophie, has Leader Myker been listening to this? I assume he has the support of the council to make decisions?"

"Yes, Lizbeth, as you surmised, Myker has been in constant contact with the council," replied Sophie quietly.

"Leader Myker, I believe Ms Zhang Nianzhen is interested in negotiating a trade agreement to obtain Helium 3 for Earth in exchange for resources Lúth may need. Is this something your people would consider?"

"Hello Lizbeth, yes we would be willing to develop some sort of trade arrangement with Earth. There are materials available on inner planets like Earth that are difficult and expensive for us to obtain. It would also seem preferable to conflict. I will have my people set up communication channels".

Lizbeth turned to the camera and turned the audio on again. "Speaker Zhang, I am informed that Leader Myker of Lúth is agreeable to such an arrangement and will set up communication channels. Will you have Alexi call off his warships please?"

Zhang Nianzhen turned to Alexi who started to protest but nodded in agreement and returned to the camera. "Elisabeth, it seems you have averted a crisis here for the moment. We can't allow you into Earth orbit until we have some agreement in place. If your Leader Myker were willing to leave us two fuel pods as a gesture of goodwill so we can fuel our reactors it would go a long way to defusing the tensions here on Earth."

She heard Myker's voice in her head agreeing. "Yes Alexi, I will deposit two tanks in Lunar orbit where you can retrieve them. I hope we get a chance to speak again."

Alexi looked at her one more time. "Elisabeth, if that is

still you, I hope you find some peace," he started and then continued in another vein, "Please let us know about the rest of the crew."

She smiled and replied, "I will Alexi, I am worried about them as well." She closed the link, left the bridge and headed back to the cockpit.

LIZBETH SETTLED INTO the pilot's chair and reconnected to the ship systems. She still wasn't used to the immersive environment, it always felt like she was floating in space. The excitement of piloting like this still hadn't worn off and she suspected it never would. She just sat there for a few minutes, taking in the immensity of the surroundings, Earth and the Moon and the background of stars and planets. Everything she knew about the Solar System had to be tossed in the rubbish bin. If they were so wrong about Uranus, what did that say about the rest of the planets? She would have to find out. In the meantime, she needed to find Ivan and Jimmy and Marika, if they were alive.

"Sophie, can you get us back to Lúth?" After a minute she heard Sophie's now familiar voice in her head. "Yes Lizbeth, based on your previous mission trajectory, I can navigate us back".

"Thank you, Sophie, I think I want to just watch and enjoy the view this time." She could even imagine what her future would be at this point but at least there was a future and there were amazing things to learn and discover. She turned on Mozart and flew through space, alive again.

Ron Mucklestone resides in Toronto, Canada, where he works as a consultant and spends his free time engaged in organic gardening, carpentry, mystical pursuits and raising a family. He has recently resumed his childhood passion for writing science fiction and other forms of fiction.

There are plenty of reasons to enjoy tales of the Old Solar System, but one of them is the sheer kaleidoscopic color of a setting full of planets where quite literally anything can happen. Ron Mucklestone's The Horse-men of Ganymede is a grand example—a lively adventure tale full of strange creatures and dire perils where the unbelievable is ordinary...

THE HORSE-MEN OF GANYMEDE

Ron Mucklestone

I: Captured

SAM COLLINS AIMED his gun at the giant bat-like raptor that had taken notice of him from about fifty yards up in the air and pulled the trigger. The gun jammed. Third time this week. *What's with the new issue from Planetex? If there is one thing that they need on this god-forsaken planet, it is a properly functioning fire-arm.*

Sam gave the gun holster a few firm bangs on a flat rock and pulled the trigger half-way again. The green light glowed reassuringly. Now if only he could get a clean shot at it before it decided to make him its dinner…

Before Sam realized what was going on, his head felt like it was exploding and he was face-down in the sand. Something big and heavy was on him and it was definitely not friendly. He used all the senses he could to figure out who—or what—his assailant could be. Several hundred pounds for sure, with rough skin and what felt like gravel digging into his thighs and lower back. Smelled like a combination of overcooked broccoli and rubbing alcohol. Silent. That narrowed it down to one thing in this world: a Smaggot. The question was what did the Smaggot want with him?

(Meanwhile the raptor swung away and disappeared in the glare of the sun to the west.)

Sam's right hand was pinned under his left hip. The coarse sand was digging into the back of his hand. He hoped it wasn't bleeding because if it was, in a few minutes the little sand worms would smell the blood, find the wound, and burrow into his bloodstream to breed. No idea where his gun had gone to.

Slowly, Sam wiggled his right hand to move the sand underneath and slipped it under his abdomen until it was free. He looked right and left for his gun. No luck.

The Smaggot shifted its weight and rose. Before he knew it, Sam's right fore-arm was enclosed in the thing's huge hand and it lifted Sam off his feet in one smooth motion. Dangling by his arm, Sam faced his assailant. Yup. It was a Smaggot alright—huge, droopy, fleshy ears the colour of decaying broccoli; practically no nose, but with two gigantic round nostrils to let in the thin Martian air; a single red eye in the middle of its mustard-yellow forehead; and a frog-like mouth equipped with 66 razor-sharp teeth. Sam had definitely experienced better days.

The Smaggot finally spoke. "Oongh oye opifif slong," it drawled. Sam tried his best to remember the rudiments of the Smaggot tongue he had learned on the voyage to Mars—one of the four languages he had had to cram during the 9-month journey. "I'm not going to eat you"—ok, that was good news. The Smaggot continued: "Oongh hoosh marangake shloo Gammam." Sam could only catch some of the sentence—"I'm handing you over to… Gammam."

Who was Gammam?

Now suspended about 10 feet off the ground, Sam frantically looked for his gun. In the scuffle created when the Smaggot attacked him, the gun had gone flying a few feet to the right of where he was standing, but luckily it had sunk partway into the loose sand. Just a bit of the handle was peeking out. The question was whether or not the Smaggot had noticed the gun.

With its left hand, the Smaggot searched Sam's gun holster on his left hip to ascertain whether he was armed. Satisfied that the human was defenceless, the Smaggot let out a confident grunt to itself. It then checked the holster for the walkie-talkie on Sam's right hip, clumsily removed the device and proceeded to crush it in its left hand. Suddenly, Sam felt all alone in this alien world.

Then an enormous explosive noise rang out and echoed against the nearby escarpments. The Smaggot dropped Sam and covered its ears with its two huge hands. Sam fell hard to the ground on his back, winding himself. As if breathing the thin Martian atmosphere wasn't difficult at the best of times! He was determined not to pass out.

Ears ringing from the noise, Sam quickly searched for his bearings and his gun. It was within the reach of his left hand. With as little commotion as possible and as deftly as a stage magician, he stuck his hand into the sand, pulled the gun under the sand and slipped it into his holster. A split second later, the Smaggot turned to Sam and grabbed his right hand—none the wiser about the gun. Not as though the gun would be any use against a Smaggot: excepting right under the chin, the creature's hide was as thick as armour plates. Its only other vulnerable spot was its single eye. No, shooting the thing was not much of an option, but there was more to be scared of on Mars than just these lumbering ogres. A human without a gun in this brutal world would last 24 hours at best.

"Hak shok" said the Smaggot. "We walk" translated Sam to himself.

The Smaggot and its human captive walked up the gradual slope of the dune. At the crest, they could see the lap of the Utopia Basin spread before them. And the source of the loud noise. Sam's head reeled and his stomach felt like it fell to the ground. At a distance of about 2 miles (crystal clear in the dry Martian air), the satellite communication dish established by his crew last week was now a crumpled, smoldering wreck, with pieces strewn a hundred yards in every direction. It looked as though it had been bombed.

"Gammam" said the Smaggot as it faced Sam and contorted its face. Sam had the sick feeling that it was smiling.

They trudged along towards the gradually setting sun -- two hours until dark, Sam guessed. With each step the distance between him and the safety of his Earthship (the "Jolly Roger") increased. If he didn't make it back to the ship by sundown, a search party would go out. But they had only an hour before it got too dangerous even for the tank-like rover to venture forth. Even though they know that Captain Stroud had assigned Sam to the west for the day, he was now more than 10 miles from the Earthship and far from where he was supposed to be. Only if they were very lucky would they find Sam under these circumstances.

The two moved along at a sedate pace. One doesn't rush a Smaggot. They know how to conserve their resources in this parched land. Some of Sam's experienced crewmates compared these beasts to camels: they can walk day and night for a whole week without rest, food or water. Sam just hoped that this particular Smaggot was at least somewhat familiar with human limitations.

Gathering up his courage and practicing the words to himself a few times, Sam asked: "Oola hashmat?" ("How far?") The Smaggot turned its head down and to the left, fixing its big red eye onto Sam's eyes, its face expressionless and silent. Sam knew that it had heard him—its ears were four times more sensitive than a human's—and likely understood him too, but for whatever reason, it decided not to reply.

As the shadows of the small dunes and scraggly bushes before them gradually lengthened, Sam's mind wandered to his decision to work on Mars. Jobs for young geologists on

Earth were hard to find these days and prospecting on Mars was the only guaranteed job. Desperate to pay off his student debt, he had signed up even though it was common knowledge that only two-thirds of the workers made it back to Earth alive after one six-month stint on the red planet. Sam was a survivor. He'd had a rough scrabble life growing up in downtown Detroit. Handling a gun was part of growing up. But it was Mr. Williams, Sam's Grade 10 geography teacher, who'd lit the passion of geology in Sam's mind. Even though he had to borrow a lot of money to get his Bachelor's degree, just getting a degree seemed an opportunity to escape the inner city squalor in which he had grown up. Sam also saw geology as a great opportunity for a person like him who wanted to live in exotic locations—maybe the Andes, or the jungles of the Congo, or Canada's arctic tundra, or the Australian outback. But when violent revolutions broke out over much of the globe over the course of only two years, mining companies gave up prospecting on Earth in favour of Mars. And now he was prospecting on another planet with increasingly dismal chances of ever making it back to his home world.

His mind also turned to the huge blast that had made scrap metal out of his team's satellite dish. What could have happened? The dish itself had no explosives—not even compressed air. Some outside force must have destroyed it—but what?

Sure, Mars was a hostile place: a lot of life here was brutal or downright deadly, but so far in the three years of manned prospecting missions on the planet, there had been no sign of advanced intelligent life. Yes, four species were capable of speech—the ogre-like Smaggots of the deserts that practically encircle the planet, the flamingo-like Orfus of the wetlands in the Hellas Basin, the wild wolverine-like Krupas of Olympus Mons and other volcanic peaks, and the winged humanoid Feebees who dwell in the Valles Marineris. But all of them were primitive by human standards: none had mastered chemistry sufficiently to produce explosives and while they had tools, they had yet to graduate to building machines. So, unless there was an undiscovered species as technologically advanced as humans, the destroyer could not be Martian.

Could it have been human? Not likely. Even though the US was in an arms race with the Russians and Chinese, neither of those foes of America had yet sent a human mission to Mars, and from all the talk Sam had heard, it was at least a couple of years before that would happen.

What about a stray asteroid or meteor? Mars' pocked surface is testament to the ravages of these extraterrestrial rocks due to its thin atmosphere and proximity to the asteroid belt. And some of Sam's team-mates who had made two or three tours of Mars swore that they had seen a meteor hit the planet. But the chance of a space-rock making a direct hit on a newly installed satellite dish strained credibility too far. Besides, there would be a crater, and Sam did not see one.

What other explanation could there be? Sam was stumped.

He thought again about the destination to which the Smaggot claimed it was taking him: Gammam. The Smaggot had used the same word when the satellite dish was destroyed. Sam felt like kicking himself for not having studied the Smaggot tongue more diligently during the voyage. But then again, the crew was not expected to have much interaction with the fauna of Mars—they were there to interact with minerals and find the telltale signs of diamonds. That was what they were paid to do. What could "Gammam" possibly mean? And why were they not walking to the destroyed dish when the Smaggot called it "Gammam" and told Sam that it was taking him to "Gammam"? Nothing was making sense, and now Sam was too fatigued to think clearly.

II: Attacked

THE SMALL WAN Martian sun had set only thirty minutes ago,

but with practically no clouds in the sky, twilight was a short affair. Soon it would be too dark to see where they were going. And, unlike on Earth, there was no big brilliant Moon to shed light at night—just the two little rocks Phoebus and Deimos, which looked like bright stars in an already star-jammed Martian night sky. Maybe Smaggots had really good night vision; Sam didn't know. The air grew chill; Sam was glad that Planetex had invested in really warm jackets and pants for these missions.

In the twilight gloom, Sam started to see movement among the small dunes around them. Sinuous, but indistinct. Maybe it was the combination of poor light and oxygen deprivation that was getting to him. He had never been out after sunset, nor had he gone so long without the rich oxygenated atmosphere of the Earthship. Maybe he was just hallucinating. There it was again, but this time it looked like he could see a diamond-shaped head and several spindly limbs. Now he hoped that he was just hallucinating—because if he wasn't, then he and his captor were in mortal danger. In the deserts of Mars the nights belonged to the Martian equivalent of Gila monsters. Smaggots called them "Skarjul."

The Skarjul were equipped with poisonous fangs and were fond of biting anything that moved at night. To make things worse, their bodies were covered with poisonous spines and if for any reason one touched a spine, an excruciating death was assured within the span of a minute. Apparently, Skarjuls were the main source of fatalities among the first missions to Mars and that's why night missions were banned. Even a rover-vehicle is not immune to the wily Skarjul: if they see one, they leap into the wheel wells and find their way into the cabin. Only two humans had ever survived such attacks. Now Planetex was trying to outfit the next round of missions with rovers with completely sealed cabins. Those who had survived missions to Mars shook their heads when they heard such plans and wondered how long it would take before the Skarjuls figured a way in regardless.

Another movement in the sand a mere 15 feet ahead grabbed Sam's attention. This time, he saw not only a head and spindly limbs, but also a spiny body and long spiky tail. The thing looked about 2 feet long. And it was crawling straight towards Sam.

The Smaggot whacked the top of Sam's head with one fat finger from its right hand and pointed to the Skarjul coming towards them. Then it let go of Sam's hand. "What next" Sam wondered, "is the Smaggot going to leave me to my fate?"

The next thing that happened took Sam totally by surprise. The Smaggot stuck its right hand right into its left side. The hand disappeared! And then it re-emerged, but holding a twisted foot-long stick that ended with a claw-like appendage. The Smaggot transferred the stick to its left hand. Then its right hand disappeared into its left side again. This time when it came out it was holding a sphere about the size of a bocce ball, but which glowed a rich purple very similar to ultraviolet lights back on Earth. The Smaggot fixed the luminescent ball into the stick's claw and then held it close to its mouth. Then the creature sang a single pure note for about 5 seconds. But when the singing stopped, the note continued, now with a more crystal texture. The ball seemed to be vibrating sympathetically. It glowed brighter. Sam didn't know which surprised him the most: that Smaggots were like marsupials with built-in pockets, or that these primitive creatures had a technology that was barely dreamed of in his world.

Holding the end of the stick, the Smaggot swung the ball down low over the sand, almost like the sweeping motion of a person on Earth hunting for treasure on a beach with an electromagnet. The Skarjul stopped dead in its tracks for a moment. Then it dashed to the left and out of sight.

Looking around in the purplish light, Sam could see that other Skarjuls were keeping their distance—a good 30 feet in every direction from the glowing ball. Whether it was the light, or the sound, or both that repelled them, it certainly worked!

Shortly afterwards, Sam thought that he saw the faint reflection of white lights on the sides of some dunes a few miles to his left, but after a minute or two it grew dark again and did not return. "Probably the search team out looking for me," thought Sam; "they've likely given up on me by now."

After about an hour walking this way, the Smaggot suddenly stopped. "Oofa" it said to Sam, who both thought and hoped that this meant "drink." He was getting frightfully dehydrated, which made it all that harder for him to walk. The Smaggot thrust the "handle end" of the stick into the sand about six feet away from Sam; the two of them sat down on the cold sand bathed in the purple glow. The Smaggot eyed him carefully while Sam slowly took off his backpack, unzipped it and took out the last remaining canister of water. Should he try his escape now? No, he told himself—as desperate as he was to get out of this mess, his captor was too attentive right now. Wait for the moment when it was less focused on him. He opened the canister and drank, savouring the blissful feeling of water sliding down his parched throat.

Suddenly the Smaggot became tense and looked in all directions, swivelling its head, owl-like, almost completely around. It sniffed the air. Then there was a mighty thrashing, with sand flying everywhere, and near total darkness. Keeping his wits about him, Sam realized that they were being attacked by some large winged creature. "Damn," thought Sam, "are those scary raptors nocturnal too?" Fortunately for Sam, the Smaggot seemed to be the main object of the winged creature's attention. Now was his chance to escape. Ignoring the danger of the Skarjuls lurking in the sand, Sam bolted. Within a few steps Sam found himself upside down, with his left leg in a vice-like grip. Sand was swirling around with the steady beat of immense wings. He no longer felt his body on the sand; he was airborne. Before he knew what he was doing, Sam had his gun in his hand and fired six times into what he figured was the under-belly of the creature. Hot, foul-smelling liquid was soon spraying about and the creature let out a most horrid loud scream. It moved its head back to see what was tormenting it. Sam could faintly see its open beak in the starlight and shot directly into it. The creature convulsed and dropped hard onto the ground with Sam partially pinned underneath.

Dazed, Sam could see the Smaggot running towards him with the glowing sphere aloft. He was able to pull the trigger three times before the Smaggot was upon him. Either he missed the Smaggot entirely or the bullets bounced off its hide. It didn't matter; Sam's escape was a failure and he dreaded what would happen next. The back of the Smaggot's hand was enough; Sam lost consciousness.

When he came to, Sam was bound tightly and was bobbing to the slow steady rhythm of the Smaggot's gait. "How many things does this Smaggot have in its built-in pockets?" Sam wondered to himself groggily as his mind cleared. Apparently, he was now the Smaggot's back-pack. He was facing backwards; it was still night, but in his peripheral vision he could see the deep violet glow of the Smaggot's "ball". Of course, his gun was gone now. So was his back-pack—although it was practically empty anyway, excepting a first-aid kit and a few high-energy snack bars. His throat was parched again and his feet were tied so tightly together that his ankles poked into each other. Given the height of the Smaggot, his feet were probably a yard off the ground.

Sam's head was free to move from side to side. After some time, he noticed that the light in his peripheral vision was no longer the same purple—it now had a reddish tinge, which grew brighter over the next few minutes until the light was now pure red. Then the Smaggot stopped. It mumbled some words that Sam could not make out at all—staccato with a lot of "t" sounds, which the Smaggot-tongue rarely uses.

Then, from both the right and the left of Sam's vision appeared a half-dozen or so beings that were totally unlike any creatures Sam had heard of living on Mars. They were the same height as a human but were quadrupedal and had four arms. They were covered from head to foot in a shiny silvery suit and wore metallic helmets which were broad and flat on the top and pointy in the front. Sam could not see inside the helmets. More alarming, though, was the clearly shotgun-shaped weapons that each being held in at least one hand.

III: Transported

THE SMAGGOT SAT down on the ground. One of the "silver centaurs" approach Sam and untied him with two of its hands. Sam could see that their hands had eight fingers -- four opposed four—which were extraordinarily supple and nimble. Within a few seconds, he was unbound. One of the centaurs took Sam by the arm and brought him around to face the Smaggot. The centaur was holding a small bag in one hand, which it passed over to the upward-turned right palm of the Smaggot. Turning to Sam, the Smaggot said "Gammam" and then rose up and lumbered off into the night illuminated by the purple sphere.

Sam now got bearings of his surroundings. The red light was coming from what looked like the porch-light of a one-storey house. In the strange light he could not make out what the house was made of. His quadrupedal captors then led him inside. In the reddish light that illuminated the interior of the house, no furnishings were visible. The door closed. Sam could feel the air change in the room: still thin but more oppressive like the air pollution in his hometown of Detroit. But he was a prisoner of totally unfamiliar beings whose reason for getting a Smaggot to kidnap him were unknown. So, these were the Gammam.

The Gammam took off their helmets, revealing what looked like dark skin (it was hard to determine real colour in the blood-red light that these creatures seemed to like), and a face that consisted of a bird-like beak and (Sam practically guessed it) four large, round, ink-black eyes in a line from one side of the head across the front to the other.

The group of six Gammam in the room started to chatter in their staccato whistle- and click-filled language. The Gammam who still had Sam's arm firmly held in its grip talked to him in broken Smaggot-tongue. Sam tried his best to figure out what it was saying and it was something like this: "You are a creature we have rarely seen... you are not welcome on this land... Angira [the Smaggot word for Mars] is ours... if you are not alone, we will find others like you... and kill them... we destroyed your primitive communication device... you are our prisoner... we need to learn about you even though your form and smell disgusts us."

Sam tried not to take the comments about him personally. Based on his very limited experience, these Gammam looked pretty ugly and smelled pretty bad (sickly sweet) to Sam. Their body chemistry must be very different from that of Earth life-forms.

At this point, Sam was wondering if he was just dreaming all this. Nothing made sense. Who were these centaur-like Gammam? Why didn't the Smaggots ever tell Earth missions about them? And why did they like polluted air and red light? Of course, it was true that most of Mars was still unexplored and where his team was presently stationed was on the northern edge of known territory, but these beings were odd indeed. Maybe they dwelt deep underground... Fatigue and lack of sleep were quickly getting the better of Sam and he simply could not think clearly anymore. He just wanted this bad dream to end so he could wake up in his cot in the Earthship.

Sam jolted awake. But, unhappily, he was not in his cot.

He was lying on the floor in the same house he had been forced into by the Gammam. But he was alone now. Groggily he got to his feet and in the weird red light looked for the door. He found it, but there was no knob or any other protuberance to make the door open. He squinted and looked closely at the sides of the walls beside the door to see if there was any button or latch. Nothing. Turning around, he saw a second door on the opposite side of the empty house (if it could be called that—it was more like a barn). Again, no means to open the door. And that meant no means of escape. But realistically, if he escaped, what were his chances of getting back to his Earthship alone and without provisions across many miles of desert?

Then Sam noticed two things: one, the window beside the second door seemed to be letting in sunlight. And second, he could hear what was clearly the sound of machinery. Curious, he went to the window. There, bathed in the weak rays of the Martian morning, Sam saw spread out before him a vast crater—easily 5 miles wide. The noise was coming from inside the crater. At the bottom he could see centaur-like figures and large truck-like machines. "I was right," said Sam to himself, "they ARE subterranean Martians." As he took more details in, he saw the now familiar bulky shapes of Smaggots. But the Smaggots were labouring, walking up a long incline that lined the inside of the crater carrying something heavy on their backs. And there was a Gammam in front and in back of the line of Smaggots. At the top of the slope was another house. Or was it? At the distance of a couple of miles, and with the sun shining at an acute angle, it was hard to tell. It glinted like metal and seemed to gleam a golden colour. But it looked long and low and oddly angular to be any kind of house that Sam had ever seen or even imagined. And the more Sam looked the more he wondered: is this a crater… or is it a mine?

Sam didn't have more time to wonder. Quickly and almost

silently the door close to where he was standing opened. Two Gammam were standing outside. One entered the house and immediately grabbed Sam's arm. He couldn't tell if it was the same one who had held him captive before, as it was wearing its helmet. Not as though it made a difference—they all looked the same to him: a weird four-eyed flat-headed bird face atop a centaur body with too many appendages. A sight only a mother could love—and Sam wasn't even sure about that.

He kept pace with the Gammam beside him; the other Gammam walked behind him with a gun-like weapon in each of two hands. They walked near the edge of the crater/ mine towards the golden house that he had just been looking at. His captors were silent.

When they were within a couple hundred yards of the golden house, Sam could see how mistaken he was. This was no house; it was a spaceship lying on its side. And by the looks of things, he was going to be forced into it.

Now it made more sense to Sam. The Gammam were not Martians at all... they were from another world. But where? And why did his captor tell him that Mars belonged to them?

Soon he was being led into the spaceship, flanked by Gammam. Again, that wretched red light!

The Gammam walked Sam through a long corridor to a room near the end. Turning into the room, he was presented to a Gammam who must have been in a senior position. After his captors chatted with their commander for a couple minutes in their unintelligible tongue, Sam was led back down the corridor for about fifty yards and put into a smaller, cramped room that contained several cages of various sizes. Sam could guess what would happen next. As they tried to push him into the cage, Sam squirmed and struggled and swore his head off—not because he thought he could escape, but to demonstrate to his captors that he was not willingly cooperating with his forced captivity. After about half a minute of struggling, his captors gained control of him and Sam was forced into a cage that was about 8 feet tall, wide and deep. The cage's bars were thin and so closely spaced that Sam couldn't squeeze his hand through. The Gammam left the room and Sam was left alone to his thoughts. He looked around the room. All the other cages were empty.

Within his cage was a bottle and a box that could be easily opened. Sam felt like a gerbil.

Now that he was alone, Sam noticed how hungry and thirsty he was. He was terribly fatigued too, but with all the adrenalin racing around in his bloodstream from being shoved into a strange spaceship and a cage, he knew that only after satisfying thirst and hunger would he be able to relax. Reluctantly, he opened the bottle and sniffed the contents. It was odourless like distilled water. He took a long draught. Yes, distilled water for sure, but judging by how relaxed he suddenly felt, Sam figured that it contained a sedative. He tried to fight the grogginess, but it was futile. Within a minute he was out cold.

He awoke totally disoriented—probably the lingering effect of the drug, he figured. Gradually the shapes that filled the room made sense to him. There was no way of knowing how long he had been asleep. But judging by his near-weightlessness and the continuous light vibrations that he felt in the cage, he figured that the spaceship was headed to whatever world these Gammam called home.

As soon as he was fairly alert, Sam realized how hungry he was. He opened the box to see what was inside. It was full of a kind of wafer, neatly stacked and of uniform size. Breaking off a corner, he stuck his tongue onto the small piece. It reminded him, of all things, of graham crackers. He ate one and waited a few minutes to see if there was any adverse reaction. He felt fine. Slowly he ate the remaining crackers, fighting the urge to eat them quickly as he was so famished. But knowing that he had nothing else to do, Sam decided to keep his body and mind occupied with food for as long as possible. While eating, Sam's mind inevitably turned to his predicament. He was prisoner of an unknown species headed to an unknown world. It had to be farther than Earth's distance from Mars—and that trip takes a minimum of 6 months. How long would he be in his cage? Years? Undoubtedly the solitary confinement would render him a raving lunatic long before he arrived at this ship's destination. Well, with time on his hands he had plenty of opportunity to explore his prison and determine what he could do to either escape or (if worst came to worst) find a way to scuttle this mission. Sam figured that if he was destined to be a slave—and at this point he had no idea what he was destined for—it was better to die on the slave ship than prolong his captivity.

The dull red light that filled the room made it difficult to clearly make details out. *Looks like it will take a long time for my eyes to adjust*, thought Sam. The room seemed to be well ventilated. He focused on one of the vents: covered with a grill similar in nature to the bars of his cage, he saw that the vent itself was generously proportioned: about two feet square—big enough for a human to fit in but not a Gammam. It might work as a passageway for him once he figured out how to escape the cage. Sam deliberately thought "once" rather than "if", for if there was one thing he learned in life on the streets, the more he dwelled on the positive within the context of his situation, the better his chances of survival. Sam looked back at the vent: he could almost make out a human face in the grill—a feminine face with straight hair. He tightly closed his eyes and looked again: nothing was there other than the straight grill pattern.

His hunger and thirst satisfied, fatigue quickly settled back in. Sam's thoughts became incoherent. Soon he was fast asleep in his cage.

Sam awoke, disoriented again, with the sound of his cage rattling. One of the Gammam was unlocking the cage. Sam feigned sleep, hoping that he could find a way to shock his captor and gain his escape. The moment that the rattling stopped and Sam guessed that his cage door was being opened, he sprang to action. Keeping low, he dove out the door and under the belly of the Gammam—which, strangely, had all four feet on the floor as if held there by gravity. Not knowing the anatomy of the strange creature, Sam got on his back and with his feet he landed blows along its abdomen. While it bent over to address the assault, Sam slid to the Gammam's left side, jumped up and sat on the beast's back. He then put a choke hold around its neck in the hope that it had a collapsible windpipe like mammals on Earth.

The Gammam dropped the items in its hands (a couple of shiny bags and a short cudgel, from what Sam could see in the blur of action) and with its lower two arms, grabbed Sam by the waist, and began to squeeze its two eight-fingered hands. Sam felt excruciating pain. Then with its upper two arms, the Gammam grabbed Sam by the arm-pits, let go of its lower two hands, and lifted Sam over its head. Sam realized at this point that he could not possibly win this fight.

The Gammam suddenly jerked its body and let out a loud, high-pitched shriek. To Sam's ears, this did not sound like a roar of victory, it was more like a cry of pain. The Gammam dropped to the floor, its arms and legs flailing. Sam rolled on the floor. He was at a loss as to what had just happened.

Sam saw a gaping wound in the Gammam's left lower torso and some dark blue liquid was quickly issuing from it. Then there was a bright flash of green that leapt from one of the walls to the Gammam's head. It became still and silent.

Immediately glancing to the origin of the bright flash, he saw a very human-looking face looking back at him from behind the grill of the air vent. The face disappeared and was replaced by feet, which quickly but expertly kicked at the grill until one edge pried loose. With another kick and it swung open. An all-too-human voice firmly whispered to Sam in English, "Come quickly, idiot!"

Before having time to think, Sam speedily crawled towards to open vent, just as the door to the room opened and three more Gammam came gambolling in. As he slid through the first few feet of the vent he could feel the hand of one Gammam touch the heel of his boot, but it was too late for it to get a good grip. Sam was free!

He squirmed in the total darkness for about two minutes until he spilled into another room with his new human companion. The lighting was dull red, as always. It looked like a store-room filled with boxes and barrels in strange shapes and sizes. Finally, he got a look at his liberator. Female, short and wiry, with shoulder-length hair and a wild look in her eyes. She looked vaguely familiar, but Sam could not figure it out while his mind and body were filled with adrenalin.

"Grab some of the pouches over there, hurry," she said to Sam, pointing to his right. Fortunately, he still had his backpack. Sam quickly threw them into the pack and sealed it. "We've got to keep moving," she said, and disappeared back into the vent as if it was the most natural thing in the world.

Struggling through the vents was not as unpleasant as Sam had thought, once he got used to the dark. The inner surface had some grip and so he could move swiftly. And most of the vents were about three to four feet square. After about ten minutes of further scrambling, the woman said, "Now we can stop." It was dark but not totally black, as there was a vent opening nearby. Sam floated cross-legged in the vent.

Sam was the first to speak. "Who are you and what are you doing here?" he asked her.

She turned to Sam and replied, "My name is Ella Hermoza. I was on the third, ill-fated mission to Mars. I am the only survivor of that mission."

Sam immediately put the face (now changed somewhat) to the name. Ten months ago, while Sam was being trained for his Mars trip, news came about the Purcell mission to

Mars. The trip was uneventful in all ways until three days before it was expected to go into orbit around the red planet. Communication suddenly stopped. And never returned. Everyone back on Earth assumed that the ship and crew must have been taken out by a stray asteroid—highly unlikely as the chances are of that happening. With multiple back-up systems, if the ship had experienced some mechanical or electrical failure, it still should have been possible for the crew to message Earth.

"Our ship encountered the ship of these beings," Ella told Sam. "We were totally caught by surprise," she continued, "because we all thought that humans were the only space-faring species in the solar system. How wrong we were...

"These centaur-things have amazing technologies," Ella continued. "Their ship was incredibly massive—like the size of a small city—and they were able to remotely disable all our transportation and communication systems. We were a sitting duck. They boarded our vessel and started to slaughter us with their weapons. One of them grabbed me and took me hostage. And I've been stuck with them ever since."

"You've been on their ship all this time?" enquired Sam.

"Good heavens, no," replied Ella. "I only got on this ship on this trip to Mars. Though I don't know which is worse— their spacecraft or their world. There is so little difference between the two."

"What do you mean?" asked Sam.

"They live on one of the moons of Jupiter - Ganymede, I think. The sun shines red there because of all the air pollution. Much of its surface is covered with huge metallic cities. I've hardly seen any wildlife there; even a plant. The place is high tech on steroids," she replied.

Sam sat quietly letting it all sink in.

"I think," she went on, "that I was the first human they encountered. When they took me to Ganymede they poked and prodded me with many different instruments. They tried to interrogate me in their unintelligible gibberish. And they put some instrument around my head that I suspect can read my thoughts.

"At one point during their tests and experiments I saw an opportunity to escape. I had noticed that while their hearing is far more acute than ours, their vision is not nearly as good. In particular, if something is motionless or moves very slowly it seems to be invisible to them. Kind of like frogs in that respect.

"All during the escape, the rush of adrenalin was telling me to run as fast as I can—and run I did when the coast was clear—but at the times when I was most in danger of being caught, I had to be either like a statue or no faster than a snail. It was the hardest thing I've had to do in my entire life!

"Of course, once I was free from the examination chamber, I was not free from their world. It's not as though I could catch a bus back to Earth! But I didn't care then; nor do I really care now. I am free from being forcibly confined by them. I go wherever I think is safe and keep moving. I've been at it for ten months now and, barring a miracle, will likely do so until I die."

"So, why are you on this spaceship?" enquired Sam.

"A vain hope to get back to Mars and human company," Ella replied. "They use a fair number of spaceships, but most of them are to other moons of Jupiter judging by how fast they return. I found a number of hide-outs near their main spaceport. A few days ago, I saw one ship return and it unloaded a few species from Mars, so I saw my chance and crept aboard. But I didn't have a chance to escape, as the ship was on Mars for only a few hours. I suspect your capture contributed to their early departure."

"Just a minute" interjected Sam, "are you telling me that this ship made it from Ganymede to Mars in a few DAYS?"

"Yup," replied Ella, "like I said, these creatures have high tech on steroids. Beats me how they power their ships—

there's only so much you can learn from inside an airduct—but they take off with an incredible kick."

"Speaking of airducts," interrupted Sam, "they must know that we are here. We're trapped."

"True," said Ella, "but I think that as long as we are on route to Ganymede we are safe. They need their air. And fortunately due to their size and shape these space centaurs can't pursue us in the airducts. We are safe for now. Relax. But be prepared for the unexpected when we land."

During the two-day voyage to Ganymede, the two humans became well acquainted with each other. Ella—like Sam -- had a rough childhood and was very proficient in self-defence and survival skills. Together, they made a number of elaborate contingency-ridden plans for eluding capture once they landed, and dreamed of returning to Earth someday, somehow. Both of them felt relieved to have human companionship during their perilous journey.

IV: Offered

DRASTIC CHANGES IN the sound of the engines—which permeated the ship—told Sam and Ella that they were soon to be landing on Ganymede. Ella told Sam the details about re-entry and what happens upon landing, based on her initial visit to this strange world. Sam felt as prepared as he could be, under the circumstances.

Once the ship landed, Sam and Ella heard the crew scurrying about for about ten minutes. Then silence. Sam and Ella looked at each other in disbelief. Then they heard the sound of rushing water: the Gammam were flushing them out!

Not having time to find an escape, the two were caught up in the torrent, banging their heads and limbs against the sides of the ducts as they were swept away. Within a minute they found themselves shooting out the side of the ship and into a large, shallow pool. Within seconds, each found their arms grabbed by grim-looking Gammam and were pulled clear from the pool. Each of them tried to wriggle free—their jackets were slippery when wet, but the Gammams' grip was vice-like and after a minute of trying, they switched to a different tactic by assaulting their captors. Sam no longer had a gun, but he still had a blade. With a lightning-fast motion honed by years of tight situations, Sam grabbed his blade and slit the throat of the Gammam that was holding him as well as the two Gammam closest to him as he fled. Blue blood spurted in all directions as the three Gammam dropped to the ground. Slipping on the blood, Sam fell as well, but sprang to his feet and dashed under the bellies of several other Gammam who were gathered around. He quickly looked around for one of the hiding spots that Ella had so meticulously described to him and recognized one immediately.

Two Gammam were in hot pursuit of Sam. He glanced back, hoping to see Ella in the clear, but could not. He realized that the quadrupedal Gammam would easily out-run him before he reached safety, so he changed tactic. He turned around and ran straight towards them. He could see the puzzled looks on their faces as he neared them. The ground was smooth and hard—almost like polished marble. Once he got within a yard of the Gammam to the right, Sam put out the sides of his heels and slid right under the belly, slashing away as he coursed underneath. He could feel the blade hit bones in some spots and dig deep in other spots. As he slowed down and neared the end of the now disembowelled beast, he rolled over to the left and slit the underbelly of the second Gammam. Again, he sprang to his feet, and headed back to the hide-out, when his legs gave out from under him and he fell. He tried to get up again, but he had lost all sensation to his legs. Looking to his left, Sam saw a Gammam looking straight at him with a strange-looking weapon drawn. It pulled the trigger and Sam could no longer feel his arms.

Again, it pulled the trigger, and Sam blacked out.

When he came to, Sam was lying down in some kind of examination room, with his arms and legs secured and a metallic device encircling most of his head. The lighting in the room was a dull red. One Gammam was standing behind an instrument panel of sorts and was shrieking and whistling at him in its bizarre language. Sam had no idea what it was trying to communicate to him—these creatures were emotionally so alien to Earth life forms, he was totally perplexed. The Gammam became quiet. A low mechanical hum then filled Sam's ears and he felt what seemed to be static electricity around his head. He passed out again.

The same thing happened again. And again. Sam lost all track of time. Had he been examined for six hours? A week? He had no way of telling. Once he thought he saw a large window in the room and Ella on the other side, bound to a cot like he was. But the next time he saw neither Ella nor the window. It all seemed to be surreal.

Eventually the examination, or interrogation, or whatever it was that the Gammam were doing to him, stopped. Sam felt woozy as his restraints were removed and he was walked out of the room. He was led by two white-clad Gammam into an elevator which moved swiftly down for a couple of minutes. When the doors opened again, they were on ground level. The two Gammam were met by another Gammam who looked very different. Until now, all the Gammam that Sam saw wore either silver garments (the astronauts) or white garments (all those living on Ganymede). But this one wore brilliant red, with what looked like gold thread on the borders around the neck and at the sleeves of the four arms and four legs. This different Gammam also had a thin red streak running along the ridge of its beak and its eyes were pale blue in colour, instead of the impenetrable black eyes of all Gammam he had seen until then. The red-attired Gammam inspected Sam closely and seemed to enquire about him with the other two Gammam.

Then they all started walking: the red-attired one in front, and with Sam behind, flanked on both sides by other Gammam, each of whom was tightly holding one of his upper arms. For a moment, he wondered if he was being sold into slavery, but he figured that such a high-tech world had enough "energy-slaves" (machines) that made "biological" slavery terribly inefficient in comparison.

As they walked, Sam got a good look at Ganymede for the first time. It was daytime: the sun, about 40 degrees above the horizon, looked small and weak from nearly 500 million miles away. It also looked red and hazy, bathing this world in weird red light. But far more imposing than the sun was the giant Jupiter a mere 600,000 miles distant. It dominated half of the sky and even through the pollution-filled atmosphere Sam wondered at the sight of the bands of clouds with intricate swirling currents, back-eddies, cyclones and, of course the Great Red Spot, which was bigger than Sam's fist held at arm's distance. Also, for the first time, he noticed the cold. He had felt cool in the examination room, but at least that was well above freezing; outside, the temperature hovered around freezing. Yet how a world so distant from the Sun could be even at the freezing point was a mystery to him.

He also looked around at the environment around him. Buildings of all imaginable shapes and sizes, from house-sized to dizzying skyscrapers. And every one of them silver in colour. He looked for signs of life other than the Gammam but found none. No winged creatures in the sky. No small creatures crawling upon the ground. Not even a weed peeking from between the polished paving stones. The streets were occupied only by Gammam and what looked like a menagerie of metallic robots. The air was eerily silent and pungent with the smell of sulphur and various acid compounds. "What a wretched world," mused Sam as his thinking became clearer and he felt strength returning to his limbs.

After about ten minutes of walking, they approached what looked like a steep-sided pyramid. Unlike the other buildings, this one did not seem to be metallic: it was light in colour (making it look red) and had the texture of well-hewn stone. Sam gazed in wonder—it must be half a mile tall. As they got closer, he saw what looked to be an infinite number of broad steps going to the pinnacle. They began to ascend the steps. Even though each step was large and steep, owing to the low gravity compared to Earth, Sam found the ascent easy.

The moment they began their ascent, the air filled with a deep booming metallic sound reminiscent of a large bell or gong. Sam suddenly felt that he was stuck in some B-film from the 1930s. "Great," he thought, "I'm going to be sacrificed by savages to their blood-thirsty god. But this can't be happening! These are rational, high-tech beings not benighted animals..." His wits fully about him at this point, Sam moved his body in various ways to feel for any concealed weapons that he might still possess. No luck. The Gammam must have cleaned him out when they examined him. All he had left was his wits and bare hands. He must plan some kind of escape—no way was he going to be a willing victim.

As they ascended the pyramid, Sam noticed that ranks of Gammam were filling the seried "blocks" on the side of the structure—each block being about 20 feet tall and 20 feet wide. Each Gammam had some flat rectangular device in one of its hands—it didn't look like a weapon, so Sam figured it must be some kind of screen. "The event is being televised," he conjectured.

Once they had ascended about 200 feet, a different sound accompanied the first sound: a similar kind of gong, but at a higher pitch and in counterpoint to the beats of the first gong. At about 500 feet in altitude they paused on a broader step. This gave Sam a moment to look around. Glancing downwards he saw about 200 feet below him a group of three

Gammam surrounding a much smaller human form. Ella. He shouted to attract her attention. But the sound of the gongs—which increased in volume as they ascended the pyramid—drowned out his voice. "Well," thought Sam, "at least I have an accomplice. With two of us street-fighters working together, our odds of foiling their plans increase greatly."

On the way up, they stopped three more times, it seemed at every extra 500 feet of altitude.

Eventually, Sam was brought to the pinnacle. The pyramid was flat on the top, about 100 feet square. There were four gongs—one on each edge—each suspended by a large metallic arch. In one corner grew a twisted and spongy-looking tree with all branches bare—except for one branch that had at the most five or six large purple leaves. There were about 20 red-clad Gammam stationed on the pinnacle's terrace, all standing stock-still and looking at him. And in the centre was a pit about 20 feet square. He started to size up his situation and identify possible means of escaping and defending himself, and of distracting the Gammam to aid in his release.

Within a couple of minutes, Ella joined Sam on the pinnacle. Their eyes met. Half expecting to see terror in her eyes, he was relieved to see mere confusion, quickly replaced with determination. "That's the look of a street-fighter," he said to himself in relief.

The gongs stopped; the ceremony began. What looked to be the eldest of the red-clad started to chirp and squeak and click in its staccato Gammam-ese for several minutes and the rest listened intently. The old red-clad Gammam suddenly fell silent and walked over to the two human captives. All the red-clad started to whistle a melody in unison: slow, sad and with very different tuning from anything human ears had ever heard. Sam was conducted over to one side of the pit, Ella to the other side. The red-clad continued with their melodic whistling. Suddenly, each of them was flanked by a third Gammam. These held in their hands some sort of large bag. Judging by its size and shape, Sam figured it held about half a gallon of some liquid or maybe sand. As they raised their bags to go over Sam's and Ella's heads, the two humans wriggled their hands free in unison and struggled with their captors. They dodged among the Gammam and tried their best to wreak mayhem. For their size, the Gammam were surprisingly weak (except for their hands) and slow, apparently due to Ganymede's low gravity and possibly many generations of letting machines do all the work. Then four black-clad, beefy-looking Gammam appeared on the terrace and going straight to Sam and Ella, quickly put an end to their escape plans by putting a cudgel to both of their heads. The eldest red-clad shrieked at the black-clad Gammam.

Sam and Ella were brought again to the precipice of the pit. The Gammam with the bags returned to their places. For the first time Sam looked down into the pit, which he now knew would be his final resting place. He expected to see spikes or fire or a ravenous beast or something equally gruesome, but instead he saw what looked like an egg cut in half lengthwise, its smooth oval nearly filling the pit. Inside the egg was a surface that was red and lumpy. Sam didn't even want to imagine what this was. The Gammam with the bags emptied their contents over the heads of both Sam and Ella. The liquid was red and a little sticky and smelled of perfume. As soon as the red shower was over, the red-clad shouted in unison, "kap kap," and the two humans were pushed into the pit.

V: A Conversation

SAM EXPECTED A bone-crunching thud when he hit the bottom of the pit, but it felt more like falling onto a mattress. Then he expected some excruciating pain to course over his body. But he felt nothing of the sort. In fact, he felt comfortable.

He looked to Ella, who had the same surprised expression on her face. Before they could say a word to each other, they heard a high but faint mechanical humming. A clear lid in the shape and size of the "egg" was emerging from one side of it and proceeded to close and seal it in the matter of two seconds. Sam and Ella were trapped once more.

Then they felt the egg shake and rattle slightly; within a few seconds it was rising out of the pit. As the clear portion of the egg rose to the level of the terrace, they could see that all the Gammam assembled there were moving to the outer edges of the terrace and were looking intently at them.

The next moment, the egg leapt skyward. The force must have been 5 or 6 Gs and Sam and Ella were forced onto their backs into the lumpy red mattress-like material. After a few minutes the force reduced to about 3 Gs and they started to look around and take stock of their situation. Obviously, they were in some kind of spacecraft, but there were no visible means of controlling it, nor did they have any idea of the voyage's duration or destination.

Sam and Ella brought each other up to date on their experiences on Ganymede (Ella's was not too different from Sam's, apparently) and speculated on their fate. Clearly, the small craft had only enough air to last them a few hours. Were they being sacrificed to some space-god?

Initially the craft was headed in a direction half-way between the Sun and Jupiter. But shortly after leaving Ganymede's gravity, it veered and moved gradually towards Jupiter. And while Sam and Ella marvelled at the spectacle of the phenomenally huge world before them, they felt fear in the pits of their stomachs that they would end as pulpy messes torn apart by the awesome gravity of the solar system's largest planet.

To distract themselves, the two of them whiled away the time chatting about their main events of their lives, their highest hopes, deepest fears, greatest loves and biggest disappointments. They both felt that they were basically decent people who had been given a raw deal by life—both back on Earth and since then in space—yet they were not bitter or even fearful. Their consciences were clean and they would each try to face their end as bravely as they could.

Within an hour they could feel the inexorable tug of Jupiter's gravity. At the force of 1 G it was comfortable and familiar. Presently, though, it became oppressive. An hour later they felt the force of 2 Gs and could see that Jupiter's multi-coloured clouds formed many tiers. Soon they were whisking past the highest clouds and the sky now looked ocean blue instead of inky black, and they felt the full force of Jupiter's 2.4 Gs. Sam and Ella looked at each other in wonder. Their egg-ship was slowing down but still moving at an extraordinary rate. They passed another couple of layers of wispy clouds and the sky looked pale blue.

Suddenly, the egg-ship began to convulse. Cracks formed on the clear "windshield" and the ship spun out of control. And then the whole thing shattered into a thousand pieces before their eyes. They knew that this was their final moment of life.

Yet it wasn't the end. Both of them were clear of the wreckage, and unscathed. Strangely, each seemed to have their own translucent "bubble" surrounding them. They were five feet apart, hurtling towards darker clouds below in this utterly alien world. As they looked down, they saw the wreckage plummeting faster than they, and then they saw what appeared to be spikes poking out of the clouds. Or not exactly spikes, as they were somewhat twisted. And there seemed to be balloons and other hard-to-distinguish objects floating about. It was impossible to make sense of what they were seeing.

The wreckage punched through the deck of darker clouds, but Sam and Ella seemed to be falling at a much slower rate. In fact, they seemed to be slowing down as if a force countering gravity was exerting itself upon them. And instead of heavier, they now felt lighter, as if they were experiencing only 1 G.

Their bubbles came to a halt just above the dark clouds, near one of the twisted spikes. But the more they looked at the spike, the more it looked like a tree. It seemed to have branches. And something translucent on the ends of branches, like leaves. Truly immense, this "tree" seemed to tower more than a thousand feet above the clouds. Gradually their bubbles moved towards it and halted a hundred feet from the massive trunk. Above them, they could see that the "balloons" that they had seen earlier were like giant aerial whales about twice the size of the Hindenburg, "swimming" about in the air. And they saw flying beings, with wingspans the size of a football field or more, fluttering above and around the "balloons".

Concentrating upon the tree they saw what looked like hundreds of large-winged green bees buzzing around the branches, while thin creatures and snake-like things clung to the trunk and moved slowly along the branches. Their bubbles edged closer, so that they were only a few feet apart from each other and ten feet from the gnarled tree trunk. Their attention was drawn to a pale green raccoon-sized creature that had a face like a frog, with big yellow eyes and very long, thin limbs ending in three fingers and toes. It was seated on the crotch where a tree limb met the trunk. The frog-being looked at Sam and Ella, and blinked its eyes.

Then it spoke. Sam heard it say in English, "Welcome to the world you call Jupiter," but the frog-being's lips did not move. Sam immediately turned to Ella and pointed to his ear, saying to her, "Did you just hear it speak?" Ella with a baffled look on her face replied, "Yes, I did!" And they both realized that they could clearly hear each other.

"OK," Sam said to Ella, "now I know this has got to be a dream."

"Well then," replied Ella, "I guess that I am in your dream... or you are in my dream... or we are both in somebody else's dream..."

"I am sure you must find this very strange, or perhaps surreal," they both heard a high, raspy voice say in their minds. "Let me introduce myself: you may call me Hoga. What are your names?" Sam and Ella told their names mentally, and Hoga confirmed that it understood. Hoga continued, "You have been sent to Jupiter as a sacrifice by what you know as the Gammam because they worship Jupiter as their god. As far as they know, you are now dead and their sacrifice has been successful. The protective bubbles you are presently in are my creation. You are protected from the gravity and atmosphere of this world which are incompatible with your bodies. Don't consider them to be your prison; consider them to be your temporary shelter."

Sam and Ella had no fight left in them. They had already given themselves up for dead and this unexpected deliverance (or perhaps reprieve) made them grateful and calm, yet curious.

They both spoke at the same time, asking Hoga many questions: "How do you know English? How can you be speaking to us mentally? How do you know what conditions we need to survive? How are you creating these 'bubbles'? How do you know anything about where we have come from?" Hoga with a calm look on his face said to them, "These, and all other questions, will be answered," as if he clearly understood the mess of bewilderment that had just been thrown at him.

"First of all, let me explain something about this world. You see that even though your scientists say it is not possible, there is life on Jupiter. And not just life—animals and trees. These huge trees are the keystone species here. They are hundreds of miles tall and are immensely old: the one I am sitting on here is over 100 million Jupiter-years old—

that's 1.2 billion Earth-years. Some trees here are even older. People in your world totally underestimate the tree life-form. Trees, though they have no organ called 'brain' and have very restricted movement, are immensely intelligent in ways that you cannot understand. They are in touch with the world around them and with each other and live in harmony.

"The worlds that we know—the planets, the moons, and even the Sun itself—are full of life. And nearly all of them harbour organisms which in form or function are trees, whether or not they are made out of carbon. The trees on Jupiter have knowledge, experience and memory that are unrivalled in this solar system. And they are able to communicate with their counterparts in all the other worlds. The trees are always watching, listening, understanding and communicating. This one has watched life in your world grow and diversify and nearly get snuffed out and diversify yet again several times over the millennia. And the trees on Earth have told it all it needs to know about your world, and it, in turn, has told me much about you. Likewise, the shrubs on Mars told about you, Sam, and the tree on the top of the pyramid on Ganymede told about both of you being sent here.

"This tree is a store-house of many energies collected by its roots from deep within core of Jupiter. It permits beings who live on it to make use of these energies as food as well as for their own purposes. There are still many energies that are not known to your world. One of these energies we can use to create a 'bubble' with specific atmospheric and other conditions so that visitors to our world can survive for some time. In fact, sometimes we visit your world in a subtle form and on occasion are seen by your people as bubbles or balls of light with small beings inside—fairies and such.

"No doubt you want to learn something about the beings who inhabit Ganymede. But first you must understand something about the worlds you can 'planets'. Each planet has a particular 'theme' to its life. The ancients of your world knew this well. The trees silently taught it to them as they sat in contemplation in the forests, with their backs against the trunks. Much of this knowledge has been lost or corrupted—but not all. As you have seen, Mars is a world of struggle, harshness, and aggression. Jupiter, on the other hand, is a world of knowledge and peaceful co-existence, of acceptance and expansion of awareness.

"Those satellites that orbit the planets take on some of their host-planet's nature, but because they get caught in the "shadow" of the planet that they orbit, they manifest quite negative energies as well. Ganymede has great knowledge but mostly on the physical level, and their world has been blessed with extraordinary material wealth. Beneath its surface is an ocean of hydrocarbons which the Gammam have been making use of for a million years. This has allowed the Gammam to progress technologically to an impressive degree, but in the process they have transformed their atmosphere and nearly destroyed life on their world. The first wrong turn the Gammam made in their history was to declare war on their trees—and as a result they stopped listening to the good voice of their world.

"Even though the Gammam have great material wealth, they have run out of certain key elements that are crucial for the operation of their energy-powered technologies. So, they have gone to the other moons of Jupiter to take what they want, and in the past century, Mars as well. But they hate Mars and they fear it, for in the Martian sky the Sun looms large and yellow, and Jupiter is merely a bright star. The rulers of Ganymede have even seriously discussed settling down on Mars once Ganymede becomes uninhabitable—but the common folk of Ganymede refuse to support it: "Better to die with our god Jupiter in our sky than to live on another world without Jupiter," they say. And so, they will never colonize Mars. But just the same, Mars is theirs for now, as they got there first. And the people of Earth need to leave

Mars alone. As it is, the Gammam have found out where the "Jolly Roger" is located and have already destroyed it and all its occupants. They will never tolerate another Earthling on Martian soil. "But soon enough the Gammam will have killed their world, and themselves along with it. And life in the solar system will go on fine without them. In that respect, the people of Earth must learn to move away from the Gammam's mindset. For, of all the other worlds, Earth is most similar in nature to Ganymede. Stay clear of Ganymede and the other moons of Jupiter, and of Mars if you want to survive the Gammam and yourselves. But there are other worlds to explore: Venus and Mercury in particular have many valuable lessons to teach the people of your world, and there is much for you to gain from such contact. So does Saturn, especially if you are going to learn to live within limits and get over your mindless pursuit of growth for its own sake.

"That is why you have come here today. Don't think for a moment that your coming here was accidental. Your world stands in the balance—both in its history as well as in relation with other beings in this solar system. Since you contacted the Gammam—Jupiter's negative counterparts—you had to meet us—the positive side, so to speak. And you can help to tip your world back to the positive side."

Hoga paused, while Sam and Ella let all his words sink in.

"I still am not sure if this is real or not," stated Ella, "but if we get back to Earth—and at this point I cannot see how that is even possible—nobody is going to believe the stories we tell them. Even our descriptions of Ganymede and Jupiter are at odds with what our astronomers and astrophysicists say, and to argue with them is a one-way street to ridicule and notoriety."

"She's right," promptly added Sam. "There's no way that anyone will listen to our story except the tabloid reporters and then it is downhill from there. Perhaps you don't understand our world as much as you think, Hoga."

"I make no claim of being all-knowing," replied Hoga, "but I trust what my tree tells me. It has never led me astray in the hundreds of years we have been together—although sometimes it likes to pull my leg. I am sending you back to your world, not only with a message but with a gift."

The two bubbles floated towards Hoga and stopped mere inches from him. Hoga then shoved its little hands through the bubbles and motioned to Sam and Ella to open their palms. They did so and glanced down into their left palms. Each of them saw about a hundred tiny yellow seeds similar in shape and size to sesame seeds.

"These seeds," continued Hoga, "are specially designed by my tree for your world. My tree is able to split and recombine DNA in its flowers to whatever it wants. These seeds are safe—that is, they will not go wild—and they can grow in nearly any environment: hot, cold, wet or dry. And your medical researchers will find that the entire plant has numerous properties to treat (but not necessarily cure) many illnesses. There is no plant that even remotely resembles this in your world. This will be the proof that you are not just making things up. Also, there will be no rational explanation for how you return to Earth. That will help your story immensely."

"How do you mean?" both Sam and Ella asked simultaneously.

"No spaceship is required," replied Hoga; "the bubbles you are in can traverse billions of miles in a fraction of a second."

All were silent for a moment. "The time of your bubbles runs short," said Hoga, "as they are an unstable energy form. Any final questions?"

"Will our two species be in touch again?" asked Ella.

"On Jupiter, not very likely—unless the trees will it, as there is no way that your beings can visit us and survive. But we can easily visit your world as we have in the past. However, that depends on your species. If you learn once again to respect the trees of your world, let them grow, and listen to them, the beings known as fairies will become common again, and sometimes it will be we Jovians who appear as fairies."

Hoga said to them in parting, "I bid you good-bye and wish you well."

The next moment, Sam and Ella saw a bright flash of light all around them. When the light faded, they were standing on the launchpad at Cape Canaveral with seeds in their hands and a bewildered look on their faces.

Joel Caris is the editor and publisher of Into the Ruins, *a quarterly magazine of deindustrial science fiction. He is a gardener and occasional homesteader, advocate for local food systems, sporadic writer, voracious reader, and both deeply empathetic toward and frustrated with humanity. Living in Portland, Oregon with his all-too-patient wife, he works for a local food nonprofit and at times takes on too many side projects. Aside from regular editor introductions in* Into the Ruins, *his story "An Expected Chill" was published in the Winter 2017 issue. Further information about his literary activities can be found at* joelcaris.com *and* intotheruins. com.

Of all the worlds of the Old Solar System, Mars was developed most richly by the classic writers; its ancient ruins and windswept deserts occupy a permanent place among the landscapes of Earthling imaginative fiction. In Exodus, *Joel Caris offers a vivid and engrossing tale set in a classic Mars—with a twist of its own...*

EXODUS

Joel Caris

SUFFERING FROM THIRST and eager to return home to Laithos, clutching absently at her canteen, Alinda scrambled her way down the graveled bank, dirt and stone cascading down around her feet while her eyes remained locked on the middle of the sprawling, near-dry canal. A thin trickle of clear-flowing water could be glimpsed there in the occasional gap found in the mat of twisted vines and deep purple leaves that had come to mark so many of the wastrel canals veining the northern lowlands of Mars. The dry air and parching heat; the scratch of her throat; the incessant burning sun; the need for provision before her turn home; all of it drove her forward, shimmering between her and the water buried beneath those vines. It severed the thread of caution she normally bound her movements in. It blinded her to the tell-tale sign of bone-white spines peeking out from the red earth of the canal.

The creature to which those spines were attached suffered no such blindness. Buried shallow in the sand, it moved ever-so-slightly—and if only Alinda had stopped and held her breath and listened, and if the wind did not howl or mutter, and if the trickle of the water was soft enough, she would have heard it: the shifting sands, the vague way it stirred its tentacles through the martian soil. The raalech waited for anything living to cross its path, to set a foot wrong and in that instant turn into prey. She set her foot wrong and it struck.

Alinda could not say how many tentacles this raalech had; probably not more than three or four, but in that moment of attack she would have sworn to a dozen. They erupted from the ground, spraying her with dirt and grit, blinding her, and in an instant twisted around her right leg. Squeezing and flexing, they pulled on her, and in so doing the rows of bony spines—teeth—that lined the cool, fleshy underside of the tentacles plunged ragged into her bare legs, catching and tearing at her flesh and knocking her to the ground as she struggled against the creature's grip. It happened within the briefest of moments and she had failed even to register the initial pain before the burning of its digestive fluids ejected hot into her wounds, acting as a powerful anticoagulant to speed the flow of her blood.

The raalech's spines not only were sharp and rigid, perfect for tearing into flesh, but also hollow, holding a reserve of saliva that ejected into its prey upon attack to stimulate bleeding before transforming into a straw, the raalech slurping its victim's blood as fast as the wounds would release it. As Alinda had learned long ago, though, she was a good bleeder—anticoagulant or no—and despite the raalech's known thirst for blood, it could not keep up with her hemorrhaging. Its tentacles quickly grew slick with her free-flowing blood and, as she struggled against the creature, she could feel its grip on her slipping. Spiked with adrenaline and well aware that she had only moments before the blood loss would begin to fatigue her and allow the raalech to further wrap her in its vampiric grip, Alinda rolled into a crouch, leveraging her still-untangled left leg against the sandy slope of the canal and heaving herself forward with every bit of force she could muster. Feeling the pull of her attempted escape, the raalech tightened its grip on her leg but slipped against her blood-slicked flesh, its shallow spines raking through her skin as her leg tore free from its entanglement and she tumbled face first into the sandy side of the canal, rolling forward and away from the monstrous creature even as she spat out dirt and gravel, her eyes stung and watering, her vision blurred.

She scrambled, frantic, as the sounds of the raalech clawing its way free from its self-burial tore at the air behind her. Its thrashing tentacles showered her with dirt and raked across her upper thigh as she plunged forward along the run of the canal, her right leg faltering but her left leg strong. Instinct screamed at her to mount the canal's wall and push farther into the relative safety of the surrounding desert, but a small-but-focused part of her mind zeroed in instead on the clusters of broad, purple leaves twisted in and around the canal's piteous flow of water; if she wanted to live, she first had to gather a handful of those vines and leaves, a plant known as arethus.

Daring a glance behind her, she saw the struggling raalech using its tentacles to ratchet itself forward, but already falling behind. While its fury of limbs looked impressive and worked well to entangle its prey, the raalech's strength lay in the element of surprise—not, given its physiology, in the quick movements of a hunter. Its numerous tentacles extended out of a small and spherical, rough and knobby base from which a mass of extremely long, thin white roots dangled. The roots dragged limp and flaccid through the sand as the creature heaved itself toward Alinda.

Seizing her advantage, she angled toward the middle of the canal, limp-running her way toward the tangled vines while assuring herself in a steady mantra that the worst of the pain would be over soon, that she had only to endure for a few more minutes to ensure her survival. Coming to the middle of the canal and within reach of the arethus, she bent and ripped up a mass of tangled vines and leaves, then pivoted and risked another glance at the raalech—still coming, but several yards away and flagging. Belonging to a kingdom of creatures that could best be described in Earth terms as a cross between plant and animal, raalechs depended on their roots to provide them a needed draw of water during their long wait between meals buried in the Martian soil. Most often found in or along the planet's canals, the creatures pushed their roots deep into the soil to find small reserves of moisture and nutrients to keep them alive until they could feed on the blood that truly sustained them. The raalech spent most of its life buried and in wait, its only movement the interminable flexing of its tentacles to maintain their musculature, which created a steady and rhythmic—but very subtle—movement through the sand. Otherwise, it often went years without moving, except in the occasional, often futile burst of surfacing to pursue prey that had just slipped from its grasp.

Alinda angled herself back toward the edge of the canal, relieved at her adversary's distance but not yet feeling safe. The pain gnawed at her and she knew she needed to stem the bleeding, but she also wanted out of the canal and into a greater separation from the raalech, not to mention from any others that might be buried in the sand and awaiting another wrong step. She pushed off with her good leg and hobbled as best she could on her blood-slicked, burning right leg.

Soon back at the edge of the canal but farther down the way from her near-fatal encounter, Alinda managed to boost herself up and out of the channel and onto the fine, dry sand of the surrounding desert, still clutching tight the mangled bouquet she hoped would be her redemption. Thirty yards down the canal from her, the raalech had given up its pursuit and was now methodically digging itself back into the sand to await its next opportunity to eat. She watched its oddly compelling, rhythmic movements for a moment: something of a steady back-and-forth rocking of its knobby base, assisted by tentacles on either side, the body working its way into the ground while the creature's roots penetrated deep into the soil, searching out moisture. With a few hearty twists of her hands she crushed the mass of vines and leaves she held, releasing a sticky purple juice that she smeared over her wounds. The plant contained powerful procoagulant proteins that served to neutralize and reverse the anticoagulant effect of the raalech's saliva—not to mention containing antibacterial and pain-relieving properties as well. Dressing her wounds and then chewing cautiously on the bitter plant, Alinda hoped it would be enough to keep away any infection—several strains of Martian bacteria were particularly fatal to humans—and allow for enough clotting to keep her from bleeding to death while providing enough relief from the pain so that she could make her way back to the village. Failure on any one of those fronts would leave her dead before the day was out.

Silently cursing the red planet, her heart began to slow as a tentative sense of safety settled over her. An intense loneliness swept over her as she continued to chew on the arethus, trying to ignore the plant's bitterness. In that moment she wanted nothing more than another human—*anyone*—to lean against, to weep out her stress and terror with. Breathing deep instead and waiting to see how her wounds would react, she watched the distant raalech rock back and forth, back and forth, slowly sinking its way into the sand, its tentacles occasionally slashing at the air as if it were a dancer at a rave.

It did not take long for Alinda's blood to crust in the dry Martian air. An inspection of her leg showed numerous shallow cuts and slashes, some small and others jagged, spaced at semi-regular intervals up her ankle and calf to just past her knee. Already they were beginning to close, aided by the healing effects of the arethus. The pain lingered, though, and as she began her tentative trek home to Laithos, it stabbed across her skin in accordance with her staggered steps, webbing out along her nerves.

The desert wind cut across the expansive surroundings of sand and red rock outcroppings, drying and chapping her exposed skin while raking her cuts with erratic blasts of grit. Gods, she hated this desolate planet with each erratic step, each lightning burst of pain. How could she have been so stupid, so thoughtless and unaware, like some babe off the ship, some easy prey who would not last the day? How many times, in how many canals, had she filled her canteen with the utmost care, scanning each step before taking it, eyes sharp for the the slow shift of sand and the spined tips of a buried raalech?

Her throat cracking in the desert's harsh aridity, she had to fight against taking the few final gulps of water she carried. In the end, she had not refilled her canteen, too shaken by the consequences of her cavalier pursuit of water to risk another approach. She regretted that decision now, telling herself that in the aftermath of her attack she would have reentered the canal with the proper caution, attentive to any lurking danger. Yet at the outset of the day, she would not have believed herself idiotic enough to earn a raalech attack in the first place; confidence shaken and thirst not yet extreme—and Laithos not more than a mile away—a quick return home for further medical care and recuperation had seemed most prudent. Her thirst now claimed different, but she resisted the urge to empty her canteen. The village was not far now and the promise of the last water she carried was too great a balm for her to release until she came to one of Laithos' canal-fed public pools and its greater promise.

Thirst and pain gnawing at her, the wind-swept desert sprawling stark to the horizon at every turn and not a single inch of it, she was certain, home to another human, she yearned in that moment for the comfort of the gods she had known back on Earth. But she knew better than to call on them here; they would not answer in this place, settled instead on the planet she had grown up knowing as home and unconcerned with whatever follies she suffered here on Mars, her existence likely long forgotten. Aching with a deep sense of isolation and abandonment, she wished she better knew the Dekari gods in recompense, knew some power to call upon in such dark times. Yet Grijval—her Dekari steward and teacher, a great four-armed hulk of bristled fur and impossible strength, genetically cut across thousands of millennia to fit the harsh Martian environment, and the keeper of Laithos' religious life—had refused her any Dekari religious teachings of substance, insisting that the gods had given him no permission to speak of them to an outsider; that unless she revealed herself to them and they chose, in turn, to enter into a relationship with her, she could only be as nothing to them: an inconsequential creature unworthy of consideration.

Wishing now to reveal herself to them, she cast her mind out into the edged desert air, imagining herself unsheathed and exposed to whatever higher beings might be waiting in the bleak surrounding environs, her body vivid against the dull desert landscape. For a brief moment, she even convinced herself it might work; that some god would find and absolve her, providing some kind of indistinct salvation that would clear the pain of her wounds and desiccation of her throat. Such easy redemption was not how the gods worked, of course, but still she allowed herself to hope, imagining the many ways in which her salvation might be delivered and falling into those fantasies for an unknown bout of merciful time, pain somewhat fading in her distraction.

In that time, in that distraction, the familiar desert landscape began to shift around her, the sand thinning into patches of slick red shale and a modest rock ridge rising steadily from the horizon as she approached. By the time her inner vision cleared enough to reassert her outer, the ridge sloped gentle in front of her, a small and familiar obstacle waiting between her and Laithos. Facing it, she stopped and blinked and allowed her futile hopes of divine rescue to fade and be replaced with a very real one instead: the pooled expanses of cool, fresh water waiting in Laithos, promising relief for her withered throat.

As she scrambled over the ridge, her battered right leg tensed and seized, threatening to give out on her. She paused only a moment, just long enough to allow the convulsions to pass, before continuing to push toward the village and its relative safeties and comforts. It waited just over and beyond the ridgeline, she knew; and indeed, as she crested the top of the weathered and pockmarked stone beneath her, the undulating rock peaks of Laithos came into view before her, a clustering of so many dwellings rising from out of the rocky ground, sculptures standing against the rusty sky. The sight brought her immense relief, pushing the pain far enough from the forefront of her mind for her to speed her steps as she scrabbled down the backside of the rock ridge and reentered the desert's shifting, rolling sands.

EVEN BEFORE SHE came to Laithos' southern entry—an expansive rock stairway that led thirty feet down into the narrow and twisting pathways of the village—an uneasiness settled over her. Nothing stirred in the visible dwelling uppers and no sound came to her other than the ceaseless wind hissing over the desert terrain and her own labored breath, shallow and ragged from pain and exertion. It made little sense: never had she approached the village without seeing at least a few Dekari climbing between buildings along the gnarled saaverña timbers that connected so many of the towering stone structures; and while the Dekari did not speak aloud, a sussuration of bustle and movement normally arose from the depths of the village, audible from the head of the village's stairway entrances even if not at a distance. Yet as she came to that entrance, no sounds emerged from the village below.

She waited at the head of the stairs, a disquietude continuing to rise in her as no signs of life greeted her. After a moment of indecision, both her need for water and the pain in her leg gnawing at her, she started down the stairs. Whatever waited below, she needed drink and recuperation; without both, she might not survive.

Descending with caution and as little noise as possible, she followed the stairs down into the depths of the village. The steps were smooth and even, carved directly out of what had once been a towering red rock cliff. The entire village came from the same: the result of years of painstaking, meticulous work by Dekari sculptors and carvers and architects, some of the finest craftsmen in the solar system. Alinda often marveled at their work, at the utility and creativity they coaxed from the massive stone edifices of Mars. Every Dekari dwelling across Mars had once been a great rock outcropping, which served as the raw material of their architecture. Upon choosing a site for a new dwelling, a multitude of Dekari would descend upon the monolith in question and begin the years-long process of carving a new village out of it, laboriously creating smooth and narrow, towering dwellings by hand that rose phallic against the sky, their midpoints at ground level while their bases sank deep into the Martian substrate. They carved out twisting walkways and public squares between the buildings, shaped the entire village into something of a rough square, then created massive stairways in its corners aligned with the cardinal directions. Each stairway served as a main entry point into the village, their steps encased by rock walls that seemed to tower ever higher as one descended, curving gently up and outward to the expansive sky above.

Those walls now loomed over Alinda as she followed the stairs down toward whatever mystery awaited below. She took the steps one at a time, nursing her injured right leg while keeping her eyes sharp for any movement. Pausing halfway down to rest, her attention turned to the walls alongside her and the elaborate tapestry of looping, intricate design work carved into them. It was the Dekari's written language, sloping along the wall in a gorgeous band of storytelling that tracked the angle of the stairs in their descent down into the depths of Laithos. Something of a cross between words and pictographs, the Dekari's language had stunned Alinda when she first saw it: to this day, the writings remained one of her favorite sights on Mars. She could not read it well, but thanks to her friendship with Grijval, she had advanced to a rudimentary understanding in the past year and hoped eventually to gain a fluency that would allow her to better appreciate their rich culture. It was challenging to learn, though: epic in its narrative and poetry, non-linear and circular in its references, immensely complex in its number and combination of characters, and made all the harder to understand by dint of its evolution on a planet that, no matter how familiar she had become with it, was alien at its core. Still, she studied it in the hopes of learning, and now she traced her hands along the stone wall's embedded language, a partial history of the village's Dekari community that amazed her in how it could spin entire worlds out of stone.

As her gaze traveled along the written history, she noticed a white flower emerging from the rock wall ahead, just above the carved writing. Confused, she took the three stairs down to bring her just below it, the five-petaled flower blooming six feet high on the wall. "What the hell?" she mumbled, reaching tentatively to touch the blossom. It emerged directly from the wall, stemless, as if the stone itself gave it life. As she touched its lower petal, all five began to tremble and a bead of ruddy liquid appeared at the end of the flower's pistil. The droplet filled and fattened and, fascinated, Alinda touched it with the tip of her index finger; immediately, the liquid broke upon the end of her finger and a small burning sensation leapt to life with its dispersal along her skin. She gasped, pulling back her hand and pressing her finger against her shirt. The liquid smeared red along her chest and the burning sensation dissipated, the tip of her finger throbbing and red but otherwise unharmed. She looked back at the flower; it remained, but had ceased trembling.

Stepping to the side, she tried to catch glimpse of some source of the bloom: a camouflaged vine spread across the rock, perhaps, or thin tendrils of root that might connect the flower to something other than the wall. She saw nothing, though, and the sense of unease that had settled on her at the top of the stairs deepened. Suddenly aware of her vulnerability—of her distraction and inattention—she snapped her gaze back to the bottom of the stairs. Nothing awaited her, though, and a quick glance behind her revealed the same lack of danger above. The quiet remained broken only by the desert wind and an almost inaudible skitter of sand along the steps.

Resisting the urge to return to the surface and set off elsewhere—she knew, after all, of nowhere else to go, and would surely die if she set out into the inhospitable desert without sufficient supplies and a clear destination—Alinda continued down the stairs. It did not take long for her to traverse the final steps. A wide greeting square opened out from the bottom of the stairwell, empty of any life or activity, with tall and narrow buildings standing silent on the far side and the sky opening wide above her. The emptiness of the square was eerie; plenty of Dekari ventured out daily into the surrounding landscape to hunt and forage, but plenty more remained in the village and a typical day saw the public squares alive with activity, the Dekari meeting and conversing in their unique way and always some hurrying past on their way to bathe or mill about in the public pools, or heading to the tunnels to go tend to their underground gardens. Never had she seen any part of Laithos so empty, nor so quiet.

Certain now that something had gone wrong but clueless

what to do about it—or even how to determine what exactly ly *had* gone wrong—she veered off to her left, heading for the closest public pool via a familiar, narrow pathway that wound between a zigzagging row of towering buildings along the village's southwestern border. Her steps were tense as she scanned the path ahead and looked up at the buildings above, passing far below a series of connecting saaverña trunks running twisted between the rock structures. These served as skyward links, a sort of alternate pathway for the four-armed Dekari, who were great climbers and often preferred to move between buildings by swinging or scurrying along the connecting beams and entering through the auxiliary doorways the beams led to. Over time, she had become used to the idea that creatures moved and waited and crouched above her, traveling along these makeshift catwalks or sometimes even sitting hunched upon them, ruminating while looking out across the desert landscape typically revealed by the beams' height. But now the idea unsettled her and she continued to glance up as she traveled the pathway, imagining some unknown horror waiting to drop down upon her, the source of the Dekari's disappearance eager to tear her apart as easily as it surely had the village's other inhabitants.

Rounding a corner and closing in on her destination, a sight above stopped her cold. No creature lurked on one of the walkways, but something was there: a ragged row of white flowers twisted around a short and thick saaverña bole thirty feet above her. They appeared the same as the one she had seen in the stairway; however, these, she saw, did not emerge directly from the trunk but instead blossomed out of a vein-work of thin gray vines that webbed across the wood's surface and disappeared into the stone edges of the above-ground entryway of the dwelling to her right. The flowers trembled in the wind and, as she stood and stared, a drop of liquid fell from one of them, hitting the ground near her feet and emitting a faint hiss. Crouching down to inspect the impact point, Alinda saw that the stone path was pockmarked with small, uneven depressions a few millimeters deep, a pattern vaguely reminiscent of the spatter of heavy desert raindrops she remembered from so long ago on Earth. *Get out from under them*, some part of her brain hissed, instinct made audible. Another drop fell from above as she straightened, burning another hole into the pathway beneath her. She hurried on, clutching her canteen and eager to get to the water ahead, both to drink and wash her wounds. Curving around another Dekari home, something flitted above at the outskirts of her vision. Halting and scanning the upper stories of the three tall dwellings crowded around her and crisscrossed high with still more saaverña timbers, she searched for the source of movement. She saw nothing, though, and after a moment continued on, the village now stifling, everything looming and pressing in toward her. The path narrowed yet more even as she moved closer to her destination, the tight confines of the stone walkway that on her initial arrival to Laithos had struck her as fanciful now proving restrictive and claustrophobic, an open-air coffin waiting to take her into a terrifying darkness. She resisted the urge to break into a run and continued to glance upwards as she navigated between buildings, certain now that something tracked her, sensing its focus but clueless to its intention. And as though in response to her surety of its presence, something—a shadow, a heft, some shifting and scurrying apparition clawing its way across wood and stone and dropping fast toward her—blossomed in her vision, indistinct but tangible and almost upon her; and breath hitching and wounds beginning to burn with pain, she flung herself forward—*now* running, trying even for something more, desperate—and struggled with a screaming dilemma of whether to keep running or turn and fight (but did it even hold enough solidity to fight, to struggle with?) and was on the verge of turning and facing the menace when she broke out between two pressing red stone walls into another expansive public square, and a mass of white flutter bloomed in front of her even as she whirled and grabbed at her canteen—something, anything—in the certainty that whatever pursued her now loomed within clawed reach—

and nothing.

Behind her was nothing but the smooth, reaching walls of the dwellings and a ten foot curve of the path she had just traveled disappearing between those buildings. Looking above her, she saw only stone wall stretching into the sky, not even a saaverña connection visible from her vantage point, nothing odd or out of the ordinary except for the continued heavy silence and sense of emptiness present from the moment she entered Laithos. Heart pounding, breath beginning to normalize and the oppressive sense of attack receding, she turned back around and the glimpsed white from before unveiled itself as a sprawling mass of tangled, flowered vines cascading over the village's thirty-foot-high southwestern wall and spilling over a large, clear pool of water abutting that wall. The massive tumble of white flowers rippled in the swirls of wind that whorled down to the village floor from the desert landscape above, appearing almost as though they were crawling down the side of the rock wall. At the base of the cliff, the vines floated on the top of the pool, and a closer look revealed near-invisible roots, thin as hair, that clung to the skin of the water and trembled in the wind, sending out tiny ripples that reminded Alinda of the water skippers she used to see in creeks and streams back on Earth. The longest of the vines had reached the edge of the pool and were beginning to creep onto the rough-hewn floor of the public square, rootlets clinging to the stone as the protuberant tips of the vines hovered a half inch above the ground, as though tasting the air.

The pool was one of four such public baths in Laithos, open to the Dekari for bathing, swimming, and playing in, fed by wooden piping that tapped Laithos' main canal in the desert above and wound a steady flow of water from it through the rock wall and to the village below. Alongside the pool, not more than ten feet from Alinda, a series of wooden-levered faucets jutted out of the rock, placed three feet from the ground to provide on-demand water. She had hoped to take advantage of both, washing her wounds in the pool and filling her canteen from the faucets, the first steps in regrouping before making hard decisions. The unexpected invasion of the pool short-circuited her plan, though, and as she stared at the flowered vines, the underlying unease that had been with her since entering Laithos grew stronger still. She glanced behind her, eyes sharp for the presence of any dark spirits—of any looming, disembodied assailants emerging into the public square in pursuit of her. But nothing appeared to hunt her. The only movement was the wind and the soft flutter of flowers.

Something else arose, though, coalescing out of the background sibilance of the wind: a whispered scratching interspersed with tiny hisses and sizzles, sporadic but continuous. Eyes sharp, studying, she saw a stray drop fall from the pistil of a flower a third of the way up the rock wall, dropping with a tiny splash in the pool. A moment later, another; and this one hit stone just to the side of the pool, evincing the source of the hissing. Moving forward and circling around the side of the pool, stepping closer to the rock wall upon which the vines tumbled and clung, she saw rivulets of grainy red running down the stone, etching tributaries into the rock and dripping pale pink blooms into the water. The soft scratch grew, as well, and as she looked even closer she began to see the tremble and twitch of root and vine, the movement of the plant and its flowers not accountable to wind alone. No, it was growing—almost impossibly fast. It was visible but not; an optical illusion, but real. The vines seemed to thicken as she stared at them and she could see the gentle shifting of the roots upon the stone: movement similar to what she had seen on the skin of the water, a physical restlessness, as though with minute movements the roots were exploring the rock to which they clung. The scratch and rustle of growth came to her as the murmur of some incomprehensible creature, and for all the impossibilities she had seen on Mars since arriving those years ago, this one somehow unnerved her most of all.

"*Shit*," she mumbled, backing away from the rock wall.

Pain lightninged through her leg and a glance down at the dirty and wound-riven skin, rusty red with dried blood and a layer of clinging Martian dust, confirmed her need to wash and bandage it. She needed medicine, as well. The arethus had helped, but the wounds were not fully healed and their exposure on a planet that, despite her growing familiarity over the years, was still mostly alien to her immune system suggested too high a risk for a deadly infection. She had seen others die in such ways and did not want to recreate their fate. Nor did she want to spend any more time among these restless vines, waiting to see what they might do next.

Favoring her injured leg, she angled her way down a pathway different than the one from which she had arrived, directed toward the village center and her own home. She kept a close watch on the stone and saavernã around her as she walked, intent on scoping out any flush of flowers or another dark specter plummeting toward her from on high. She was becoming increasingly certain that something permanent, disruptive, and destructive had encroached upon the village, and that whatever her life had been over the past several years, it no longer would be. The village felt doomed, invaded—and as she traveled its eerie and empty, windblown paths, she considered the possibility of losing the only true home she had known on Mars, the place that four years ago had taken her in upon her scrambled, desperate arrival, far more torn and bloody than she was now and still aching from the fresh, clawed memory of her companions' torturous deaths at the hands of nightmarish Martian megafauna.

HER ACCIDENTAL ARRIVAL at one of Laithos' grand entryways those years ago had proved fortunate, even if at the moment of her first tentative descent down the stairs she had assumed, bleak and dejected, that she was entering what could only be a charnel house. Somehow, in her trudging, head-down approach, she had not seen a single Dekari swinging along the saavería bridges or even taken particular notice of the stone structures towering out of Laithos' sunken square; had she spied one of the hulking beasts—appearing as some kind of alarming cross between human and wolf, but yet also unnervingly alien—surely she would have turned and fled, hoping to keep her condemned life at least a little longer. Thankfully, her arrival in Laithos came both in her ignorance and Grijval's insight: he awaited her, having been warned (he would much later inform her) of her approach by a particular god with a contemptuous curiosity about humans, and having thus committed himself to her stewardship even before laying eyes upon her.

That stewardship had not proven easy. Upon sight of him, she had attempted to flee. He easily seized and subdued her, however, with a witchcraft she to this day did not understand—a touch and series of hand gestures that brought her to mental heel, captive to a psychic fog and bodily lethargy for days—then patiently refused her at least a dozen desperate attempts at escape with gentle but immovable physical restraint. It was in those attempts she realized that she physically was nothing to him, hardly even a nuisance in her desire to flee and his desire to keep her in Laithos. Again and again he refused her sought-after exit; again and again he kept her from running to her death. She didn't understand at the time, for he said nothing to her, nor did the other Dekari she saw on occasion. Only later, in ongoing frustration, would she so slowly learn their language, at least at a rudimentary level, as Grijval took her under his tutelage and began to open in her an understanding of his alien world. And only then would she begin to learn to communicate to him her own reality, snippets of her former life on Earth and the circumstances that had brought her to Mars as part of a group of abandoned political prisoners, suffering the all-too-common outcome for citizens who had been deemed problematic and dispensable. "Better red than dead," their government compassionately claimed to their citizenry as they jettisoned the prisoners into space—never mentioning that the prisoners were abandoned on the planet with few provisions and no safe harbor, therefore ending up as often as not both red and dead.

The initial months of her captivity had proved excruciating for Alinda. Isolated from humanity, unable to communicate with her captors, and deeply sick for weeks as her body rebelled against the unknown Martian environment and suffered a series of exhaustive illnesses, her weight plummeted while her mind hollowed out into a dull and repetitive yearning for some final condemnation, the release of a death she believed inevitable. Grijval would not allow it, though; he brought her blistered hunks of strangely delicious meat that he forced her to eat, steeped her a variety of astringent teas he forced her to drink, treated her with a series of ointments and rubs, and insisted she walk daily, even if only for a few minutes. The first time he pushed her out into Laithos' pathways, she felt for sure it was for a death march to her own execution. Only later would she come to realize that the force with which he brought her out into the village's open was nothing more than gentle insistence; at the time, given his immense strength and her extreme weakness, she thought it a violent fury. It took a few occurrences before she understood the walks to be benign, to in fact be in service of her health and recovery, and it was not until then that she began to pay attention to her surroundings, to marvel at the carved intricacy of Laithos and shrink at the passing Dekari, all of them varying degrees of imposing in their stature, the village blanketed with their heavy musk.

Over time it all became familiar to her—and as her health improved, her body strengthened, and the possibility of imminent death grew more remote, Laithos, and Grijval in particular, began to bring her an odd sense of comfort. While neither of them understood the others' language, they could communicate at a basic level—and he seemed to understand her even better than that, as though he could sense her mood and emotions, her needs and desires and fears. After a few months, when she no longer sought her escape and had recovered physically, she began to grow restless. Despite her newfound comfort with Laithos and Grijval, the sense of isolation that came with her residence in a village populated with alien creatures incapable of clearly communicating with her began to overcome her. Coupled with a claustrophobia born of her inability to imagine any other place to go despite her desperation to find other humans, that isolation fostered within her a wave of panic that grew by the day. It was as that panic overwhelmed her that Grijval finally, in one desperate afternoon during which she rebelled against him, took her in his arms, all four of them, pushed up her shirt, and began to trace his language upon her back in uncertain but swift movements, bringing upon her a sensation of such immense complexity and depth that she could never properly explain it to someone who had not experienced it, and bursting upon her vision a kaleidoscope of searing color that brought both pain and wonder and, within moments, an unconsciousness that lasted days.

When she awoke, her first sight was of Grijval crouched in the corner of the room in prayer—something she would understand only later—and the one coherent thought that echoed through the pain and hunger and disorientation of her rebirth into consciousness was that she was Grijval's student now, she had much to learn, and that Mars now had purpose for her. She understood little more than that, except for a deep and aching realization imparted by Grijval that no other humans survived on Mars, that no hunkered community waited for her somewhere in the midst of the planet's vast deserts. That entwined knowledge etched in her mind and from that day forward she lived it steadily, with certainty, and began to make herself a creature of the planet she would die upon, first coming to know Laithos and the Dekari and then, with Grijval's grudging acquiescence, the Martian geology and ecology itself, setting out often into the harsh and at times deadly environment with minimal provisions and an intent to explore, an intent to learn to survive or die trying.

In this rhythm, and in her study under Grijval, the years passed. Grijval in particular offered her a kind of relief from her loneliness, but it was a tempered one; despite her affection for him, he could not substitute for the necessity of human companionship. As the months and years unwound, nightmares of friendship and sex and conversation plagued her: aching comforts offered at night and torn cruelly from her upon her awakening. She would wake up crying; she would lose herself in the middle of the day in hazy remembrances of laughter and friendship from her days on Earth; frustrated with desire, she would touch herself with a resolved necessity, climaxing sometimes in distracting relief and other times in angry resignation. The faded memories of her family and friends slowly morphed their faces into disturbing fusions of human and Dekari. The closest thing she had to a mirror was a large, flat, polished stone, strangely reflective, found one day at the bottom of one of Laithos' pools. She guarded it jealously, but the clouded countenance it showed her was no sharper than her memories.

Often the greatest comfort she took came from her explorations of the Martian landscape surrounding Laithos. While Grijval's companionship at times mitigated her loneliness, it was in those isolated expeditions that she felt most released from the prison of her circumstances. She could imagine in those long days of trekking through the desert, observing the planet's scope and character, that she was not stuck on an alien planet in absence of humans, but that she was out on an adventure and might yet return home. She could not imagine the same in Laithos, surrounded by the Dekari and their representation of her condemnation, but the solitude of the desert gave her the smallest of openings for such self-deception. And so day after day she would plunge into it, always returning to her relationship with Grijval and his patient teachings, the soft sorrow she sensed from him in response to her loneliness, but maintaining her sanity through her frequent excursions into the desert emptiness.

That emptiness always contrasted against her return to Laithos and its liveliness, though, and so nothing prepared her for the day she came home to the empty pathways of Laithos, a village bereft of the life she had come to take for granted, haunted in its abandonment and yet whispering with something shadowed and alien, disorienting in a way it had not been for her since her arrival. Traveling the familiar paths now, suddenly guilty for her loneliness, she ached for Grijval and his guidance—for a return of his stewardship that had saved her life so long ago. But the empty village gave her nothing but a creeping sense of abandonment, of a community whose time had passed, and so she moved silent through its walkways, eyes sharp for any shadowed beings—any apparitions dropping from on high—as she angled her way toward a familiar home for which a sense of loss was already beginning to settle within her.

THE STONE DWELLING she knew so well, within which she had lived from her first days of physical restraint in Laithos, was one of the more modest in the village. Roughly the height of a two-story house, it was narrow, but all the dwellings in Laithos were; the Dekari tended to live upwards rather than outwards. Indeed, the structure was truncated and oddly decorated in comparison to most of the rest of the village's homes, with the entrance opening into a main living room with several chairs and a table, along with two walls of bookshelves anchored into the rock, weighted with a large collection of Dekari reading material she had yet failed to crack. To the left of the entrance, a large fire chamber extended out from the wall—the heart of the home's elaborate piped heating system—and two shelves to the side of the fire chamber held a small collection of rock dishware and tumblers, as well as finely carved wooden utensils. On the right, a secondary chamber served as a washroom, where a small cache of medicinal and hygienic items were stored. A sturdy wooden ladder led up to the second story—more of a loft than a second room—where a makeshift bed consisting of fragrant dried leedow fronds covered in furs served as the room's primary furniture, alongside a series of wooden boxes lining one wall that contained her modest wardrobe.

Alinda sought out her medicine, moving gingerly, exhausted, into the washroom. She stripped out of her clothes and settled herself into the strangely comfortable carved rock outcropping that served as a sitting spot for washings and personal care. Originally sculpted to fit a Dekari, one of Laithos' carvers had reworked the stone impression to better suit her body, sensing with only a brief study of her form the best way to re-mold the seat. Her initial skepticism fled on her first seating; the Dekari's skill in working stone never ceased to amaze her, despite the abundant evidence all around her that they had long ago mastered the skill at a depth unmatched in the entirety of the solar system.

Hearty, adapted to the dry Martian climate, and nowhere near as thirsty as humans, the Dekari did not pipe water to their homes, opting instead to visit the public pools for drinking, communal bathing, and playing. They washed daily, though, using gravity-fed draws of water from small tanks anchored to the washroom ceilings that they filled on occasion from outside access points. Filling a stone pitcher, she first took a long drink of the water, cooling her throat. Then wetting a rag, she began wiping down her injured leg, wincing at the pain as the crusted blood and grime washed away, revealing the angry red wounds beneath. They did not look nearly so bad as she had expected, though, already closing and healing, and a sense of relief came over her at the thought that her wounds may not be infected, that she wasn't facing a flight from Laithos while crippled. Still vulnerable, yes, but the guillotine had lifted, if only somewhat; perhaps she would survive the day, after all.

Taking her time, she finished washing her wounds and then rinsed the rest of her body, wringing out the rag again and again while watching the dirty swirls of water trickle down the drain set into the stone floor, carrying the waste water to the underground gardens. She wondered if any Dekari were down there, crouched in darkness, perhaps unaware of the exodus above. But she doubted it; the Dekari communicated even across distances, using some kind of low-grade telepathy, and whatever had happened to empty Laithos surely had not gone unnoticed by any of them, whatever their location. They were likely as gone as the others, the village left abandoned.

Finished with her cleaning, Alinda dressed her wounds with a powerful salve, bringing fast relief to their dull ache. Sitting, breathing, she considered her next steps but no clear course of action came to mind. Thinking of the vines, their rustle as they grew, she knew that she had to leave Laithos. But no destination waited and, at this point, she wasn't even aware of how far off another village might be. It could be hundreds of miles away; Dekari settlements tended to be sparse and spread out, never permanent for some reason she had never quite grasped. It was possible the departed Dekari were not far away, but she had no way of knowing. Their long-distance communication was not functional at the interspecies level—hell, she could barely communicate with them even when within reach. And even if she could communicate with them across distances, that did her no good if they were dead, which they could as well be. For all she knew, the underground gardens were not empty but instead filled with the bodies of dead Dekari, Laithos' former inhabitants heaped in the dark tunnels.

Pushing back against a rising panic, she decided to dress—the only obvious step in front of her. Leaving the washroom behind, she climbed to her room and fetched a fresh set of clothes, heavy jeans and a favorite long sleeve shirt made of a rough fabric she nevertheless found comforting. But dressing only took a moment and a fresh indecision settled upon her once it was done, her brain cycling through the impossible idea of what to pack for an indeterminably long foray into the harsh desert surroundings. She did not get far in the mental exercise before something else wormed its way into her attention, though: a soft and persistent scratching coming from the stone wall at the head of her bed. It was tiny, almost nothing, the faintest reminder of a long ago home on Earth where mice lived in the wall, scrabbling and tumbling and scratching in the dead of night. But the walls here were thick and solid, without space within where mice could live—and no mice lived in Laithos, anyway.

Leaning close to the wall, hunting the sound, her eyes soon settled on a trace-thin vine, or perhaps a root, something brown and desiccated and clinging to the stone wall. It emerged from the rock for a few inches and then reentered it, as though a fossil unearthed by erosion. And even as she watched, and listened to the muffled *scritch* of something murmuring from behind the rock, a tiny green protuberance swelled from the vine and, with impossible speed and grace, unfurled into a single trembling white flower.

"Gods," Alinda whispered, stepping back from the wall, her heartbeat ratcheting into a fury.

She fled her home, feeling sick as she emerged out into the dry air with a pounding sense of entrapment. Glancing along the outer walls of her home, she saw what she had missed before, or what perhaps had not been there only minutes before: a tangled mass of vines growing up the side, clinging tight to the stone walls while sporadic flushes of white flowers rippled in the wind.

The entire village was being overtaken. Fighting back panic, wanting to get away but with nowhere to go, Alinda tried to think of a course of action that wouldn't lead her to a quick demise. But all she could think in that moment was how much she missed the steadying, comforting presence of Grijval and how she wished he was there to explain to her what the hell was happening. For he would know, she was sure of that, and an explanation of the impossible was all she needed to steady herself and better understand her options, to move forward in this alien world and keep herself alive for another day. Yet he was as gone as the others, and—

She realized suddenly where he might be.

THE TEMPLE'S ENTRANCE was an archway framed in one continuous piece of thin saaverña, carved into elaborate twists and loops and swirls that Alinda could only imagine must have taken months of cautious work. She hesitated outside it, every sense of decorum telling her to turn and leave, not to enter into the village's one space where she had always been forbidden to enter; where, indeed, all but Grijval had been forbidden to enter. Yet the empty archway called to her, as did the sense that the temple alone might reveal to her where the Dekari had gone. She feared entry, believing the warning Grijval had once imparted to her that entering the temple would bring an end to her existence (not death—at least, not in the translation; *cessation of existence* was the closest words she could associate with the sensation his touch had given her) but she knew also that to not solve the mystery before her would just as likely end in her death. Even if her wounds healed, she could survive alone only so long.

So she entered, holding her breath as she stepped past the threshold of the archway. Nothing happened; she did not cease to exist, nothing came crashing down upon her, nor did any great sense of horror or foreboding envelope her. She simply entered into a modest interior chamber with rounded stone walls, approximately fifteen feet in diameter and the same in height, the walls some of the smoothest stone she had ever seen. The room was empty except for two thick, gnarled saaverña trunks in the middle, roughly six feet apart and each set into carved depressions in the stone floor and braced diagonally against the wall opposite the entryway, settled sturdily upon the fitted ledges of two more half-moon depressions carved into the stone wall. Between them, another archway hovered six feet off the ground, a window emptying into a further chamber from which Alinda could make out nothing—just a sense of space and anticipation, of the next step of her journey.

Unwilling to turn back now, she pushed forward before doubt could seize her. Shimmying up the saaverña trunk on her right, she brought herself to the bottom of the archway and clambered onto its ledge, which she quickly realized was the edge of the next chamber's floor, raised above the room behind her. Clearing the archway and rising from her crouch, the room beyond materialized before her out of a weak light filtering down from far above.

The chamber was massive and cavernous, at least fifty feet across and circular, with walls sloping inward as they rose high above her and eventually curved into a narrow domed ceiling. The room's modest illumination came from two small openings at the ceiling's apex, filtering in weak sunlight from without. The light illuminated the room's most awing element: every square inch of the towering sloped walls was blanketed with carved writings in the same vein as the flowing histories traced along the village's entry stairways; yet these narratives were presented not as simple carvings within the rock but as infinitely complex and looping saaverña inlays, each wooden thread at least as delicate and intricate as that which outlined the temple's entry, but easily thousands of meters of such carved saaverña layering the walls of the chamber. The sight stunned Alinda to such a degree that it took her a few long moments of awed study before her attention finally settled to the middle of the chamber and onto the bristled and hulking figure that crouched therein, its muzzled head bowed and shoulders gently rising and falling with a deep and steady breath.

Grijval.

She almost cried out but stifled her voice at the last moment. Her mere presence in the temple already broke important rules laid down with an utmost solemnity by the creature in front of her; to speak, as well, in a place of unquestioned silence could only accentuate her affront. Grijval had yet to look up at her and as she studied his countenance, her mind racing with considered courses of action, a great desire to flee the chamber took hold of her. Surely she had miscalculated in coming here; whatever worship enveloped Grijval could only be disrupted by her presence. Worse, she might bring dreadful consequences down upon the both of them. She did not know what levels of tolerance the Dekari gods held, but what little Grijval had told her of them did not suggest much. While she knew the Dekari worshiped multiple gods, those gods were a mystery to her outside the fragments of religious myths she had gleaned from her incompetent readings of the creatures' writings, as well as the occasional vague allusion made by Grijval during their conversations. For all he had taught her, time and again he had refused to elaborate on the gods he worshiped and the details of his and the Dekari's religious beliefs, despite the fact that he stood alone as the religious leader of Laithos. All he had been willing to tell her was that he stewarded the relationship between the village, its inhabitants, and the gods they worshiped; that he alone was allowed to enter the temple she now stood within; and that the exact relationship between the gods and the Dekari could not be spoken of to outsiders. The rest was mystery.

Before she could make any decision as to her next movement, Grijval raised his massive head and locked eyes with her from across the room. She froze as he huffed in surprise, slitted yellow-green eyes flashing in the chamber's murk, his body rising as his muscles stiffened. Alinda took a step backward, unthinking, all instinct screaming for her to leave the temple, to scramble back out into the dry desert air, get out of the village as quickly as possible, and plunge into the desert—somewhere, anywhere other than Laithos and the empty madness that had consumed it. But she remained and Grijval, instead, was the one to move. Breath heavy, massive in stature but lithe in movement, the creature crossed the floor of the temple to stand towering in front of her, seven feet tall and thick with muscle, large even by Dekari standards. He stared down at her and she could not help but meet his gaze. Even in the dim light of the temple, the details of his rugged visage sharpened into focus: the wiry dark fur that covered his face; his elongated snout so reminiscent of a dog's; the dried-blood brown of his meaty, cracked nose, three nostrils carved ragged out of the flesh; the bioluminescence of his kaleidoscopic yellow-green irises, severed by the thinnest slit of a pupil; his crooked mouthful of chipped and ragged teeth, chapped and blood-red lips strained tight against them and a tenuous pool of dirty saliva gathered in one corner. His thick chest, woven of striated muscle and covered in downy black hair, heaved with ragged breaths that imparted a sense of vulnerability on him she had never before experienced; always he had been in her presence in perfect control, impervious, expansive with knowledge and gentle in his willingness to teach her, even as she betrayed her own ignorance with her struggle to grasp the basic concepts of Dekari culture. Now he seemed only fear and wildness, wrapped in instinct and response. She did not know even if he recognized her.

"Grijval," she whispered, "what happened?"

Of course he did not speak, not words, even though he had come to know hers—or at least, he had come to understand her, though more through his ability to tap her mind and read her emotions than through the actual words spoken. But he did speak in his own way: stepping forward and kneeling, bowing his head close to hers—hot breath steaming past her, blooming sour—and wrapping his front right arm around her to gently trace an impossible symbol on the back of her skull.

He wanted to tell her something.

Again the screaming urge to leave the temple, to run from it, flooded over her. But she had no place to run and right here in front of her was Grijval, the one Dekari who meant everything to her, who had taught and welcomed and trusted her, who asked now to speak to her with a sense of wild uncertainty—of some kind of pending devastation, good or bad—in a village disappeared of all its inhabitants. She could never turn from him. Terrified and desperate to understand and wanting only for all of it to be different, *normal*, she leaned back from Grijval as he slipped away his hand and in a swift motion pulled her shirt over her head, exposed now but unembarrassed—her body meant nothing to him, as his nudity meant nothing to her; and besides, how many times had she been this way in front of him, bared and waiting to try to understand what he would try to tell her?—and then he leaned back in, his phosphorescent eyes spiraling with delirium, and he wrapped her in his four arms, his two back ones unfolding from behind his shoulder blades and gently settling upon her upper back as his two front arms settled upon her lower. Sixteen fingers flexed and traced and tested her skin with the opening movements of a familiar conversation even as Grijval leaned his head in so close to hers that they soon touched, the soft fur of his face tickling her left cheek, his weary breath cavernous in her ear and an intense moist heat rolling off him to envelop her, his presence dominant and overwhelming—and then the chamber fell away and a fathomless universe burst within her.

THE RED DESERT coalesces around her: the cutting and cold wind-blast of sharp sand across an eternal expanse, stone edifices hunkered on the horizons, the endless world a great sweep of aridity and loneliness. Each heavy step falls exhausted on the shifting ground—sand and stone and tumbling, scheming rocks—and the pressing pain and isolation of this impossible, interminable journey slowly gives way to a sense of massive legs, of tangled fur, of strained muscle and too many arms and a perplexing weight that breaks her out of her internal world into the external, into Grijval, into his Dekari body and resigned search across the Martian landscape. A deep sorrow fogs her mind—*his* mind—weighing as heavy as physical exhaustion, as heavy as the gnawing hunger and intense thirst weighs, as heavy as the necessity of this ritual hunt for home. It's a sorrow of abandonment, of banishment, of the loss of community and comfort and familiarity, and its familiarity aches within her as brutally as it does within him. But for him it was expected, something he understood inherently as requisite and even at times anticipated, longed for—until the day it arrived and everything he knew shattered.

It comes to Alinda as flashes, his memories as hers: the great stone spires, the scent of sand and hot stone and Dekari bodies, the gorgeous and cool Martian nights, the ritual bathing as a mass of Dekari mill and mingle around the public pool, calling out silently and joking and breaking off again and again into talkative embraces, their arms moving swift across each others' backs before finding a new partner, the ongoing conversations resembling nothing less than a complex group dance. She feels Grijval emerging from the pool, the cleansing water sluicing through his fur, and him standing a moment watching, the background mumble of the Dekari's silent calls to each other blending with the soft rustling of movements, of gentle huffs and snorts, of the tracing of backs. She remembers the great contentment that took him at such times.

It is gone now. Silently they pushed him from the village and only the desert remains, immense and infinite, promising somewhere the raw material of a new home and the long and lonely wait for its readiness. He imagines the long days of isolation, those first months of painstaking carving, the search for the nearest stand of saaverña and the slow harvest and endless trips back and forth. He imagines the underground gardens and their slow taming and cultivation, the long work of preparing them to feed hundreds rather than just a few. He imagines the hunt for the closest feeder line for the canal; the long, slow dig of tributary; the boring of water lines to the village's eventual floor. The thought of so much work makes him restless.

Night falls. Time stutters. Weary, they cease and hunker for the night. His memories continue to flash as hers: the bone-lock of her back arms, clinging to a saaverña beam throughout the night as she sleeps, aloft, nestled in the smooth stone cubby of an upper room that could best be described as a Dekari bedroom; the slide of wind-troubled air as she swings easily along saaverña beams, moving swiftly between stone structures, the village uppers a series of navigable byways; the comings and goings of the psychic calls between Dekari, her mind nearly always open to them by choice, born of a curiosity of her community—of who these creatures are, always a partial mystery even though she is one of them.

The night is wind, as the desert so often is, and it is troubled. Before the end of it, just as the horizon begins to lighten but long before the sun appears, the constant murmuration of the wind coalesces into something more, into a whispering, gibbering chatter. Somehow Alinda thinks she catches it before Grijval, even though they are the same, even though she cannot understand these words, spoken in a Dekari language she never even has heard—only has felt upon her skin. And yet she does understand them as Grijval does, recognizes them anyway, as there is not enough clarity in the wind's whispering to suss out the actual words, only to know it as a background murmur, as the confused and interwoven grumblings of an undefined number of . . . *something*.

It shakes Grijval and the combined sense of awe and terror that infuses him takes her, as well. Their vision sharpens, then blurs, and then, in an impossible blink, the sun is a third high in the sky—time has tricked them, or the voices have mesmerized them, or perhaps this is just the reality of memory, of the tracings on her back that unweave this world into her mind and then demand that she bring it back into tapestry. The voices now are so loud and while she cannot understand, Grijval sets back off into the harsh desert with a renewed purpose and vigor, with the ever-present hunger and thirst pushed as deep as it can go, with all the pain and discomfort ground under foot. The voices are a revelation. He knew to expect this but could not really know until he heard, and it has made the world bloom anew.

And so they walk, and the days unwind, even as they grow more fatigued as the endless desert unspools around them, dry and unforgiving, the land rising and falling and them scrabbling, wishing for the option to swing—for something other than this interminable walking. Fat and muscle burns, ticking away even as the wind keeps whispering, the words growing more clear and varied with each passing hour but still a gibbering mess of what sounds like a hundred tangled voices. The source of these voices tugs at her—or, more specifically, Grijval's understanding of them tugs at her as she struggles to tease that comprehension out into something understandable to her, in him a roiling mass of emotion that imparts to her something of importance that she cannot translate into human terms. At least, not until the third day of wind-whispered travel, when the concept untangles itself into the most foundational of concepts: *These are the voices of gods.*

By now their skin has shrunk, grown taut, parched and cracking with thick blood spotting out into the harsh air. Their heavy steps are weak and faltering. Grijval pushes himself with an eagerness, though, with a dedication to these voices that call him forward with an opaque grumbling of fate. He knows what lies on the other side and all the shaded imaginings of it before—of the endless work, the isolation, the repetition and cruelty—are beginning to brighten with a sense of destiny fulfilled, of his own great importance. Memories of those he left behind waver and flicker into new faces: into those who will someday come, who will eventually look to him for guidance, who will trust more than anything in his bond with the gods forged during these very days, in this hellish trek through an endless desert, and confirmed in his ability to withstand it unbroken. Years of arduous work still await him but he can almost see it now, the temple that will tower high in the middle of this new village to come and that will serve to house him and the gods and from which wisdom and trust and awe will blanket the resident Dekari; a place of great worship that will serve as illumination for all else.

Their muscles seize and contract at the thought and a particularly harsh blast of wind sends Grijval staggering to the side, onto a slick of shale stippled with gravel. Losing his footing, he crashes to the ground, the sharp rocks tearing open a long gash in his right leg. Heat and pain bursts from the wound but already Alinda, Grijval, the both of them are looking up from the ground toward the sky, to the great desert lumbering in front of them, and they see that the horizon is broken by a massive cliff face, cragged and cracked, perfect for sculpture. It is so close, impossibly close. How could they not have seen it before? It shimmers as they stare at it, the wind howling and churning around it—around them—sand whirling through the air and the dusty scent of the gods that Grijval finds so familiar radiating out from the rock. The full weight of the discovery settles upon them, a final revelation wrapped in exhaustion and reverence, in the haunting incredulity that this epochal moment finally has arrived.

Grijval soars. He climbs to his feet and it is as though his entire body opens to the looming cliff, welcoming it into him. He staggers forward and now Alinda is only just along for the ride, the majesty of this moment overwhelming any sense of self and giving her over completely to the flood of emotion Grijval experiences. It is a holiness and wonderment, a knowing in that moment that the world is everything it is supposed to be and that it offers him everything he could want. The wind, its grit—none of it touches him. The sense of loss and loneliness has vanished. All but one of the garbled voices of the gods have fallen away, and the remaining voice rings through with a perfect lilting clarity: an intent and pronounced flood of words she cannot begin to understand, but that she senses as sacred.

As Grijval stumbles forward on his injured and bloody leg, the fur on his body standing on end in the whipping, whirling wind, the coming years are again flashes of his foreknowledge that becomes hers: the dank and humid underground gardens, promised by the whispering god to be already in their nascent state, buried beneath the great monolith before them in a network of long-formed catacombs and ensuring a steady source of sustenance for him and the coming sculptors; the great, slow process of shaping a new village out of the immense tower of rock before them (*Laithos*, the

god whispers, naming the village, the final syllable lengthened out into a trailing sibilance), the commitment and condemnation of Grijval's coming years promising a culmina-
tion in priesthood; the patient and intricate work of crafting
miles of saaverña inlays to christen the majestic stone temple
once it is unearthed by the carvers of the village, one of his
great works finally at hand; and the long lessons of the gods
awaiting him in that work, in the endless days of tedious,
critical carving, their intermittent background whisperings
interweaving with the carving of myth to lay the foundation
of wisdom and knowledge he will later bring to all those who
form the community of Laithos. It has all been traced upon
him a thousand times in preparation for this moment, and
the realization that now the great trial begins overwhelms
him as he approaches the remainder of his long life, its ending so far away but still glimpsed in the fog of the future, in
his understanding of the day that will eventually come when
the bloom of death begins.

The base of the cliff is littered with great, jagged boulders, a ragged heap of tailings shrugged from the looming
rock wall above. Lurching forward, Grijval stumbles on the
rubble, his right foot slipping into a crevice and twisting him
forward to slam his knee into a boulder, his hands against
sharp stone. A lacerating pain starbursts from both impacts
and in the clarity of the shock Alinda latches onto the continued oratory of the singular remaining voice within the wind,
the one god that has separated itself from all the others. The
words break apart the pain, fade the desert, quiet the wind;
even the disorienting effect of her presence within Grijval
falls away and he disappears; and the words then become
everything to her—or, more specifically, the voice becomes
everything, ringing through to stab deep within her, its rough
texture but profound urgency wrapped in an alien eloquence,
the deep intimacy of its presence within her mind tying her to
something elemental and infinite within this planet that has

never yet been able to prove home to her. The voice is born of Mars, and deep within it, at its very edges, she senses the source of the planet itself, feels the comfort and familiarity and love for the planet which this being holds, and somehow understands it. The barren planet falls into place, its beauty clear; and now she looks up at the cliff above her and the world opens up to her—and Grijval's presence returns, and the both of them stare forward with a perfect affection, with the certainty that this is where they belong, and the merciless pain engulfing them blooms with joy, as well, brought upon them by a world that has nurtured this moment, brought the both of them into its embrace and whispered their belonging into their ears.

They have found home, and in that realization Alinda almost begins to understand the urgent whisperings brought to her by the wind before the desert suddenly plummets away and she slumps out of Grijval's twisting, tracing hands onto the cold stone floor of the temple, rolling onto her back to stare upward at the thousands of white-blossomed flowers above her, come to take Laithos back to the stone and soil from which it came.

THE SAAVERÑA INLAYS were mostly gone, the temple's walls now obscured by a clinging network of thick and twisted vines laden with white flowers trembling in the soft swirl of the chamber's air currents. The weak sunlight from above had dimmed almost to nothing thanks to the heavy tangle of vines, which not only climbed the adjacent walls but knit themselves together near the openings at the chamber's apex. Blinking, Alinda could just make out the room around her, the vines and the flowers, Grijval's hulking, heavy-breathed form crouched beside her. The stone floor pressed cold and rough against her bare back. Her right hand clung to a handful of shirt—*her* shirt, never quite released when Grijval had taken her into his arms and begun to invoke in her the trial that brought him to the great stone edifice from which Laithos had been carved; to this eventual temple; to the blooming death that now trembled above them, promising the completion of a long-held cycle. Weakly, she pulled the shirt close and covered herself.

Grijval leaned in toward her, his massive body looming above and blocking much of her view. His heavy musk enveloped her, the scent tinged with a sour acidity she had never before noticed. Each breath heaved his chest and his exhalations ran hot against the bare skin of her shoulder. The intensity with which he gasped at the air alarmed her. His eyes seemed somehow now even a greater riot of color and as she stared into them she could not tell if he truly saw her or if he still existed somewhere else—in the past, perhaps, or lost in the anticipation of—

Her breath hitched and she gasped, her inhalation a stifled sob brought on by newfound comprehension. This death had come not just for Laithos, but for Grijval, as well. It would dissolve and take both of them back to the earth. She knew this; knew it as he did, his foreknowledge from so many years ago burned now into her understanding of Laithos and the land upon which it stood, of the gods who both watched over and were a part of the cycles of death and rebirth that churned ceaselessly throughout the planet.

The gods gave her no time to struggle with this newfound knowledge. A process had to be completed. From the trembling flowers above came a stray drop of fire, a splash of acid that spattered against her bare right arm holding close her shirt. Flinching and gasping at the sear of pain, she caught sight of the angry red pockmarks on her skin and smelled the acrid scent of scorched flesh. This again; only for a moment did she freeze, her realization coming swift that the entirety of the chamber's inside now grew coated with the offending flowers, her mind already clearing out of necessity and returning with force to the present world, leaving behind the aching echo of Laithos' origins and Grijval's discovery of his long destiny. Exposed, vulnerable, she pushed herself into a sitting position and ripped her shirt down over her head, arms tangled for a brief moment in the rough fabric and another burn of pain bursting on the tender flesh of her exposed stomach, then yet another on the ring and pinky fingers of her left hand. Hissing with the pain, she finished wrestling back on her shirt and pushed herself into a sitting position, her eyes wildly scanning the steep-walled chamber in an effort to gain her bearings.

The flowered vines had taken over the entire room. It seemed to her an impossibility; how long could she have been in Grijval's arms, the swift tracings of his memories taking her back years into the past? Surely it could not have been more than several minutes, maybe half an hour? And yet the thick vines and matted flowers coating the chamber walls looked as though they had grown over months, even years. They shuddered, rippling along the curved and arching stone, and Alinda watched as across the room a scatter of drops fell like rain, hitting the chamber floor and emitting a hiss as they ate into the stone.

She looked back toward the entryway from which she had entered the chamber. Rather than an empty opening, though, it now stood obscured, a curtain of flowered vines draped over the archway. She wondered what the consequences of pushing through those vines would be, but even as the consideration unnerved her the understanding that she had to leave the temple burned just as bright.

Grijval's angry growl erupted behind her. Whirling, she unsteadily began to climb to her feet, the force of his outcry overwhelming her frayed nerves. He loomed close to her, flinching as a series of acidic drops fell upon him, singing his fur and eating into his flesh; almost simultaneously she felt a dizzying pain of her own on the back of her skull, a hammerblow of hot agony, a burning spike hungrily seeking out brain matter. Her vision blurred and pitched and she stutter-stepped backward, the chamber careening around her as her balance faltered. She fell, but never hit the floor; Grijval caught her mid-drop, her vision jerking as she fell rough into two of his massive hands, his body bent over her and two of his four arms braced against the floor, holding both him and her up off the rough stone. Even as she lay there—arched in his arms and trying to bring her vision back into focus, the pain in her head strong but receding from a hot agony into a harsh and throbbing ache—she saw drops raining down from above, Grijval shaking and grunting as they hit his back and shoulders like gunshot burrowing into his flesh.

The chamber faded as her focus locked into Grijval, his hunched body shaking with pain and exhaustion. Blood seeped down the side of his face, leaking into his eyes, and he furiously blinked it away, snorting and shaking his head. Shifting, he pulled her in close to him, his body arched and protecting her from the devastation falling from above. Carefully he crept forward, using his two back arms and legs to crawl across the chamber while holding her close to his chest with his two front arms, one looped just below her shoulders and the other under her knees, pressing her up against him. Her body rising and falling with each of his breaths, she attempted to shrink herself into him, staying shielded from the hot burn of acid even while regretting his protection and what it cost him. As he crawled forward he flinched and hissed, unsteady, his body swaying and listing to his right.

Leaning her head back, she glimpsed his face again, now at an odd angle, and the twist of his features stabbed at her. If only she had not come into the temple; if only she had left him at peace with his gods. He had told her she could not enter. He had warned her of the consequences, even if she could never have foreseen this nightmare reality. The responsibility of it overwhelmed her and for a moment she wanted him to drop her to the floor, to step back and let death find her, to release her from his protection and let her suffer for her actions rather than take it upon himself.

And then, in the slightest pause of movement, he craned his own head to look beneath him at her, to catch her eye, and she saw the affection with which he regarded her even through the agony of the assault upon him. On her back she felt the twitch of his hand, the subtle movement of his fingers, and as it netted her mind she realized it was not inadvertent but necessary, a final tracing of knowledge from him to her. It was like nothing he had told her before and in it was not forgiveness but resoluteness, understanding—even a purpose the depth of which she could not comprehend. It was a release for both him and her. It was, in that briefest moment, a revelation passed to her—and as she understood what he told her, the chamber and its denouement faded almost to nothing, replaced by the soft whispering and muttering of something more. It came from every direction, from every inch of the chamber's interior, and Alinda wondered with amazement if it could be coming from the flowers themselves, each delicate bloom a conduit for the voice of the gods. Or no, the voice of a god. Of the one that had come for Grijval, for Laithos, for the return of everything that had been given. The god whose voice she remembered.

The chamber swam with a wild darkness and her vision spiraled across fur and flowers and stone. She rocked and swayed in Grijval's grip and tried to focus but could not. Grijval's hands stirred beneath her, carving some knowledge she could not quite grasp deep into her—until she did, in a moment of hope and devastation, in anger and sorrow. Briefly her mind broke with the knowledge, then raged. Arching back against his grasp, she again caught sight of his face, turned now from her and intent on their destination, and glimpsed the delirium and wildness of his eyes, the singularity of his focus. Just beyond she saw a web of flower and vine.

It swayed and parted and then the world shook as Grijval growled, the sound cavernous, and fire and flesh and sulfur consumed them, and she closed her eyes but could not stop hearing the mutterings, the rumblings, the gibbering cries of the all-consuming god around them.

Then cool air broke across her and she dropped sharply toward the floor, Grijval's grip loosening, and pitched forward, her hands grasping instinctively for some hold, for something safe and steady. Her fingers curled around wood as Grijval released her and she fell heavy onto a sturdy saaverña beam, clinging to it. Shifting herself, she looked back at where she had come and saw a gruesome montage of Grijval's face and arms, blood and gore and a tangled drapery of flower and vine. Rivulets of acid burned channels through Grijval's fur and flesh. He hunched against the offense, straining his face from the worst of it, his eyes locked on hers and his arms braced against the bloodied stone ledge, the hiss of acid everywhere and the stench of his flesh whirling within the clean, sandy scent of desert air billowing in from the outer doorway. Even as she watched, the twisted pain of his expression transformed into release and relief. Pain revealed itself to her then, the result of thin streaks of acid scorching her arms and burning along the right side of her face. But a quick glance at her arms showed the injuries as superficial, with her greater ruin negated by Grijval's protection and taken, instead, upon himself.

She wanted to reach for him, this creature who remained her friend, her teacher, her betrayer, the most unlikely of connections upon this impossible planet, but already he was withdrawing back into the chamber behind him. He paused only a moment to lift his right hand and twist it into a flowing symbol, a transitory pattern that stirred something deep within her and filled her with an aching sadness she saw reflected back at her in his own eyes—a regret, but one tempered by a belief in its necessity—and then he disappeared back through the flowered vines, shedding blood and fur and flesh upon their white petals, turning them into a grisly curtained entryway into what was now the charnel house she had once feared Laithos to be so long ago.

She heard only the softest of stirrings from within the chamber after Grijval's disappearance. Then even those sounds disappeared. After a moment she realized the whispers and mutters she had heard within also had ceased. The flowers draped over the entryway did not stir, not even in the soft breeze that entered from without the temple. She clung to the beam, her breath slowing, the aching sadness unceasing, anger fighting with affection and confusion, but the smallest of conflicted comfort available to her from Grijval's final expression as he had withdrawn back into the chamber of horrors beyond: one of intense peace and the achievement of something long desired—of expectations fulfilled.

ALINDA STUMBLED FROM the temple into a remade world. Vine and flower and acid had come for Laithos, dissolution and reclamation the order of the day. Alternating with the hot, sandy scent of the wind came regular wafts of sulfur. Creaks and cracks echoed across the village, sharp but muffled by the flowers that now blanketed nearly every surface. Rivulets of acid, ruddy with dissolved red rock, ran along the pathways while searching out the drains that would take them deep into the underground gardens. Laithos' primary food source would soon be no more. It hardly mattered.

She scrambled to exit the village, to escape into the unforgiving surrounding desert. Acid ate at her shoes and fell from above. Only a few drops hit her, but their stings still clawed. From somewhere off in another part of the village, a magnificent crash sounded. She carried no canteen or provisions except one; the madness of her descent into the village and all that had happened since had left her distracted and unprepared, the canteen she had carried forgotten and discarded within what remained of her home and no food or medicine gathered in her hurry to leave it. She dared not go back now—her survival would have to depend on other means.

Navigating her way to the same stairway from which she had entered Laithos, Alinda found a drapery of weeping flowers half covering its entrance. Ducking beneath, she caught only a drop or two of fire; the acid seared her back but she hurried up the stairs, paying as little mind as possible to the pain. Then she broke out into the desert and its steady wind, its dry air, the clarity of its scent. Only in breathing it did she realize how tainted Laithos' atmosphere had been with the acerbic scent of the village's ongoing destruction. Stumbling away from the stairway, she took deep breaths of that clean air, working to calm herself, trying not to imagine Grijval's fate.

Eventually turning, she stared at the peaks of Laithos' buildings. A thick matting of flowering vines covered them all. The ongoing wind rippled through the petals and the view looked to Alinda like some odd, hilly pasture, blanketed in flowers and extending far into the distance. The occasional crack sounded from within, but no buildings fell while she watched. At a distance, the slow destruction of Laithos looked almost peaceful.

Grijval's bloody face flashed through her mind, twisted by what he had revealed. She closed her eyes but it did not help, providing only a blank canvas for more visions of his demise.

What he had told her, given her in his soft tracings upon her as he carried her out of the temple's chamber of worship, echoed now in her mind. It was, first and foremost, a story of his gods, the Dekari gods, the gods of Mars—or at least some of them—who carried the planet's spirit and history, who saw to its cycles and renewals, who entered into relationship with the Dekari and their priests, and who could be kind and capricious, cruel and caring. It was the understanding of what happened below, in Laithos, now that the village had run its course. It was the knowledge that Grijval had held for many, many years—since even before he had first come upon the great stone edifice that once had stood near her, from which Laithos had been carved—that when the day came that the gods reclaimed Laithos, they too would take Grijval in the same manner, as they took all priests. It was the knowledge that in his final moments, he would await his own return to the earth in the great temple that he had built, all the other resident Dekari of Laithos already evacuated from the village and in transit to their next community, Grijval alone left to face the gods: a return to the same vulnerable place from which he had originally come to them in banishment, in search of the village for which he would serve the rest of his life in priesthood. It was the realization that this cycle continued indefinitely; that years ago, another young Dekari priest-to-be had been banished from a different village elsewhere on the planet, had found another great stone edifice, and had begun the work of carving a new village from it with the help of a special guild of carvers sent from Laithos upon demand of the gods; that upon the arrival of Laithos' population, she would become their new priest and help bring them into relationship with gods both old and new; and that some day many, many years in the future, she would suffer the same fate as Grijval.

The cycle did not account for Alinda, though. He had given her this knowledge with a certain sorrow, a deep weariness, and then he had given her his final revelation: that she was not alone as human on Mars. He did not know where those other humans were, only that they existed, scattered across the planet in a mixture of tiny communities and isolated individuals, the remnant survivors of political exile. Not wanting to lose her and certain that if she went in hunt of them she would die in the unforgiving Martian ecology, he had lied to her so long ago and condemned her to a loneliness and devastation that nearly had killed her.

But in his final moments, he had given her something else, as well: a small hope and glimmer of a possible new life. Tracing the knowledge upon her, he had gifted her the language of the god who had come to take Laithos—the same god who so long ago had told him of Alinda's arrival, who took an odd interest in humans, who had told him as well that other humans existed on Mars. While Grijval did not know where they lived, in his final act of saving her life he had also passed to her knowledge of a ritual to call upon the god who did.

A ritual he had received no permission to give her.

That could as well be her death as her salvation.

FIRST WATER, THEN ritual. Turning from her view of the crumbling Laithos, she traveled in a fog toward where she knew the main feeder canal for the village waited. Coming to the water, she knelt and drank, incautious, oblivious to the possibility of a raalech or any other predator. She splashed water on her face and struggled to focus, her mind a whirl of possibility and anger and sadness, of betrayal at what Grijval had kept from her for long torturous years. Yet a tentative forgiveness for his act stirred, as-yet-unrealized, deep within her. Far behind her came the rumbling crashes of Laithos' demise; glancing halfheartedly behind her, she saw a distant building fall. It no longer mattered; nothing about this past life of hers did. It was dead.

She stood and backed away from the canal, vaguely aware of the desert's whipping wind and the scrape of blasted sand against her skin. For a long time she stood, vision swimming, thinking back on the ritual Grijval had outlined in her mind, desperate to enact it right. Slipping her hand into her right pants pocket, she took from it the one thing she

254 • Vintage Worlds 2

had thought to retrieve from Laithos: her makeshift mirror, the polished stone. She stared into it and only the vaguest outline stared back, the closest she had to a reflection, the closest she had to another human being. After a moment, she realized she was weeping.

She put the stone back in her pocket and began.

THE RITUAL REQUIRED nothing but a single saaverña staff. Having none, and with no material available to fashion such a tool—with most of the land about her an expanse of sand and rock, and the vining arethus within the canal too slight to substitute for wood—she opted to use careful movement and her hands, hoping the god proved to be in a forgiving mood. Searching out four large rocks, she placed them in a diamond shape in the sand, equidistant, each three feet from the diamond's center. Standing outside the diamond, she removed her shoes and then stepped carefully within, striving to remain on her toes so as to minimize the impressions left in the sand. Bending and reaching, her balance at times wavering, she traced two twisting, interwoven lines from each rock to the diamond's center. *The village is the map*, Grijval had told her, and she thus worked off her memory of Laithos' layout to recreate the twisting paths she had walked so many times before—casting her memory back to the pathways that had run between each of the village's four public pools and the central temple in which Grijval had just met his grisly end. She never had known them as anything more significant than walking paths laid down at random by the initial carvers of Laithos; now she knew they signified much more: a geographic recreation of the Dekari creation myth, each pool a representation of one of the four original Dekari settlements and Laithos' central temple a representation of the birthplace of the first eight Dekari.

With four pairs of interconnected lines traced and connecting each rock back to the center of the diamond, the pattern appeared a jittery cross drawn by an unsure hand. Alinda stepped within and settled herself at the central point of the tableau, the place of Dekari birth. Taking several deep breaths to clear her mind, she called back to the ritual words Grijval had given her and began to speak them into the dry desert air. Her voice startled her: shaky and brittle, edged with fear. She nearly faltered, but then pushed forward, calling back so many years, across a solar system's impossible distance, to remember the respect and reverence with which she brought herself to the gods she had worshiped on Earth and striving to reenact the same, hoping it would translate to this planet and this deity.

She did not truly understand the Dekari words that tumbled from her lips, but understood the rough outline: the enactment of protection, the obsequious incantations, the recitations of history. Facing each rock—a representation of one of the original four Dekari villages, the same as the pools in Laithos—she traced its connecting lines upon her own body one by one, starting at her groin and winding her way to the top of her head. The first line represented a canal and the second the arduous trek of discovery taken by two of the first eight Dekari. As she traced them slowly upon her body, she spoke of Dekari creation: how eight of the creatures were made by the gods, two at a time; how the gods, working with the energy and substance of Mars, birthed the four pairs within a great hollow stone; and how each pair had been sent forth upon one of the four radiating canal lines to discover one of the first Dekari settlements, their journeys assisted by their god of birth and their path a meandering one that would bring them back again and again to the canal but would not keep them along its banks for long. She faced each of the four rocks in turn, tracing twice upon her body the paths of water and life. She praised the god upon which she called, speaking of the greatness of the god and her creations. Yet as she enacted the ritual, imaginings of human companionship tugged at her, threatening her concentration; furiously, she fought the anticipation and brought her focus back to the task at hand, to the god she hoped to bring before her.

As Alinda closed the ritual, its final words slipping into the tumultuous desert air and her hands now quieted, she let out a long, slow breath. Swaying for a moment, suddenly dizzy, she crumpled to the sand beneath her. Staring at one of the rocks, she felt the presence of no god. Far behind her she heard the continued crumbling of Laithos and, for a moment, the horror of the thought that she had performed a ritual to invoke a god far too busy to respond enveloped her. Just as quickly, it left. No, she had simply failed.

Closing her eyes, she fell back against the sand, lying flat against the warm ground with the four rocks resting about her. She lost herself to the sound of Laithos' destruction and the certainty that death would come for her next, in whatever form this godforsaken planet felt most appropriate. The world around her fuzzed and faded as exhaustion took her. The disturbed air eventually calmed. Slowly the light ceased to illuminate her eyelids as the planet turned and the sun went to rest. Hours passed—or what felt like hours. Alinda lost herself to crazed, half-dreamt fantasies as her mind unspooled all that had happened that day. And then, at the night's seeming darkest, the world bloomed with voice.

She knew this voice. In the temple, in Grijval's arms, it had come from the flowers. In Grijval's memories, at the great stone edifice that long ago had waited to form Laithos, it had come from the wind. Now it came from the sand and rock. It emerged from the ground to envelope her and take her into its embrace. Tumbling and mellifluous, daunting and formidable, it brought her a sharp focus. The voice wormed into her brain and flowered there. It burst visions within her—flashes of strange and unfamiliar Martian terrain, of towering trees that were not the saaverña specimens she knew so well, of swampy canals teeming with lurking, twisting creatures. And in that wet, humid place—that environment so inappropriate to the Mars she had come to know—a human. A man. Disheveled, sunk within himself, alone, but with a home.

Then more flashes, other strange terrain, though some of it more familiar than the first. Somewhere far, a place of horror called "The Darklands." Elsewhere—in the opposite direction?—a small cluster of rough-hewn stone structures, incompetent but sturdy, and a group of weary, wary outcasts. Twenty, perhaps thirty? The possibility shook and thrilled her. Somewhere else again—she struggled to map these places, to place them on some mental atlas of the planet—a couple living a hardscrabble existence, but thankful at least to have each other and to wake up each day yet alive.

Dear gods, she breathed. Or thought. She did not know what she did, and she realized in her sickening excitement that still she had not opened her eyes to the surrounding world, only her ears. And so she brought the dim, twin-mooned night into focus. It spread around her as a still, cool landscape, a vast difference from the daytime desert. She feared that upon opening her sight she would close off the voice of the god, but it was still there, still speaking a cascade of words Alinda did not quite understand but that wove visions into her mind regardless. The language felt adjacent to the intricate tracings of the Dekari, but different yet, born of some other element of Mars. It brought the fine grains of sand and cracked rock around her into a sharper focus.

Standing, retrieving her shoes, not quite knowing why, Alinda returned to the edge of the canal. The flow of water appeared heavier now, fuller. Phobos' misshapen visage reflected upon the water and for a long moment she lost herself in it, the small moon rippling with the water. Aside from the god's voice—quiet now, barely more than a murmur—the night was silent. The sounds of Laithos' destruction, she realized, were no more. She assumed that meant it had finished

falling and for a moment imagined Grijval's crushed, mangled body beneath the stone wreckage. Or perhaps there had
been little or no body left by the time the temple fell.

Then the voice of the god quieted, and the night grew
silent.

Startled, Alinda's heart began to pound. She glanced
around wildly in the nighttime dark, as though she might see
some fading outline of the deity. But nothing appeared and a
deep dread welled in her at the thought of being alone on this
planet, with no Dekari to comfort and keep her, no god to
look over her, no water or food at hand—just a depth of isolation beyond even the recurrent loneliness she had felt over
the years. Her acquiescence to death from just a few hours
ago no longer held; the thought of dying alone on an alien
planet terrified her. Her mind began to churn, trying to imagine some way to safety, straining to dredge some memory of
her earlier visions that might clue her to the location of one
of the other humans the god had shown her.

Just as quickly, though, something else arose to counter-
act her panic: a foggy mental vision of herself, trudging weary along the banks of a wide canal. It drifted into her mind,
depicting her no more clearly than the polished face of the
stone in her pocket. Yet she recognized herself, and saw in
the distorted outline of her form some ragged, limp creature
slung over her back. As she marveled at this vision, she felt
something as well—the sense of another human, far in the
distance and beckoning her home. Not in explicit knowledge
of her coming, but in some connected yearning, an unreal-
ized recognition of her approach cast across a great distance.

This too was the god speaking to her. Not in voice now,
but in instruction: for her to go forward along the canal, to
move with subtle guidance toward a reunion with another of
her kind. The offer hung tentative in the night air, as if this
god—*she*, Alinda could sense, though not so much in form
as in energy—could not decide if helping Alinda was a good

idea or not. Alinda sensed that this being could be capricious, that she might decide at some point deep in the desert that she no longer cared to guide and coddle this simple human, but Alinda held no other option. And the thought of guidance to another human, of rediscovery of a kind of companionship she had long since given up hope on—it both thrilled and terrified her, but demanded her in a way nothing had in years.

Aside from the stone, she carried nothing. Travel along the canal would at least promise her water, but she could not know what food she might eat. While she had explored the surrounding Martian terrain in the intervening years and learned a cross section of its fauna and flora—including some edible plants—she had few hunting skills and no weapon. She could not begin to imagine how she would eat. Yet the sense in the vision of some creature slung over her shoulder offered her a small confidence that the god might offer her still more in the coming days. Clearly it beckoned her forward along the canal; if it truly wanted to guide Alinda, then surely it would help her find food.

Alinda did not stand long in indecision. Offering a small thanks and holding fast to the vision of her travels, daring to believe in another human being waiting somewhere in the far distance and a renewed life in accompaniment, she began to walk. The cool, dark desert spread out around her, shadowed with distant cliffs and slopes. The night air hung still and calm. Off somewhere far on her right, the small scratch of some nocturnal animal skittered through the air while the comforting sounds of the canal's flow of water attended on her left. Above, the stars shone bright. With each of her soft steps she remembered Grijval's heavy ones so long ago, in search of his final home and in banishment from his first. She remembered his joy upon gazing up at the great cliff that would one day become Laithos and wondered what kind of similar transcendence might await her at some future point in some far off place. She wondered what, in the coming weeks and months and years, Mars yet promised her—and dared hope, at the end of her long journey, to discover some remaining small piece of Earth within which she might nestle, might rediscover what it was to be human so far from home.

Joel B. Jones is a playwright, performer, and improv teacher in Charlottesville, Virginia, where he resides with his wife and daughter. His interest in sci-fi goes back to the Traveller role-playing games run by his older brother in the late 1970s. He currently works as the co-director of Charlottesville's Big Blue Door, a theater and comedy troupe.

Joel Jones' contribution to the first Vintage Worlds *anthology, Death Songs of Saturn, introduced Captain Dido of the space sloop Antigone, one of six immortal travelers sent on a mission to our solar system from far beyond. In* Blood Prince of Venus *Dido is back, caught up in a complex and deadly game of interplanetary politics that involves the clades of Mars and the nobility of Venus in a conflict some will not survive...*

BLOOD PRINCE OF VENUS

Joel B. Jones

1.

ORIGIN SENT SIX of us across the galaxy to your solar system to study and report, but after Altinus died— after in a sense I killed him—I refused my mission. I dug the soma beacon from my neck so the others from Origin could no longer track me. I thought if I could be separate I would be free. But I found I couldn't stay apart. I could live without love and friendship, but I could not live without purpose. Maybe that's true of all creatures. It was true of Bast and her beloved prince of Venus. I think it was true of the dancing girl most of all.

Zkala was one of the refugees from a decimated Stlk village. I hoped to smuggle them off Mars to safety on Venus where Bast's prince had offered protection. I led them along the sunken ditches of the ancient collapsed waterways, hiding by daylight, moving by night.

Origin had grown the six of us to observe our surroundings and remember details, so I noted the girl with the others. She was dark-eyed, sullen, and haughty—even for a Martian. She was very agile, moving toe-to-heel noiselessly. She was of that age which humanoids in their various languages call a 'young woman', either to empower or exploit. But to me Zkala was a girl.

I'm no expert on Martian clades—there are hundreds— but I guessed she wasn't Stlk. Her skin had more copper in its redness, she carried two knives under her cloak, and the other women called her 'dancer' with contempt. She traveled with a Stlk war chief named Tnlaz, who seemed to love her and hate her.

By 0800 hours on the third day, we reached a Chtlu village on the shoulder of low mountains. My ship, *Antigone*, was hidden under holonet on the far side. I wanted to use the Chtlu tunnels to get to it. Once in orbit we would rendezvous with a transport hopper and head for Venus.

The Chtlus were at peace with the Stlks, but they were also at peace with the more-powerful Dyrellians—the clade who had destroyed the Stlk village—so it was a difficult negotiation. My being female for many in the Chtlu headman's crowded hut made it worse. Cup after cup of black calda, speeches in Martian Warcant invoking the Goddess, stacks of platinum bars. Then the breakthrough: Could I not take an octad of Chtlu warriors to Venus along with the Stlkmen? The wars in the valley below had disrupted trade and left the mountain villages poor. The octad could send money home. Should not the Chtlu benefit from this generous and rich prince of Venus? Are the Chtlumen not brave too?

We emerged with an agreement but the courtyard was empty. Shouts drew us to a disturbance around the corner. A crowd had gathered. Zkala, the dancer, was crouched, lip bleeding, struggling to free herself. Tnlaz held her wrists, shouting, "You will do as I say!" as he hit her in the face with his knee.

"Stop!" I shoved through the bystanders, broke Tnlaz's grip, and pushed him back. For a moment Tnlaz was too shocked to reply, but then his surprise hardened into rage that an off-worlder, an alien, a *woman*—would challenge him.

"How dare you, demoness!"

Zkala muttered a single insult, *shngwal*—'bloodless'—and lunged at Tnlaz, one of her knives arcing toward his face. I caught her wrist and swung her around, as the onlookers fell back.

I held her knife hand. "No, Zkala!" She glared, the clear dust lids of her Martian eyes giving them a fathomless blackness. She could have slashed me with the other knife, but did not.

"Demoness!" Tnlaz bellowed to the crowd as much as me. "You steal away a life, a life that is not yours! I challenge you to fight to the death according to the laws! Chtlus, lead us to your place of battle!" He tossed his belt and holster to a messmate.

"Foolish Stlkman!" said the old Chtlu headman, leaning on his brn-metal staff. "Did Captain Dido not lead you out of the jaws of your enemies? Is Captain Dido not taking you to Venus where you can earn platinum and fame?!"

"I will earn fame now by bringing death to this deathless one! Where is the fighting place?"

"Tnlaz," I said, "The Dyrellians may be following."

"I do not fear the Drlu! And I do not fear you!" He spit at my feet.

"Captain Dido is a woman and a guest," the headman offered, "Under Chltu protection!"

I didn't need protection. Origin had grown us to be quicker and stronger than the Martians, Venusians, and Earthlings who ruled the Primacy. In the two centuries we'd been in the system, we'd mastered their weapons and fighting styles as we had their languages. Moreover, our bodies regenerated from ordinary wounds. We were not deathless, as Tnlaz proclaimed, but we were close to it. The problem was, Martian honor was deathless too.

"If Captain Dido can drink black calda with men, she can fight with men!" said Tnlaz. "I am within my rights! Lead us!"

The crowd clicked their tongues in acquiescence and started moving with Tnlaz toward the edge of the village. They saw the absurdity of fighting someone whose ship they needed to get to Venus, and they surely knew, as Tnlaz knew, he didn't stand a chance. But to the proud Martian military clades eking out squalid lives in the shadows of the Primacy they once ruled, honor was all that was left. *A Martian lives by honor and tarzha* as it's said.

The old Chtlu headman had witnessed futility for three generations. He sadly leaned on his staff, spit pala juice, shrugged at me. "You should not have interfered. You dishonored him."

"What about her?"

"She is Krshi. Not Stlk or Chtlu. A tkra dancer. Young but well-known already. She would have survived." The headman shrugged again as if to say, *Too late now.*

So we followed the crowd through the village's twisting, sunken alleys between stone and pack-gravel hovels, until we emerged from the draped holonet into a clearing. Below us to the east the Martian plains stretched to the horizon. To our south high cliffs loomed of ancient carvings worn by wind and desecration. To the north the clearing broke into craggy moss-and-lichen-covered hills. Without holonet we were exposed to the sky. Dyrellian micromotes would be searching for us. Helimotes too. I wished I had equipment to counter but in the eighty cycles I'd spent on Mars, I had almost nothing left by my pistol. The crowd formed a semicircle on the western, village side. Tnlaz was already pacing on the north. He deftly flipped a scimitar to test its weight.

"Choose," said the headman. Another Chtluman held up several swords. Instead I handed him my pistol belt and grabbed the brn-staff from the headman. "Captain, that is not a sword!"

"It is enough," I said as I walked to take my place on the south. "Friend Stlkman, I meant no offense. Here we are not hidden by the holonet and the Dyrellians may be following. Instead of fighting let us go to Venus. *Who cannot forget their wrongs in the glistening joys of glory?*" This was a quote from a Martian epic.

"Demoness," he spat, "my glory is the justice of your destruction!"

He uncurled and charged, his scimitar whipping in a wild backhanded swing. It was bold, but too slow. Sidestepping, I lifted one end of the staff, deflecting his blade, and lowered the other end to sweep his legs. He tripped, fell, rolled, but sprung to his feet.

He attacked again, this time with the cross-armed *tvin-dru*. Again I laid him out. He rolled and rose, slashing wildly to drive me momentarily backward with repeated *tvin-mars*. Spin, slash, spin, slash. I could feel my lungs strain in the thin Martian air. I had given him enough to save face.

Pacing his rhythm, I waited between strikes, then hammered. I struck the nerve of his right forearm with the staff's top. In the instant when his muscles fought to recover, I dropped and swept his legs, and with an uppercut I dislodged his sword. As he hit the ground I knocked it out of reach, pinned his chest with my knee and held the staff across his collarbone to trap his arms.

He struggled to rise, but when he realized he was helpless, the rage in his eyes fell to panic.

"Goddess, kill me! I am without worth!" he howled.

The crowd wanted his death too, out of pity. Instead I jumped up and pulled Tnlaz to his feet.

"Friend Stlk, I praise the *dance of your dvin-mar*." I said. "I pray that we will be friends so that you may show me your technique." The crowd was confused. The humiliation of others is one of the few pleasures left to dying civilizations. Tnlaz was especially bewildered. But the Chtlu headman realized what I was doing and took my lead. He embraced Tnlaz as if he had won, praising him for daring to challenge a 'demoness'. Now having proven himself he could lead the brave young men to Venus and get rich! As I hooked on my belt and the headman talked, I noticed the girl Zkala was gone.

Three Chtlu women were pointing out to the east. They shushed children and held their windcloak hoods out to block the glare. One knelt and placed her palm on the ground. The headman stopped talking. All the Martians were now studying the plain.

Zkala was suddenly next to me, pulling my arm. "Drlu," she said, using their word for the Dyrellians. "We must go."

The Stlkmen were unshouldering IRP-7 inductor rifles and taking positions on the ridgeline. The Chtlumen who had their long guns—mostly old Martian radon rifles—took positions on the flanks. The women and children were melting back under the holonet into the village's sunken alleys. Not because Martians believed only men could fight but because they believed only men were expendable.

On the plains below two wisps of dust coughed and spat. Suddenly two spinning points split the ground. Metallic spiraling cones lurched upward becoming two armored sandtracks. They thrust in the air, front ends trembling, suspended an moment, and then crashed flat with a mechanical groan as their treads gripped the slinging sand. They rumbled toward us, low turrets lifting with stubby black cylinders. The guns recoiled. One of the Stlks to my left burst into bloody pulp before the cannon's boom reached us. The Stlkmen and Chtlumen returned fire. I wished again that I had equipment, a rifle of my own, canisters, RPGs, anything, but all I could do was fire my bannock pistol. The Martians are the finest marksmen in the solar system and gamely aimed into the yellow dust clouds for weaknesses in the sandtracks' armor. Chtlu warriors were returning now from the village with rocket launchers and spanner guns.

From the sandtracks two helimotes shot upward—one

immediately destroyed by a well-aimed shot, the other escaping skyward. A few Dyrellian infantry were jumping from the back of the sandtracks, but they only crept along behind the vehicles for cover.

"We must go!" said Zkala again, pulling my arm back toward the village shadows.

The headman was beside me now too. "Go. I will send the others."

The Chtlu would keep the sandtracks on the slope while the refugees escaped. Then they could nominally surrender and a few Dyrellian troops would be allowed to search the village. Everyone would pretend no Stlks were ever here.

Zkala pulled on me again. "We go now!"

"She cannot go," said the headman. "She is Krshi; she will have no protection."

"I must go!"

"The others will kill her."

An explosion hit one of the spanners. We had to move. "I will be her protection," I said finally. The headman sighed. Zkala pulled me under the holonet and we zigzagged through the village toward the village center. When we rounded a corner out of sight of the others, Zkala stopped us and turned.

"Don't be afraid," I said, "The Chtlu will hold them while we escape. The prince of Venus will help you, and I will help you. I promise."

Zkala seemed to stare into my soul as if the battle around us were a mere illusion compared to the grandeur and horror of the world she knew.

"I am Zkala, who serves the Goddess. The Goddess commands that I dance for the prince. The Goddess commands that I help you."

2.

EVEN BY MARTIAN standards Zkala was a religious fanatic

making the trip from Mars exhausting. She worshipped Shrgu. Long a minor goddess called Athlaka, a naming taboo a century ago had allowed the Unspoken One to grow in power, poaching the stories of other divinities as their epithets became her monikers. Zkala's speech was filled with them: Canal Digger, Beast Slayer, Moon Spinner. I'd heard of Zkala's clade, the Krshis, as itinerant entertainers, mystics, and thieves. About Zkala herself she revealed only that her parents were dead, she'd lived mostly in the shantytowns of the great Martian cities, she had a musician brother—a neuropenthe addict squatting somewhere in the slums of Earth—and she was a *tkra* dancer. I'd seen versions of such dancing but only in newsreels and diplomatic events with prop knives.

We'd come in off the Kang Tai space current, my sloop Antigone leading, the transport hopper behind. Venus was still only a blinking crosshairs on the naviscope. I'd signaled our position and we drifted now awaiting response.

The Kang Tai is the slowest and longest current of the inner planets. It approaches Venus from windward from the sun. Its length discourages shipping, which discourages pirates, which discourages Primacy naval patrols. Just empty space with the occasional rock, solar eddy, or drifting colony of tardigrades. The problem of smuggling, though, is always the arrival. For this I was counting on Ubastu.

Of the six of us sent by Origin, Ubastu was the first one to go native. She was not disloyal to our mission; she was indifferent to it. Compiling and transmitting reports was not something she saw a reason to do. Forty annos ago the Third Primacy realized that trying to subdue the six of us had contributed too much to the destruction of the Second Primacy. So they sent a delegation to barter a truce. Among them was Alawan-Tey, the youngest, most accomplished, and most handsome of Venus's seven *teydeevalic*, princes of royal blood, a step from Venus' queen.

Ubastu returned to Venus with Alawan-Tey, fell in love,

and eventually became his 'lifemate' as the Venusians call it.

Alawan-Tey made his own decisions—that's one reason Bast loved him—but through Bast he had agreed to hide the Martians. When a Martian military clade's village is destroyed the men often go off-world to fight as mercenaries, hoping to earn enough to rebuild or resettle. They were popular mercenaries for the clades were utterly loyal to their employers. "Follow orders like a Martian," as it's said. So I took pride in having found one place where the Stlks could follow their fighting creed without actually fighting. They would be folded into the Teylafaw palace guard, with the women and children settled on nearby Teymakan.

The transvox buzzed with a clear Venusian voice. "Foundry to iron shipment, foundry to iron shipment. Come in iron shipment. Over."

I grabbed the handset. "This is iron shipment."

"Proceed to delivery, iron shipment. Over and out."

I hailed the transport. "Shadow Two, Shadow Two, confirmation received."

The transport pilot was a Jovian savdo named Vanza, an adept smuggler I'd worked with often. She answered in her guttural voice of forced air (since Jovians lack vocal chords). "Copy that, Shadow One. Over." Our plan was to quickly enter at a high vector, furling sails only in the cloud layer, and ignoring all communications until we were in Alawan's territories.

I opened the *Antigone's* plasma sails one quarter, and the solar wind filled the radiant netting into bulbous spheres as the ship pulled forward. Behind, the transport did the same. Two ships meant if we ran into a Primacy patrol, I would engage while Vanza escaped with the Martians.

All the Martians but Zkala. I was stuck with Zkala since Tnlaz's messmates had threatened to kill her and as the headman warned me neither the Stlks nor the Chtlu would protect her.

I flicked the navmech switch. "Navmech, alert me when we reach Venus sector."

"Navmech obeys," said the mechanical voice of the autopilot.

I released the gyrogrips, unfastened from the chair, and slid down the bridge railing into the middeck below. Zkala was in the galley staring at the luminous screen of the infomech, absorbed in old holopix of Venusian royalty. She turned the electrofiche knobs till the smears of moving light solidified into each new oddity or scandal. I assumed her interest in the prince was the usual humanoid fantasies about the distantly powerful being less awful than the locally powerful. But I couldn't get her to say how she came to be with the Stlks—other than to tell me her goddess brought her.

When the six of us came to this system we struggled to conceptualize humanoid religion for most Venusians, Earthlings, and Martians are superstitious. Altinus saw humanoid religion as the contemptible fantasies of frightened and deluded children. Bast saw humanoid religion as a fun and intriguing game. Hamilcar insisted it was an expression of sublimated political rebellion. To me, since it was so common, religion must be a natural instinct, but since its details were so varied, there couldn't be much truth in it.

"We have a confirmation from my friend on Venus," I said to Zkala. "We'll be there soon."

"The Goddess told me this already," said Zkala, not looking up. She was gawking at a decade-old holopic of a 'dusk' ceremony from Alawan's court.

"Zkala, I'm sorry we didn't leave Tnlaz on Mars. I didn't want to endanger the others with another fight."

"I do not care where Tnlaz goes or stays." She turned her head away and spit on the deck.

"Zkala, please stop spitting on my ship."

Zkala sighed as if I had said this too many times—which I had--and half-heartedly rubbed the wet spot with the ball of her foot. She pointed in prurient disgust at a blue-skinned, nearly-naked man on the screen. "That is Prince Alawan-Tey?"

Venusians show emotion in the color changes and patterns in their skin. Because of that and the tropical heat most Venusians wear only loincloths. The ruling classes add a long sheer vest, a *malalana*, to give their emotions a plausible deniability while seeming to be hiding nothing. (So it is with ruling classes everywhere). To the Martian military clades bare skin is abhorrent, a sign of humiliation. *Only animals and the dead show their flesh.* I tend to agree with the Martians, but there is something about Zkala's confidence that made me want to argue.

"Zkala, Martians long ago went through a period of dressing like that, at least near the equator. Those ancient carvings on cliffs and temples were defaced because they showed nakedness."

"The Nameless One saved us from that, and taught us what was shameful and forbidden."

"According to the writings doesn't the Nameless One also forbid dancing?"

"You cannot interpret the will of the Water Bringer because you are not her obligant."

"Maybe you can't interpret the will of the Water Bringer since you can't read."

"I don't need to read. The Moon Spinner speaks to me directly."

"By the way, it's either Prince Alawan or *Alawan-Tey*. 'Tey' means prince in Venusian." I pointed to the non-Venusian woman in the holopic. "That's Alawan's consort Ubastu. My friend Bast. She has arranged our landing. We have her to thank for saving your Chtlu and Stlk friends."

"I have no Chtlu or Stlk friends. I am Krshi!" Zkala turned her head and spat again.

"Stop spitting on my deck!"

"Do you not clean your deck with water?"

"*Antigone* is *my* ship. *My* ship. *My* rules."

"Ubastu is a demoness like you?"

Here was one problem with religious ideation. When Zkala told me her brother was a neuropenthe addict, she used the Martian word *bzra*. That's the most common word among Martians for drug addicts, but it literally means 'ghost'. Martians don't consider addicts to be actual ghosts; they simply pressed a vivid old word into service for a current condition. But how much of that was true of the Martian word *pathu*— 'demon'? *Pathu* seems to carry more of its original supernatural connotation than *bzra*, but how much more? And the goddess? An amorphous force, a flesh-and-muscle person, something in between?Did Zkala truly think the goddess slew the two-headed beast and threw its skulls into the sky to become the Martian moons?

"You do know I'm not an actual demoness, Zkala. We were sent here from the far side of the galaxy by non-humanoids, but still biological creatures like you. Our bodies were made to regenerate, to regrow, in order to survive the long journey, and to change gradually so that we would fit with Martians, Earthlings, and Venusians. Origin wanted us to record information about your worlds and send it back. But we stopped, so now we are just here. Like you."

"You are not like me," she said calmly. She pointed to the screen. "I had heard the prince is sickly."

"He might be now. I don't have more recent VIMs."

VIM originally stood for 'Verified Information *Matrix*' but changed to 'Verified Information *Medium*' when one conglomerate bought the contract from another conglomerate in exchange for a share of Neptune. VIMs were the Primacy's latest newsreels, announcements, census records, maps, legal dictates, directories, and public redactions.

"Zkala, did the Goddess tell you that the Dyrellians would attack the Stlk village? Or that I would be coming there?"

Zkala turned from the screen to stare at me, as if looking for something. "Some say you demons cannot die. Others say one of you has already died."

"Altinus died. He died on Saturn. He and I loved one another."

"You will avenge his death?"

"I can't. I'm the one who killed him."

She was not shocked by this the way others are, and I felt gratitude to her for it. "You made a mistake not to kill Tnlaz," said Zkala, as if a sisterly confession. "Now he must live in disgrace. If you had killed him, one of his kindred could have avenged him and tested himself against you. Now no one can."

"Zkala, first, why would I want to kill his kindred one after another forever until one of them happens by some fluke to kill me? And second, don't these feuds harm Mars more than the Primacy and the Dyrellians combined? How many Martians have to die for the sake of revenge killings and vendettas?"

She looked at me as if I were an idiot. "The same number as would die without the revenge killings and vendettas."

"But I mean, individual Martians would live longer."

"They would exist longer. The Goddess does not command that we *exist*; She makes us exist so that we might *live*."

The mechanical voice of Navmech saved me: "Approaching Venus Section. Approaching Venus Section..."

"Strap in here. Or follow me."

Zkala followed me up the ladder to the bridge deck. I made sure she took the observation chair behind the copilot chair so she couldn't reach the controls. I didn't trust her.

"If you spit on my bridge I'll jettison you."

3.

Venus was a growing disk on the central videoscope. On

the smaller surrounding screens the mech scanners identified and magnified distant military frigates, gun decks, orbiting toroids, and the criss-crossing swarms of commercial shipping. Venus was one of the three ruling planets of the Primacy and had the space traffic to prove it.

"Navmech release controls."

"Navmech obeys."

I raked the gyrogrips to test the helm and hit the switch to ignite the sloop's jets. In the rear videoscope I saw the transport hopper doing the same. Our course would bring us down across the northern hemisphere bearing southwest, a path far from the toroids and gun decks, so it was only a matter of being lucky with patrols.

"Time to run the gauntlet."

As we accelerated the videoscope magnifications clicked downward to keep the planet on the screen. Then I tripped the cowling levers to open the cupola armor, and through the lucetine bow windows the planet engulfed the horizon. We raced past the distant ships, stations, satellites. Hailing signals lit our transvox panels, gauges bouncing in amber squibs as voices questioned us in Groupspeak and Venusian:

"Unidentified ship. Please identify yourself...!"

"Attention sloop. You are at full speed with sails out...!"

"Unidentified sloop. You are violating Primacy protocols...!"

I could see on my right, as we plunged into the upper atmosphere, Zkala's fingers gripping her chair arms, and it pleased me far too much, this rare sight of Zkala rattled.

As the clouds engulfed us I furled sails, but the jets and gravity still drew the ship downward. Down. Down. Now I too felt panic. The clouds brought memories of Saturn, of Altinus' death, his doomed eyes glaring at me in fear and confusion. Then in an instant we were beneath the cloud layer and I hit the jets full to slow descent. The transport hopper appeared behind. Darker thoughts vanished in the panorama of Venus. Below us stretched to the bent-haze horizon was heaving, slate-green ocean. Only occasional islands broke the watery expanse.

Zkala was stunned. "All that is water?"

"All of that is water."

We leveled and were soon speeding beneath the gray clouds, passing over seas and more islands scattered in strings and clusters like thrown pebbles. On the larger islands volcanic cones rose above the jungle. At their rims ancient basalt statues had been usurped by pteradons for their nests. Further down the lush slopes villages of stone and wicker crouched and clung. Occasionally a rotorcraft hovered over the trees where the sheerka fruit was yet unharvested, the last crop before the long night. At the shores the jungle finally unspooled into dense coves, coral shoals, and sand beaches, and out past the breakers were patches of light-green and dark-green, the kelp berries and sea beans, rolling on the waves, being harvested by squat, tub-like boats.

There is no time on Venus, it is said. The planet's climate is tropical and oceanic, so it varies little from pole to equator. The sky is always overcast, so the stars aren't tracked, nor is there any moon. Even the sun is but a barely-moving smudge of light, crossing the sky only 150 times in the life of the luckiest Venusian. *On Venus a day is the only year.* So goes the joke. But it is that slow daily cycle that orders everything.

I had mentioned this to Zkala before, but it was the most difficult transition for off-worlders so I alluded to it again. "Be warned, Zkala, Venus turns slowly. When it finally gets to night you'll have darkness for about 90 straight Martian days."

"I have visited Rshgu." Rothak in classical Martian, a city near the Martian arctic where it was dark for much of the year.

By the geometer we were in Alawan's territory now. The islands were larger, closer together, busier. The basalt statues shared the volcanic rims now with power plants, the slopes in places cut to make paths for pipes. Out at sea were many more boats, bounding catamarans piled with cargo, raised hydrokoras skating on streaks of foam. Through skies above the larger islands flitted small rotorcraft—mostly TG-90s and other 'skimmers' as they were called—from dirigibles aloft to coastal docks to cliff-side landing decks.

Skimmers were common on Venus because they could take off vertically from such tight spaces. They were simple grav-plate disks little about two meters in diameter with four moveable propeller housings. The pilot stood or leaned against a seat backing in an open frame and piloted the skimmer with gyrogrips like a spaceship. On their undercarriages skimmers could mount winches, davits, or mechanical arms depending on the weight or type of cargo they were moving.

Zkala was watching a group of skimmers hover and dart like a swarm of Martian sand gnats. "Those people are foolish to fly exposed." She used the Martian word kntumu, which has the connotation of 'exposed to gunfire'.

"In the major principalities there is so little violence that most Venusians don't carry weapons. Not even knives. Honor killings and feuds are unheard of. And illegal."

Zkala stared at me like I was insane, and after 80 cycles on Mars it seemed quaint and far-fetched even to me. "They do say there are isolated islands that are wild, and in ancient times there was constant war," I offered as if the exceptions would help prove the rule, "But right now Venus is at peace and the Venusians want to keep it that way. Don't expect Venus to welcome Martians even with the prince's blessing. Everything has to be discreet."

Zkala studied the passing scenery. "How far is the prince's island?"

"Teylafaw. We should be there about 0600 hours. We're already in his territory. I charted the course to cross open sea and minor principalities so we'll attract as little attention as possible."

Administration of the major archipelagos was divided among seven major or 'blood' princes. 'Blood' was not because the princes were *descendants* of royalty (though distantly many were) but because the seven blood princes were the queen's nominal mates, the *progenitors* of royalty.

I find all humanoid sexuality disgusting, but Venusian especially so. The seven princes are officially hosted at the queen's palace during its prolonged dusk. In the Shin-am-keer, the ritual of the 'unknown chambers', the queen invites each into her private rooms in an order chosen by lots, each turn marked by a water clock. When all seven princes have done their reproductive duty, they return to their own territories and none of them, nor any other Venusian, can be certain who is the father of the next queen. In their home territories the princes have their own 'lifemates'—wives in all but name—who bear their own children. In ancient times, when the queen died, every prince was expected to throw himself into his local volcano in a public ceremony. Newborn male offspring of the queen and female offspring of the princes were also thrown in. And when a prince died before the queen, if his lifemate had no young child to raise, she too was expected to give herself to the fire.

In reality, at least in recent times Third Primacy *Shin-am-keer* visits are reputed to be spent playing card games, old princes and lifemates peacefully retire, and children born of the 'wrong' sex are quietly found careers in the bureaucracy. But the ancient, supreme willingness of the princes to do their duties in the queen's bed or on the volcano's rim is the founding myth of their legitimacy.

Finally, amid the din of the transvox I heard what I was waiting for.

"Repeat. This is Teylafaw wing of Venus Command." I turned up the volume dial. "This is Teylafaw wing of Venus Command. You have entered Teylafaw airspace. Please identify yourself. Over."

I hit the reply: "This is the far-running sloop. Repeat. This is the far-running sloop. I have the iron shipment." We slowed our advance. Soon on the horizon I could make out the archipelago of Teylafaw, Teymakan and the smaller islands.

The voice returned: "Welcome to Venus, Captain Dido! Stand by for escort to the capital. Over."

I was surprised my name was spoken on a public frequency—this was supposed to be discreet—but Ubastu must have a reason. "Thank you, Teylafaw wing. Standing by." I flipped the switch position. "Shadow Two, Shadow Two, standby for approach. Over."

"Copy, Shadow One," said Vanza in her forced-air speech. "See you on deck. Out."

We slowed further by engaging the grav levels and swiveling the jets until both ships hovered over the open water. This would use a lot of fuel and I had hoped to get Vanza and her transport to space again quickly, but she could siphon from the *Antigone* if necessary, and I'd get fuel from Bast. It was a minor problem. I let myself stop worrying. I had nearly done it. The Martians would be safe.

Twenty skimmers had lifted off from a hydrokora sailing below. Coming closer they were identifiable as TG-90Ms with military insignia and light arms slung next to the controls. On their undercarriage they dangled retractable metal tendrils trailing as they flew so they looked like Earthling jellyfish. The blue-skinned Venusian pilots were visible in their breechcloths with gloves, helmets, and elbow and forearm guards, not worn for protection against weapons but against cable burns. Unlike their Martian counterparts, Venusian women could serve in military forces, and I wondered what Zkala thought of the female pilots.

One skimmer flew directly in front of my cupola, its pilot deftly maneuvering with an easy touch of the gyrogrips. The pilot was a tall, muscular, and handsome Venusian wearing an officer's breastplate. He motioned with hand signals for me to follow. The skimmers started ahead, eight surrounding the sloop and six the transport, and the others flying along our flanks, escorting us toward the volcanic cone in the distance. There was nothing intimidating about skimmers as military craft—indeed after so long on Mars it was a relief to be around a vehicle that I knew couldn't hurt me—but they flew so close to the ship I worried about hitting one. As we approached the taller Teylafaw, we passed over its larger, flatter sister.

"That's Teymakan," I said, pointing to our right. "On the north shore there is Teymakan City. They'll probably land us at the spaceport there. Lots of traffic so we won't stand out. Remember when we disembark, we want to attract as little attention as possible."

Zkala nodded.

As we neared the spaceport, I prepared to slow, but the TG-90s in front kept going, and the leader sternly motioned us on. Maybe we were circling before landing, but as we headed out over the inlet between Teymakan and Teylafaw no one turned. I could feel Zkala's look. "I guess they changed plans," I said meekly.

We crossed the channel to Teylafaw. On the shore facing Teymakan were docks and a town piled up the slope. We ascended, gradually circling clockwise around the volcano's conic slope. Above us near the summit was the power plant. The Venusians used pipes with gravity coils and pressure hoists to pump seawater into the crater where the heat turned it to steam. The steam ran turbines—mostly Greer vaporware units—creating the planet's electricity.

As we rose above the volcano, passing the statues on the rim, we could see in the mouth cables, turbines, and pipes bridging and bisecting the billowing steam. There was something new above all this, a defensive tower with two SAM-casters, probably Divul-3s, guarded by mounted strakers. The strakers were intended to cover the slopes below while the Divul-3s could fire missiles at anything passing to or from orbit. The tower was poorly placed for the strakers. Whoever placed it probably had the right idea but no military experience. But the SAMcasters were deadly. And then I hated how time in war zones poisoned everything—I couldn't look at a peaceful island without denigrating its defenses.

We circled farther westward, descending now, corkscrewing clockwise as we passed over a series of warehouses, a guard station, an orchard. I wondered again why were they bringing us in this way, visible to the entire island? It all seemed wrong. We were heading right to the palace. I caught the first glimpse of a gleaming new landing pad jutting out over the far side of the island.

The skimmers rushed ahead descending over the ridgeline out of sight. As we cross the ridgeline ourselves, suddenly there was a boom.

Instantly my left hand swept to unlock the forward guns and I started to press the trigger. But before I had a target, the air around us filled with unspooling colorful streamers. A shout went up. The far end of the entire landing platform that now came into view was packed with cheering crowds. On high poles hung electronic ampliboxes blaring music. A line of blue-skinned palace guards stood between the crowds and the open landing area. In front of them on the landing pad itself was written in Venusian glyphs:

"WELCOME MARTIANS!"

The cannons boomed again and more colorful streamers unspooled in the air.

"You said Venusians would not welcome us."

"I guess they've changed their mind."

4.

THE AIRLOCK DECOUPLED, hissed, and slid open. The tumid

Venusian heat and noise engulfed us heavy and wet, thick and slow. I reluctantly picked up my duffel, Zkala looped a satchel strap over her shoulder. We stepped out into the chaos. The band was blaring a Martian folk song of the Grsh clade, incredibly inappropriate since they were enemies of Stlks, but fortunately almost unrecognizable played on electronic sonoharps.

We descended the gangway. A distorted voice echoed over the ampliboxes. "Welcome Captain Dido and the Martians!" The row of Venusian palace guards lifted their piezospears and snapped to attention. The tips of the spears danced in purple sparks. Behind them to the left the cheering Venusian commoners stamped and waved strings of colorful jengi flowers. On a riser in the center Venusian noble families stood fluttering leaf-shaped fans whilea dozen Primacy dignitaries clapped. To the right, a roped-off section of Primacy chroniclers pointed their holocams.

Everywhere was the shock of bare Venusian blue skin. Male and female guards in breechcloths, commoners and obligants in simple loincloths, nobles in decorated loincloths somewhat covered by their *malalanas*. Only among the dignitaries and chroniclers were there Earthlings sweating in pinsonweave suits.

Behind us the transport hopper was perched high on its landing gear like a disporlian crab. Vanza's greenish, tusked head was visible in the cockpit—laughing at me probably. I had told her to get back into orbit at the first sign of trouble and she'd replied that *she'd been paid*—pirate slang for don't worry, you're on your own. The transport's underlift was lowering with the rest of the Martian belongings covered by a tarp so no one could see it was military gear. Down the transport's gangway stumbled the first dozen confused Martians, Stlkmen brandishing their guns. I needed to get their guns stowed as quickly as possible.

Suddenly, a voice was so familiar it cut through the din. I turned to the crowds to search for it.

"Di! Didona!"

A tall, beautiful woman descended the steps from the dignitaries' platform. She was not Venusian but dressed in the loincloth, jewelry, and wispy white malalana of the nobles.

This was Ubastu.

Origin grew all our bodies to be attractive to the Martians, Venusians, and Earthlings who ruled the Primacy, but Ubastu was the most beautiful. And she enjoyed her beauty thoroughly. Altinus had loved his looks for the power it gave him over others. Pabil and Nanshe only had interest in one another. Hamilcar and I were unsettled by the attention our appearances brought. But for Ubastu beauty was a feast that she delighted utterly in, as she delighted in wealth and fame, like a wide-eyed Venusian child discovering a glistening *kanshina* shell in a happy cove.

She started across the landing platform toward us accompanied by several palace guards, one holding the taut leash of a pair of massive scylas, cousins of the Earth's therapsids from the second primordial exchange. Two other guards carried spears. A tiny Mercurian in a parka and spherical guide helmet hurried after. Mercurians were often employed for their language abilities.

"Didona!" she called in Venusian as she reached us and pulled me into an embrace! "Di, oh Di, it's so good to see you!"

Over the amplibox the distorted voice announced, "Ubastu-Tem has greeted Captain Dido!" Another cheer went up.

I switched to our Origin language: "Bast, this was supposed to be discreet!"

"I couldn't resist a little party. I've missed you so much! Where is your soma beacon? I'm sorry to hear about Altinus. I can't wait to talk about *everything*! You've carried your own bags? Who carries their own bags?" She turned the Mercurian. "Summon two porters. And let everyone know that Captain Didona has the run of the palace. She is my sister and can go anywhere and do anything she wants!"

"Yes, Ubastu-Tem."

Zkala shrank from the huge Scylas trying to nuzzle her. Bast noticed and barked a command at the beasts. They instantly sat back on their haunches and licked their fangs through the gaps in jewel-inlaid muzzles. Bast turned to the guard with the scylas. "They're scaring this woman; take them away!"

"Yes, Ubastu-Tem." The guard bowed and retreated with the beasts.

This drew Bast's attention to Zkala. "And who is this utterly exquisite creature?" she said to me in Venusians. "Wherever did you find her?" Bast brushed her fingertips against Zkala's face. Zkala winced and I pulled Bast's hand away quickly.

"Please don't touch the Martians."

"With those knives I'd best not," laughed Bast, notiing the tikras in Zkala's belt. "Oh, I love her! What a wonderful little find!"

Noise and wind interrupted us, as the commander's skimmer lowered twenty meters way. Its segmented metal tendrils curled into a tight bundle as the four rotors eased it to rest on the deck. The haughty young Venusian jumped down.

The amplibox voice rang out, "Protector Fassan returns!" Another cheer.

Bast embraced him as he approached. Like all Venusians the commander's face was nearly expressionless, but the skin along the side of his thighs and abdomen paled and swirled in Venusian embarrassment. Two porters came and took my bag but Zkala refused to let them take her shoulder satchel. Bast told them to ready a room for Zkala next to mine.

Behind us there was confusion at the baggage pallet. A skimmer was aloft with the claw end of its metal tentacles open to break up the pallet and other skimmers hovered behind with hooks underneath to move the contents, but the skimmers were afraid to approach and the Martians wouldn't back away, not sure what was happening. I needed disarm them but didn't dare leave Zkala alone here. Meanwhile all around was still chaos.

"Ubastu," I said in Origin language, "There shouldn't have been all this."

Bast laughed. She bowed to Zkala with her hands out in Venusian style, and spoke in flawless HIgh Martian. "I am Ubastu, the lifemate of Prince Alawan. Welcome to Venus."

Zkala replied in Warcant, awkwardly trying to imitate the gesture. "I am Zkala of the Krshi..."

"Krshi?! I thought we were only getting Stlks and we have a Krshi! You are famous prophets and magicians, if I remember?! Tonight, you must tell the prince's fortune!"

"I do not cast the sacred bones nor read the skies. I am a dancer," said Zkala with pride, as if Ubastu should have heard her reputation. "The Goddess commands me to dance for the prince."

"Then you must dance! Oh, the prince will love you!" Ubastu turned and switch to Venusian. "She's a dancer, Fassan! She'll dance for the prince!"

"No," I said in Venusian.

Zkala glared. She didn't speak Venusian but she got the gist. "I will dance for the prince," she repeated.

"Absolutely not. She's a knife dancer, Bast."

"I will dance!" she repeated and spit on the pavement.

"Stop spitting!"

Bast was very amused. "Oh, she can spit wherever she wants! Let's all spit!" Bast spat herself in solidarity. The commander's skin darkly swirled in disgust. Bast noticed.

"Fassan doesn't agree. He's more stubborn than a scyla, aren't you, Fassan!" She absently ran a finger over his forearm. "Protector Fassan, I present Captain Dido and her friend, the esteemed dancer Zkala of the Martian Krshi. Protector Fassan is the commander of our palace security."

Fassan bowed his head. "Captain Dido, welcome to Venus." He pointedly ignored Zkala. I had never read the name Fassan in the VIM logs of military or police commanders, and he seemed awfully young to have the rank.

Behind us some of the Martians and the Venusians were still at an impasse.

"Bast, I need to go deal with..." I started to say, but Bast beat me to it.

"Nonsense! Fassan is more than capable," she said, "Fassan, don't you think it might be a good idea to welcome the Stlks?"

Fassan bowed. "Yes Ubastu-Tem."

"Wait," I said. "I can go too, if you wish. You must disarm them and stow their weapons. The clades take pride in always following orders, so if you command them directly, they'll disarm, but..."

"Protector Fassan is more than capable," said Bast.

"Also," I said. "There are eight Chtlus. It's a mountain clade. But you'll want to put them in a different unit."

"We were only expecting Stlks and you bring us Krshi and Chtlus too! Do Chtlus speak the same language as the Stlks? Fassan has been learning the Martian languages, haven't you Fassan? He's made amazing progress."

"Martian languages are primitive and therefore inferior but interesting," said Fassan in stilted Martian, looking directly at Zkala. He said this arrogantly, but his skin swirled in signs of embarrassment—whether self-conscious about his linguistic abilities, or unsettled by her, I don't know.

He bowed again and set off towards the Martians. Bast's eyes followed him, and I noticed that Zkala's did too.

Then locking arms with Zkala and me, Bast led us to the palace. The single guard and the Mercurian followed.

"How are Pablisag and Nanshe?" she said in Groupspeak,

"I miss them so much."

Of the six of us from Origin Pabilsag and Nanshe had settled on Mars, running a combination hospital, orphanage, and refugee camp in the ruins of one of the ancient cites. It was Pabilsag and Nanshe who asked me to get the Stlks off planet.

"You may have endangered them by making this public, Bast."

"Nonsense. Now you *must* let me know if you need anything after the journey. Neuropenthe?"

"No."

"Let's pause here and wave." At the guard line we stopped. Ubastu waved toward the cheering crowds and Zkala and I stared stupidly.

"Bast, speaking of needing anything, the transport pilot may want to leave, so I'd like to get her refueled and cleared by your air command. I noticed the SAMcasters. Also fuel for the *Antigone* too if possible, and medicine, ammunition, food supplies, micromotes, holonets..."

"The SAMcasters were Fassan's idea. He is doing a wonderful job learning about tactics and strategies and that sort of thing. I'll call the tower about the transport. But I'm not sure about the weapons. There are some of those nosey Primacy people here wanting to speak with you. Mitigators or Dispositors—so many police these days, who can keep up?"

"Bast, if you hadn't made this a public event, the Primacy agents might not have heard about it!"

"Darling, I am sorry for the ceremony, but we just had to express our enthusiasm for your visit—we're so excited!—plus we need a good event. Something positive for the VIMs."

"I'm shocked that your people are so happy to have Martians here."

"Oh, we paid them," said Bast waving toward the cheering crowds. "We told them the Martians would pay off their taxes for them."

"We cannot," said Zkala. "We have no money."

Bast laughed. "Of course not! We just told them that. Public relations, it's called."

The phrase and the scene around us brought to mind that I'd seen Fassan in VIM newsreels of rotorcraft races.

"Bast, was Fassan a rotorcraft racer?"

She beamed. "Three regional championships! That's how the prince and I met him."

"You promoted a skimmer pilot to be commander of your entire palace guard?"

"Di, darling, everyone has to start somewhere." Then she looked at me again. "You really don't keep up with the news, do you? The prince and I adopted him. Fassan is our son."

Before I could react the chroniclers had rushed forward on cue to surround us, shoving their holocams in our faces. Bast told them in Groupspeak that I was a hero who had once saved an entire Primacy garrison from Jovian Cossacks in Saturn Section, single-handedly captured thirty pirates on Pallas, and now rescued eighty innocent Martians from the barbaric civil wars of that unfortunate planet. All lies. The Chroniclers, ignoring Zkala, who had little idea what was going on, spewed questions at me:

"Captain Dido, can you describe how you felt when they learned of the Prince's generosity?"

"Captain Dido, how would you respond to critics who say the Martians need to learn to help themselves?"

"Captain Dido, what will bring an end to these unprovoked attacks against the Dyrellians?"

"Everyone please!" Bast interrupted, "Captain Dido is very tired from her long heroic journey. The Prince will have a statement at the feast tonight." Bast took our arms and whisked us onward passing beneath an arching roof of spiral-form metalwork into a long vaulted entrance hall of the palace. In the last glance behind us Fassan was giving orders to the Martians. They still had their guns.

5.

ALAWAN'S PALACE SPRAWLED like a stranded sea creature flung on a hill. A central, domed rotunda, surrounded by a smaller domed chambers was the body, and from this what Venusians called 'vine-arms'—*luma-kis*—spread out like long, undulating tentacles. Each luma-ki consisted of a corridor with rows of stilt-perched rooms on both sides, and a veranda running along the outside of the rooms. Alawan's palace had a shorter, central luma-ki extending to the landing platform gate. Two longer luma-kis form a bow around a swath of the volcano's jungle-covered slope. My suite was next to Zkala's near the bow's southern tip. From the veranda the view up the slope to the volcano's rim was obscured by the thick vegetation, but I could see Venusian palace guards ocassionally patrolling the jungle with leashed syclas.

The suite had a comfortable sitting room that ran from the hall to the veranda. Off the right a third door opened to a small dressing room with a bedroom on the veranda side and a bathroom on the other.

Obligants came to ask if they could help with anything. I gave them my clothing to launder, and stowed the duffel in the bedroom. On Mars a fine, gritty dust coats every person, place, and thing, and I looked forward to being clean.

I showered and felt the wars and death and hardness of Martian life wash away.

As I stepped from the shower to dry off, I heard a chime. A voice reverberated from both the hall and outside. "Prince Alawan cordially invites you all to feast in the rotunda at 1900 hours." This was Bast's doing. She had not only adopted Primacy time, she had installed those infernal ampliboxes everywhere. An array of clean sovyas hung in the dressing room. I pulled one over my head, and still drying off, I stepped out into the sitting room.

On the low stone table rested a black case. In the chair

behind it sat an Earthling. A Martian stood behind him. Both sweated in pinsonweave suits. The Martian looked broad and tough, and wanted everyone to know it. The strap of a shoulder holster crossed his chest where the coat opened to show he was armed. The Earthling looked frail. He wore on his nose two glass lenses joined by wire frame to compensate for the poor eyesight so common among Earthlings. He fiddled with the brim of a hat on his lap.

"Mitigator Lin," I said, "What an unpleasant surprise."

The Earthling politely rose and nodded his head. "Hello Captain Dido. I hoped to ask you a few questions. I am sorry to intrude." Mitigator Lin of the Inquiry and Redaction Bureau was not as corrupt as most Primacy agents, which he seemed to consider a tremendous accomplishment.

"Ubastu-Tem told me you wanted to speak to me," I said, "But she didn't say you'd break into my room."

"We did knock, Captain," said Lin politely, "But there was no answer. I am sorry."

"Your flunky doesn't look sorry." I nodded toward the Martian. "I see the Primacy has its usual quality recruits."

"Sit down and shut up," barked the Martian. I remained standing.

Lin smiled. "I was about to introduce my associate, Submitigator Tarl."

Submitigator Tarl said nothing. Lin opened the black case and took out a small dark metal sphere about .2 meters in circumference. "Captain Dido, this is an Origin scouting sensor, I believe. As I understand it you and the other five were sent in hemistasis. These devices were shot ahead and returned with genetic information. That information was used to modify you so that when you arrived you looked like us."

"Is any of that a question?"

Tarl started to come toward me but Lin gently stopped him with a palm. "Now now, Tarl," he said. "Captain Dido, if these sensors were gathering information and returning to you so long ago, why was this found near Neptune?"

I touched the sphere with my fingertips but could detect no micropulses. It did look newer than I would have expected but there was no telling what Primacy scientists had done to it. "Thousands of these were sent out, Lin. It probably malfunctioned and never returned. Anyway, this one is dead."

"Lifemate Ubastu said the same thing."

It unsettled me that Bast hadn't warned me that she'd been questioned, or that they might come into my rooms without permission, or that they had a sensor, but I tried to show nothing.

Lin put the sphere away and held up the case until Tarl took it. Then Lin sat again. "There were six of you, yes, Captain? Lifemate Ubastu is here. You are here temporarily. Pabilsag and Nanshe reside on Mars. Commodore Altinus died, or so you've told us. Where is the one named Hamilcar?"

"I don't know."

"Lifemate Ubastu said she thought he was dead. But you say you don't know."

"If you already questioned Lifemate Ubastu, why are you questioning me?"

"I trust you more." He took off the lenses from his eyes and polished them with a cloth from his pocket. "My final question is, may we search your ship?"

"No."

Lin returned the lenses to his nose. "I really do apologize, Captain, but my superiors are quite explicit in this matter. Let me assure you we are not here to investigate your illegal smuggling of Martian refugees in violation of Primacy Valued Practices."

"Which I never agreed to follow."

"Nor are we here to raise the question of why Admiral Grsh still believes you destroyed a military battery of trebuchets on the rings of Saturn."

"There couldn't have been a military battery on the rings

of Saturn since that would have been a violation of Primacy Valued Practices."

Lin laughed. Behind him Tarl clenched his fists.

"Captain," said Lin, "We realize that your ship has devices that will explode if we try to break in, and we defer to your superior technology. But I have been expressly instructed to inform you that nothing prevents us from dumping your ship in the bottom of the nearest ocean trench and covering it with hydraulic Venusian concrete. If we cannot search your ship we may prevent you from flying it."

"That would make us enemies, Mitigator Lin, and I don't die very easily. Do you?"

"Captain Dido," Lin looked uncomfortable now. "I am also expressly required to inform you that if your friends on Mars contributed to your smuggling, the Primacy may stop permitting their charitable efforts." Tarl smiled as if it were a great joke.

"Tell me, Lin, why do rulers and their flunkies always do this? The Primacy controls 90% of everything that's worth anything in the solar system. Your rulers have everything they could reasonably want, and all they have to do is maintain enough stability that people can live their lives. Maybe every now and then they have to step in and fix a problem or two, but it's not like they don't have the free time. Why can't empires ever leave things alone? Are your bosses just bored? Or do they really think creating enemies helps them rule?"

"I assure you, Captain, I do not want you for an enemy. But I'm wondering what you want?"

"So you can buy me?"

"So I can understand you."

"Here's something you can understand... I want you out of my rooms." I slid open the door.

Lin stood and bowed his head. "I am truly sorry that our meeting did not go more auspiciously."

He walked out and put on his hat. Tarl walked after him,

glaring up at me as he pushed by: "I'll see you again real soon, Captain," he said.

"I hope not, Tarl."

When the door was closed I walked out on the veranda for air, but the languid humidity and diffused gray light clung to everything, wet and heavy and wearisome. On the far end of the veranda, a hundred meters across the open jungle, were the Martians. Bast or Fassan had quartered them there. Stlks and Chtlus were sitting out on chairs, stools, and the banister railings. Tnlaz was with a group of men cleaning their induction rifles. Either Fassan had been too stupid or too fearful to take them away. Behind them on the tarkwood deck women were chatting as children played.

When Tnlaz noticed me he leaned to the Martian next to him, gestured toward me, and lifted his rifle. Tnlaz's firing mechanism was in a cloth on his lap so the rifle was inert, and he knew that I knew that, but he aimed as if to shoot me, and pressed his lips together to mouth a firing sound. Then he and the other Stlkmen laughed. It sent a chill through me. He could probably shoot me through the spine at 180 meters. Anyone—Chtlu, Stlk, Venusian, Primacy Mitigators—could be out in the jungle waiting to sneak in and knife me in my sleep. On Mars every village was a camouflaged fortress, every house a redoubt, but here everything seemed exposed.

I turned to retreat and almost ran into Zkala. She must have been standing silently watching me.

"You startled me."

Her windcloak was off, she wore a blouse and leggings and the knife hilts prominently jutted from her belt. I wondered if she had been thinking of stabbing me.

"Is that the way to the volcano?" she asked pointing up the slope of the jungle.

"Yes, we flew in over it from the northeast. That way."

"Teymakan is beyond?"

"Yes." I walked past her into the sitting room. She turned

but waited in the archway. "Ubastu does not have a true son?"

Of course, Ubastu couldn't have a 'true son' in the humanoid sense. None of us from Origin could. Our regenerative ability took the place of the biological capacity or desire to bear offspring. But I'd learned not to explain this to humanoids.

"If he's adopted then I don't see why he isn't as true a son as any other. Zkala, you can't go near the prince with those knives."

She looked at me, and I expected her to argue in her usual stubborn way. I think I wanted her to argue because I wanted to compel her—or someone, anyone—to do what I wanted. Instead she took the knives from her belt and offered them to me handle-first.

"I do not need them to dance. Give them to my brother. The one on Earth."

I took them. "I'm not going to Earth, Zkala."

"The Goddess says you are going to earth. Plus the Goddess says I might have the honor to die here serving Her."

"Zkala, how many humanoids must die because of your gods and goddesses?"

She looked at me like I was a child. "The same number who would die with no gods or goddesses."

This answer irritated me. "When I leave Venus, I'll give you back the knives. Then you can stab whomever you want. It'll someone else's problem."

She watched me a moment as if she would say something more, but we were interrupted by obligants bringing back my laundered clothing. They asked if there was anything else they could do for me. When they'd left, Zkala was gone. I dressed. Then I wrapped the knives in a damracloth and packed the bundle midway down the duffel, surrounded by folded clothing. I closed the duffel's fastenings almost all the way but left two centimeters open.

6.

AS OBLIGANTS CAME to escort us, an announcement chimed and reverberated through the halls: "Prince Alawan wishes to welcome his guests in the rotunda."

Zkala was wearing a new blouse and leggings. Somehow Ubastu's palace workforce had created brand-new clothing that looked like her old clothing, but cleaner. Instead of boots Zkala wore leather dancing shoes. The low heels were heavy enough to click as we walked the luma-ki passage.

I was happy at the prospect of a Venusian meal. Not the food itself. I much preferred the simple tarzha grown in the caves of rural Mars. But after eighty cycles of squeezing into tight benches at long tables, I'd devour all the turspice, sea breads, and sheerka paste in the solar system to choose my own food from the central trays and sit wherever I liked with whomever I wanted, Venusian style.

At the rotunda carved cantawood doors opened and Ubastu was there. "Darlings! Look!" She swept her arm to reveal the room, which had been set up with long tables and benches. "I thought it would be so much fun to dine Martian style!"

There were nine tables, three by three. Venusians nobles mostly filled the middle and left, in their loincloths and glistening jewelry, except for half of one table with Earthlings. The Martians filled the three tables on the right. Along the wall to the right a Venusian duo played popular tunes on sono-harps. In the corresponding position on the left an Earthling operated a holocam on a tripod. Bast led us to the central Martian table. "Zkala, you'll naturally want to sit here with your friends. We'll look forward to the dance later!"

Poor Zkala was left stranded at a table of Chtlu—safer than the Stlks perhaps. Tnlaz glowered from the next table over. Of course, Bast, despite insisting on authentic Martian dining, would never allow women and men to sit at different tables—"Darling, we won't let men push women around on Venus"—so the dining was no more Martian than it was Venusian.

Greeting guests as we passed, Bast brought me to a raised, perpendicular table at the room's western side. In the middle was a carved chair of cantawood for the prince. Fassan to the immediate right. Farther to the right Submitigator Tarl and Mitigator Lin and others. Lin bowed from a distance. Tarl glowered. To the left of the prince's throne was Bast's chair and an empty chair for me. Farther to the left sat some Venusian nobles. As we circled around behind them to reach our seats, Bast introduced them and they pointedly ignored me. On the floor behind us Bast's twin scyla dozed, sides lifting and lowering.

Obligants held our chairs as Bast and I sat.

"If we're eating Martian style, does that mean we get tarzha?"

Bast scoffed. "I wouldn't dream of serving something so bland. These poor people have finally reached civilization; they'll want some decent food for a change! Isn't this going to be so much fun?!"

The rotunda's encircling wall was trisected by the double doors, interspersed by colorful mosaics of Venusian history, and small single doors. A balcony ran above us. Above that the high dome spiraled with rows of small circular windows—translucent sunstones facetted so that, despite the cloud cover, each gleamed whenever the sun was directly over it. Ancient priests had used sunstones to mark the progress of the protracted Venusian day.

Finally, the doors closed, the musicians stopped, and we all stood, as two valets from the door directly behind us led in the prince. I'd shamefully hoped to see Zkala's girlish fixation crushed by his age, but when the valets gingerly steered him in by his thin, frail arms, it was I who was shocked. Alawan-Tey had seen 123 Venusian days—quite old for Venus—

but he looked older still. He was small, his back hunched, his skin sagging where muscles had been. Blue flesh that had danced in the vibrancy of youth now was dark blue mud.

Ubastu hovered behind the valets. Several times she reached out, her face desperately solicitous, but each time she drew back again—not in disgust or shame—but seemingly out of a fear that she would hurt him. This helplessness of hers felt more heartbreaking than the prince's. Fassan finally stepped in front of her, taking the place of one of the valets, and helping the prince to sit. Fassan's skin shone pale swirls in dark striations. He revered his adopted father.

"Friends," Alawan-Tey said in Venusian, his voice thin and wavering. "Thank you for feasting with us." The prince paused for interpreters to catch up in Groupspeak and Martian. "Welcome to those from Mars. Welcome to my kindred here on Venus. Welcome to our other guests. I recently return from the chambers of the queen, may she ever rule us. She is well and reminds us that with our own dusk approaching we have reason to be grateful. The fires and the seas have been good, the harvest rich, we are at peace. Let us live well." He raised his glass. "By the fires and the seas!"

"By the fires and the seas!" said the Venusians raising glasses.

The Martians and others did the same, for humanoids know a toast in any language.

I looked at Zkala but she only regarded the prince blandly.

Bast next spoke. "The red Dusk is soon here so it is fitting that we have guests from the Red Planet!" A few Venusians laughed at the pun, but there was only an awkward pause among the Martians, since their word for sunset red is different from their word for the color. Bast went on in her way to praise me, the prince, Fassan, the Martians, the Primacy, and even Mitigator Lee and Submitigator Tarl. Halfway through the Venusians shifted and looked off as if bored and their blue skin rippled in irritation. Bast's greatest gift had always been her genuine enthusiasm for everything, and many annos ago when I had last visited here, Bast's ephemeral joys were apt. But now with the planet's old queen near death, their own prince near death, and Martians sitting across from them, the Venusian nobles seemed sullen and petulant. Finally Bast said, "By the fires and the seas!" and the room half-heartedly did the same. Ubastu sat.

Fassan stood. "Noble Venusians, I can say nothing except that my father, Alawan-Tey is a great prince, never equaled. He is the fire. He is the sea."

Fassan started to sit, but Bast waved her hand to him, and he stood again. "Now, please enjoy the good things before you, the bounty of the fire and sea."

A steward rang a chime, musicians played their sono-harps, obligants set out plates of food and ramekins of spices. The scyla behind us jumped to flee the smell and I felt relieved to have the drooling fanged beasts far away.

Ubastu grasped my hand. "This is just perfect, Di. I have all the people who matter right here."

"It's good to see you too. Did you happen to contact the tower about the transport hopper?"

"I forgot! We'll go to my chambers right after this, and I'll call with you right there so I can't forget." Bast was interrupted frequently by stewards with various issues. Finally, after more wine she switched from Venusian to the Origin language, and turned to me again. "Di, I'm so sorry about Altinus and Hamilcar dying."

"We don't know if Hamilcar died. He disappeared. Altinus may have killed him."

"They were always fighting over you."

"Not this time."

"You dug out your soma beacon. It's strange not to sense you when you're next to me, Di."

"Yes. Well, you're the only one at this point who hasn't."

"Pabilsag and Nanshe too? Are they still in love? I envy

them. It was delightful to hear from them. I rarely do. I invite them to events but they don't come. Neither do you, by the way. But I'm glad all this worked out."

"It hasn't worked out yet, Bast. The Martians should have their weapons stowed. They're hardened fighters."

"Fassan has his reasons, I'm sure."

"Bast, why didn't you warn me about Lin?"

"I did."

"You didn't tell me you'd talked to them. You didn't tell me they would come into my rooms."

"I'm so sorry, Di. The Primacy officials are getting more and more pushy. I think Martian barbarism is so ingrained it must take generations to undo, don't you think? "

I heard snippets of Venusians around me detailing Martian barbarisms too, probably assuming that I couldn't understand their language, or that if I could I would agree with them. Earthlings and Venusians, as all humanoids in the peak of their power, like to imagine barbarism as a past they left and not a future where all empires go.

"Do you ever remember the nest, Di?"

"Some things. It's vague. I remember songs, I think."

"I remember the closeness, so many of us together sharing everything. I miss that." Bast dropped her voice to a whisper. "I loved the prince. I love him still of course, but you know that I loved him from the start, don't you?"

"Yes. Of course."

"What will I do when he dies?"

"Bast, I don't think this is the place or time to discuss it." No one could understand our Origin language, I was sure, but they could see our facial expressions and hear the tone. "Besides, nobles don't have to dive into the volcanoes anymore. Just retire quietly."

"And do what?"

Ubastu noticed a table complaining to the steward that their turspice ramekin was gone. She immediately excused herself, whispered to the prince, rose, whispered to Fassan as she passed behind, and hurried to resolve the confusion. Bast seemed genuinely energized by these details of entertaining. Zkala was not eating her food. From beyond Bast's empty chair, I heard the prince addressing me in Groupspeak.

"You are Captain Dido."

"Yes, Tey-anak. You honor me to remember."

"You do not visit often, but I remember your visits. Even more than this I remember when we first met. I had the honor to speak with you and the others from what you call Origin. And I had the honor to take one of you home for my lifemate."

"It was our honor to speak with you, Tey-anak."

"You are too polite. Remember, I am an old man, but you are older, even though your appearance does not show your age."

"Tey-anak, we all age. There is no shame in that."

"Ubastu does not age. That is my shame. I have failed her as a husband."

I started to disagree but he lifted his hand. "Do not say it. You have never been skilled at flattery, Captain. That is my favorite of your virtues. No, you and Bast both look young, but you have aged and she has not, and I have failed her in that. It was said by our poet Sisima that all stories end in either love or death. But marriage should teach us that love and death are the same. The same." He nodded to himself. "Somehow I have failed to teach Bast. I leave her as helpless as the day we met. This is my great regret."

Bast was returning. She happily touched the shoulders of Fassan and the prince again as she passed behind them. "What are you two discussing?"

"We were wondering," the prince said affectionately, "When will the Martian girl dance? Is she here?"

Bast beamed. She stood and signaled the steward. Servers quickly cleared the tables and brought pasga-tea, calda, liquors, and small bowls of neuropenthe. Meanwhile four Martians crowded onto two small benches replacing the Venusian musicians.

Ubastu rose: "Friends, we have a very special treat tonight. The famous Zkala of the Krshi will be dancing for us."

The Venusians clapped in the fashionable Earth way, and Zkala stood and walked around her table, eyes downcast. She stopped before our perpendicular table, facing the prince, but did not look up.

A Chtlu began to play on a bowed fazho a long improvised passage of bent notes and semi-tones between quick arpeggios and tumbling scales. Then three Stlks joined in on shawm, Pngr tambourine, and a second bowed fazho, until they carried a repetitive, droning, eerie tune. Then when it seemed the song had settled and would change no more, the Stlk fazho-player lifted his bow, straightened his back, and began to moan. The moan thickened into syllables. The syllables stretched into hypnotic archaized Martian:

Thou shalt never again see the water paths
Where gardens are burning burning
I am burning too...

Zkala's upper body stiffened and bent backward. Her arms stretched above her head. Her hands moved, gracefully, precise, and her feet moved, step by deliberate step, clapping the floor with her heavy shoes. She found the rhythm, fell into it, and then the rhythm seemed to come from her.

I understand humanoid dancing even less than humanoid religion. I remember songs from Origin but no dances. But humanoid dancing to that point had always seemed either exultant joy or calculated seduction. But Zkala's dance was neither. Her chin raised, her fathomless eyes half-closed, her face a study of whole lives she'd known, enemies she'd defeated, lovers who'd broken her heart, triumphs, mistakes, hopes, and fears. The conversations in the room died away.

The lyrics lost their quality of speech. Even the music becmae only a distraction. The dance pulled the peripheral detritus of my memories and emotions into poignant floating tableaus. Altinus's embrace. Altinus's death. Hamlicar. Bast. Old battles. Deaths of friends. Love in the eyes between Nanshe and Pabilsag. Love between Bast and young Alawan long ago. The wonder of these humanoids. Existences as fleeting as the mist of a wave, the swirl of dust. Perhaps only they know true courage because they realize the short span of their lives yet struggle on anyway.

I realized the song was over and the room was sitting in stunned silence. Zkala had ended the dance directly in front of the prince with her eyes lowered, breathing heavily, returning gradually from her trance. Then the applause erupted. Everyone was on their feet. Bast was studying her husband. For the first time there was blue cascading in his limbs. He was enrapt. Bast seemed not jealous, but pleased.

"Zkala of the Krshi!" said Bast standing as the applause finally ebbed, "By fire and sea, what a wonderful dance! You must dance again for the prince soon. Everyone, thank you for attending. The prince is tired and wishes to retire to his chambers."

Fassan and Bast helped Alawan to his feet. "Thank you," Alawn said to Zkala. "You are an artist." He addressed the room. "Until we meet again let us live well."

Zkala was confused, not knowing what she was supposed to do, but everyone around her was moving toward the doors.

As the valets led the prince out the back, Bast leaned to whisper to me in Origin. "He likes her. I'll arrange it now."

"Arrange what?"

I saw or imagined I saw Bast share a look with Fassan before she slipped off. The Mercurian approached Zkala and led her out of the room. I noticed Tnlaz watching her departure. He sank to his bench and reached for more wine.

Then when the prince, Bast, Zkala, and Fassan were all

gone and the guests crowding out the doors, Submitigator Tarl jumped up, drunk and angry. "Dyrellians are true dancers!" he insisted loudly as if he couldn't let one more guest leave without the truth. "Don't be fooled by these cheap savages!" Stlkmen jumped up to hold Tnlaz back. Lin tried to stop Tarl but Tarl was on a mission: "Dyrellians have true passion because Dyrellians have fought for everything against everyone and we still prevail!" Lin pulled him out the door.

I had suspected Tarl was Dyrellian, but it was an ugly proof. I left the rotunda myself for the long walk back to my suite, and suddenly I wanted to leave Venus now. It wasn't the ugliness of humanoids that I'd felt on the veranda. It was the strength I saw in Zkala. I had to tell Bast that I wouldn't be staying long, and get her to clear Vanza's departure too. So only forty meters down the passage, I turned back, and cut through the side passage to Bast's chambers. I passed through a door where an obligant bowed, ignoring her when she asked if she could be of assistance. In the second foyer there no attendant, but as I reached for the second door, an obligant entered from the opposite side of the room and called out, "Captain Dido..."

"No, I don't need assistance!" I said sharply. They're relentless. I pushed through the door and curtain into Bast's chambers. Amid the luxurious furnishings of jangwood tables, deslin silk pillows, and savdo rugs, Bast and Fassan were embracing on sofa, both naked, pressing against one another as they moaned.

7.

I WASN'T SHOCKED that Bast and Fassan were lovers. I was shocked that they were so reckless about it. I am always shocked at the recklessness of humanoids. Ubastu froze and blurted out, "Di?!"

"I'm sorry." I tried to turn but Fassan suddenly pushed

Bast off him, and the violence of it drew back my attention.

"Fassan, no!" She reached for him, but he shoved her again, and seizing his meager clothing from the floor, ran past me. I jumped out of the way as he exited, his skin pale blue in utter humiliation. Bast grabbed her malalana from the floor to cover herself a little and tried to run after him.

"Wait Fassan!"

But I blocked the door. "Bast, no, you can't!" The prince's lifemate could not be seen running naked through her own palace chasing her adopted son. "Stop."

Bast silently nodded and sank to the floor. I knelt, not knowing what to say or do.

"I'm sorry, Bast."

"He doesn't love me anymore."

"Alawan?"

When she didn't answer I felt stupid because, of course, she meant Fassan, but the name broke her trance. She looked up. "Di, I didn't want to betray Alawan. I know you think I adopted Fassan to have an affair."

"No. I don't."

"But that's not what happened. Alawan needed an heir and it was wonderful to give such a dream to Fassan. And then I fell in love. We tried to stop, but you don't understand because you don't really love like I do. I'm a passionate person. You're not." She crossed to petulantly curl up on the sofa, covering herself with her malalana as if it were a blanket.

"Does Alawan know?"

"The people still love me, Di. And I look young, don't I?"

I could see where this was going. I beat down the panic to sit next to her, keeping my voice as calm as possible. "Bast, look at me. When the prince dies, you must retire. You can never be with Fassan. Fassan will marry a Venusian. And you must retire. You do understand that, don't you?"

"Of course," she said collecting herself. "It's just a fling.

We can stop."

"Bast, was it your idea to add the Martians to the palace guard or Alawan's?"

"Alawan's." Bast gathered her clothing, such as it was, and went behind a screen.

So the Martians weren't here out of charity. Alawan wanted them in case the native guards rebelled against Fassan's succession. Which meant Alawan knew or suspected what was between Bast and Fassan. But the Stlks and Chtlus wouldn't be enough if too many rumors got out.

Bast emerged, her jewelry and meager clothing in place. She picked up the intraphone transceiver from the ornate writing desk. "Yes. This is Ubastu. See to it that Captain Dido's sloop and the transport hopper are refueled from my fuel stories, and give them clearance to leave Teylafaw whenever they wish. Also give Captain Dido access to the armory. She can take anything she wants." Bast waited a moment for a confirmation and hung up.

She looked at me, sadly. "Goodbye, Didona." She turned and walked out through the archway into the sleeping chamber.

I walked back to my suite. I walked into the bedroom and looked out through the slatted window. Down near the north end of the veranda no Martians were visible. Turning, I noticed my duffel. The fasterner was completely closed. I tore it open and rifled through. The tkra knives were gone.

I rushed into the hall breaking into a run. As I passed two obligants I yelled for them to find palace guards and meet me in the prince's chambers. Near the hallway's end I rounded the corner to the cross corridor and yelled for another attendant to find Bast. Across the main hall to the last section of the smaller corridor, the prince's chambers were ahead. Thick, solid doors with two guards in front.

"Get back!" I shouted. Before they could lift their spears to stop me, I ploughed shoulder-first into the heavy wood and felt the cracking sound of the breaking latches.

The doors gave way and I was in the prince's chamber. The room was as sumptuous as Bast's—curtains, settees, couches, upholstered chairs, all luxuriously appointed—with a vaulted dome overheard, only a bit less grand than the rotunda's. Venus' gray light suffused the air with stillness. The room was covered in blood, Venusian blue blood dripping from sofa edges, pooled in carpets, splattered on the bric-a-brac, as two valets and the prince lay dead, flesh shredded to ribbons

8.

SOON UBASTU WAS slumped over the dead prince. The palace guards stood in shock.

A skylight overhead was open. There were burn marks in the roof beams that looked like laser burns. Zkala must have climbed up through the ceiling rafters and escaped through the skylight. There were no weapons in the room now. Maybe a valet had had a laser pistol that discharged in the struggle and Zkala took it after killing him. Or maybe someone shot at her as she fled, which meant someone else was in the room. Zkala would move across the roofs, maybe pause at our rooms if she saw patrols, then head for the jungle. She'd make for the docks on the far side of the island. If she could sneak onto a boat to cross the channel, she could hide in the slums of Teymakan City.

Fassan rushed in with four more guards. "You and you," I said to two of the new arrivals, "Stand outside that entrance." I pointed to the first two guards. "You both watch the other entrance. Don't let anyone in. You two," I pointed to the final two, "Don't let anyone touch the bodies." Then I told the obligants to bar the doors from the inside.

Fassan and Bast were embracing. Not as lovers it seemed to me, but as shared sufferers of loss. The blue of Fassan's face and sides flowed downward like azury sand. But it was not pure sadness. What else was there—fear of ruling? Guilt at his affair? Relief? I didn't have time to find out.

"Ubastu," I said as sternly as I could, looking directly in the eyes. "Find Mitigator Lin to look at all this. But only him. Don't let Tarl come with him."

"Look at *what?*" shouted Fassan suddenly enraged. "That Martian whore you brought has killed my father!"

"If that's true we don't know why, or if anyone helped her, or if she was working for someone." I turned to Bast again. "This is critical. Do not announce anything until I've found Zkala and until Lin has investigated. More importantly, if anyone does find out, and you have to say something, don't lie. Understand? If possible, say nothing. If you must talk, make sure what you say is true. Got it?"

Bast nodded her head.

"Fassan, deploy the Martians on the far side of the island to keep anyone from crossing the channel. Venusians will have friends and relatives that they'll be tempted to let cross. They might even go with them. But the Martians will lock it down. Got it? I'll find Zkala."

"If you know where she is you must tell me!" shouted Fassan.

"Just do as I say."

"You do not give orders!" Fassan shouted. "I give orders! I am the Protector!"

"Really? Well, you're doing a bang-up job."

I took a piezospear from one of the two remaning guards. Jumping onto a table I planted the spears end, and vaulted upward, grasping the balustrade with my left hand. I swung over it. In a few steps I leaped up into the expanse of the dome, slipping the spear ends horizontally across two beams. Then I swung forward for momentum, came around to lift, planting my feet on the spear, and jumped toward the skylight, kicking the spear up behind me with my trailing left foot.

I pulled up and slipped out onto the roof. I ran between

the rotunda's dome and smaller domes of the royal chambers, half-stepping, half-leaping across the flashing, to come around to the southern luma-ki. There I raced along the woven-wood peaked roof, using the spear sometimes as a balance bar, sometimes as a testing prod, up and down between the roof's valley and ridge. As I approached the end, near my rooms, I could see back to the left the Martian wing of the palace was empty now, even the women and children gone.

When I guessed I was roughly over Zkala's suite, I flipped down onto the veranda, and slipped into her rooms. There was no sign of her or her satchel. I could sense movement next door, and I hadn't been quiet, so they'd know I was here. I crept along the veranda wall to the edge of my suite's door. I heard a belligerent voice. "Come on in."

There was Tarl, his jacket off, a Triton K80 pistol in his hand. "I've been waiting for you.

"Wait a little longer." I spun below the barrel's trajectory, flipping the spear underhanded and around to burn his forearm with the piezo's dancing purple tongues. That stunned him long enough for me to roundhouse kick his chin, knocking him out cold.

In a few steps I vaulted the veranda railing into the thick, soft jungle floor below and raced up the hillside.

A hundred meters up, the chimes chimed and I was shocked when the voice over the ampliboxes was Bast's. It stopped me in my tracks. "Venusians, our beloved ruler Alawan-Tey has received an unfortunate head injury." I turned to look down the slope as if I might see Bast on the veranda below and somehow stop her. "But Alaway-Tey has declared that Protector Fassan will have temporary regency until he fully recovers, which we're sure will be soon."

The breath left me. My head spun. That's when the scylas attacked.

Only a murmur of clawed feet on the soft ground, only a rustle of parting leaves, presaged the assault. My involuntary reflexes lifted the spear, which blocked the right-side beast, but it knocked the spear enough that the other scyla's fangs plunged into my left hip. I spun toward the bite, trying to keep the jaws from locking. I flung the spear sideways at the right-side scyla to disorient it, while I jabbed my free arm into the left-side creature's mouth. I punched down on its head, while digging my thumb into the roof of its mouth. It opened its jaws and drew back in confusion.

Meanwhile the right-side creature lunged. I punched its eye and kneed it upward in the throat, but this caused my left leg almost to collapse when there was weight on it. The scylas swiftly regrouped, and lunged. As the left-side creature led, I sidestepped and punched its head, as its mate plowed into it. They tumbled together, snarling, snapping at the air, and spinning to attack again.

But I'd kicked the spear up into my hand now, and they no longer had surprise. I thrust the spear's electrical tip deep into the first scyla's throat, then jerked the shaft sideways to block the second scyla. Wild scylas would have run, but these were trained to fight to the death. So blow followed blow as my initial adrenaline rush of fear curdled into nausea at the creatures' pathetic deaths.

Slowly around me a crescent of Venusian palace guards emerged from the jungle. They stared at the dead scyla and my bleeding left hand and hip. Using the spear shaft as support I knelt on my right knee to relieve pressure on the hip. I concentrated to constrict the arteries and redirect nerve endings. I probed the wound with my hand gritting my teeth to manage the pain. "Help," I said simply.

Two of the guards quickly came and took my spear and helped me to my feet as I slung my arms around their shoulders for support. The bleeding was mostly contained but therapsid saliva is toxic.

"We thought you were the dancer," explained one of the guards.

"Who ordered you to let the scyla off leash?"

"Protector Fassan told us to capture the dancer using maximum vigilance," said the woman holding me up. Humanoid police and military forces use euphemisms like 'maximum vigilance' when they don't want to admit they're killing.

From the palace below the chimes chimed and the ampliboxes reverberated with Fassan's voice, this time. "This is Protector Fassan. All members of the palace guard, all Venusians of Teylafaw, your directives are updated! In addition to Zkala, the Martian, Captain Dido is also to be arrested immediately for threats against our wounded prince. She is also armed and extremely dangerous and should be subject to *maximum vigilance*."

Strangely I always feel a partial sense of relief when my worst suspicions are confirmed. The betrayal was complete. For a moment I felt pity for the dozen guards awkwardly looking at one another, unsure of what to do. I could not bring myself to harm them.

Then one brave guard—the one on the right who had helped me, actually—stepped back, tossing my spear away, and began to lift her own. This prompted others to do the same. And that hesitant aggression drove me to action. I let the pain of my thigh wash through me.

With the arm I still had over his shoulder, I flung the man on my right into the woman on my left, as I twisted and wrenched the spear from her hand.

Several of the guards now struck, and I parried, swung, and thrust, retreating step by step backward up the slope. I mostly counterattacked their flanks to keep them from surrounding me. Four or five of the guards stayed behind, but to those who didn't I showed no mercy. Driving the electrical tip into their faces, necks, and crotches, pounding their skulls, kneecaps, and jaws. Two were down, then three, then four.

Soon I heard commands and movements in the jungle. Reinforcements were coming. With a wide swing to put my immediate assailants on their heels, I wheeled for the slope, ducking and dodging through the brush, whirling back to level any pursuer who managed to keep pace.

As the reinforcements closed in from both sides, I changed speed and direction to spread them, sometimes cutting behind or charging through, laying them out on the run. The slope was steeper now, underbrush sparser, trees farther apart. Above us the underside of the defense tower was sometimes visible through gaps in the canopy, which meant I was near the volcano's rim. I knew the guards were getting more and more disorganized, the bleeding in my hip had stopped, and the pain was manageable.

Ahead was a clearing. Venusians were come from the right-side tree line. If I could draw them into the open, I could make a break, cutting behind them down the hillside into the denser brush. They wouldn't know if I was going toward the docks on the north or back to the warehouses southeast of the palace.

I started across the clearing and the Venusians took the bait, but as I began to double-back, I slipped, losing half a step, and when I regained my footing, I saw only forty meters ahead on the left, an octad of Stlks with their induction rifles emerging from the trees. Led by Tnlaz. They formed a rank and aimed. I glanced around for cover but there was none. From this distance eight Martian riflemen would kill me. Eight shots to the head. No hope of regeneration.

I dropped my spear and raised my hands. "I surrender!"

The treetops on the north side of the clearing rustled, then shook. Engines hummed. Three BR-90 skimmers, gleaming silver, flew in, descending as their undercarriages dangled snaking metal tendrils terminating in snapping claws. The lead skimmer, piloted by Fassan, came to hover above the Stlkmen. piloted by Fassan.

"She has surrendered, Protector Fassan," reported Tnlaz glowering at me proudly.

"Shoot her."

Tnlaz's eyes instantly snapped to Fassan, unsure what he'd heard.

"Shoot her!" Fassan repeated sternly.

The pride in Tnlaz's eyes withered to shame, and for a split-second it seemed the Martians glanced at one another as if there might be some other possiblity. But Martians follow order. So Tnlaz and the Stlks fired.

It felt like a handful of pebbles hit my body, and there was some pain, but then, only then, my insides suddenly exploded in a new pain, a burning agony as if pierced through by shafts of fire. I fell. As if in a dream, as I stared up helplessly at the gray cloudy sky, I saw a tiny space ship flying upward as two missiles on spitting tails joined it in an explosion. Everything went black.

I thought that was death, but I came back to consciousness suspended in the air. The regenerative instincts Origin had given me went to work, locating wounds, sealing off arteries, rerouting nerves, releasing painkilling hormones, but I knew it was hopeless. Then I realized my face, neck, and torso--they had no gunshots. There was the bite on my hip, but no gunshots. I checked again: right leg twice, right arm twice, left thigh, left shoulder, left arm. The Stlks had somehow missed my vital organs.

Then I realized they hadn't missed. The Stlkmen shot me as ordered, but without a word somehow agreed not to kill me. Even Tnlaz. Gratitude? Honor? I don't know why.

But the mercy of the Stlks brought me to full consciousness. I was floating in the air above the tree line approaching the edge of the volcano. I was being carried by the dangling claws of Fassan's skimmer. He knew I couldn't regenerate from lava. He was going to drop me in. I had to climb the tentacles and attack the vessel from below. I tried to move but my arms were too ravaged. No, my arms were useless.

Think. I had to cling. Wrap my body and my one working

leg around a tentacle and refuse to drop. No, Fassan must have some way to jettison the entire tendril structure, since skimmers often switched to different undercarriage tools. He'd jettison me with the tendrils. Yes. That's it. Like rolling into the scyla bite. I'd get him to drop me too soon, just inside the volcano's mouth, where there was a chance the tendrils might tangle me in the wires and pipes and scaffolding.

I swung my torso back and forth, then wrenched it more sharply, jerking until I could flip up and wrap my good calf and ankle around one of the tentacles. I coiled it as tightly as I could and began to violently pull and jolt, throwing the entire skimmer off-balance. Fassan expertly shifted the blade housings to level off, but I lurched again. Again. Again. He struggled to keep the vessel from capsizing, until it happened. We were over the volcano's mouth, and Fassan would risk no more.

I felt the claws slacken, the tentacles lose their internal pressure, and suddenly I was in free-fall. The skimmer had jettisoned the tendril structure. It vanished above as I plunged into the billowing steam.

I stretched as far as I could my tortured form, until a guide wire hit me and spun me. I plowed into the rocky wall, slid downward, twisting and turning, smashing into a pipe, then a ledge that I was too weak to grab for, then another guide wire, and another ledge. I bounced away from the wall and thought all was lost, when a third wire lodged between my chest and arm, wrenching my shoulder from its socket. The pain enveloped me and all was black again.

9.

I CAME IN AND out of consciousness dangling like a battlefield corpse strung as a warning, lost in the scalding, rufous steam. At first it was dreamless or perhaps the dreams were too recondite to be sensed even by the dreamer. I came to again and I was moving. I wondered if the wires were breaking, or my ligaments, but I didn't care. I could not even concentrate enough to fight my own pain or check my own injuries. Again all went black. This time I did dream. Of the Nameless One with the Martian dead passing the cup of the black calda, but I couldn't remember why they drank it together. Did the dead honor her, or did she honor the dead?

When I came to again, over me was Zkala. She poured water into my mouth. My senses wavered, faded, coalesced again. The sheer rockface was to my left. I was lying on a narrow ledge. The hot clouds billowed around us, red glowing through it from below.

Zkala was sawing through a cable with the serrated back of her tkra. A loop of the cable was around my chest. Zkala must have used it to swing me to this ledge. The metal tendrils were gone. My shoulder had healed in a dislocated position, so I'd have to break it again. Most of the bullets had passed through and the wounds were healing, but the two bullets in my right leg were lodged there. I'd have to dig them out. The deep scyla bite on my hip was infected too, despite my body's powerful natural immunities. I needed a medipract.

When the cable was freed and Zkala realized I was conscious, she poured more water into my lips. Her blouse was torn and her face was filthy, but it somehow suited her more than the fresh-pressed luxuries of Venus.

"Why did you save me?"

"The Goddess saved you," she said plainly. She fed me a small piece of stale breadfruit unwrapped from a cloth in her shoulder satchel, and ate a piece herself.

"What happened to the prince?"

"It was the Chtlus. They brought knives."

"To make it look like you did it?"

Zkala half-nodded, half-shrugged. She did not care the reason. "I knew there was danger. That is why I took my tkra from your bag. But I failed. Chtlu." She spat at the thought and for once I agreed.

Maybe the Dyrellians arranged it? Maybe the Chtlu were working with the Dyrellians all along? Maybe that's why the headman stalled the negotiations? No. The headman didn't know.

"It was Fassan," I said. The Dyrellians would had promised to support Fassan whenever Alawan died, if he would see their side on Martian issues. But they'd have no reason to assassinate Alawan prematurely. No, when I caught Fassan with Bast, he panicked.

"How long have I been unconscious?"

"I do not know time in this place. The sun is near the horizon I think, but with the clouds I am not sure even of this. I have observed the Stlks who are guarding the docks on the far side of the island. They changed watch twice, I think. Your ship has not been touched but the Shrgu's ship was destroyed trying to fly away." Shrgu was the Martian term for savdo.

"I thought I saw it but wasn't sure."

"Other soldiers have landed. With guns and armor. I think Tnlaz's Stlks were arrested and many of the palace guards."

"Fassan is covering his tracks." If Tnlaz had been willing to kill me they might not have been arrested. "Have they announced yet that the prince is dead?"

"I do not know. The announcements are only in Venusian, and I cannot get as close to the palace as I did before." Zkala finished sawing away the last bit of cable. She looked at me sadly. "I thought the Goddess had sent me to protect the prince and help you. Now I do not hear the Goddess as I did. Is She ashamed of me? Did I fail Her?"

It was the sort of moment I had longed for, the chance to free a humanoid of their superstitions, but I could not. Zkala with her superstition had saved my life and almost saved the prince, while I'd brought about the deaths of two octads of Martians already and the prince.

"No," I said, "No, you didn't fail her, Zkala. The Moon Spinner is proud of you."

Zkala smiled weakly.

"How do you move around without the scyla smelling you?"

She reached into her pocket and drew out a handful of turspice. "At the feast I saw the creatures did not like this."

I laughed. I pulled myself up enough to roll on my right side. "Tnlaz and his octad could have killed me, but they chose not to. Why was he angry with you that day?"

"He wanted me to stay on Mars. He said the Drlu would not harm me since I was neither Stlk nor Chtlu. I told him the Goddess had commanded me to follow you, and he demanded I not do this. He said the Goddess would want me to stay on Mars and dance so that true Martians could be proud of something."

"I'm sorry, Zkala. I'm sorry for everything. If I hadn't told Fassan to post the Stlks on the docks, maybe you could slip across."

She shrugged again. "Then he would have used them to patrol the woods and I would have been found already."

"Zkala, what does your Goddess tell us to do now?"

"She does not speak as she did."

There were no good options. The *Antigone* would be guarded and the jungle would be patrolled, and even if we got to the ship, we couldn't make orbit without first destroying the SAMcasters, and I was too damaged to fly well-enough for that. Nor could I stay. Without a medipract my hip infection would worsen till I slipped into a coma again. But I trusted Zkala's instincts more than mine, and her instincts seemed to be wired to her superstitions.

"Ask the goddess, Zkala, and we will wait."

So Zkala asked and we waited. We waited until the food and water was gone. Then, still with no word from the divine, Zkala announced that we would wait no longer. We would go. In uncounted hours of fumbling through the steam she'd mapped the volcano's cone—tunnels, conduits, and ladders. I could only walk by leaning on Zkala, but we stumbled along the narrow ledge until we reached a concrete pipe she'd used to slip into the jungle and back. We crawled meter by meter down its length. At the end Zkala slipped the grate off and dropped into the jungle brush, returning to pull me out. I guessed we were about a kilometer from the palace. Zkala quietly put the grate back in place and sprinkled handfuls of turspice over us. The gray sky and lush green felt cool after the time in the volcano. The pteradons squawked. The distant waves crashed.

"Hold it!" came a voice.

Twenty Venusian infantry with laser carbines surrounded us.

10.

ALL TRACES OF blood had been scrubbed away and the silks and plush furnishings were gone too. What had been Alawan's private chambers were empty except for a simple table, a bench, and some chairs. I noticed even the laser burns high above had been sanded out. Venusian infantry stood at every door. They freed our legs but our wrists were still bound in zipcuffs. I could barely stand.

Bast and Fassan strode in with more Venusian infantry. Mitigator Lin and Submitigator Tarl followed as Bast rushed to embrace me. "Darling, you look awful." She gently lowered me to a sofa. "I am so grateful you are alive."

"Speaking of alive, has the prince recovered yet? Has he had a chance to reaffirm his declaration of Fassan's *temporary* regency?"

"Gag them!" shouted Fassan, his skin rippling in the darkest blue.

Zkala shouted *shngwal*—'bloodless'—and spat towards

him. Tarl and Lin cooly observed the scene, Tarl smirking, Lin polite. They did nothing and Bast made only token protests as an infantrywoman gagged us.

The commander of the unit that captured us showed Fassan the knives, waterbag, and satchel emptied of its meager contents—laid out on the table like evidence.

"Darling, we really ought to free her!" said Bast to Fassan. She touched him and lighter blue momentarily swirled, but was quickly reabsorbed in darker tides of his rage.

"Leave me!" shouted Fassan to everyone. "Now!"

"Yes, Fassan-Tey," said the infantry and attendants. Tarl lingered but Lin coaxed him. Finally, only Bast, Zkala, Fassan, and I remained.

Fassan was circling the room, locking doors. "You also," he said to Bast. "I will question them alone."

"But Son, Dido must heal first..." Fassan charged her and grabbed her by the neck. "I am not your son! You are an offworlder, a monster like this one! I will be the blood prince now! Get out!"

He thrust her toward the door by the nape of her neck. Even after so long in luxury, Bast was still from Origin. She was stronger than Fassan. She could have free herself and dropped him with a single blow, but instead she meekly, penitently, scurried out leaving us to die. Fassan locked the door behind her.

Fassan picked up one of the tkras form the table. As he approached me I tried to move but my wrists were bound behind. He straddled me across my waist. He looked in my eyes. He looked at my throat. He held up the knife. I tried to throw him off but my left leg buckled. I saw Zkala moving in the periphery of my sight. The cold blade dug into my neck cutting swiftly toward the arteries.

Zkala was on him. She'd rolled backward bringing her bound hands under her to the front of her body. She looped her zipcuffed wrists over Fassan's head and neck from behind. As she pulled they fell, writhing, Fassan tried to break free, then tried to stab backward, while underneath Zkala choked him.

I rolled to the floor looking toward the table where the other knife waited, but it was too far. I'd never reach it. I tried to shout but couldn't get sound past the gag. I had to get my arms in front. Pain exploding, lying on my side, knees against my chest, centimeter by centimer, I working my cuffed wrists down my back, under, up my shins—almost there.

I saw the blood. Fassan had managed to stab Zkala's thigh and turned toward her.

With a violent jerk my wrists were in front. I dove at Fassan as he stabbed Zkala's chest. He drove him onto his own back, blocking the knife with my arms, pushing it towards him, closer, closer, the blade to his neck, closer, the blue skin swirling in terror as a glistening line appeared. Then the blood ran and Fassan struggled, quivered, choked till his hateful eyes were cold and dead.

I cut my zipcuffs and Zkala's. I pulled away our gags. I hopelessly screamed toward the doors for them to come, to bring a doctor, though I knew they wouldn't hear. I tried to stop Zkala's bleeding with pressure on the chest wound. She clung to me. Her eyes opened.

"Give the knives to my brother," she whispered and smiled a little. "I am happy now. The Goddess spoke to me again."

"Zkala? Zkala?!"

The doors rattled open. As the soldiers entered, Zkala the Krshi was dead.

11.

MITIGATOR LIN WAS brisk, Tarl behind him carried my duffel. Lin ordered the soldiers to stand down and they did, perhaps stunned by his confidence or shocked by another death. Kneeling, Lin put a medipatch over my neck to slow the bleeding.

"Captain, you really do not die very easily."

So Lin had guessed I would kill Fassan. Or probably he had a contingency plan either way. He wiped the tkra blades and put them in my duffel, then fastened it closed. "I have secured clearance from Teylafaw air wing and the tower. We must hurry before minds change and doubts set in."

Lin helped me down the passage to the landing platform as Tarl churlishly carried my duffel. Ubastu ran past us in the other direction, ignoring me, rushing toward the room we'd escaped. We heard her scream in crazed grief.

They put me in the *Antigone* but did not try to search. I made it to orbit. I flew on jets alone since I was too disoriented to steer the solar sails. I reached the Kang Tai. I flew until the fuel ran out. Then I drifted like the tardigrades.

I was too injured to know or care why Lin let me go, but much later I found he'd had fabric woven into my duffel for a tracking echo. He didn't search my ship, but he found a way to follow it.

I never saw Ubastu again. While I was adrift in space, she invited the chroniclers and holocams to hear her confessions, which turned out not to be words. With the entourage following her, in her finest jewelry and loincloth, beautiful as ever, she strode up the hill like the Venusian nobles of old, and in the full view of obligants and soldiers, she threw herself into the volcano.

Both Tnlaz and his octad of Stlkmen, and the Chtlu who assassinated the prince, were executed. The other Martians who'd been deployed to guard the docks were spared, as I'd hoped; that's why I told Fassan to deploy them there.

But the executions of the others, unprecedented in the recent history of Venus, plus the chaos and scandal of Alawan's death, and Fassan's, and Bast's in quick succession, shook the ruling order of the planet, and the queen's subsequent death moved it to its downfall.

The dancer Zkala died too young for her reputation to outlast her, but I remember her always.

I wish there were a Nameless One, an immortal who dug the Martian canals with her tkra knives, and sent the twin moons of the slain beast hurling through the heavens. I would challenge her. I would battle her to the death in the fighting place according to the laws, that she would steal a young woman's life for the sake of a doomed prince and to twice save a worthless thing like me.

ACKKNOWLEDGEMENTS

WE WOULD LIKE to give a special thanks to the following people for their support as backers through Kickstarter: Steve Tanner, Garrett L. Ward, John Conner - Coop Janitor, Mark Carter, Anaxphone, Robet C Flipse, Jay Skiles, Michael Gonzales, Stephen Ballentine, E.M. Middel, Jason Miller, Jim Kosmicki, Richard Sands, Ryan A. Fleming, BuddyH, Robert Gibson, Eric Richetti, David England, John Robert Mead, Thomas Biros, Clifton Roberts, Serpent Moon, Mog, Hiram G. Wells, Thomas Bull, Olivia Rohan, James Lucas, Thomas M. Colwell, Don C, Justin, Will A Oberton, Daniel G., Catherine Trouth, Jeff Huggins, Mary Gibson, Stephen Rubin, Jim Gotaas, J. Sobieraj, Jerry Koehr, Ruth Ann Orlansky, MJ Silversmith, Luis Manuel Sánchez García, James W. Murphy, Chris Bekofske, Raul Castro, Jill Grow, John J. Senn, Emilia Marjaana Pullianen, Digby, Jeff Hotchkiss, Trip Space-Parasite, Alastair Palmer, Joshua Palmatier, Michael D'Auben, Katy Manck - BooksYALove, Yankton Robins, Eric, Vince Kindfuller, AlmostHuman, Robert Claney, Michael Barbour, Mark Newman, Bobbi Boyd, Gary Phillips, Marko Deablo, Ben Haskett, Richard Dulik, Tim Stroup, Stephen Frede, Edmund Boys, Jen Witsoe, Rob Szarka, Kevin Moreau, Robin E. Douglas, Jean-Pierre Ardoguein, Joseph Guzzo, Cliff

324 • Vintage Worlds 2

Allred, L.E. Roncayolo, Per Axel Stanley Willis, Sister Crow, Jennifer Barber, Matt Staples, E. Ashby, Sc Fi Cardre, Linda S., Travis Siegel, Jillian Harker, Peter Borah, Andy Dwelly, Daniel C., Keith West: Future Potentate of the Solar System, Silvina & Keren Cohen, Eron Wyngarde, Tanner Nash, Brett Carlson, Michael Ball, Walt Freitag, Justin Patrick Moore, Doug Forand, Orange exiguous piglet - the name bestowed upon me by the Cosmic Oom. Who am I to argue, Harvey L. Lesser, Michael Mudgett, R.J.H., Terrence Miller, Jeff Sigmund, Erik T. Johnson, Joan, Charles Rivers, Ross Richey, Rick Ohnemus, Jeff S., Quin Arbeitman, John Markley, Tim Jordan, Joel Caris, Dagmar Baumann, Niall Gordon, Stacy Shuda, Jonathan Hodge, Ivan Donati, Dan Mollo, Thomas Gaudaire-Thore, Matt Trepal, Howard J. Bampton, Tracy 'Rayhne' Fretwell, P. Robert Thorson, Fred W. Johnson, Dillon Burke, Fenric Cayne, Jeffrey Scarpace, Bill Kohn, Brian Holder, Adrienne, Zack Fissel, Camille Lofters, Michael Carroll, Russell Graves, SwordFirey, Peter Klimas, Ed Matalka, Kelly Mayo, xorx, RvR, Ane-Marte Mortensen, Benjamin, Old Man Sparck, John H. Bookwalter Jr., Robert L. Vaughn, Frank Lewis, M. Phelps, Troy Jones, neeneko, R. Gregory Conners, and John J. Senn.

Made in the USA
Middletown, DE
05 December 2020